THE STARQUEST

THE LEGEND OF Q'NTANA
BOOK TWO

MARK DAVID GERSON

THE STARQUEST

This is a work of fiction. Names, characters, places, events and incidents are either the products of the author's imagination or used in a fictitious manner. Any resemblance to actual persons, living or dead, or to actual events is purely coincidental.

First Paperback Edition 2014

Fourth Edition 2024
Published by MDG Media International
Beverly Hills, CA
www.mdgmediainternational.com

Library of Congress Control Number: 2024902517

ISBN: 978-1-950189-39-7 (paperback)
ISBN: 978-1-950189-40-3 (ebook)

Cover Image: Kathleen Messmer
www.kathleenmessmer.com

I have decided to stick with love. Hate is too great a burden to bear
MARTIN LUTHER KING, JR.

An open heart knows no limits.
ASTEL LEV

To all those with the courage to open their hearts.
And to my mother, whose sacrifices made my choices possible

PRAISE FOR THE LEGEND OF Q'NTANA

Leaves you turning every single page, hungry for more!
DAVID MICHAEL – AUTHOR OF "THE UNITED SERIES"

Compelling…a magical journey!
KAREN VAUGHAN – AUTHOR OF "DEAD TO WRITES"

An intriguing and exhilarating magical tale.
DAN STONE – AUTHOR OF "ICE ON FIRE"

An evocative and emotionally moving tale.
"MIDWEST BOOK REVIEW"

*I read "The MoonQuest" three times and couldn't wait for
"The StarQuest" to come out. Well, it was worth the wait.
I loved this book, and you will too!*
AMY ROBBINS-WILSON – AUTHOR OF "TRANSFORMATIONAL MOTHERING"

*An enjoyable journey into a wondrous world
that will leave you yearning to return again and again.*
JUDY SMITH ADAMS – SPRINGFIELD, MO

Stunning, magical and inspiring.
PAOLA RIZZATO– GLASGOW, UK

*Magic, music and universal truths
masterfully woven into a gripping tale.*
BETTY DRAVIS – AUTHOR OF "1106 GRAND BOULEVARD"

*Of the hundreds of books I own and hundreds more I've read, this is
the only book I've ever finished and immediately picked pack up and
read a second time. Amazing masterpiece of literature.*
LYNN HUDSON – ALBUQUERQUE, NM

*A fantastical ride to another world…the kind of book
the world should clamor for and read more of.*
MICHAEL HICE – SANTA FE, NM

*Fans of quest-centered fantasy and visionary fiction
as well as New Agers should enjoy this emotionally solid tale.*
"LIBRARY JOURNAL"

More from Mark David Gerson

FICTION

Sara's Year

After Sara's Year

The Emmeline Papers

MEMOIR

Acts of Surrender: A Writer's Memoir

Dialogues with the Divine: Encounters with my Wisest Self

Pilgrimage: A Fool's Journey

SELF-HELP & PERSONAL GROWTH

*The Way of the Fool: How to Stop Worrying About Life
and Start Living It…in 12½ Super-Simple Steps*

*The Way of the Imperfect Fool: How to Bust the Addiction to Perfection
That's Stifling Your Success…in 12½ Super-Simple Steps*

*The Way of the Abundant Fool: How to Bust Free of "Not Enough"
and Break Free into Prosperity…in 12½ Super-Simple Steps*

The Book of Messages: Writings Inspired by Melchizedek

BOOKS & RECORDINGS FOR WRITERS

The Voice of the Muse: Answering the Call to Write

The Voice of the Muse Companion: Guided Meditations for Writers

From Memory to Memoir: Writing the Stories of Your Life

Organic Screenwriting: Writing for Film, Naturally

Birthing Your Book…Even If You Don't Know What It's About

The Heartful Art of Revision: An Intuitive Guide to Editing

*Writer's Block Unblocked: Seven Surefire Ways
to Free Up Your Writing and Creative Flow*

*As you step from your world into the worlds of Q'ntana, you
will experience foreign lands, sample exotic foods and encounter
all manner of uncommon individuals and peculiar creatures.*

*Look for "The Worlds of The StarQuest" at the back of the book
to ease your journey through this unfamiliar territory
(and to assist you with some unusual pronunciations).*

*If you'd prefer to have this guide by your side as you travel these
pages, download a free copy of "The Worlds of The StarQuest"
at www.markdavidgerson.com/qntanaworlds.*

§ § § § §

*With its compelling story, engaging characters and rich,
multilayered themes, "The StarQuest" is an ideal selection
for any book club.*

CO'AN: THE LAND OF LOST MEMORIES

one

The face in the glass was a stranger's. The face in the glass was my own. I stared up at it, willing it to reveal itself to me. But it, like me, knew nothing. Nothing of who I was. Nothing of where I was. Nothing of how I got here.

Nothing of what "here" was.

All I knew of my world was this round room lit by round windows and filled with a scattering of round furnishings, all draped with the same coarse, unbleached floor-length cloth stamped with the same faded design: an eight-pointed star enclosed in a sunlike circlet. All I saw of the world I viewed through the round mirror suspended above my round bed. All I heard of the world was my breath, resonant against a pall of absolute stillness.

How my body ached. I couldn't say why, only that each time I tried to sit up, I collapsed impotently back onto the bed. Time passed…or didn't, as I lay motionless and bewildered, waiting for…for what?

"Does she still sleep, I wonder?" A throaty voice, deep and drowsy, interrupted my half-wakeful wondering. It wafted toward me from the other side of an opaque-glass door leaded with the same sun-star motif, the sound accompanied by the syncopated thump-*thump* of a pronounced limp.

Thump-*thump*.

Thump-*thump*.

"How long has it been?" A second voice, in the high-pitched tone of the very young or the very old. And a second pair of feet, shuffling in barely perceptible counterpoint to the first.

Shuffle-thump.

Shuffle-thump.

"Too long."

The door latch clicked and I shut my eyes as hinges squeaked open.

Thump-*thump.*
Shuffle-thump.
Thump-*thump.*
Shuffle-thump.

The footsteps drew nearer, stopped. I feigned sleep, too wary to open my eyes.

"How does she feel now?" Rough skin gently stroked my forehead, magically soothing my achiness. Curious as I was, my eyes remained closed. Too much remained too strange in the too few moments since my sleep had ended to trust this strange couple.

"Hmm."

"Is she still like ice?"

"Oh my no, thank the stars." A slight instant's slight pressure squeezed into my chest. "Her breathing is more regular as well."

They said nothing, with whispers of breath my only clue to my visitors' continued presence.

"She sleeps so long," I heard at last. "It is worrisome. No?"

"At least the thrashing has ended. Oh my yes."

"Indeed." The high-pitched voice paused. "If she awakes—"

"*When* she awakes, brother."

"*If* she awakes, sister, she must be away from here. We cannot keep her presence secret much longer. It is not safe — for any of us."

"It is not safe in any event, brother."

"Indeed," he harrumphed loudly. "Then there is the b—"

"Co'anra!" She pushed against him and I heard him tumble to the floor. "Hush, brother," she whispered loudly. "Now is not the time, nor is here the place. Oh my no." Another touch, on my cheek and then on my hand, suffused me with warmth. "She *is* better. Oh my yes. Close to waking too, I warrant. It is best to let her rest."

Co'anra scrambled to his feet. "It is best," he muttered, "to have many things be otherwise."

"It is best, brother, that you ee'jin. Presently. You become so ill-humored when you go past the time."

"Indeed," he snarled.

A door shut on their whispered bickering and opened more fully into my anxiety. Not safe? What was this place? How did I get here? How could I leave, not even knowing who I was? Where would I go?

I clenched my fists, hugged myself and opened my eyes, studying yet again the stranger's face that so intently studied me back from the mirror: a woman of late mothering years, attractive but for a hawk-like nose, cracked lips a bit too full, eyes impenetrably dark, and auburn hair knotted and tangled as seaweed. I watched her trace her features with long, slender fingers and prayed for some shard of memory to emerge.

None did.

Reluctantly, I tore my eyes from my reflection and once again surveyed my surroundings. Soft, uncertain light filtered gauzily through the windows' cloudy glass and through the weave of translucent thatch that formed the ceiling, bathing the room in a dreamlike half-reality. *Was* this a dream? I pinched myself, hoping to awaken.

I didn't.

Cautiously, I pushed myself up to sitting. I let my feet touch the ground, breathed in deeply and tried to stand. My body refused the attempt. Dizzy and nauseous, I grabbed onto the bed, my heart racing. As I did, I glimpsed a light-flash of movement.

The door handle. It turned.

The door. It opened. A sliver.

Before I could again pretend to be sleeping, a silvery sphere glistering with starlight slid gently into the room. It hovered briefly over my bed, then gamboled playfully from wall to wall to wall, growing larger and brighter until it enveloped me, first in its light then in a wordless song at once alien and strangely familiar. For a timeless time beyond forever, I floated inside this globe, freed by its gauzy light and hypnotic melody from all yearning. Who I was didn't matter. Where I was didn't matter. All that mattered was the song emanating from its center, from the center of me.

A black thunderbolt thrusts itself at the sphere. The sphere parries left to avoid it. The thunderbolt aims again. The sphere lurches right, left, then right again.

Not swiftly enough.

With a screeching hiss, the thunderbolt strikes. With a deafening blast, the sphere explodes.

Shards of light flare out in every direction. One by one, they dissolve into a blackness blacker than any night sky. With the sphere gone, I hurtle through darkness, toward a grim, soot-gray fortress built forbiddingly into the tallest in a chain of craggy, angular mountains. Giant birdlike creatures circle the castle, their shrieks piercing the wailing winds that whip the snake-emblem pennons flying from its tallest turrets.

One creature spots me. Wings pinned to its sides, it charges toward me, its needle-nose beak trained on my heart. As it nears, I see the black, troll-like drone that pilots it, spittle dripping viscously from its sharp-toothed grin.

"Astel Lev," I cry out in the breath before it strikes me. "Astel Lev!"

Everything stops: creatures in mid-flight, flags in mid-flutter, my descent toward the castle.

Nothing moves.

Nothing breathes. Nothing. No one.

I gasp for air.

Choking, I force myself back into this stranger's body, back into this stranger's bed, back into this stranger's life.

"Astel Lev."

I heard the dulcet voice before I saw its speaker, who glistened into the room on an infinity of tiny twinklings, her pearlescent hair rippling to her waist, shimmering as though it was starlight itself. She smiled and glided toward me, a cascade of flickering sparks trailing behind her.

"You are beginning to remember," she said, taking my hands in hers. Like her face, they were pale, almost gossamer. They felt neither warm nor cold; rather, some ineffable combination of both. And they felt barely solid, as though rays of moonlight held me in their incandescence. She wore a silvery robe that flashed and flared as she moved, just as her silver-green eyes did as they traveled the length of my body before resting on my face.

"Do you know who I am?" Her voice, too, shimmered, as though it emerged more from the aura that surrounded her than from her throat.

"Yes." I nodded in amazement. "You are Àna. B-but how…"

"Good." Her smile broadened so warmly that I couldn't help but grin back. "You are beginning to remember," she repeated.

"No, I'm not. I don't remember anything." The corners of my mouth dropped into a pout. "It doesn't make any sense. How I can know you when I don't know any of this?" I swept my arm to take in the newness of…everything. "Or that." I pointed up to the mirror.

Àna touched her index finger to my mouth.

"You are beginning to remember," she insisted.

I shook my head childishly.

"Your remembering will continue," she said softly. "Not in your time. In Star Time."

"Star Time? What's Star Time? What's Astel Lev?"

Àna's hands slid to my eyes. "More knowingness comes," she crooned.

"How?"

"Let your questions answer themselves, as they will...though not through *your* will."

"When?"

Àna's fingers played gently on my eyelids. I tried to force them to stay open. They refused.

"Soon..."

A moment later, I was asleep.

I float...freely and easily, so high above the ground that I see the world in its entirety spread out beneath me. Regal mountains crowned in snow...frothy surf pounding a relentless heartbeat..sapphire river chains flung casually onto crazy-quilt blankets of myriad textures and hues... Around me, cotton puffs scud through endless azure, brushing my cheeks with their damp softness.

"I'm home," I sigh.

Without losing its richness, the scene below becomes translucent, revealing a second world underneath it. This one is golden: vast seas of undulating sands flecked with emerald isles. The scene below is so real that I taste the waters burbling up into these oases, sift the velvet grains between my toes and touch my cheek where the warm breeze has kissed it.

This too is home.

A third landscape tiers below the first two. A fourth, fifth and sixth...then uncountable others. I experience each with equal clarity and with a giddy exuberance that swells with every added layer. Oceans, mountains, jungles, prairies, forests, lakes: I belong to each...I belong to all.

Skeptical, my mind's reality slices through the euphoria.

"How can this be?" it shrieks. "It's not possible. None of this is possible. None of it!"

A crippling vertigo overtakes me.

I tumble from my celestial perch, plummeting through a dizzying succession of colors, sounds, smells and tastes so overwhelming that I squeeze my eyes shut and slam my hands against my ears — to no effect. My awareness only heightens.

Deeper and faster, faster and deeper I fall — tumbling, turning, barreling, hurtling — until lifetimes later, I slam into the earth with a bone-jarring thud.

two

"Don't move. Let Co'anri make sure you're not hurt first." The young man who spoke knelt next to me on the floor, where I lay aching and bruised. Blond hair, curly and unkempt, framed a sun-browned face tight with worry. He wore the same coarse cotton pants and tunic I did. Like mine, they bore the ubiquitous sun-star pattern stitched onto the left breast, over his heart. His clothes, though, were stained and brightened by a flaming red neckerchief. He stared at me with sea-green eyes almost alarming in their intensity. I stared back, unable to look at anything but his face.

"You are okay, aren't you?" he asked.

"I'm fine." I groaned, tried to stand. He reached toward me, but whether to stop or steady me, I never knew. He didn't vanish. That would have been strange enough. Instead, the air around him flickered and the young man's body shrank steadily until he was an infant. Only the tanned, curl-framed face peering intently out at me from soft, white swaddling linked him to who he had just been. I blinked. The infant was gone. The young man was back. The look was the same.

"I— Did you—?" I turned to my other two visitors. Their faces, identical as twins, were nothing but creases and wrinkles so deep that I could barely make out eyes, mouth and nose. Wisps of wiry gray hair spilled down the sides of their heads, over quivering ears topped with three starlike points. They squatted next to me on short, stubby legs, their chubby, finlike hands — two fat fingers and a thumb — folded on their laps. All that distinguished their clothing from mine was a jagged, chevron-like rip through the sun-star embroidery. Nothing distinguished one from the other.

Again, I tried to stand. With a shake of the head, one of them placed a hand on my leg.

"You must not get up. Oh my no. Not yet, leastways." I recognized the throaty voice, and the touch. It was the sister.

"She is Co'anri," said the other in his familiar high-pitched tone. "I am Co'anra." He turned to the young man. "You should not be here, you know."

"Let him be, brother. He has all right to be here. More, perhaps, than we do." She touched her free hand to the young man's shoulder.

"Indeed," Co'anra muttered. "Well, get on with the s'ken, sister. It is not proper to leave a guest on the floor like this." Co'anri creaked to standing and pulled Co'anra up after her. His body complained even more loudly than had his sister's. At full height, they barely reached my shoulders.

I shrank back. "S'ken? What's that?"

I turned to the young man, my jumbled mind still trying to make sense of what I had seen of him. "Who are you?"

His eyes widened, furrowing his brow into dark creases of confusion.

"You don't know me?" He leaned in closer. His breath mingled with mine.

"How would I know you?"

He looked away, his face pale.

"Hmm." Co'anra tapped his cheek with his two fingers. "Worse than I thought. Much worse. Sister?"

She nodded. "The s'ken. Assuredly." She nudged the young man's shoulder. He turned back. His eyes were wet.

"You do not know his name?" she asked gently.

I shook my head.

"Ben," he whispered hoarsely.

Ben. I knew the name. But how? I clenched my fists until my nails bit into my palms. Nothing.

Tears rolled down my cheeks. "I don't know Ben. I don't know you." I stared up into the mirror. "I don't know her."

Ben looked at Co'anra. Coa'nra looked at Co'anri. Co'anri studied me closely.

"If you know anything," I cried, "anything at all, please tell me."

Co'anri shook her head almost imperceptibly.

"Please!"

"There is a season for telling and a season for kenning." Co'anri rubbed her hands together briskly. "Now is the season for kenning."

"The s'ken." Co'anra nodded his head so vigorously the flaps of skin on his face quavered.

Co'anri and Co'anra inched closer. I edged away. "What are you going to do to me?"

"Can you stand?" Co'anri asked. "Aid her, Ben."

I shrugged off Ben's help, awkwardly offered, and rose. For an instant, the room swayed. I braced myself on the bed.

"What's a s'ken?" I asked again.

"It is nothing to fear, indeed not," Co'anra replied.

Co'anri stood on tiptoes and pushed her face into mine, so near that I saw more clearly the features buried within the deep creases on her face: tiny, black, slit-like eyes, an O-shaped mouth that barely moved when she spoke, and a slight indentation, triangular in shape, in which three nostrils shivered. She nodded, rubbed her hands again and hummed softly — a single tone that vibrated all through my body.

Co'anra tilted his head and swayed. "It is a way my sister can ken your fli'aq."

"Can do what to my what?"

"Your— How would you say it, Ben?"

Ben looked at me then quickly averted his gaze. I could see that he longed to engage me but was offended because I didn't recognize him. If he wouldn't tell me who he was and no one would tell me who I was, what was I supposed to do? I only wanted answers.

"It's like she's studying your body," he said coolly, watching Co'anri. She swayed too. "She's trying to make sure nothing's damaged after your—"

Co'anra shook his head so slightly I almost missed it. What was everyone hiding from me?

"After your fall," Ben continued. "It's more than that. She's looking deep into every part of you, including parts others can't see."

"What about the parts I can't see?"

Ben shrugged.

Co'anri's monotone dropped to a gargly growl then coughed into staccato yips that lurched gratingly and increasingly loudly up the scale. The glass in the windows and door rattled. So did my skull. It didn't hurt. But it was unsettling, as though she was whipping up my insides with a giant churn.

With a piercing squeak, she stopped. The sudden silence jarred me off balance. Ben reached out to steady me.

"She couldn't ken you before now because it only works if you're upright," Ben explained, his earlier pique forgotten. "And you haven't been standing since—"

"Since when?" I asked eagerly.

Co'anra touched Ben's arm. "Not yet, Ben."

Ben's face darkened. Mine too.

"If you know something," I said as evenly as I could. "If you know *anything...*"

"Of course, you are anxious to know more," Co'anra said with uncharacteristic gentleness. "For Co'anri's s'ken to work appropriately, though, she must ken you as you are now, not as you would be with more knowingness. All we ask is a few minims of patience more. Can you give us just a few minims of patience more?"

I sighed. Did I have a choice?

Once more, Co'anri rubbed her hands together briskly. This time, they changed color with the friction — from blue to gold, then to orange and crimson before returning to flesh. She circled me twice, pausing each time to place one hand on the small of my back and the other on my right hip. When she faced me again, she stepped back and stretched both arms as high as she could reach, just past the top of my head. This time, her hands didn't touch me, but they were near enough that I could feel their heat. She didn't move for what seemed a long time, never breathing.

"Breathe, dear," Co'anra whispered to me. I hadn't realized that I'd stopped too. "The s'ken cannot work if you do not breathe."

Co'anri matched my exhalation with a startlingly loud intake of breath. Then she breathed out with what sounded like a violent sneeze. After that, she breathed in counterpoint to me, gulping air when I exhaled, discharging it explosively when I inhaled. Slowly, her breathing steadied. She lowered her arms to her sides, circled me a further two times, then stopped in front of me, humming. This time, it was gently melodic, a sweet sound that teased the edges of my memory. I closed my eyes and relaxed into it, only to be jerked back to the present moment when, once again, her voice bumped up into a dissonant, eardrum-shattering shriek. Then, in silence, she passed her hands up and down my body, hovering longer over my elbows, knees, nose and heart. At each stop her hands changed to a reddish-orange, where they lingered until the color dissipated, then moved on. In those moments of pause, I caught the slightest shake of her head and heard, from Co'anra, who followed her movements closely, an almost inaudible "tsk."

Throughout this unsettling diagnostic, waves of conflicting sensations engulfed me. I felt hot enough that I wanted to tear my clothes off yet so chilled that my body shook with cold. I was frantic with fear, while at the same time peacefully calm. I wept from an unbearable pain that coursed through me then giggled uncontrollably as though I were being tickled. I was exultant and dejected, grateful and angry, and both solid on my feet and so wobbly I expected to faint.

"Nothing bruised. Nothing broken," Co'anri pronounced. "Yet there is mending to be done. Oh my yes. Mending to be done."

Without warning, my legs collapsed. I clutched at the bed. My fingers refused to make contact. The floor rushed at me, its sun-star pattern fading to a fuzzy, indistinct blur, its pocked off-white tiles darkening to black.

Something jerked me onto the bed.

"Wh-what happened?"

"The foraa'a, Co'anra," Ben shouted. "You forgot the foraa'a!"

Co'anri swatted at her brother. He ducked.

"You pohrià," she exclaimed. "How could you forget the foraa'a?"

Co'anra ignored Co'anri, nodded at Ben and then, I'm certain, winked at me — though his eyes were still largely concealed.

"What's fora'aa?" I asked weakly after Co'anra had shuffled from the room. With all the questions tripping over each other in my mind for attention, only this least important of all emerged.

"A special broth," Ben replied when it became clear that Co'anri wouldn't. "What you're feeling is common after a s'ken. Fora'aa helps alleviate the symptoms. Dizziness, weakness. You'll feel better after you drink it. I know I did."

"You? When? Why?"

"No more questions," Co'anri replied before Ben could, her gaze fixed warningly on him. He shrugged.

An acrid odor invaded the room with Co'anra's return, a wooden tray balanced precariously on his head. Perched atop the tray was a silver cup nearly obscured by a billow of green-and-purple steam, a cup that threatened to tumble to the floor with each halting step. Ben rescued the tray from Co'anra's head. Co'anra thrust the cup in my face.

My stomach heaved. I pushed it away.

"No, no. You must," he insisted, his face so close to mine that only the cup he pressed to my lips separated us. Now I could see his eyes, mouth and nose too. They were just like his sister's.

"Oh my yes." Co'anri inserted her face next to her brother's. "You must. Indeed there is no choice. Not after a s'ken."

"Indeed," Co'anra repeated. "Not after a s'ken."

Even this near, they were indistinguishable, the folds and furrows on one face directly matching those on the other. Co'anra winked at me again.

I inhaled the steam, trying not to gag, before swallowing the hot, treacly liquid. To my relieved surprise its taste — sweet and spicy — bore no resemblance to its noxious smell. By the third and final sip, my head had cleared and all weakness had evaporated. I passed the cup to Co'anra.

"Oh my no" Co'anri thrust it back at me. "You must drink it all. All of it, if the mending is to be truly commenced. Oh my yes."

"I did. I drank it all." The cup was empty.

"Not." Co'anra flicked the cup with his fingernail. It refilled itself. "The fora'aa knows what you need. Indeed, it does." He nodded his head.

After four more cups, the refills ceased and the cup vanished from my hand.

"Now," Co'anra proclaimed. With great effort, he shuffled to the farthest corner of the room and pushed something only he could see toward my bed, stopping every few steps to wipe perspiration from his forehead with a white kerchief pulled from his sleeve. When he reached my bedside, he lowered himself achingly into the nothingness until he sat facing me on a cushion of air. "No," he muttered. He rose and stared at the invisible chair with disgust. He nudged it backwards then forward, to the left then to the right, each new adjustment more subtle than the last. Finally satisfied, he sank back into it, sighing contentedly. Co'anri stood behind him, one hand on his shoulder. Ben stood several paces behind her, a full two heads taller.

"Now," Co'anra repeated. "Now is it time for storying."

three

"Once," Co'anra began, "so many seasons ago that time itself had a different measure, the world was ruled by the stars."

Co'anri nodded. "By the stars. Oh my yes." She stroked the rip in her tunic and murmured an inaudible invocation.

Co'anra drummed his fingers on the invisible arm of his invisible chair and stared into the ceiling.

"Go on, brother." She placed a hand over Co'anra's.

He pulled his hand free and continued drumming. Only when Co'anri stepped back did he go on. "The stars, in that time before time, arranged themselves into the patterns you know as constellations. These patterns held the land and its people in a loving embrace that denied none their true character and united all in the Heart of the Star. This star, known in those ancient times as Astel Lev—"

I gasped loudly.

"Astel Lev?"

"Indeed, yes. Is that not what I said?"

"Yes, but—"

"You must let him finish, dear one," Co'anri cut in. "He hates when anyone interrupts his storying. Don't you, brother?"

"Hmph."

"But—"

"You'd better let him finish," Ben said.

"This star," Co'anra declared loudly, "known in those ancient times as Astel Lev burned most fiercely in the heart of Reesa Kam'ana, the Star Chantress…"

"Alla ka tchù, tia à." A voice, strong yet ethereal, sings these words to a haunting, minor-key melody. Her voice swells, becomes more insistent, drowning out Co'anra's story.

The room darkens then disappears as her chant continues.

Stars twinkle alight overhead. First a few, then a few more until, all at once, the night sky bursts into a diadem of constellations.

I know it to be the night sky, for everywhere around me are trees ripe with fruit and lush with flowering buds, all illuminated by the stars of a moonless night, which sparkle reflectively in a trio of silvery waterfalls whose music underscores the song. On an island in the center of the stream created by the cascading waters stands Reesa Kam'ana, her arms outstretched to the heavens. Timeless and translucent, her face is both ancient and childlike, gentle and fierce. She radiates a silvery light that glints in the dark.

"Alla ka tchù, tia à," she sings. "Alla ka tchù, tia à."

Co'anra's voice rose over Reesa Kam'ana's and my vision faded, though her chant still played in the dim recesses of my hearing.

"Then one day," he continued, "in the timelessness that is the truth of all time, Astel Lev vanished from Reesa Kam'ana's care. Without Astel Lev, she could no longer sing. And without her chant…"

Reesa Kam'ana's voice stopped, mid-chant.

Co'anra took a deep, trembling breath. He gripped the invisible arms of his chair to steady himself. Co'anri pressed her hand into his shoulder. After a few moments, he sighed and continued.

"Without her chant, the stars lost their moorings and, one by one, the celestial tapestries unraveled. Once all constellations had scattered, the unraveling could not be stopped and the land of M'ranna fell into chaos."

"Into chaos. Oh my yes," Co'anri added. She knelt next to Co'anra and squeezed his hand.

"What happened to Astel Lev?" I asked.

"They say the Stone People know," Co'anri said.

"Indeed," Co'anra nodded. "If that is true, they hold that knowledge close."

"Why is that?" I asked.

"That knowledge, too, they hold close," Co'anra replied.

"There is more," Coa'nri added. "The Black Lord."

"Indeed. Bo'Rá K'n. He surely has had a hand in this."

A clammy sweat chilled me at the mention of Bo'Rá K'n's name.

"B-Bo—" I couldn't speak it. I didn't know why.

Co'anri pulled her hand free and swatted her brother across the forehead. He pushed her away.

"What is it?"

"You left out the most important part of the story." She swung at him again. He ducked. "How could you forget the most important part? You neglected to ee'jin, didn't you?"

"Hmm? Oh. Indeed. No. Yes." He nodded. "The most important part."

He leaned back and closed his eyes. Co'anri stood and resumed her place behind his chair. "The unraveling?" she prompted.

"The unraveling. Once the tapestry's threads unraveled, tangled and knotted, the kep'chas awoke from the dead to do the bidding of S'kryssna S'kyaga, the Serpentine Sorceress..."

The room again darkens. Sconces leap to light and I see the flickering gloom of an elegantly appointed sitting room high up in a castle turret. Outside on a balcony, stands a tall woman silhouetted against the chaotic night sky. She croons sibilantly to the birdlike creatures I recognize as kep'chas as they swoop past her, piloted by their thorag drones.

A flash of lightning scars the sky. The kep'chas scatter into the night.

A second flash of lightning.

A giant kep'cha, many times larger than the others, thrusts itself toward the balcony, its wingspan so broad that it veils all starlight. Just before impact, it shrinks and swoops past the woman and into the sitting room. The woman turns and follows the kep'cha inside. It lands next to her.

"My Lord," S'kryssna S'kyaga says, with the slightest dip of her head. Startlingly beautiful, she is willowy, with pale, creamy skin and straight, raven hair that cascades to her waist. Only her cold, washed-out gray-blue eyes suggest the evil I know to dwell in her heart.

The kep'cha re-forms itself into a tall figure cloaked in black, a swirling mass of dusky mist partly veiling his face. As tall as S'kryssna S'kayaga is, Bo'Rá K'n towers over her.

"She is here," he says, in a voice that could turn blood to ice.

"So I have heard. They both are. I thought—"

"I will tell you what to think...and when to think it."

"My Lord."

"You still believe you can stop her? Because if you cannot—"

"I know I can."

"I have been deceived before."

"I as well, my Lord. No more."

"No, S'kyaga. No more. You desire to rule M'ranna. Eternally. Only I can give that to you. In exchange..."

"In exchange, I destroy the Fayr'Owyn."

Bo'Rà K'n circles S'kryssna S'kyaga slowly. Silently. She waits, in such perfect stillness that she might not be breathing. He stops in front of her, his face a hair's breadth from hers. She blinks but will not flinch.

"The thorags will have their body, S'kyaga." He pauses, his eyes blazing. "Hers or yours."

Without waiting for a reply, he strides outside and leaps off the balcony, becoming once again a giant kep'cha that blackens the sky as it flies off, screeching angrily.

His screech melts into the distance, taking the vision with it.

Co'anra looked at me curiously, as though he sensed I had seen something and was waiting for me to share it. I said nothing. Ben handed him a goblet. He sipped slowly, gazed at me again and, after a few moments' silence, continued.

"Yet in the midst of the terror that S'kryssna S'kyaga wreaked on the land, the stars did not lose the entirety of their power. Within them lived the legend of the Fayr'Owyn, who, it was said, would emerge from the angry mist to rekindle Astel Lev and return it to the Star Chantress, its rightful guardian. Only then would the storied pattern be restored. Only then would M'ranna fulfill its destiny. Only then would S'kryssna S'kyaga and her nightmare master be thwarted."

Co'anra looked up at Co'anri and nodded.

"The StarQuest," she said.

"Indeed."

With Co'nari's help, he stood, shakily, and touched his hand to the ripped sun-star stitching.

"Only the Fayr'Owyn can make things right again," Co'anri said, touching her heart.

They gazed dreamily into the some imagined realm. "O, Fayr'Owyn from ages far-distant," they chanted, "where are you? M'ranna waits."

four

Co'anra and Co'anri stood, hands on hearts, for what seemed forever. I had so many questions I was sure that I would explode. But Ben touched his finger to his lips and I held still. Finally, they dropped their hands and Coa'nra lowered himself back into his armchair.

"What's a Fayr'Owyn?" I asked.

Co'anra hesitated. He looked from me to Co'anri. Although he said nothing, I sensed that some knowingness passed between them.

"I cannot say," Co'anra said when Co'anri looked away, "other than that her arrival has long been prophesied. I know the prophecy as I know this story. Beyond that, I know nothing."

"You know something more, brother," Co'anri countered.

"What is that?"

"You know that the Black Lord is determined to undo the prophecy."

Co'anra nodded. "He will try."

He rose painfully and pulled himself to my side, once again bringing his face so close to mine that I could see his tiny eyes. "He already has."

"With the sorceress's help."

"Indeed."

"No matter what they think," Co'anra continued, "other forces are more powerful still. More powerful than her. More powerful than him. Mightily so." He collapsed, coughing, back into his invisible seat, and his features folded back into the furrows of skin on his face. "Mightily so," he wheezed.

Co'anri patted his arm and whispered something in his ear. He nodded wearily. Almost immediately, his head dropped to his chest. A soft snore vibrated from the creases around his mouth. Co'anri stroked the top of his head then limped toward the door. With one hand on the handle, she turned back and cocked her head inquiringly at Ben. But Ben, who stared at me so intently that I had to look away, ignored her. Co'anri sighed and was gone.

"How can you say you don't know me?" Ben's face was hard and angry. I forced my eyes to his.

"If you know me," I said, "tell me who I am. Tell me who *you* are. I don't know anything. About anything. Every time I ask a question, someone tells me to wait."

"Who? Who tells you to wait?"

"Co'anri. Co'anra…"

"You've seen something…someone."

"What do you mean?"

"A vision. More than one, maybe."

I shook my head.

"You have." He scanned the room as though looking for clues that I was lying, then he drilled his eyes into me again. "I know you have. Tell me."

I shook my head again, fiercely this time. "Why would I tell you anything?" I pointed to Co'anra, who still slept. "Why would I tell any of you anything? I ask who I am and how I got here, and all I get is an ancient legend about this Fayr'Owyn, whatever it is. You either know who I am or you don't. You either know why I'm here or you don't. *You* know what this place is. But you don't tell me anything. All you do is demand and accuse. I'm tired of it. Just go away." I curled up, my back to him, my eyes closed.

I felt Ben's hand on my neck. I didn't turn.

"You really don't know who I am?" he asked softly.

I said nothing.

"You really don't recognize me?"

I saw no reason to respond.

Ben breathed into my silence. "You really don't know anything, do you?" he asked, as much to himself as to me.

I ignored him.

"I'm sorry, Q'nta," he said softly.

I jerked my head around. "What did you call me?"

"Q'nta. Isn't that your name?"

I bolted up and grabbed his shirt. "How—?"

"Huppapra-sh-sh-*SHA*!" Co'anra lurched awake and shook his head until all the wrinkles in his face quivered like gelatin. His eyes darted blindly around the room. "Oh," he exclaimed when he noticed us. "You."

Ben pried my fingers from his shirt and placed my hands on my lap.

"Did we wake you?" I asked, trying to regain some composure.

"Wake me? *Ha!*" Co'anra roared. Ben and I both started at the uncharacteristically large sound. Co'anra blushed a light pink. "Pardon me," he said in his normal, high-pitched voice. "I was in ee'jin. I drop into it quite unexpectedly sometimes. Now, I have dropped out of it." He stood and stretched, then plopped back into his armchair. "My, how I feel better. Indeed, I do."

He looked better. The folds in his face had flattened enough for me to see a yawn morph into a tiny smile and diamond-like sparkles glint from his dark, knowing eyes. He tipped his head ever so slightly at Ben, then at me, then at Ben again, where his glance lingered.

"Please find Co'anri," he said, "and let her know that our guest requires comestibles." He turned to me. "You do, do you not?"

I hadn't noticed how hungry I was until that instant. My stomach growled loudly.

Co'anra laughed. "You had best hurry. There is an impatient belly waiting to be filled."

Co'anra waited until Ben was gone before speaking again. "You *are* impatient, Q'nta."

That name again.

"I know what I know," Co'anra said before I could speak. He closed his eyes and let his head drop to his chest. After two snuffling rasps, he opened one eye and grinned. "And I hear what I hear."

"You weren't asleep!" I didn't know whether to be angry or laugh.

"I was not asleep." He giggled, opened both eyes and sat up. "Ee'jin looks like sleep but it is not sleep. Not at all. I cannot see what is going on around me when I'm in ee'jin, but I hear everything and I sense even more."

"So you didn't know my name?"

"You are just like that Ben." Co'anra laughed. "Questions, questions. Always questions."

I dropped my eyes and twisted my sleeve. "I'm sorry."

"Do not be. Indeed not. Of course you have questions. So many that it is hard to know which to ask first. Yes?"

I nodded my head.

"If I allow you to ask me any one question right now, which would it be?"

"Who's Ben?" The question slipped out before I could think.

Co'anra said nothing. He seemed to be waiting for an explanation. I didn't have one.

"A good question. Indeed it is," he said at last. "Ben asks it every day."

"Why? Doesn't he live here, with you?"

"For now."

"I don't understand."

"How could you? There are always more questions than answers and never time enough for the answers there are. Indeed not." He leaned in toward me, whispering. "You are not safe here. Not you. Not Ben. Co'anri will not like me to say this. No, she will not. Still, what she likes and what she does not like cannot change what is. I have told Ben; now I tell you: You will have to leave. Both of you."

Numb to my rising panic, I slid from the bed, smoothed my tunic and ran my fingers through my knot of hair. I slipped on a nearby pair of sandals. "Are these mine?"

"No, no." Co'anra heaved himself from his chair. "Impatient and impetuous," he muttered. "Just like the Ko'leya."

The Ko'leya? I kicked off the sandals.

"Sit," he ordered. "Of course, I am not throwing you out. Indeed, I am not. But it will not be long before S'kryssna S'kyaga discovers that we are harboring Outlanders. When she does, it will not matter what you know or do not know, who you are or who you are not. Indeed, it will not." He made a slashing motion across his throat. "Or worse." He dropped his voice. "My sister thinks we can keep you hidden. Not one Outlander, but two. I say nothing remains hidden for long from that sorceress."

I buried my head in my hands and wept. How could someone know me enough to want to kill me when I didn't even know myself?

"Oh, dear," Co'anra sighed. "There is no need to weep. Indeed, there is not." He patted my head. "The sandals. They are yours, you know," he added, not knowing what else to say to comfort me. He glanced nervously at the door. "If Co'anri sees that I have caused your tears—"

"You made her cry, brother!" Co'anri exploded into the room, Ben at her heels, pushing a cart overflowing with strange foods. "What have you been telling her? Why have you been frightening her? Can I not leave you for one minim without you making a bother?" Limping as fast as she could, she hurried to my side. She pushed Co'anra away, so violently that he tumbled to the floor.

"Liar," she snarled in his direction. She turned to Ben. "Haven't I always said so?" She pressed her head to my bosom and held me tightly. "Pay no attention to that—that… He is no brother of mine. I disown him. For all time. What did he say? Whatever it was, it was a lie. Why would not you stay? You too, Ben." She glared at Co'anra. "A liar. A liar and a bully. Yes, he is. Oh my yes." She limped to the door and blocked Co'anra, who was trying to slip out. He swatted at her. She dodged with surprising agility. Then she kicked him so hard he yelped. Recovering, he bent over and rammed her stomach with his head.

"Shouldn't we do something?" I asked Ben.

"They'll get over it. They always do. You'll see." He grinned. "I'm sorry I got angry before."

I smiled back weakly. "You're not from here either."

"No."

"Did you get here the same way I did?"

"I— No. Food first." He pushed the cart over. "You've got to be hungry. I was ravenous when I got here." He plucked a plump, crimson fruit from the center of the tray — kiribà, he called it — and forced it into my hand. "Eat."

"But my name. How did you know it?"

"How did you know mine?"

"What do you mean? I didn't. Until just now, I mean."

He looked at me quizzically. "Are you sure?" He shook his head. "Never mind." Gently, he pushed my hand toward my mouth. "If Co'anri sees you haven't eaten, she'll go at me just like she's going after him."

I bit into the kiribà. It was as juicy as it was crunchy, with flesh as red as its skin. The sweet-sour flavor was surprisingly satisfying, and I reached for another. By the door, Co'anri slapped her brother's arms and chest. Co'anra dropped to his knees and bit Co'anri's ankle. She kicked him. He grabbed her leg and she tumbled noisily on top of him.

"Are you sure we shouldn't stop them?" I asked my mouth full of yàmana. "Aren't they hurting each other?" This fruit's rough, mud-colored skin peeled away to reveal a stringy flesh braided in strands of bright orange and shocking pink. It was sweet, almost too sweet, and left a tingly aftertaste on my tongue.

"Best not to get in their way. I learned that the hard way." He picked a thomé from a gold-stemmed cluster of fluorescent violet nuts. "Try one of these. They're messy but really good."

He was right. My questions forgotten, I devoured fruit after nut after bread until a scattering of skins, pits, crumbs and shells was all that remained. Only then did I notice that Co'anra and Co'anri were hugging and blubbering.

"It always ends this way." Ben rolled his eyes and laughed. He pulled a sticky, orange twig-like confection from behind his back. "I saved the best for last. It's filiamo."

When I bit into it, the filiamo burst open with a startling crack and squirted sticky, green juice all over my hands.

Co'anri bustled over with a damp, scented cloth. "Are you still hungry, my dear?"

"Only for knowingness." I wiped my hands and face and inhaled the perfume. It reminded me of something pleasant. My mind refused to make the connection. "I know this smell," I said. "What is it?"

"It is time for Ben's story," Co'anra said, ignoring my question.

"You do it," Ben said.

"It is more yours than mine. Why will you not speak it?"

"I will," Ben replied. "Through you."

I looked from one to the other. "I don't care who tells it. Will someone just do it?"

Co'anri nodded at Co'anra then limped from the room, pushing the food cart in front of her.

"Very well," Co'anra said. "To hear Ben tell it, you— You tell it so well, Ben…"

Ben said nothing. He stood statue-still, his eyes trained fixedly on my face. Co'anra sighed. "To hear Ben tell it, you materialized out of nothing. Indeed, you did. One minim he stood alone atop the Ko'Ba, watching the Ma's waters throw themselves at the rocks. The next, in the space between the Ma's in-breath and out-breath, you appeared."

"Appeared? What do you mean?"

"You appeared." The voice was Ben's, but his lips never moved. The sound emerged from Co'anra's mouth.

Ben's stare drilled into me so intensely, it was as though he saw everything about me. I blushed and looked back at Co'anra, who continued, as though he was Ben.

"It was like you took form from the water droplets that hung in the air. There was this one breaker that crashed onto the Ko'Ba, reaching higher than I'd ever seen before. I've always been safe and dry up there but this one drenched me. It hit so fast and hard I thought it would throw me off the ledge. And loud. I don't think I've ever heard anything so loud. Like thunder crashing in my head. I should have been scared. I don't know why I wasn't. But I wasn't."

Co'anra slumped in his chair, his face more deeply wrinkled than I had yet seen it. He faltered as Co'anri returned, carrying a goblet so clear it would have been invisible but for a sparkling gold cider that bubbled inside it. She passed it to her brother. He sipped slowly, gathering his thoughts and marshaling his strength. When he spoke again, he sat straighter. He still looked tired. As before, his voice was Ben's — youthful and passionate.

Ben hadn't moved, had barely blinked.

"I jumped back to save myself from the worst of it. As soon as I did, those water droplets came together where I had stood. They came together. They were you."

Co'anra finished his cider and passed the cup back to his sister. "Are you ready for more?" he asked, in his own voice. Finlike fingers reached for my hand and squeezed. I nodded, my heart racing. He inhaled deeply and, once more, the voice that moved through him was Ben's.

"It had to have been magic." Ben's face had lost its expressionless stare. Instead, the words seemed to speak from his eyes, as well as from Co'anra's mouth. "Magic," he repeated. "What else could it have been?"

"What happened?" I whispered.

"You looked at me. The look on your face was, was— I can't even describe it. Like you had seen a ghost? Water was streaming down your face. Not only from the Ma. You were sobbing the name 'Ben.' Louder and louder. Louder than the waves. And they were pretty loud."

BEN!

A thundering noise crashed in my head, loud as any breaker, in wave after wave of pain. With each wave, I heard myself cry out his name.

Ben! Ben! BEN!

"You reached out to touch my face. It's like you couldn't believe I was real. I know I didn't think you were. Before your hand reached me, you fainted. I couldn't wake you. I tried and tried. Nothing worked. So I half-carried, half-dragged you back here."

Once more, Co'anra collapsed in his chair. Co'anri knelt by his side and forced more cider into him.

Now, Ben spoke his own words, his eyes rimmed with tears. "Who are you that you appeared like that?"

I could barely hear him over the thunder still smashing against my skull.

"Who are you that you called me Ben?" he implored. "Who are you?"

When I said nothing, he fled from the room, slamming the door behind him.

five

"Do not fuss about Ben," Co'anri said. She patted my pillow and smoothed my bedclothes. "He will be back after he cools off. He is headstrong, that one."

I wanted to go after him. Co'anri wouldn't let me. "Rest time," she insisted. "Then answer time."

"My sister is right," Co'anra added. "You will need strength and wellness." He leaned into me so Co'anri wouldn't hear. "For the journeying ahead."

Co'anri elbowed him aside. "I heard that, brother," she growled. "Oh my yes."

"Oh my yes," he mimicked back. He punched her in the side as they shuffled, limped and bickered from the room.

With my eyes closed, sleep eluded me. With them open, the image in the ceiling mirror mocked me. I climbed out of bed. There wasn't much to see in my round room. Apart from the bed, a nightstand, a small table by the door, a low stool by the far wall and Co'anra's invisible chair, which I immediately bumped into, the only "furniture" I was aware of was a fringed cotton cloth suspended chest-high in midair in front of one of the windows. Atop it sat a cream-colored basin and pitcher. I moved toward the window slowly, sweeping my hands in front of me as I walked, trying to avoid colliding with anything else I might not be able to see.

"Prakk," I swore softly, when my foot smashed into whatever supported the cloth. I hopped in circles on one foot — only to bump my elbow. "Prakk estafi," I swore again.

"Don't let Co'anri hear you talk like that." Ben shut the door behind him. "She may swear at Co'anra, but she doesn't like anyone else to do it."

I glared at him.

"Sorry. I shouldn't laugh." He took my arm. "Lean on me and let's take a look." A greenish-purple bruise had spread over the tip of my toe. "Just be grateful for the cloth covers. Without them, you'd be bumping into everything like I did."

He touched my toe gently. I gasped.

"I came back to apologize."

"It's okay."

He shook his head. "It isn't. I shouldn't have slammed out of here like that. It's just that—" He examined my toe. "Can you bend it?"

I tried, and flinched.

"The water will help."

"What water?" The pitcher was empty, and the basin held nothing but an encircled eight-pointed star.

Ben passed me the pitcher. "Does it feel empty?"

It didn't. Although I saw and heard nothing, liquid seemed to be sloshing around inside.

"Pour some into the basin."

I felt foolish as I tilted the pitcher. Its shifting weight was so disorienting that I nearly dropped it.

"Are your hands still sticky from the filiamo?"

"A little bit."

"Wash them."

"How?"

Ben laid my hands palms down in the basin. I felt nothing at first.

"What?" I asked.

"Wait."

"For what?" I wiggled my fingers. A vague warmth coated my hands, as if someone were breathing on them. I rubbed them together, and all stickiness dissolved.

"For that."

"This place just gets stranger and stranger. Now what?"

"Do you need to dry them?"

"Funny."

Carefully, Ben lifted the basin and placed it on the floor. "Put your toe in."

"Why?"

"Do you always ask this many questions?"

I smiled. "Co'anra says you ask even more."

Ben laughed. "Just do it. You'll see why."

I dunked my toe. All soreness dissipated. A moment later, the final flush of purple had vanished, as had any swelling.

I replaced the basin next to the pitcher. "Nothing here makes any sense," I sighed. I would be repeating versions of those five words often.

"There's more."

What more could there be?

"Look inside the basin."

Ben whipped up its invisible contents with his finger. Bleached spots appeared on the cloth where unseeable liquid slopped over the edge. They disappeared almost immediately as they dried. Inside, the basin's cream-colored bottom darkened to blue and lost its solidity, taking on an ocean-like depth so entrancing that I felt myself dissolving into it.

I stand on an ocean floor. Around me, a forest of giant ferns sways to music that permeates every water droplet.

Alla ka tchù, tia à

Alla ka tchù, tia à

Alla ka tchù, tia à

That music again…the same music Reesa Kam'ana sang. I know I must sing these words. I know, too, that my heart will explode if I do not free this song into the sea. But how can I open my mouth? I will drown if I do.

Still, the music calls. Insistently. Still frightened, I hold my breath. The water churns. The ferns' dance turns menacing. My lungs burn.

If I sing, I will die.

If I don't sing, I will die.

I hum the melody through watertight lips. It's not enough. The words demand equal time. The ferns whip at me. The water froths and roils. I can barely see, barely hear. The music fades…fades…

I cannot hold back. I must sing. If die I must, I will die with the music.

My mouth opens…

Alla ka tchù, tia à

No water rushes in.

Alla ka tchù, tia à

I breath. Normally.

Alla ka tchù, tia à

I sing. Naturally. With each sung word, waters calm, ferns relax, music swells.

Alla ka tchù, tia à

Alla ka tchù, tia à

Alla ka tchù, tia à

Other voices join with mine. Other songs blend with mine. I sing them all — all at once.

The ferns part in front of me. Through the opening, a kaleidoscope of many-hued lights flash and dart hypnotically, then slow into pyramid-like formation. They are not lights at all. They're luminescent ovals, the rarest of fish, the same fish that helped save my father—

My father? I don't know how I know this and I don't know who my father is. Yet this shard of memory fills my eyes with tears. They fall from my face in silver droplets that float fizzily toward two ovals that have broken away from the others. The fish swallow my tears as they glide toward me.

I had thought all the fish to be indistinguishable, one from the other. But as these two swim closer, I realize that they are not at all the same. One's colors are vivid; the other's, more muted. One is larger, with glistening black eyes and thick lips that form a perpetual smile. It butts up against the smaller one, whose eyes so match the ocean's changing color that they seem to disappear altogether. Its thicker lips form an O, out of which bubbles gurgle in threes and fours.

For an instant, the bubbles distort my view. In that same instant, the larger oval looks like Co'anra, the smaller like Co'anri. Then the bubbles clear and all I see are twin ovals. They flick their tails at the fern opening and merge back into their pyramid. The ferns melt into each other, taking fish, ocean and music with them.

I'm back in my room, staring into the cream-colored bottom of an empty basin.

"You saw it too?"

I jumped at Ben's voice, barely a whisper.

"The first time I saw the fish in there, and the sea, I thought for sure I was going crazy. The second time, I asked Co'anra about it. He looked at me funny. Then he started talking about something else. This time was even stranger. This time I heard the music. I've never heard music before."

"What does it mean?"

Ben shrugged.

"What is this place?"

"M'ranna."

"What is that?"

Ben shook his head. "I don't know."

six

Co'anri shuffled back in, supported by a rough, twisted-wood walking stick that she poked at Ben. "You should not be in here," she scolded. "Oh my no. Not by yourself." She poked him again. "Not a word," she interrupted when he tried to speak. "Out. Out. This Q'nta needs to rest. Oh my yes. She needs to rest."

Co'anri must have been right. Before the door closed, I was asleep.

I slept, but without rest. I woke frequently, alternately hot then cold, thirsty then unable to swallow, fidgety then still — all the while too tired to do anything other than rearrange my tossed and rumpled bedclothes and try, once more, to sleep.

Although my room darkened as time passed, flickering half-light from the windows never dimmed. Vague shapes played like shadow puppets from the other side of the glass. I watched, wondering who or what they might be until, as they faded with dawn's first glow, I fell into a deep, dreamless sleep.

*　*　*

"Good morning, sleepybones." I forced my sleep-crusted eyes open and squinted at Ben. His tight face relaxed into a generous smile. "I brought us breakfast." A tray overflowing with colorful fruits, nuts and breads hung in midair next to him. Cross-legged in Co'anra's chair, he also seemed to hover, unsupported, above the floor.

I smiled back weakly and grunted. My head throbbed, ached and spun. Had I really slept? If so, I felt no benefit. "Sleepybones?"

"I don't know why I said that." Ben pushed the invisible breakfast table closer to my bed. "I've never used that word before. 'Good morning, sleepybones.' Odd."

"Maybe not." *Good morning, sleepybones.* Something about that curious, strangely familiar phrase teased at my mind. I shook my head, trying to jar loose the half-memory. *Good morning, sleepybones.* I could almost hear the woman's voice who spoke it. Almost.

"What do you mean?" he asked.

I shook my head again. Reaching for the tray, I picked out a long, hairy-skinned fat stick. I turned it over and around, wondering if there was a way to eat it and why one would want to. Brown and brittle, it looked singularly unappetizing.

"How do you manage?" I asked.

Ben took it from me and cracked it open. Soft, yellow flesh spiked with tiny crimson seeds appeared. He sucked pulp out of one half.

"It's called tikinà." He passed the other half back to me. "Here, you try."

I touched my tongue to the fruity inside then, satisfied with its tart flavor, slurped it out. It dissolved before I could swallow it.

"Good, eh?"

I nodded, reaching for another.

"It's one of my favorites."

I cracked open the tikinà. "I meant how do you manage the pieces of memory that don't connect with anything? Like 'sleepybones.'"

"At least you've got a witness to your arrival." He poked himself in the chest. "All I know is that I turned up on the Co'ans' doorstep one day. I don't know anything before then. The only reason I know that is because Co'anra told me. I don't remember anything at all." He popped three kiribà into his mouth. "Nothing."

"You know something," I said. "You knew my name. You called me Q'nta."

"And you knew mine. When I didn't."

And you knew mine. When I didn't.

Ben's words echoed in my head, louder and louder until I couldn't bear it.

And you knew mine. When I didn't.

I shut my eyes.

And you knew mine. When I didn't.

His words became thunder. The thunder of ocean breakers. My tears became another day's tears, mingled with sea mist.

"BEN!"

He stares at me in fear and confusion. Salt water from the Ma slicks the hair to his scalp and the clothes to his body.

"Ben. Ben! BEN!" I rush toward him, my heart pounding.
Then blackness. Then nothing.

"You didn't know your name until I called it out?" I opened my eyes. My head still throbbed.

Ben didn't answer.

"Is it your name? Are you Ben?"

He glanced up into the mirror and touched his face. "I think it is. It feels right." He shrugged. "I don't know."

"But you knew me. You knew my name."

"I didn't. You were a stranger when I saw you on the Ko'Ba." He half-smiled. "A deranged stranger."

"But my name. You called me Q'nta."

"Sometimes, I just know things. It comes in flashes, with no explanation. That's how I knew to call you Q'nta." He stared up into the mirror again and stroked his cheek, thoughtfully. "It feels right. Like 'Ben.' Is it true?" He shook his head. "I can't say." He dropped his hand into his lap and looked at me, still in the mirror. "I don't know any more about you than I know about myself. That's why I was so angry before. Co'anra and Co'anri can't tell me anything. Or won't. Then you turn up, call me by a name I don't know and promptly faint away." He laughed bitterly. "All the time you were sleeping, I figured you'd tell me all about me when you woke up."

"I didn't."

"No." He picked up another tikinà, cracked it open and sucked out the fruit. Crimson juice dribbled down his chin.

"Doesn't the not knowing make you crazy?"

Ben laughed. "You've already seen that it does."

"Me too." I didn't feel like laughing. "I know I've heard 'sleepy-bones' before. I almost know how. I just can't touch it. It so frustrating."

"Yeah."

"Then there's Àna." I told Ben the story. "How did I know who she was?" I groaned. "I still don't know who she is. Just her name."

Ben slathered a sticky green paste on a slice of orange bread. "I haven't seen your Àna. I've seen plenty of other strange things."

"Like what?"

He glanced at the door. "Later. Maybe we can sneak out for a bit and I'll show you." He poured red sauce on the concoction and stuffed it in his mouth. "I don't know how I manage. I just do. I know you're discouraged and angry. I still am, sometimes. Not as much as when I first got here. Ask Co'anra. I threw things around. A lot."

"What happened?"

"I gave up. Nothing I did brought much memory back. Just unconnected pieces of…of I don't know what. I don't even know if they've been my memories or someone else's. Or even memories at all." He shrugged. "Even when you called me Ben, I couldn't be sure it was my name, or that you even really knew me." He grinned. "You weren't exactly calm and rational."

"I suppose not." I laughed.

The sound of approaching footsteps — the distinctive shuffle and limp of the Co'ans — silenced me. "Should you be here?" I whispered.

Ben stuffed the last kiribà into his mouth. "Co'anri will be annoyed and Co'anra will say it's okay. Or the other way around. They're always disagreeing with each other." He swallowed. "It'll be all right. For all their bickering, they're good people."

Co'anri's stick pushed at the unlatched door. It swung open, banged into the wall. "Good morning," she sang. "A beautiful morning. Oh my yes."

"Indeed it is, sister." Co'anra shuffled in behind. "Indeed it is."

Co'anri beamed at the empty tray. "You have eaten! Wonderful. Is it not wonderful, brother?"

He nodded his head so vigorously that the flaps and folds in his face slapped loudly. "Indeed. Indeed."

"Tell them, Co'anra." She prodded him with her stick.

"Tell them? Oh, yes." He followed Co'anri to the edge of the bed. He patted Ben's back. "Good to see you here, my boy. Is it not good to see him here, sister?"

"Oh my yes. Yes, it is, brother. Have you told them yet?"

"Told them?" Co'anra laughed — somewhere between a forced laugh and a nervous one. "Yes, yes. I am to tell them. You are right, sister." He turned to Ben. "Can you push another chair over for me?" He pointed to the far corner. "You probably don't even know that one is there."

When Ben had set the chair in place and Co'anra had sunk into it, Co'anri leaned her stick against her brother's chair and picked up the tray. Ben grabbed the last tikinà.

"I will return this to the gabaya," she said, "while you tell them, brother. About the surprise."

"The surprise? Indeed, yes. The surprise." He turned to me. "We think you are strong enough—" He turned to Ben. "We think she is strong enough — and you too — to go on an outing."

"An outing?" Ben and I replied in unison.

"Yes, to the Ma."

"To the Ma?" Ben exclaimed. "You *never* want me to go the Ma. You never want me to be alone with Q'nta." He narrowed his eyes. "What's going on?"

"What is going on?" Co'anra shifted uneasily. "It's just that… We think… Maybe…" He looked down at his fingers, which were tapping loudly on the chair's invisible arm. In mid-tap he jerked his head up, as if he had just remembered the rehearsed answer to an expected question. "Maybe the Ma will take you home again? I know it has not until now," he added before Ben could argue. "Maybe with both of you there? Or maybe it will bring back some memories if you both go together?"

Ben leaned forward and fixed Co'anra with an intense stare. "You know I don't believe you. Right?"

Co'anra tapped harder and glanced hopefully at the door. Co'anri didn't return. Ben snapped his tikinà open with a loud crack. Co'anra jumped.

Ben passed me half the stick and smirked. "I'd love to show Q'nta the Ma and the Ko'Ba."

Co'anra exhaled loudly and stopped fidgeting.

"Maybe you're right," Ben continued. "Maybe we will remember more if we're out there together." He sucked his half of the tikinà dry and discarded its husk. Frowning, he studied Co'anra and said nothing. Co'anra squirmed.

"I still think you're hiding something." Ben's eyes twinkled. He winked at me.

Co'anra ignored him. "Would you not like that?" he asked, looking at me hopefully. "Would you not like to see the Ma and revisit the Ko'Ba?"

I felt sorry for him, but that wasn't the only reason I said yes. Going back to the Ko'Ba felt like a real chance, finally, to remember something more than a meaningless fragment.

Co'anra pulled himself up from his chair. "That is that, then," he mumbled to himself.

"Wait." Ben gently pushed him back into the chair. "Before you go, can you tell Q'nta how I got here?"

"You could tell her yourself, Ko'leya."

"What's Ko'leya?" I asked.

"Another name," Ben replied. "Co'anra will tell you."

"It would be a fine story for your outing. Indeed, it would. Why not tell her while you are walking?"

"I could, but I don't remember any of it. I only know what you told me."

Co'anra's look begged me to say no.

"Maybe there's something in Ben's story that will help me remember. Something." I winked back at Ben then turned to Co'anra. "I'm sure it will be better if you tell it."

Ben coughed to cover up his laughter.

"Very well," Co'anra sighed. "After it's told, I must go, as must you two. Indeed. Co'anri has already prepared picnic foods for you." He leaned back into his chair and gazed into the distance. "One morning," he began, "barely a single moon ago, I opened our front door to welcome morning's light. What I saw instead was this." He pointed to Ben. "I saw him, indeed I did. Yet I could not see him."

"Oh my no." Co'anri stood at the threshold. Slung over her shoulders were two full backpacks. "I was there too, and I could not see him either."

They shared a knowing glance and fell silent. I looked from one to other, waiting for an explanation.

"What we mean," Co'anra said at last, "is that with morning sun so bright behind him, we could not make out his face."

Co'anri dropped one backpack on my bed, the other at Ben's feet. "All we could see was a halo of white sunlight around him. It was wonderful strange. Oh my, yes it was."

"Indeed. It was as though the sun had dropped him on our doorstep."

"Dried him off too, maybe. Because if he arrived as you did, he would have been wet."

"Soaked." Co'anra nodded. "But he wasn't. He was dry when he got here. Indeed, he was." His reluctance had fled. He waved his arms animatedly as he continued the story.

"The sun must also have burned all knowingness out of him. It must have," Co'anri added, "because he did not know his own name."

"Like you," Co'anra repeated.

"Like you, that is not all he did not know. Is that not right, brother?"

"Indeed. He did not know where he was."

"Or where he had come from. Oh my no." Co'anri sounded enthusiastic, but her arms twitched nervously as she stood behind Co'anra and pressed her hands forcefully into his hunched shoulders.

Co'anra inhaled sharply at the pressure. He breathed out slowly then continued. "Of course, we took him in. Indeed, we did. It was the only thing to do. Is that not right, sister?"

Co'anri's face reddened. Her voice rose. "You *pulled* him in, brother. Oh my yes. Did not want anyone to see him. Is that not right, brother?"

"Of course, we took him in," Co'anra repeated firmly. "We called him Ko'leya—"

Co'anri turned to me. "Until *you* named him Ben, dear one."

"We called him Ko'leya. Indeed, we did. It was my idea," he added proudly.

"Does it mean something?" I asked.

"Indeed it does. Many things."

Neither Co'an said anything for some breaths.

"Son of the sun," Ben said. "It means son of the sun.

TO THE MA

A single sun angled down on us as we stepped outside, its golden rays capturing us in a spotlight of warmth. I closed my eyes and tilted my face to meet its gentle heat. For a moment, it burned away my anxiety and for a briefer moment, imprinted a vision of not one sun but two in the sky, a vision that seemed compellingly real.

"You need to be going now," I heard Co'anra say. I opened my eyes and squinted. Only one sun. I shook my head in familiar confusion.

"We'll see you when we get back," Ben replied. Co'anri had said her goodbyes in the gabaya while stuffing our packs with yet more food. Co'anra hovered uncertainly in the doorway

"Oh," he said. He studied the tall, flower-studded grasses surrounding his house and gazed up into the sky before gazing lingeringly at each of us in turn. "Yes. When you get back." He pushed us off the front stoop, waving his hand slightly. "Indeed," he said distractedly. He turned into the house and slammed the door behind him.

"That was strange," I said.

"Uh-hm." Ben nodded distractedly. He looked to the left then longer to the right before staring straight ahead into the distance. I followed his eyes but saw no sign of ocean.

Where the interior of the house had been cool, damp, gauzily lit and largely colorless, the land around it was bright, warm, dry and dressed in infinite shades of green spotted with vivid bursts of purple, yellow, red and gold so vibrant they barely looked real. To the left and behind us, a scattering of circular, white-stucco cottages hugged the prairie, their conical, translucent thatch glinting in the brilliant daylight. To the right and ahead of us, jagged vermilion cliffs thrust up from the flatlands, forming a backdrop to a grassy hill in the middle distance.

"Which way is the Ma?" I asked.

Ben sprinted off toward the hill. "I'll meet you at the Kora Kì," he called back. For an instant, with morning sun in front of him, I saw him as the Co'ans must have, surrounded by a halo of light. Then, not knowing what a Kora Kì was or where to find one, I took off after him — across the field and up the rounded hill. I caught up with him easily, collapsing on top of him when he stopped abruptly next to a stand of scrub.

"This," he announced, dusting himself off, "is the Kora Kì. It's the only tree I've seen anywhere near here."

"Tree?"

"Look up." As I did, foliage shivered into view. Narrow near the ground, the Kora Kì grew denser as it rose, its smooth purple-blue limbs ultimately thickening into a broad, rough-barked trunk that shot up and disappeared into the sky.

"Where does it grow down from?"

"The future."

"What do you mean?"

"It shows me things that haven't happened yet."

"Like what?"

"It sent me to Ko'Ba Rock. The day you…arrived. It warned me about the wave, though it didn't tell me you would be inside it. Other things too. Things Co'anri hadn't said yet. Then she said them. Things I don't understand. Or maybe they're things that just haven't happened yet."

"But not who you are."

"No. Never that."

I looked down at the village. All the cottages were identical. I was no longer certain which belonged to Co'anra and Co'anri.

"Wait," I said. "If we can see buildings from up here, why couldn't I see the Kora Kì from down there? And if it's so big, why couldn't I see it until you pointed it out?"

"Look up again," he said softly. As I did, the color of leaves and branches faded tremblingly to match their surroundings. "The trunk is almost sky color, so it's easy to miss. But everything else… Well, you see what they do."

"How did you find it?"

"It found me. I came up here a lot early on. Mostly for the views. To see if I could see anyone coming out of any other houses. At first, I never saw anything of the Kora Kì. Not even the shrub you saw. Then one day, its colors changed, right in front of me, and there it was. Just like this." He stroked a leaf.

"Did you ask Co'anra about it?"

"I didn't have to. As soon as I saw it, I knew everything I've told you. And I knew it would be smarter not to say anything to the Co'ans about it."

"Why?"

"I don't know. Co'anra can be kind of funny. You saw how he was when we left. Co'anri too."

"Oh my yes." I giggled.

I looked back toward the village. It appeared uninhabited.

"Does anyone live in those other houses?" I asked.

"I've never seen anyone." He shifted his gaze to one house, the farthest from the Co'an's. "Not from up here..."

"You've seen something?"

His eyes watered. He nodded.

"What's wrong?"

"It doesn't make any sense."

"What here does?"

He sniffed and wiped his eyes and nose with the back of his hand. "You have to promise not to tell Co'anra or Co'anri."

I nodded.

"Other Co'ans live down there. I haven't seen it, but the Kora Kì showed me. Two in each house. Just like Co'anra and Co'anri. Exactly like Co'anra and Co'anri. They could all be twins. But..." He turned away, crying softly.

"But what, Ben?" I touched his arm. "What is it?"

"Remember your washbasin? How you saw fish that reminded you of Co'anra and Co'anri? How they *didn't* look the same?"

I nodded.

"I saw something like that in one of the houses, the only one I've been able to see into." He dropped onto his stomach, his feet playing with Kora Kì branches. He plucked a long stem of grass and chewed on it reflectively. "It was just after you got here."

I kicked off my sandals and sat cross-legged next to him. "Which house was it?"

He nodded at the farthest. "I wanted to be sure Co'anra and Co'anri wouldn't see me. Besides, it was the only one with a window you could see through. All those houses have that same frosted glass we have. You can't see in or out. There was this one window in that one house that was scratched enough that I could see in. Sort of." He sat up and hugged his knees. "There was nothing inside. I mean nothing I could see. I'm sure there was furniture — I know there was. But without coverings, it was as invisible as Co'anra's armchair."

"What about the people inside?" I tried to imagine creeping up to the window and peering in. I wouldn't have done it. I was glad Ben had.

"I watched for a long time. I was scared someone might see me. I was about ready to give up and leave, when one came into the room. Then a second. Like the Kora Kì said, they looked just like Co'anra and Co'anri. They were dressed the same. They even shuffled and limped the same. Probably, if their furniture had been covered, I would have thought I was looking through one of the windows into our house." He buried his head in his knees.

"What is it?"

"The longer I looked, the less alike they seemed…even though nothing ever really changed. It's so hard to describe because it's nothing I saw. It's what I felt." He tapped the center of his chest. "Here." He wiped his eyes again. "This is going to make no sense…"

I tried to imagine what he could have seen that was more extraordinary than anything else that had happened. "Us being here makes no sense. This tree certainly makes no sense."

He nodded. "It was like I was seeing my mother and father…like I was looking into *our* house. I know I'm not from here and I know they couldn't be anything like my parents. But I felt it." He tried to swallow his tears. He couldn't. "I don't know who they are… I don't know who *I* am. But it's like I saw them, like they were so close…and close as they were, I couldn't touch them, couldn't talk to them." He stood and turned his back on the Co'an village, his face to the sun. "It only lasted for an instant…but it's never gone away. The feeling, I mean. Being homesick for a home I don't even know…missing parents who feel as though they're close by…who I probably wouldn't recognize if they were right here."

I studied the houses. All still seemed empty. Yet there was something magical about two of them, maybe all of them. "Will you take me there some time?"

"I don't know. I never went back. I'm not sure I could. I'm not sure I could be there, feel what I felt and not try to get inside."

"Couldn't you knock on the door?"

He shook his head. "Co'anra knows things he's not telling. Lots of things, probably. But I believe him when he says it would be dangerous for them and for me — for us — if others know we're here. Outlanders he calls us."

I nodded.

"I shouldn't have gone exploring like that," he continued. "Usually I come up this way and toward the Ma, away from the houses. That morning, I just couldn't help myself."

"I understand."

"Do you?" Ben's eyes burned then softened. "I suppose you do."

We sat quietly for a while, each lost in our own thoughts. The sun, high in the sky, shone on Ben's face, starkly outlining his features. Was it a trick of the light that again shrank him to infancy and back? I rubbed my eyes. This *was* a peculiar place.

"I'm hungry," Ben announced and rummaged first in his pack then in mine. He laid out a spread of fruit and meats and we ate, in silence.

Only when we were done and ready to move on did I speak. "Why did you bring me here?" I asked.

Ben said nothing at first. He fingered a few leaves then gazed up the tree's trunk into the sky. "I don't know." He paused. "Well, yes, I do." He plucked a leaf and handed it to me. Pinpricks of light glinted up and down the stem, and I had an overwhelming urge to eat it. Resisting temptation, I closed my fist over it.

"This is also going to sound strange," he said.

"Stranger than an ocean in a wash basin? Stranger than what you just told me?" *Stranger than wanting to eat this leaf?*

Ben laughed. "I suppose not. Okay. I brought you here because the Kora Kì asked me to."

I nodded as though I had known this all along.

"Go ahead," he said.

"What?"

"Eat it."

"How—?" I shook my head. "You know things. Right?"

He nodded. "Do it."

I opened my fist and watched the leaf change color in my hand. At first bright green, it dulled into a flesh color that so matched my skin it was nearly invisible. Only its warmth and a slight tickling in my palm convinced me that it hadn't vanished altogether. It changed color again, brightening to pink then orange, before exploding into a sparkling rainbow of ever-shifting hues. Once again, I wanted nothing more than to eat it. I lifted it toward my open mouth, then stopped. It didn't make sense. Nothing made sense. Ben. Me being in M'ranna. M'ranna itself. Not knowing who I was or why I was here. Now, I was supposed to eat from a tree that grew down from the stars? From the future? I shredded the leaf into tiny pieces and flung them into the air.

The moment the fragments scattered on the breeze, I had to pluck another leaf and stuff it into my mouth. I couldn't help myself. It immediately dissolved on my tongue. I seemed to be dissolving with it.

"Q'nta..." Ben's voice faded into silence. The Kora Kì shimmered into nothingness. Everything dispersed into a silky haze.

I see light within the haze. A brilliant crystalline luster. The Heart of the Star. It hovers in the gauzy nothingness, pulsing with life. Slowly, it illuminates its surroundings: first Reesa Kam'ana's idyllic starlit garden then Reesa Kam'ana herself, arms outstretched to the night sky. The luster radiates from the center of her chest, more brightly with each word she sings.

Alla ka tchù, tia à
Alla ka tchù, tia à
Alla ka tchù, tia—

A distant whir grows louder...nearer. The Star Chant remains strong. But it is not strong enough to compete with the thunderous flapping of the massive wings of a menacing kep'cha, wings that in a single beat shroud the stars.

The kep'cha passes. The stars are once more visible in the heavens.

Expressionless, Reesa Kam'ana lowers her arms. Her chant continues, more melancholy than before.

Alla ka tchù, tia à
Alla ka tchù, tia à

She reaches into the center of her chest. The crystalline light now pulses in her hand. Still she sings.

Alla ka tchù, tia à
Alla ka tchù, tia à

High in the sky, tree roots twinkle into view, each anchored to a single star. From the roots a tree trunk forms, only slightly paler than the deep blue that surrounds it. It thrusts earthward, sprouting limbs, branches and leaves as it travels toward the eastern horizon, where a needle of light pricks the darkness.

Still, Reesa Kam'ana sings.

Alla ka tchù, tia à

Alla ka tchù, tia à

Expressionless, she raises her arm and flings the Heart of the Star up toward the tree roots.

Alla ka tch—

The constellations explode. The world holds its breath and nothing moves. Only the Heart of the Star is exempt. It flashes up toward the Kora Kì and, with a loud hiss, is absorbed into the trunk. There, it hovers twinklingly until Reesa Kam'ana lowers her arm and nods. Then, it streaks through the tree toward the horizon, where it vanishes as though it had never been.

One by one, the stars wink out until the world is empty of light and blackness swallows Reesa Kam'ana.

Waves of grief wash over me. I can barely breathe for the sobs that quake through my body for what feels like lifetimes. My tears barely stilled, a white star pierces the velvet emptiness. It flares toward me, illuminating a cavern so vast that all I can see is a smooth, star-shaped slab of mirrored slate set into its rough-stone floor, a simple coronet of braided white and yellow gold embedded into a raised circular platform at its center point. The light slams into that center point in a blinding explosion of multicolored light that forces my eyes shut against the glare.

A deep peace fills me.

"Astel Lev," I hear. "Astel Lev," I hear it again. And again. The words awaken a memory — not of who I am but of what I am. Not of where I came from but of where I am going. Not of how or why, but of when.

"Now," I hear through the rustling of leaves. "Now. Now…"

eight

"**N**ow, we will go to the Ma."

"What?" My vision evaporated. Ben tugged on my arm. Wind whistled through the tree.

"The Ma," he repeated. "It's time. Are you ready?" He tugged again. My body wouldn't respond. My eyes were still on the Kora Kì, tracing its trunk up into the sky until it disappeared into the distance.

Ben followed my eyes with his. "You're not crazy. You're thinking you're crazy, aren't you?"

I nodded. "Reesa Kam'ana…"

"I saw her too," he said, and described everything I had seen and experienced of the Star Chantress. "Sort of."

"What do you mean, 'sort of?' That's exactly what happened."

"I didn't see it through my eyes," he said carefully. "I saw it through yours."

"What do you mean?"

"It happens to me sometimes. I see something that someone else is seeing. It's like I'm in their head, looking through their eyes."

"I'm not sure I like that."

Ben laughed. "I can't read your mind, if that's what you're worried about."

"I wouldn't care about that if you could get into the part of my mind that I can't, the part that knows who I am and why I'm here." There was so much I didn't know, so much I didn't understand. What had I just seen? What had happened to Reesa Kam'ana? What was this place and how could I have arrived here on the crash of a wave? Where had I come from? Would I ever see it again? I shut my eyes and tried to hold back my tears.

"It's okay. I mean it's okay that you're scared and confused. I was too, at first. A lot of the time. It just seems to get worse, doesn't it?"

I tasted a slight salt tang in the air and felt thundering surf coax me from somewhere beyond the cliffs. "The Ma," I whimpered, opening my eyes. "I have to see the Ma."

"I know." Ben brushed loose grass from his pants. "That's the way." He indicated a field of gray-green grasses that rippled from the base of An Kora Mount to the cliffs, etched by the sun's angle with a series of glyph-like lines and squiggles. The markings deepened where the sun was directly overhead. Those farther away lost their sharpness, their edges fuzzing until they faded into the landscape.

We raced down the slope, through knee-high grasses, and stopped at the base, where a dense forest of tall, feathery fronds blocked our way. Ben paced back and forth, sniffing the air uncertainly. Then, finding what he sought, he turned sharply to the right and stopped, hushing me when I tried to speak. After a few breaths, the grasses in front of us parted. Ben stepped onto the narrow path and motioned me to follow. I did, nervously aware that even as the path opened in front of him, it closed immediately behind me. I edged closer to him and swatted stray stems from my face. The air was cool, damp and eerily still. An Kora Mount had been alive with birdsong and insect squeaks. Not here. Only our breath and the rough scrape of the grasses against our clothes scratched through the silence.

Arrow-straight at the outset, our path soon angled into a chaotic confusion of zigs, zags, snakes and spirals. First, we veered sharply left then right then left again, doubling back and around so many times that we seemed to be taking forever to go nowhere at all.

"Are we nearly there?" My voice sounded alien in this soundless place. The Ma still roared in my stomach.

"Yes and no." Ben stopped. The grasses' path-making stopped too.

"Remember those markings we saw in the grasses?"

"The glyphs?"

"That's what we're walking through. Those words or symbols, whatever they are. Only thing is, they're different every time I come. They feel different too. So I never know how long it's going to take. To get to the Ma, I mean. This is the longest it's ever taken me. I don't understand it."

"Are we lost?" I wheezed. My breath raced raspingly, as though I'd been sprinting. The grasses seemed taller, pressed closer. The air felt stale, hot. I couldn't breathe.

Ben gazed thoughtfully around our tiny clearing. "I don't see how we could be." He paused. "I wonder…" He paused again and took my hand. "Let's try walking side-by-side."

I squeezed next to him on a path barely wide enough for one. Dry stalks jabbed my arms and face, poked my clothes. Yet, as soon as we stepped forward together, the path widened and straightened, opening up farther ahead than it had previously. Shafts of sunlight angled down toward us, catching diamond drops of tangy mist on the way. No longer did I only feel the breaking surf in my stomach. Now, interspersed with the screeching of unseen sea birds, the Ma rumbled reassuringly in the distance. I inhaled fresh, ocean-seasoned air, and my breathing regained its normal rhythm.

Dense grasses thinned into clumps, like tufts of coarse, sage-colored hair. Scarlet cliffs paled to pink then to a dull gray that twinkled to life when sunlight licked their surface. The earth too had reconstituted itself. Black, moist, rich and spongy when we set out, then red and dry through the grasses, it now matched the cliffs in color and mimicked warm silk in texture. I slipped off my sandals and let my feet sink into the sparkling sand.

Soon my nose tickled with salt, and the Ma's approaching thunder crashed in my ears, never ebbing into silence. Instead, its intensity increased with every step. The louder it blasted, the more rounded were the rocks, as though the sound itself had worn them down.

Ben indicated the tallest of the boulders. Brilliantly lit from the front, it stood against a menacing backdrop of squall-like sky and spray. "That's the Ko'Ba," he shouted into the roar.

The Ko'Ba. It rose higher, darker and more jagged than its neighbors through a series of ledges, each smaller than its predecessor. From the final ledge, a rough black monolith spiraled up to stab storm-dark skies.

I shivered. Although the sun still warmed rock and sand where we stood, it couldn't penetrate the biting chill that enveloped me. I hugged myself to keep warm. In that same instant, a giant white bird emerged from the darkest part of the sky. It circled the spire three times, its massive wings spread wide and motionless, before gliding to a graceful landing on the Ko'Ba's topmost tip. It stared out to sea then swiveled to face me. As far up as it was, I felt its black eyes drilling unblinkingly into me. Finally, it flapped its wings once, leapt up and disappeared into the stormy sky.

"Last one up's a pohrià," Ben shouted, unaware of my discomfort.

He sprinted to the base and scrambled up to the first of the ledges with the agility of the twelve-legged kitikà bugs that shimmied alongside him. "You do *not* want to be a pohrià," he exclaimed from the second ledge, while I stood in disoriented unease where he had left me.

I longed for this rock to speak to me, to tell me where I had come from and why I was here. I stared at the Ko'Ba, probing every crevice for clues and every rune-like scratch for messages. For all its disturbing majesty, the Ko'Ba revealed nothing. I sighed.

"Are you coming?" Ben shouted down at me.

Crabbed, stunted jyp trees twisted out of narrow fissures that creased the rock, offering convenient handholds as I climbed up after him. I began slowly, cautiously. By the time I reached that first ledge, I found myself out-shimmying the kitikàs, pulled upward by some unseen hypnotic power. When I reached the second ledge, I clambered past Ben, who watched in astonishment as I scrabbled up the escarpment toward the base of the monolith.

He called out after me. I didn't hear him — and not because of the Ma. Strangely, I no longer heard the Ma. All I heard was a deep rumbling that throbbed through my body with increasing intensity the higher I climbed.

When I stepped onto the smooth, almost shiny surface of the penultimate ledge, my breath was ragged. Sweat drenched my clothes. I looked around, unsure what had drawn me to this place so compellingly. The rock was even darker up here, nearly black, but still tinged with red. And it was cool to the touch, protected from the sun's baking rays by roiling storm clouds.

Craggy steps hacked out of the rock twisted up to the final ledge. As my eyes followed the primitive staircase, the inner rumbling grew even more insistent, ordering me to the summit as powerfully as it had called me this far. I tried to imagine that the noise came from outside me, that it was the Ma. It wasn't. Three ledges below, Ben waved his arms at me. His mouth moved soundlessly. Even had I wanted to respond, I couldn't. My legs moved independently of my will, propelling me up the stairs to the spire's base. I could neither stop nor direct them. With each step, my heart hammered as thunderously as the rumbling. Or had it been my heart all along?

When I stepped onto the topmost ledge, the rock beneath me lurched. I grabbed for the spire, recoiled. The air around it was forbiddingly hot. I dropped to my knees and stared down into the Ma.

It was then I realized that the rock wasn't moving at all. It was the rest of the world that quaked. It was the Ma — a blistering, boiling stew of angry foment that pitched and churned unrelentingly. Foam-crested waves hurled themselves up at me, each flinging itself higher than the last to reach this sky-scraping slab. I squeezed my eyes shut and clung to a protruding rock, praying for my stomach to stop its heaving. Even with my eyes closed, though, everything around me spun roughly…everything inside me still twisted queasily. Had the ledge been a flimsy boat careening violently on the Ma, I could not have felt less anchored. It seemed like hours but was probably only moments before a gentle hand on my shoulder steadied me.

"Ben?" I whispered.

No reply.

"I'm so dizzy."

The hand pressed more firmly, but no less lovingly. The spinning slowed, stopped. My stomach settled.

"I don't know what I would have done if you hadn't come after me. Thank you." I inhaled deeply. "I think I will be able to open my eyes in a bit…just not yet." The hand calmed and comforted me. I sighed, relieved. "I don't know what pulled me up here."

"I did." The voice was a deep and throaty. It rumbled as loudly inside me as out.

My eyes shot open in terror.

nine

I didn't scream right away. The mix of green scale and human-like skin was so startling that all I could do was stare at the alien creature hulking over me. The left side of his body was almost human and was clothed in a white robe. The right side was covered in iridescent scales. His left foot wore a sandal; his left hand still rested on my back. His right foot was green and webbed; his right hand was no hand at all. It was a claw with curved talons so long and sharp they could have stripped the skin off me with a single swipe. His head was even stranger. At first glance it too was divided into ruby-eyed human and creature halves. As I continued to stare, though, his whole head molded and remolded itself continuously — from entirely human to fearsomely dragon-like and back.

I tried to push away, to shake off the creature's hand. But when I moved everything else moved too — in earth-quaking counterpoint. The world heaved and my world heaved with it. I wanted to vomit but couldn't. Instead, I shut my eyes, went limp and wept in shuddering convulsions. Only then did I scream, so loud and long that my throat hurt. When I had no more tears and barely any voice, I stared up at the creature.

"Who are you?" I croaked. "What are you?"

The creature smiled, a smile at once reassuring and repellent. "You need not be afraid," he said in a voice as gentle as a grating growl could manage.

If I could have fled I would have. But there was no escape other than down, onto the rocks and into the Ma.

"What do you want with me?" I whispered.

"It's what you want with me."

"I don't want anything with you," I shrieked. "Just go. Leave me alone!"

The creature laughed. As with his smile, the laugh was equal parts joyous and jarring. "Are you certain, Q'nta Ko'lar of Q'ntana?" He flickered, faded. "Are you certain, Q'nta Fayr'Owyn of Astel Lev?"

Q'nta? He knows my name? Fayr'Owyn? Why is he calling me Fayr'Owyn?

"Wait," I cried. "Come back."

"Are you certain of that too?" Only his mouth remained, still shuddering between human and grotesque, teasing me with its knowingness.

Was I certain? Terror still gripped me. Yet I couldn't let him leave. I had to know what he knew.

"Well?"

I swallowed hard and nodded.

More slowly than he had faded, the creature reformed himself, all the while humming distractedly. First to fill in was his head, which looked more funny than frightening as, disembodied, it bobbed in time with the music. Feet followed. Unattached to anything else, they tapped in time, then did a little dance.

I tried not to laugh, but the sight was so ridiculous it was difficult to keep from smiling. When, next, hand and claw took shape and waved wildly as part of his dance, I stifled a giggle. I burst out laughing when an armless hand pulled me up to dance. Twirling, bobbing and skipping in the tight summit space, I laughed so hard I was barely aware as legs, trunk, neck and arms formed to connect hand, claw, feet and head. I was still laughing when I collapsed to the ground, unable to dance anymore. The creature flopped down next to me — whole at last.

"You are a good dancer, and a good sport," he said. "I am sorry I scared you. My name is— I am the Q'ophar." He tilted his head and drummed his human fingers against his human cheek. "Yes, you may call me Q'ophar."

"I can call you that? Or is that who you are?"

"Yes."

"Which is it? What's your name?"

"Perhaps later, Q'nta. For now—" The Q'ophar rose and looked out to sea. "For now there are things you must know. That is why you called me here."

"I didn't call you here. How could I? I didn't know anything about you until just now."

"You did, you know…even if you do not know that you did."

I shrugged.

Does it matter? What matters is that I will find out who I am, where I come from, what I'm doing here and how to get back. Maybe the Q'ophar can tell me the same for Ben. Ben? Where's Ben? Didn't he hear me screaming?

I looked down to the second ledge where I had left him. It seemed forever ago.

"Ben!" I bellowed. "Come up." He didn't answer or look my way. I waved my arms and called out again.

"He cannot hear you," the Q'ophar said.

"Ben!"

Still no response. Ben stood statue-like, his right foot slightly twisted, his head tilted up toward the fourth ledge.

"What do you mean? What's wrong with him?"

"You dwell in the time between breaths." He crouched next me. "We both do. When Prithi's next breath comes, Ben will move and I will be gone. Completely gone, this time."

"I don't understand."

"It is not an 'understanding' thing, Q'nta Ko'lar."

"Why do you call me that? What's Ko'lar?" I looked back down at Ben. "Is he going to be all right?"

The Q'ophar nodded. "I will tell you what I can tell you in the time that we have. All else you will have to learn as you quest."

"Quest?"

"The StarQuest. That is why you are here. You are the Fayr'Owyn of legend. You are the prophecy, fulfilled, in part, to this moment." The Q'ophar gazed out to sea. "Fulfilled in its fullness if you succeed, if you bring The StarQuest to Completion."

Ko'lar. Fayr'Owyn. Q'nta. The names swam in my head. Nothing made sense, and as soon as something seemed as though it might, a Q'ophar turned up to muddle my mind all over again. I took a deep breath.

"This 'time between breaths.' How long does it last? How much time do we have before you're gone?"

The Q'ophar's mouth gaped open and he convulsed with laughter. "H-how long does it last?" he sputtered. "Oh my, but that's rich. How long does it last." He shook so much that bits of his human and creature sides jogged and jumbled into each other. It was like watching ingredients that won't mix being whipped up in a bowl.

Slowly, the heaving stopped. Now the Q'ophar looked like a

misassembled puzzle. A single-fingered hand clung to his neck. The other claws and fingers protruded randomly from a body that lacked all visual integrity. Scales and skin formed a peculiar patchwork. One red eye stared up at me from the middle of an arm that lay, orphaned, on the ground. The other blinked unfocusedly from the tip of an ear that now jutted from— Well, nothing was where it belonged and the effect was at the same time alarming and comical.

Then, like a k'nrah shaking itself off after a river swim, the Q'ophar jerked, joggled and quaked. Instead of water droplets, his disparate parts flew off in all directions. I ducked to avoid being assailed by a shower of legs, ears and scales. When his body parts settled, they landed where they belonged. The Q'ophar, now restored to his former, if still-odd cohesion, heaved one final, explosive *Ha!* before smoothing his scales, robe and hair.

"My, that felt good. Thank you, Q'nta Ko'lar. I have not laughed that hard in, well…too long."

"I wasn't trying to be funny," I said sourly, handing the Q'ophar a scale that had knocked me on the head.

The Q'ophar accepted the scale and pressed it into a vacant spot above his right ankle. His whole body lurched as the scale clicked into place. "Sorry, dear," he giggled.

"All this may be funny to you," I snapped. "It's serious to me. If you have something to tell me, do it. Please. Before the next breath."

The Q'ophar twitched one final time. A few more quiet pops followed. He turned to me, soberly. "I truly am sorry, Q'nta Fayr'Owyn. Your question was sincere, I know. But it was like me asking you how long between blinks of your eye. There is no answer because no two blinks are identical. The same with breaths. When Prithi exhales, I will be gone. Whenever that is."

I glared at the Q'ophar. "Fine. Let's get on with it. Why am I here? Why are you here? What's going on?"

"Please do not be angry with me Q'nta Fayr'Owyn…" A tear rolled sizzlingly down the Q'ophar's dragon cheek. He wiped it away with the sleeve that covered his human arm.

I couldn't stay angry. For all my frustration, the Q'ophar was right. I also hadn't laughed in, well, too long.

"I'm sorry too, Q'ophar. Let's start again." I reached for his human hand. "I don't know how much time we have, so please tell me why we're together here, whoever did the calling, and what you have to tell me…and anything else you know about me and Ben. In whatever time we have."

The Q'ophar scored a circle into the rock ledge with his claw, filling it with the now-familiar eight-pointed star.

"Do you recognize this?" he asked.
I touched the stitching on my tunic. I didn't know it…yet I did. As I stared at the carving unblinkingly, the star lit up and burst beyond its circle, until its radiance seemed brighter than the sun. My eyes teared from the strain, yet I couldn't tear them away. It sang too.

Alla ka tchù, tia à
Alla ka tchù, tia à
Alla ka tchù, tia à

The song, as recognizable now as the star, rippled out from its core and embraced me until I was aware of nothing but it, certainly not of the ghostly jeers that played around its edges. Subtle at first, they burst into a fury of discordance that overwhelmed the chant and smothered the light. The Q'ophar's crude scrapings melted into the rock as though they had never been.

"Just as I feared," the Q'ophar sighed.
I blinked hard and rubbed my eyes. "What? What was that?"
"Astel Lev. It *is* extinguished."
"No," I insisted. "It isn't." I didn't know why I said it or how I knew…or what it meant. But, like Ben, it seemed, I knew things.
"You know this?"
"Yes. No. I don't know how, but—"
The Q'ophar nodded. "If what you believe you know is true, then you *are* the Fayr'Owyn of legend." He smiled, not happily. "I hoped you might be. I also hoped, for your sake, that you might not be."
"*…that the Fayr'Owyn would rekindle Astel Lev and return it to the Star Chantress, its rightful guardian.*"

Co'anra's voice sounded so real and near that I almost thought he had followed us and climbed up behind me. Then I heard Co'anri's, equally present:

"*Bo'Rá K'n…determined to undo the prophecy… to undo the prophecy… to undo the prophecy…*"

Fayr'Owyn…Bo'Rá K'n. Bo'Rá K'n…Fayr'Owyn. Fayr'O— Everything around me pitched and swayed. The ground lurched toward me. The water too. My eyes dizzied, unfocused. Was I falling? Something pulled me back. The Q'ophar? I couldn't see…him or anything.

Q'ophar, Ko'Ba, sky and Ma had dissolved into a blurring whirl that twirled faster and faster, throwing everything around me into a muddy sea of no-shape and no-color. Through it, I heard Co'anra's voice again: *"Only the Fayr'Owyn can make things right again. Only the Fayr'Owyn. Only the Fayr'Owyn…"*

I stand in the vast cavern of my earlier vision, at the edge of the star-shaped slab. On its raised center platform, surrounded by the white-and-yellow gold of the coronet, the crystalline Heart of the Star radiates its brilliant light up toward a skylight open to the stars. Part of me longs to reach for it. Another part of me wants nothing more than to flee. Paralyzed by indecision, I do neither. I stand, unable to move.

The ground beneath me rends, ruptures, bursts. Somehow, I still stand. Somehow, I'm still locked in place.

A jagged crack slices through the star slab. A thunderous blast splits it in two. The circlet snaps. The Heart of the Star tumbles into the widening crevasse, its light dimmed by the rocks and dirt that cascade after it.

"NO!" I leap after it, into the chasm.

I plummet through an endless void, miraculously unscathed by debris that hurtles past and around me. When I land, it's into a dark, dank dungeon cell. Rusty manacles clamp themselves onto my wrists and ankles. Slime ants scurry hungrily through the rank, filthy space seeking flesh to feast on. Mine.

"Astel Lev," I whimper. "Astel Lev."

A giant black-and-green snake slithers into the cell. It rises on its tail, hissing. Its yellow tongue snaps at me. I shrink back.

The snake's skin peels away. S'kryssna S'kyaga steps out.

"Astel Lev?" she shrieks. "It is mine now. All mine." She rips open her bodice. A blinding light flashes from the center of her chest. She laughs louder, maniacally. "You had your chance, Fayr'Owyn. Now it is too late. Much too late."

I reach toward the light and scream.

The light vanishes.

S'kryssna S'kyaga vanishes.

The cell vanishes.

I vanish.

One wave, fiercer and mightier than others, flung itself up from the still-churning ocean to the ledge, extinguishing my vision and soaking me in salt water. It receded as swiftly as it had appeared. I shivered. The Q'ophar gently tucked me under his dragon wing and stared at me with a curious intensity. The human side of his mouth turned up in a grim smile. The dragon side hissed a vaporous sigh.

"Is that what—?" I asked.

"It could be," he replied. "Or not."

"What do you mean?"

"I mean many things, as did your vision."

"Please don't speak in riddles, Q'ophar. I must know."

"I can only say what I can say, and that is all I can say."

"That's as much a riddle as anything else!"

The Q'ophar shrugged. "I am sorry, Q'nta Fayr'Owyn. There are many things I know only pieces of, many things I know nothing of and many things I cannot yet speak of. Of all of those, there are many things even I do not understand."

I ducked out from under his wing. "How can you know things and not tell me?" I shouted. "I need to know."

"No, Q'nta Ko'lar." The Q'ophar gently angled my head so my eyes met his. "You know what you need to know. What you want to know is not the same thing. Not at all. I do not know why that is so. I only know that it is."

With difficulty, I swallowed my mounting rage. It was pointless to argue with the Q'ophar. The more I did, the more elusive were his answers. And time was short.

"Please, Q'ophar," I said as steadily as I could, "tell me whatever you can. About anything."

The Q'ophar dipped his head. "Very well. Here is what I know to say to you and the reason, beyond what you have already seen, why you called me to this place." He stood and spread arm and wing to the Ma. Angry spray spit up at him.

"You recall your vision?" He turned back to me.

I nodded.

"You will have more like it, for that is your gift as a Ko'lar. Each vision will reveal more of your StarQuest to you, both its possibility and its reality. Each vision will restore more of your past memory and present knowingness. Each vision will propel you forward...toward Completion, if that is your destiny." The Q'ophar squatted next to me. "Each vision is a piece of the whole, yes. But it is both more and less than that. What I mean is—" He struggled for the right words. "Your vision just now. It suggested how this StarQuest might conclude?"

I nodded again, forcing myself to remain silent.

"The details may be true and they may not be. It does not matter. What matters is true truth, which is bigger than any details. It lies beneath what you saw and hovers over it as well." The Q'ophar saw the confusion on my face. "I wish I possessed other words. Better words…" He stood again and faced the Ma. "No mind. I sense the end of our time together and must say more before it is done.

"I cannot give you any more answers or explanations." He shook his head in a way that brooked no argument. "No, I cannot. All I can do now is ask — no, urge — that you trust that you are who I say you are and that your purpose here will reveal itself in its time, in Star Time, even if that time does not play out in your time." His eyes brimmed with hope. "You say that the Heart of the Star is *not* extinguished?"

I nodded. "But my vision—"

"Your vision represents a potential outcome not a present reality." He nodded once, firmly. "If you say, as you did, that it is not extinguished, then it is not. Not in this moment, at any rate. I believe you… as must you, for only three beings can be certain of the Astel Lev's state of being: Reesa Kam'ana, its guardian, Bo'Rá K'n, who would pass it to S'kryssna S'kyaga and thus destroy it forever, and the Fayr'Owyn, who would rekindle it for all." He considered the implications of what he had said. "You have arrived in time, Fayr'Owyn. Thank Prithi, you have arrived in time."

The Q'ophar dropped to his knees, tears streaming down his face. On the dragon side they sizzled into steam almost immediately. On the human side, they dripped from his cheek onto the rock. "Thank you, Fayr'Owyn," he snuffled loudly. "Thank you."

I stared openmouthed at the creature, not willing to believe that I could be this Fayr'Owyn, yet not daring to disbelieve it. What if it were true? How could it be? How could it *not* be? If it wasn't true, who was I?

Then, with the quiet certainty that comes only from Prithi, I knew. For the first time since opening my eyes in the Co'an house, I had no questions, no doubts, no concerns. Whatever it meant to be the Fayr'Owyn, I was it. It didn't matter where I came from or who I had been when I was there. It didn't matter what I was to do or how I was to do it. All that mattered was that I was here. The rest would unfold.

In time. Star Time.

I smiled at the Q'ophar and nodded. He smiled back, stroked my cheek and rose. With one backwards leap, he somersaulted off the ledge and vanished.

"Q'ophar!"

"Follow your StarQuest," he soughed on the wind. "Live the prophecy. The Heart of the Star is in your hands…your hands…your hands…"

A moment later, the Ma calmed, brilliant sunshine dispersed the squall clouds and Ben was clambering up behind me.

ten

"I guess that makes me the pohrià," Ben huffed behind me. "How did you get up here so fast?"

"What *is* a pohrià?" I asked, too startled by what had just happened to say anything else.

Ben plopped down on the rock. "It's big, ugly, bristly and *mean*, and it would sooner eat you than look at you. The good news is that it's half-blind and can't climb. The bad news is that it likes hanging around at the base of cliffs like these." He grinned. I wasn't paying attention. "Are you okay?" he asked.

I nodded. "This is where it happened, right? Where I—?"

"The Ma was rougher that day." He looked down at the water. Barely a ripple disturbed its mirror-like surface. "I've never seen it this calm," he said distractedly, then turned back to me. "Yes. This is the spot."

I hesitated. "Have you ever seen anything else, well, odd up here?"

"What do you mean?" He squinted up at me. "*Are* you okay? Did something happen up here? I mean, it couldn't. I was right behind you. Q'nta?"

I sat next to him and gazed silently out at the Ma, hugging my knees. After a while, I said, "Do you remember Co'anra's story about the prophecy, about the Fayr'Owyn and the Heart of the Star?"

Ben nodded. "Of course. I've heard it more times than I can count."

"Well, there's more." Eyes fixed on the horizon, I told him everything. I told him about my vision and about seeing S'kryssna S'kyaga in it. I told him about the Q'ophar. I told him about the Fayr'Owyn.

Ben said nothing as I spoke. He could have been gone again, for I never once looked at him. Instead, I spoke out to the Ma. She listened, lapping up each phrase and sentence and carrying it out to the open sea before returning for more. When I was done, the sun hung low in the sky, casting a column of fire into the water. Only then did I turn away from the Ma.

"I'm hungry," I said. I wasn't yet ready to discuss what I had just shared.

Ben sensed that and nodded. "It's too late to go back. Let's get down from here before it's too dark to climb. I know a place."

"Won't Co'anra and Co'anri worry if we don't get back tonight?"

"Maybe, but we don't really have a choice. There's no time to get back before dark. Besides, they seemed in a big hurry for us to be gone."

"Do you think they knew we wouldn't be coming back? They gave us a lot more food than we would need for a single picnic."

"I'm never sure what they know. Whatever it is doesn't matter now. We'll find out in the morning." He stood, wiped his hands on his trousers and pulled me up. "We'd better start down. It'll be impossible once the sun's gone."

We descended the Ko'Ba in silence. From the base, we hiked a narrow path that skirted the rock and ended at a protected cove hidden from easy view by a stand of tall, scratchy shrubs. A charred fire ring stood by the water, a stack of dried twigs and driftwood off to one side. Beyond the cove, the Ma had resumed her noisy pounding. Here, though, the tidal pool was silent and still. The Ko'Ba loomed behind us, its peculiar silhouette already merging with a darkening sky.

"Wait here," Ben said after he had lit the fire and emptied his backpack on the rocky ground. When he returned a short while later, his arms were full of green bili'i berry clusters and red bela nuts. He added them to the simple meal I had laid out from the food Co'anri packed for us.

"I try to come here every few days," Ben said. He stuffed a handful of bili'is into his mouth. "More for the Ko'Ba than this. I like this place too. It feels like it belongs to me." The fire flicked orange flashes on his face. "Nothing else in M'ranna does."

"It's beautiful, and a bit sad."

Ben nodded. "Everything in M'ranna seems a bit sad. I don't know why I keep feeling pulled to this place." He stared out at the darkening horizon. "Maybe I do."

I waiting for him to explain and, when he didn't, I asked, "What about Co'anra? What does he say about you coming out here?"

"At first, I'd get back full of questions for him — about where I'd been, what I'd seen, what I'd felt. Mostly, Co'anra wouldn't answer. Sometimes, he'd tell me a story that didn't seem to have anything to do with my questions. Like the one about the Fayr'Owyn." Ben looked at me. I didn't say anything.

"Mostly, he'd just ask me not to come back here. To the Ko'Ba or to the Ma." He bit into a bili'i berry. Wine-colored juice exploded all over his hands and face. "He never said it was dangerous. Still, I'm sure that's what he believes. Do you think it's dangerous? After what happened up there, I mean." He leaned into the water and splashed water on his face to wipe away the juice.

"Strange and scary," I said. "But dangerous? The only time I thought something bad was going to happen was when I first saw the Q'ophar." I thought of his disembodied dance and smiled. "It wasn't at all scary in the end. Or dangerous." It was the first time since the Ko'Ba that either of us mentioned what I had experienced at the summit. "Have you ever seen him?"

Ben shook his head. "No Q'ophar. Other strange things up there for sure. And not just your arrival." He fell silent, not offering any details.

I glanced around warily. "Do you think they're right to be afraid for you?"

"I don't know. I'm pretty sure they've never even been here. Which is kind of strange, don't you think?" He nibbled on a piece of pink zzyzzyby cheese. "I don't know what they're afraid of, but I don't think they're afraid for themselves."

"What do you mean?"

"It's me they worry about."

"Why? If they haven't been here…"

"I don't know. Maybe that's why they're afraid. Whatever they know, they're not telling." Ben pulled deeply from his water skin. "It doesn't matter. It really doesn't."

"What do you mean?"

Ben picked up a koka'i nut and examined its whorls and ridges as he spoke. "Not knowing who I am, where I come from or why I'm here — like you, until you met this Q'ophar — has made me...not careless..but..." He clenched the nut in his fist. "Maybe not knowing any of that means that whatever happens, happens. Maybe whatever it is doesn't matter. Do you understand what I'm saying?"

I said nothing. I didn't understand and didn't know how to answer.

"It's okay. I'm not sure I understand either."

The sky was dark now with only our meager fire to light the night. A heavy mist masked moon and stars and chilled the air. I edged closer to the fire.

"Are you okay sleeping here?" he asked. "It's the only protected place I know, and it's too dark to go looking for something softer." He patted the hard rock.

"It's fine. We'll manage." I took a final bite of cheese and wiped my mouth. "Why here?"

"What do you mean? I just said—"

"No, not why are we sleeping here. Why do you keep coming back here? There are lots of places you could explore."

"I have explored other places," he said defensively, then laughed. "Lots of them. There's something about this place…" He poked the fire with a stick and pointed its glowing end up to the now-invisible cliff. "You know how you got here. Because I was there." He threw the stick into the fire. "I think I came to M'ranna the same way. Well, maybe not exactly the same way, but through the Ko'Ba. Don't ask me why I think that. I just do. So I keep coming back…" His voice cracked.

"In the hopes of remembering something," I said, as much to myself as to him.

He stared into the fire. I watched the play of firelight and shadow dance across his face and into his eyes.

"Ben?" I tried to stifle a yawn.

"Go to sleep, Q'nta."

"Aren't you sleepy?"

"Not really." He sat stiffly, his eyes fixed on the flames, withdrawing so fully into them that he barely seemed present.

A chill of loneliness wrapped around me.

"Ben?"

No reply.

I leaned into the fire, elbows on my knees, and studied Ben. He didn't move. He barely breathed or blinked. I edged toward him then drew back. Wherever he had retreated to, I couldn't reach him. For the longest time, I watched him watch the fire, hoping he would snap out of his waking dream. When I could keep my eyes open no longer, I lay down on the hard ground and fell asleep.

I mustn't have slept long because when I opened my eyes, Ben hadn't moved and the fire hadn't gone down.

"Ben?" Had he been crying? Or had I dreamed the heaving, retching sobs that had startled me into wakefulness. Was that glint on his cheek a tear or a trick of the light? "Are you okay?"

Again, no reply.

I sat up stiffly, my body damp and aching. Ben seemed oblivious to the cold, and to me.

"What is it, Ben?" I asked softly. "What do you see in the fire?"

"Just fire," he replied after an endless silence. His voice seemed to be finding its way to me from some other world.

"You see more," I insisted. "What is it?"

His eyes followed the flutter of the flames, refusing to rise to meet mine. Then with a startling flash, they bore angrily into me.

"What if I do? Do I have to share everything I see with you?"

I flinched and looked away — into the mist, up toward the veiled Ko'Ba, back into the fire, anywhere but at Ben — and hugged myself against the chill, both Ben's and the night air's. I didn't know what to say. For all its peculiarity, I longed for the familiar comfort of my Co'an bedroom.

A squeak refocused my attention on the fire. It emerged from a bylta'a no larger than my fist. It scampered up one of the rocks that ringed the fire pit then stopped to study the flames. The bylta'a crept toward the fire then backed away, crept toward it and backed away, repeating its dance several times before moving to the next rock and doing it all over again. When, rock by rock, it had completed a full circuit, it stopped again and raised its lilliputian head toward Ben. Only then did I notice that Ben still stared at me.

"I've been watching you watch it," he said quietly. He glanced down at the bylta'a, which had turned its face to the fire in apparent paralysis — attracted by the light yet repelled by the heat.

"He wants it so much, doesn't he?" Ben asked sadly.

"We all do, Ben." I reached for his hand but immediately pulled back when I sensed my gesture wasn't welcome. "We all do, and we all have the courage."

"Do we?" A bitter edge cut through his voice. Anger flared at me from his eyes. Or was it fear?

"I believe we do. I have to believe that."

"What does courage matter if it destroys us, like it destroyed him?" Ben's long, slender finger pointed to the bylta'a. It had edged forward one last time, only to be roasted alive by the heat.

"Did it die having succeeded or failed? Is that what you're asking me?"

Ben said nothing.

"He is the one you must ask." I lifted the bylta'a from the stone, stroking its fire-singed fur gently and murmuring words of blessing, then placed it in the fire. When the flames had consumed it, I reached for Ben's hand a second time. This time he didn't resist.

"He will answer you if you ask…if you listen." I placed his hand on his heart and held it there. "He will speak to you there," I said. "Just as the fire does."

Ben's eyes filled with tears. "The fire spoke already," he said. He pulled his hand away and clenched it against his stomach. "You're my mother," he said and quickly looked away.

My heart clenched. Tighter. Tighter. Now my lungs. My chest…

Gasping, I reached for Ben.

He was gone.

eleven

I stand next to a river-smoothed boulder. The day is bright. The air is clear. Joyfully, I croon a lullaby to the infant cradled in my arms. Gently, I rock him in rhythm with the music. He gurgles with pleasure, even in sleep. I smile. This child has erased all sadness from my life…and there has been much of late.

As I continue my song, the air before me wavers, as though heat were rising from the ground. It's not hot. The breeze is as cool as ever it was. Oddly, I see the breeze. It sweeps around and past me, streaked with wisps of ghostly gray. Whatever it touches, loses color, form, substance. Nothing is spared from its kiss. Everything washes out…disperses…dissolves.

Everything.

"No!" I shriek as the bundle in my arms loses solidity.

"No!" I clutch the swaddling, tighter…more tightly still.

I clutch nothing but blankets. These, too, dissipate.

"No," I whimper. My arms are empty.

Only I am solid. Only I am present.

"Ben!" I wail as I, too, dissolve and all is black.

*   *   *

The fire pit was cold and black and the sky gray with the first hint of dawn when I stopped crying. Every part of my body ached from the night's spasms of grief. Clutching Ben's damp neckerchief as tightly as I had clutched the infant of my vision, I shivered as morning's coolness brushed against the mingled dew, tears and sweat that dampened my skin and clothes.

Ben sat next to me, poking lifeless ash with a dry stick. I didn't dare look at him. If I did, I knew tears would want to start up again, and I was certain that every tear had been drained from me. Through the night, I had replayed the vision again and again, weeping more heartbreakingly each time. I cried because I knew Ben's words and my vision were true. I cried for the mother I was but couldn't remember. I cried for the chasm that separated my heart's reality from my mind's.

"How did you know?" I asked, my voice quavering.

Ben continued to poke at the gray dust as though I hadn't spoken. With a concentration so focused it carved furrows into his forehead and around his mouth, he scratched shapes and patterns into the fine powder. When he was done, he studied them, as though they held all the answer to my questions.

"Remember what I saw in that other Co'an house?"

I nodded.

"I never saw my parents features clearly. But my mother, she had— She had your— She felt a bit like you. That's why I was so upset when you didn't recognize me, after you woke up. It wasn't just what happened up there." He pointed to the Ko'Ba summit, now sharply etched against a cloudless sky. "When you said you didn't know me, I believed you. So I let it go. Until the fire."

"What did you see in the fire?"

Ben said nothing. He stabbed at the coals with his stick. I felt his eyes on me. "I saw what you saw. I saw it in the fire and I saw it again as you saw it…each time you saw it."

With one sweep of the stick he obliterated the symbols. "I was angry. I don't know if I've ever been that angry…so angry I wanted to hit you. To hurt you."

His face was so tight with torment I wanted to look away. I didn't dare.

"Why, Ben?"

"To hurt you as much as you hurt me." He held my gaze and I knew it took all his strength, as it did mine. "Because I believed you knew all along and kept it to yourself."

"I didn't know, Ben. I swear it."

"Because I believed that if you didn't know, you should have known."

"Ben, I—"

"It doesn't make any sense. I know that. After seeing you so upset, it can't make any sense. Nothing makes any sense." He snapped the stick in two, threw it into the fire pit and turned away. His shoulders shook and he rocked back and forth. I longed to reach out to him, to hold him as a mother would…as *his* mother would. I didn't dare. I had no right.

He spun back. "How can you not have known?" he spat.

He was my son. I knew it. Not with my mind, which still struggled with all it had experienced since my reflection had stared blankly back at me in the Co'an house. I knew it with my heart. A mother's heart that remembered this young man still forming in her belly — floating…shifting…growing. A mother's heart that remembered holding him for the first time. A mother's heart that remembered holding him that last time.

My son. He was that. Yet what right did I have to claim him, to call him "son"? This young man, his blond hair alive with light, his eyes as deep and troubled as the sea…this young man was no more my child than he was the child of the sun that now rose up from the Ma.

Tears streamed down my face and I turned away. I was no prophecy fulfilled. I was no legendary Fayr'Owyn. Astel Lev, whatever it was, would have to manage without me. How could I rekindle the heart of a star when I couldn't rekindle the heart of my own son? I couldn't.

This time, the Ko'Ba didn't call me. I called up to it — to take me away from here, to a place where I could no longer hurt my son. I stroked the empty space between us, turned my back on him and walked away.

twelve

I stumbled forward leadenly, my head bowed to the ground, my body weighted with grief. I would climb back to the Ko'Ba summit and wait for an ocean wave to sweep me from this place. M'ranna would manage without me. Ben would do better without me. As for me, I could only hope that wherever I landed, the Ma would first wipe my memory clean. Maybe the Q'ophar would help. Àna too. They couldn't want me to stay where I was the cause of so much pain. I could barely see for the tears in my eyes. It didn't matter. I knew the Ko'Ba would find me. Once again, I followed a rumbling sound that could have been the Ma or could have been the Q'ophar. Regardless, it was the sound that would guide me back up the rock.

"Wait," I heard dimly through my thoughts. My body plodded on. "Wait, I'm coming." I heard a rhythmic beat. Footsteps? Or waves against rock? Still, I kept moving.

"Wait up. Why are you running?"

Running? I was crawling, too burdened with heartache to hurry.

"Q'nta, please… *Mother*!"

Everything stopped. The ocean's thunder. My feet. My heart.

A hand pressed into my shoulder. Gently. Urgently.

I reached up to cover it.

Slowly, I turned my head, letting my eyes travel from hand to shoulder to mouth to eyes. What I saw erased all doubts.

In an instant, Ben filled my open arms, sobbing. And, sobbing, I filled his.

"Ben," I whispered, stroking his hair. "Oh, my son."

thirteen

The ocean slapped rhythmically against the sentinel rocks that guarded the cove. A small fire crackled in the pit. A second helping of rainbow py'kraal that Ben had scooped out of the tidal pool roasted on a makeshift grill while we munched companionably on the first, a new ease settling between us.

"Do I call you Q'nta or Mother?" he had asked as we hiked back to our primitive campsite.

"I would love for you to call me Mother, when you're ready."

"Okay, Q'n— Moth—" He laughed. "Maybe I just won't call you anything for right now."

Two more helpings of py'kraal later, washed down with the last of our fresh water, we cleaned ourselves up and left, bound for the Co'an house. Ben wanted to reintroduce me to Co'anra and Co'anri as his mother. I wanted to find out what more they could tell us about the legend of the Fayr'Owyn. Though we never spoke of it, both of us wanted to be sure they hadn't come to harm.

We retraced our steps as best we could. At first, Ben could find no way back through the glyph grasses. No path opened for us and we paced back and forth in increasing frustration. If I am the Fayr'Owyn, I wondered after a time, do I have any special powers? I pulled Ben to where the grasses were densest and stepped forward, until the fronds tickled my nose and face.

"I am the Fayr'Owyn," I said tentatively. "Let us through." A slight breezed riffled through the grasses.

"I am the Fayr'Owyn," I repeated, with more confidence. "I have returned to fulfill the prophecy." A gust of cool wind from behind struck a blast of hot wind that blew out from somewhere deep within the grasses.

"This is the StarQuest," I shouted. "Let us through."

A whining eddy spiraled where the two forces met, noisily carving a way forward for us through the maze. This time, the path was direct, and quick. When, soon after, we reached the base of An Kora Mount and I saw the Kora Kì thrusting down from the sky, I smiled. It felt like a homecoming. Without waiting for Ben, I scrambled up toward the familiar tree.

"Pohrià!" Ben stuck his tongue out at me and grinned as he passed me halfway up. When he reached the hilltop, he gasped loudly and dropped to the ground under the tree. He pulled me down next to him, when, a few breaths later, I caught up with him. "Lay flat and don't move," he hissed. "Don't even breathe."

I pressed myself into the earth. Ben stared unblinkingly through an opening in the foliage.

A few moments passed. A few more. More still. My body stiffened. I didn't dare move. Finally, Ben edged his mouth to my ear.

"Do you hear anything?"

I shook my head.

"Do you see anything?" I parted two branches so I could see down into the valley. Co'an houses, like white flower petals, lay strewn across the meadow. Everything seemed normal. I tried to pick out Co'anri and Co'anra's house from among the identical dwellings. Again I scanned the valley, picking out each house in turn. And again.

Something isn't right. Something is different. What is it? What is it? I can't breathe…I can't breath… I can't—

"Ben!" I clawed at his shoulder. "The house. Their house. *Our* house. It's…it's—"

Gone. Razed to dust, but for a single beam whose jagged tip poked forlornly skyward from the grasses.

Nothing moved. Not even the air, which hung heavy and still.

I leapt up. "We've got to—"

Ben stood, warily. "It's too late. There's nothing there."

"But—"

"Maybe they got away," he said without conviction. "Whether they did or didn't, there's no one there now."

He was right. "What do we do now?"

Before he could answer, a kep'cha buzzed into view. Then, a second. We pressed our faces to the ground. The two creatures and their thorag drones circled first the valley then An Kora Mount in counterpoint, shrieking barbarically.

"We have to get away from here," Ben whispered. He waited until both kep'chas had passed before crawling out from under the tree.

"Where?"

He shook his head. "Back to the Ma. I've never seen kep'chas down there."

He slithered toward the slope. I followed.

With a deafening squeal, one of the kep'chas u-turned back toward us. The other swerved to join it.

We dove back under the Kora Kì. The kep'chas aimed their needle-nose beaks at us, squalling loudly.

"Do they see the Kora Kì?" I asked.

"It doesn't matter. They see us."

The kep'chas were nearly upon us.

"What do we do?"

"I don't know."

I looked up. Both kep'chas smashed into the tree — visible to us, invisible to them. They exploded on contact. The air reeked of burnt flesh and singed feathers. Bloody body parts rained down from the sky, only to be flung out over the hillside by the now-spinning Kora Kì. We each grabbed onto a branch as the world blurred out of focus.

"Ben?" I shouted. I thought I heard him reply, but it could as easily have been the Kora Kì.

"Ben?" I shouted again into the void.

"Ben—en—en—n—n—nnn," my voice echoed back at me mockingly.

I wheeled and spun...spun and twirled...twirled and whirled...

Faster and faster I spin, until the void shatters into shards of color: blue... orange...yellow. More color. Red. Purple. Brown. Pink.

I spin faster. Faster. Faster. I spin until, still spinning, I am still. Color is gone. The Kora Kì is gone. All I see is white. All I am is white, dressed in a diaphanous gown of gauzy silk. Although no breeze blows, my dress swirls and flies in the cloud of mist that surrounds me.

I hear music...familiar music. Voices. Choirs upon choirs of them. Even though I see no one, music is as close and present as the mist.

Alla ka tchù, tia à

Alla ka tchù, tia à

Did the kep'chas get me? Have I died? I don't feel dead. I feel powerfully alive. Yet nothing is real. Is that what death is? Even as I ponder that, I know the answer doesn't matter, can't matter. All answers lie in the music.

I move with the music. The mist moves too. It spirals into tendrils that billow and fly, tendrils that refashion themselves into starlike beings dressed in silver. Hoods cloak their faces but can't muffle their song.

Alla ka tchù, tia à

Alla ka tchù, tia à

Alla ka tchù, tia à

I know them to be friends, without knowing who they are. I know that I am safe, without knowing where I am.

Without knowing how I got here, I find myself dancing and singing in their misty, silvery midst. I move through them, and they part to let me pass — bobbing and bowing even as they continue their dance.

Without knowing how I got here, I find myself dancing in front, guiding them through a mist that clears only as I step into it. I can't see what is ahead, yet I feel it…anticipate it…know it: a brilliantly radiant star that draws us to it.

Faster and faster we dance toward it — turning, twirling, spinning. Faster and faster, until my misty friends melt into a cloud of silvery white. Now, strands of color weave themselves into the blur. Threads of blue…orange… yellow. More color. Red…purple…brown…pink. Now, sound: my breath… my heartbeat…a whooshing roar.

The colors pale to black…

The spinning slows…

The twirling slows…

The dancing slows…

Slower…

Slower…

Slower…

I open my eyes, not realizing they have been shut.

I stand on a star-shaped slab of mirrored rock in a cavern so large its walls and ceilings have melted into distant darkness.

I stand deep within the Ko'Ba…next to my son.

THE STONE PEOPLE

From a fissure high overhead, a thin beam of dusty sunlight pierced the shadows, picking out the same crystal, braided circlet and star-shaped slab of my vision. Now, though, I could see the crystal more clearly. More facets than I could count refracted its dancing light, which radiated a faint rainbow halo around the slightly raised platform. Immobilized by the paralysis of my vision, I waited impotently for the earth to quake and for the ground to swallow the Heart of the Star and take me with it.

Ben touched my shoulder, pulling me back to the present moment. "Is this…?"

I nodded.

"It's…they're…" He shook his head in wonder. There were no words to describe what we saw, what we felt.

Gingerly, I stepped onto the platform and knelt, mesmerized by the crystal's beauty. My hand reached toward it.

"*No!*" A male voice boomed out from the rock, bouncing from surface to surface to surface for what seemed an eternity. I leapt back and seized Ben's arm.

"Not yet," a second voice, female and softer, added when the reverberation had ceased.

Ben spun around, scanning the cave for the source of the voices. "Who are you?" he called out. His voice, too, echoed against the rock.

"Do not be afraid," the woman's voice continued. "We did not mean to alarm you. But it is not yet time."

"Not time for what?" I asked, alarmed despite the reassurance.

"It is not yet time for you to touch the Heart of the Star."

"Astel Lev," I murmured. The crystal flashed briefly. I stepped back toward it. "Then you are the Heart of the Star," I said, as much to myself as to anyone within earshot.

"Before you touch it," she continued, "you must understand what it means to do so. For once you touch it, you are bound to it. And it to you." She paused. "Forever."

"Who are you?" I asked.

"Where are you?" Ben shouted. "Come out where we can see you."

Ripples of laughter resounded against the stone.

"Why are you laughing? Show your face, if you dare." Ben backed away from the slab, nervously glancing left and right. "Tell us who you are."

"You already see us, Ben Ko'leya," the male voice said.

"Where? Show yourselves!"

"You do more than see us. You stand within us." Ben looked around in confusion. "We are the Stone People and we welcome you to the center of our beingness. I am Pri'Malaka and I am what you might call 'chief.' There is more to my name, but it cannot be spoken so long as we are bound to this place."

I squeezed Ben's arm. "The Stone People?" I whispered. "Co'anra spoke of them. He said—"

"I am Pri'Mala," the female voice interrupted. "We are here to help you, not harm you. You are safe here."

"Why should I believe you?" Ben retorted.

The cave rumbled angrily.

"No, Pri'Malaka. We cannot fault them for distrusting us." The rumbling stopped. "They do not know what we know."

"They cannot know what we know."

"Not all of it, that is true. Some of it, certainly."

"Some of it, yes," Pri'Malaka relented.

My eyes darted back to the shimmering crystal. I longed to touch it. Besides, with the rest of the cave in darkness, there was nothing else to focus on. I forced myself to look away.

"We have heard of the Stone People," I said. "But we don't know who or what you are."

"We are the guardians of stone spirits, Q'nta Ko'lar Fayr'Owyn of Q'ntana," Pri'Malaka replied. "We travel the land—"

"And sea," a child's voice interjected.

"Yes, Pri'Mikana, and sea," he continued, "to maintain their Elohia."

"Elohia?"

"Rocks and stones can hurt or heal," Pri'Mala explained. "They can build and support or knock down and destroy."

Pri'Malaka continued. "When the spirits are in Elohia—"

"In balance," Pri'Mala added.

"In balance, yes. And unity. When the spirits are united in balance, destruction can never overtake construction. Killing can never overtake healing. Death can never overtake rebirth."

"So you live in the rocks?" I asked.

"We live *for* the rocks," Pri'Malaka said.

"We *lived* for the rocks," Pri'Mala added sadly. "Not anymore."

Pri'Mikana wailed loudly. Drops of salt water splashed to the ground from somewhere overhead.

Ben brushed falling tears off his face and shoulders. "Does she have to do that?" he asked brusquely.

With that, Pri'Mikana's sobs grew louder, and wetter.

"Ben! You don't have to be rude. She's obviously upset."

"Well, I'm upset too. We're having a conversation with invisible rocks in a cave that's raining on us." He tried to dodge the falling water. "How do they know our names?"

Pri'Mikana's tears turned to giggles and the "rain" stopped. "I know. I know," she exclaimed gleefully. "Can I tell them, Father? Can I?"

Whispered arguing between Pri'Mala and Pri'Malaka swooshed around us, interrupted by pleas from Pri'Makana. In the end, Pri'Malaka grunted his reluctant assent.

"We know more than your names," she boasted. "We knew you would be coming. We've been waiting for you, for a long time. Now you're here and I'm *so* excited." She panted and swallowed her breath. "Is it time yet, Mother? Is it time?"

"Yes, sweet rock. I think it is. Pri'Malaka?"

"Not for the—"

"No, husband. For a meal. You must be hungry, children. Of course you are."

At Pri'Mala's direction, we stumbled through the dark into an adjoining cavern, but not before I glanced longingly back at the crystal. It glinted invitingly and, again, I ached to hold it.

"In time," Pri'Malaka whispered. "In Star Time…"

The second chamber was empty except for a long slate table with a rock stool at each end, all half-obscured in the dim light. Each setting was laid with a stone bowl and goblet, a slab plate, a set of wooden utensils and a flickering candelabra. Fresh cooking smells tickled my nose and set my stomach to growling. I saw no food.

"Sit, sit," Pri'Malaka's voice echoed everywhere around us.

"Eat," Pri'Mala added.

Ben and I glanced around in confusion as we took our seats. We waited for what seemed a long time, the tantalizing aromas swirling around us only heightening our hunger. Still, no food.

"Maybe they don't like our food, Mother," Pri'Mikana squeaked. "They haven't touched a thing."

"Oh dear. Is it not to your liking?" Pri'Mala asked.

"But—" I started.

"There's no food here," Ben barked.

Pri'Malaka's booming laugh quaked the ground under us. "The food. You do not see it?"

We shook our heads.

"They do not see it," he roared so explosively that chunks of rock shuddered loose from the walls and clattered down around us.

"Pri'Malaka. That is enough."

Pri'Malaka stopped mid-bellow. "I am *so* sorry. I forget that you do not see as we do."

"Laughter is good, husband…never at the expense of sustenance and never at the expense of guests. We invite them to eat, surround them with tempting aromas and give them nothing but your rock-ous guffaws. That is not right. That is not hospitable. Not at all. No when so much awaits them."

"You are right, of course," Pri'Malaka replied sheepishly.

"What kind of example are you setting for Pri'Mikana?"

"Right again."

"Tell them, husband."

"What? Oh, right, yes. Well, then."

As he explained it, so long as we looked directly forward, we would see nothing. However, once we turned our heads slightly and looked, as he put it, "from the corner of your eye," a mouthwatering array of unusual meats, broths, cheeses and breads filled our table. Once we looked directly at the food, it vanished.

"How are we supposed to eat this?" Ben groused after countless forkfuls of food shivered from view before they reached his mouth. He hurled his fork across the cavern. Another took its place in his hand. "Is it even real?"

"Oh, yes," Pri'Mikana giggled.

"It just takes practice, I think," I said, as everything on my plate faded into nothingness.

"It is simple, really," Pri'Malaka said. "All that is required to give the food substance is that you *know* the truth of its substance. Once you achieve that, even looking straight at it will not make it disappear."

Ben nodded and raised his new fork. He closed his eyes, nodded again and reopened them. Within moments he was eagerly shoveling food into his mouth. Pri'Malaka's advice only confused me.

"I don't know what to do," I cried. "Now I can't even see the food when I look at it sideways."

"Close your eyes, dear one," Pri'Mala said. "Close your eyes and smell the food before you. Smell it and breath it in. Inhale it. Can you do this?"

I shut my eyes and immediately saw and smelled the food. My stomach grumbled.

"Now, see your plate. See it heaped with all your favorite foods. See it as you smell it." She waited. "Are you able to do this?"

"I-I think so," I replied, hungrier by the instant.

"Patience, dear one," Pri'Mala chided gently. "Now, with your eyes still closed, reach for your goblet. Not with your physical hand. With the hand you see in your mind's eye."

Tentatively, that imaginary hand reached forward, fingers outstretched. Closer...closer...closer... Then...

"Oh."

My fingers closed around the neck of the goblet. I felt the solidity of the stone, the warmth of the bowl. I felt steam tickle up my nose as I drew the cup toward me.

"You see, dear one? What you see in your mind and heart is as real as what you see through your eyes. How does it taste?"

"Mmmm-mmmm," I replied as liquid passed from stone to lips to tongue. I swished its warm honey-nectar around in my mouth, felt it slide comfortingly down my throat to soothe my complaining stomach.

"You have done well," Pri'Mala said when I had emptied my goblet. "Now it is time to open your eyes, but without letting them deceive you. On the count of three, open your eyes quickly and immediately. No peeking. Nothing tentative. Are you ready?"

"I guess so."

"Of course you are. Just remember what is real. Just remember what you have already experienced. Just remember what you know. Are you ready?"

I inhaled deeply and nodded.

"All right. One…two…THREE."

I opened my eyes as wide as I could, holding within my heart and mind the image of what I had just seen and the memory of what I had just tasted. And there it was: a spread of such magnificence I could hardly believe it be real. With that spark of disbelief, it shuddered, threatening to waver out of existence.

"No!" I reached for a hunk of ripe cheese. My hand started to pass through it. Fearfully, I jerked my arm back.

"Remember," I inhaled deeply. "Believe," I sighed out. "Know." Again — "Remember…believe…know." I reached for the cheese. Not hesitantly this time. Quickly and confidently. And, like Ben, hungrily.

As with Co'anra's fora'aa, our dishes continued to replenish themselves as long as we remained hungry. The moment we were sated, though, all foodstuffs vanished as though they had never existed, and no sideways glances would restore them.

fifteen

Once more, a focused beam of light picked out the crystal and circlet glinting at our feet. Once more, the temptation to touch the Heart of the Star was almost more than I could bear. Ben's yearning was directed at the circlet, which he had eyed longingly as soon as we stepped back into the cavern, even as he tried to conceal his interest. For now, though, our hands were occupied. As instructed by Pri'Malaka, Ben and I stood across from each other, light beaming down through the diamond frame formed by our crossed wrists and linked hands.

"Now then, lean back. Lean back so that each counterbalances the other's weight. Allow your heads to fall back and your eyes to focus upward, on the source of the light. Surrender to each other. Now."

We leaned back, Ben and I. Neither of us would let go completely.

"You do not trust — not even each other, mother and son," Pri'Malaka rebuked.

"I can't," Ben said, still largely in control of his strength and weight.

"You must," Pri'Mala urged gently.

"This is as far as I can go," Ben replied. "It's the best I can do."

"If mother and son cannot trust, there is no hope," Pri'Malaka said sadly. "If there is no hope…" His voice trailed off into nothingness.

But for our breathing, the silence was complete. It was as though the Stone People had never been.

"Pri'Mala? Pri'Malaka?" I called into the emptiness. "Pri'Mikana?" All I heard in reply was the echo of my voice against the rocks. "Ben," I said, "we have to try."

"I know. I want to. I can't. What if you can't hold me? What if you're not strong enough? What if I'm not?" Panic edged his voice. "If we fall… That rock is pretty hard."

"It won't happen, Ben. You know that. Deep in your heart."

His body tautened. He said nothing.

"I left you once," I said softly. "I let you down. I want to promise that it won't happen again. You can't know how badly I want to make that promise." Ben tried to pull his hands free. His shoulders tensed. "The best I can promise is that I will do everything in my power to see that it doesn't happen again." I tightened my grip on his hands. "I will do everything in my power to see that you don't fall."

He squeezed back. "If I let go, if I let myself fall back, something awful will happen," he whispered.

"What?"

"I don't know."

He shook as tears convulsed from him. I let go his hands and stepped around the crystal and circlet to hold him.

"You can't begin to imagine how much I love you, Ben. I loved you when I didn't know if you were alive. I loved you when you didn't know who or where I was. Every night, I cradled you in my arms, even though you weren't there. Every night, I breathed with you, even though I couldn't hear your breath. Every night, Ben. And every morning, I was sure you were still with me, only to wake up alone." I stroked his hair and could almost feel him an infant again.

"I didn't remember any of that until…until just now. It's more than memory now. I know it. I feel it." I hugged Ben more tightly and wept.

"When you told me what you saw in the fire, when I saw what I saw, when my mother's heart knew you were my son, when it knew that I had truly woken up to you again, I didn't dare believe it. I was afraid that if I closed my eyes, you'd be gone when I opened them again."

As suddenly as it had started, Ben's shaking ceased. I lifted his head from my shoulder and forced his eyes into mine.

"You had those same dreams, didn't you?"

"From the moment I arrived in M'ranna until the night before I found you on the Ko'Ba. Maybe before too."

"You see? We *were* together. If we dreamed the same dreams, how could we not be?" I wiped his tears and pressed his eyelids shut. "Do you feel my arms around you?"

He nodded.

"Like in the dreams?"

He nodded again, and fresh tears leaked into his lashes.

"Keep feeling it," I said. I studied Ben's face, at once so childlike and manlike, trying to fix his features in my mind. Then I laid his head back on my shoulder and closed my eyes.

Ben's body felt solid in my arms. His size and strength reassured me, even as I feared the outcome of what I sought to prove.

"Don't be afraid, Ben," I said silently, heart-to-heart. "I'm here."

"Mother?"

"Yes, Ben."

"I love you."

I try not to panic as I feel Ben's solidity evaporate, as I feel him shrink in my arms from emerging manhood to child to infant. I feel that, too, dissolve as his presence moves from my arms to my belly. I feel tiny movements, gentle kicks, not-so-gentle kicks, until that perception also dissipates.

In its place, a young man holds me. I see him so clearly, this young man who looks so like Ben but is not, who holds me as tightly and lovingly as Ben did, but protectively, manfully. Who holds me with a love that is richer, deeper, more knowing, more mature.

Tears drench my face. Someone has died. Someone has died and I grieve. I am sad, though not for him. I'm sad for me, for me and for the tiny seed that has only just begun to flower in my belly. I'm sad the seed will never know his grandfather, will never know Q'ntana's greatest Elderbard.

He sits there, my father does, slumped over his table, his candle flame guttering in a pool of molten wax, his ink-stained fingers still gripping the quill that scratched out the words that fill the hundreds of parchment pages neatly stacked by his side. Only the final page lies beneath him, wedged between table and pen, which still rests on the final letter of the final sentences he wrote: "That is the journey. That is the quest."

Now, that young man sits next to me as I read The MoonQuest aloud to him, as I read it for myself, as I read it for the tiny seed in my belly that we know already is to be called Ben, as I read it for my father, so still next to us. I read it even before I call for help, for my father needs no help now. He has moved on to those other realms he so longed for…those realms to which these writings have freed him.

"Your legacy," the young man says when I am done. He holds me and wipes away my tears.

"Ben's too," I whisper.

"Ben's too."

The young man slowly fades and I cry out.

In an instant, his place in my awareness is succeeded by a gentle kicking in my belly that, itself, melts into an infant. I cradle the infant in my arms for what feels like a single breath and…

"No! Not you too." I wail.

Another breath and I see him again, fully grown, as he looked just before I closed my eyes. I relax and smile.

"Let's open our eyes together, Ben. Alright?"

No response. A chill so paralyzing ran through me that I could no longer feel anything.

"Ben?"

Nothing.

My throat clamped shut.

"I'm going to count to three," I croaked. "On 'three,' open your eyes quickly and immediately. No peeking. Nothing tentative. I'll do the same. Are you ready?"

No response. My lips trembled. My body quaked.

"One," I whispered. I inhaled deeply and forced my voice back to normal volume.

"Two." I inhaled again, holding my breath as long as I could, holding Ben's presence in my heart and mind.

"Three."

sixteen

"What was my father like?"

I don't know how or when we separated, or why, but Ben once again stood across from me on the other side of the circlet and crystal, his eyes closed, his face peaceful, almost childlike, his eyelids fluttering as if following a dream.

"What was my father like?" he asked again.

"Then…you saw…what?"

"Everything you did. I heard it all too." He opened his eyes a slit, reluctant to let go of a past he had never lived. "I heard The MoonQuest."

"But how?"

Ben shrugged. "I don't know. I heard some things from inside your womb and others from some place above…like I had eyes and ears even though I had no body." He shook his head in frustration. "I can't explain it any other way."

"What did you see?"

"Nothing, at first. Then something startled me. A kind of soft thud. Next, it was like someone had lit a lamp and I could see everything clearly. There wasn't much, at first. Just an old man's head resting on a pile of parchment."

"Your grandfather. Toshar."

"Yes. He was dead."

"Yes."

"Then nothing until you came into the room."

I stared at Ben, startled to be reliving my vision through him.

"You saw him — Toshar — and ran to the window. 'Akila,' you called out. 'Akila.' Akila. My father?"

I nodded, unable to speak.

"I heard him but I couldn't see him. Why couldn't I see him?"

My voice quavered. "I don't know, Ben."

"But he was there, wasn't he?"

"Yes. Yes, he was. That morning he was there. The next morning…"

"What happened the next morning?"

What had happened the next morning? I couldn't remember. I knew it. Yet I couldn't touch it, like a familiar word that refuses to be recalled.

"I'm sorry, Ben. I—" Then the words spoke themselves, seemingly from some place outside of me. With each word, I remembered something of what I had forgotten. "Akila was with me in bed when I fell asleep. When I woke up, he was gone. It was as though he never had been. His side of our bed was tidy, touched only by the brilliance of the morning sun. It was as if no one had lain there. Ever. Someone had. Akila…your father had."

I shook my head, bewildered. "Your grandfather died. I knew what happened to him. I don't know what happened to your father."

"Maybe you'll remember?"

I looked down at the Heart of the Star, hoping it might have an answer. "I don't think I ever knew," I said sadly.

"What was he like, my father…"

Ben's face blurred into Akila's through the tears gathering in my eyes.

"He was so like you," my voice cracked, "that it's almost impossible to bear."

Ben flinched, as though I had slapped him.

"I'm sorry, Ben. I shouldn't have said that. It's just that…until just now I had no memory of him. No knowledge of him. Then to remember him and see him so clearly in your face…" I wiped my eyes and collected myself. "You *are* like him, Ben. Just like him. Your face is the same. Your mannerisms are the same. I didn't know him for long, you know. He turned up one day…out of nowhere. He vanished the same way. But… but somehow I knew him. And he knew me." I smiled wistfully.

Ben smiled back. He *was* Akila: The same wavy blonde hair curling over his neck, the same childlike grin that filled his face, the same sunlight in his eyes, the same warmth in his voice…

"I never really left you, Q'nta."

I gasped.

"I have never stopped loving you."

"A-Akila?"

"Our son is maturing into a fine young man. Be proud of him."

"I remember! I remember what happened after I awoke that morning, that morning you disappeared. I ran through the castle, asking everyone I encountered

if they had seen you. No one had. With a terrible foreboding, I climbed the stairs to the library. There, on my favorite table, surrounded by quills, ink pots and parchment and propped up against a goblet, was a note to me, written in your hand."

My dearest Q'nta,

I have gone where you cannot follow me. I have left not for lack of love for you. I have left because my love for you is so great that if I do not leave now, I shall never be able to.

You will say, "What of that?" To which I must reply, my destiny demands it, as does yours and young Ben's.

It may be a long time before you understand these words, a longer time, perhaps, before you can forgive me for them. Please know that I love you more than I have ever loved another human and that that love will never diminish. Ever.

If you can, think of me kindly and speak of me kindly to our son, when your heart tells you it is right and you feel able to do so.

My love shines down upon you now and forevermore.

Yours eternally,
Akila

"Q'nta?" A hand touched my arm.
"Akila?"
"Mother?"
"Oh, Ben. I'm sorry. I thought… I thought…" I shook my head to clear it.

Ben looked at me strangely. Had he seen what I saw? Heard what I heard? I wanted to ask, but the moment had felt so intimate that it didn't seem right. He knew. I was sure he knew. I saw it in his eyes, Akila's eyes.

Ben said nothing. He looked up at the shaft of sunlight, let his gaze linger on the opening high overhead then followed the beam down to the floor. Kneeling, he leaned in as close to the circlet and crystal as he could without touching them. Their incandescence shone through his hands, illuminating bones, tendons and muscle, and lit up his face. For a stunning instant, it seemed as though his face was the more brilliant, and that the crystal and circlet derived their light from him rather than the other way around. He stood, crossed his wrists and reached for my hands.

"I think I'm ready now, Mother," he said. "I know I'm ready."

*   *   *

Nothing happened at first. We leaned back, fell into each other's weight, stared up at the light and waited. And waited.

And waited.

My wrists, back and shoulders ached from the stretch, but I held on. Ben's arms trembled from the strain. His hands grew clammy. I squeezed them more tightly.

My muscles shrieked for release, threatened to deaden when I refused. I had let go of Ben once. I couldn't again. Wouldn't. I grit my teeth, refusing to submit to the numbness. I focused instead on Ben, breathing my love for him into my hands, my wrists, my arms, my shoulders, my back…and into his.

The pain was too strong. For all my love, I felt my grip weakening, my hand slipping.

"No!" I cried as I fell backward. My arms shot out to brace myself. My eyes shot open to…darkness.

I shut my eyes and open them again. I see no cave, no crystal, no Ben. I shut them a second time and again open them. Now, darkness melts into a black mist that disperses on my breath.

I stand next to Co'anri, in her gabaya, her kitchen. She hums distractedly as she adds a pinch of this and a dash of that to a cauldron steaming over an open fire. I try to speak, to let her know that we have come back, that we are safe. Instead, all that passes my lips is the tuneless melody she is humming…I am humming.

I reach out to touch her hand. But it's too busy. They both are. One flies from shelf to cauldron, the other stirs brimiya stew with a heavy wooden spoon.

"Co'anra," I hear myself call out.

"What is it, sister?" he replies. This, too, is my voice. His is my body as well, now in an adjoining room, tinkering with a mass of fine threads and clear, jagged crystals patterned into an incomplete version of the circlet-enclosed star. The part of me that is still Q'nta watches in amazement as the part of me that is Co'anra agilely connects, disconnects and reconnects the filaments that just might revive this dusty, old transco'an.

"Brimiya," Co'anri calls back from the kitchen, where I have been all along, even as I have also been Co'anra. Even as I have also been the thorag who unwaveringly pilots his menacing kep'cha toward our house. "I have cooked it just as you like it. Come. Eat before it is ruined."

"If I can only get this transco'an working again…"

104

"You know it is not possible, brother. You know it needs a kora-stone to power it. You know there are none here…have been none since…" She sips a final taste of the stew, bounces her head in a satisfied nod and calls again: "Come. Eat. This may be your last chance. I think this is the best I have ever brewed it."

"It does taste good," I say, but whether as Q'nta, Co'anri or Co'anra I cannot know, for all distinction between us has disintegrated.

Just as all distinction between me and the thorag has vanished. I am the black, troll-like drone who single-mindedly aims his kep'cha down, down, down, nearer and nearer to where we placidly eat our stew. I am the kep'cha that catches sight of the house and the meadow in which it sits.

As thorag and kep'cha, I'm aware of nothing except my mission. As Co'anri and Co'anra, I'm aware of their approach and mission and are unconcerned. As Q'nta, I'm aware of it all and am horror-struck by my part in what is about to happen and by my powerlessness to stop it.

"Ben!" I shriek. He's in the house too. Isn't he? Maybe he can help. "Where are you?"

When I hear his voice, I know that if I cannot avert what is to be, nor can he. For his voice is not coming from elsewhere in the house. It's coming from somewhere inside me. I don't know what to do. Do I run outside? Stay with Co'anra and Co'anri? Do I hide? Do I make myself known? I can't decide, so I decide nothing. I just stand, simultaneously impotent and all-powerful, and wait.

My wait lasts less than a breath. As thorag I target the meadow. As Co'anra and Co'anri I calmly continue eating until, as kep'cha, my wings slice into and through the house, reducing it and all within to dust. Through it all, every possible sensation and emotion streaks through me — from excruciating agony to intense, orgasmic pleasure. I scream, laugh and weep uncontrollably, ready to explode from the turbulence and conflict that tear through me. I want to die yet know there is no death. And that knowledge rips at me yet more profoundly, yet more hopelessly.

"Astel Lev." I hear it faintly from some distant place beyond this one. "Astel Lev," it repeats increasingly assertively. "Remember Astel Lev. Remember the Heart of the Star."

Then I see it, its infinite facets reflecting an infinity of light. It hovers in the air then bursts explosively into a million-million starlets that also burst, and burst again. Explosions continue until all that's left is a light-shower that rains on, into and through me, until all that's left is the Heart of the Star, still surrounded by a braided gold circlet, both still framed by Ben's crossed arms and mine, which, still, are linked in the cave beneath the Ko'Ba.

"What happened?" Ben whispered.

"You saw it too?"

"I saw it and I was it. Only while you were feeling the Heart of the Star, I was feeling the circlet, Astel Elohia…the Ring of Unity. It was… awful. Awful and wonderful. Which makes it more awful still."

"And wondrous," Pri'Malaka added.

Ben pulled himself to standing. "I don't like it," he said.

Pri'Malaka's laugh again boomed against the cavern walls. "What is is, young Ben. Liking is not my concern. Choosing is. What do you choose?"

I rubbed my strained arms and shoulders and followed the beam of light, which now seemed to simultaneously rise from below the cavern floor and pour down from the sky, meeting in the Heart of the Star and the Ring of Unity. Together, they glittered with the intensity of a thousand suns. I knelt and once again leaned in toward the Heart of the Star.

"If you touch it, dear one, you have made your choice," Pri'Mala said.

"Don't!" Ben pulled me away from the platform. "You don't know what you're choosing."

I looked from my son to the crystal and back. "I'm not sure it matters. I think I have to do it. You too."

"What is it she's choosing?" Ben shouted angrily. His fingers clawed into my shoulder.

"Truth," Pri'Mala replied.

"What truth?" Ben demanded. "Whose?"

"May I, Mother?" Pri'Mikana asked.

"Of course, dear."

At first, Pri'Mikana's voice was thin and girlish. But as she continued her song, her voice grew fuller and stronger, and the beam of light broadened into a column that expanded to fill all but the star slab's outer fringes.

The truth that is
Is all that is
The truth that sings
The answer brings
The heart and ring
Apart must wing
Until each its task

Completed brings
The two as one
The star as sun.

Now, a different voice — older, more mature — repeated the song's end.

Until each its task
Completed brings
The two as one
The star as sun.

"You have your part, Q'nta," she spoke. "Ben, you have yours as well. Astel Lev and The StarQuest are Q'nta's to complete. Astel Elohia and The SunQuest are Ben's."

Until each task completed brings: The two as one, the star as sun.

In the center of the light shaft, an elderly woman in a long, white robe shivered into view. Her hair was close-cropped and her round face, folded into wrinkles, was dominated by a smile of such radiant warmth that I melted into it and by laughing, twinkling eyes of luminescent blue. She stood, tall and imposing, next to a low, three-legged table, ringed by three plump silver cushions. Carved into the table were a moon, a star and two suns, one larger than the other.

"Th-the MoonQuest," Ben stammered. "It's like in The MoonQuest. Eulisha…"

Eulisha smiled. "I am glad you know me, grandson of my grandson. You are as bright as I expected you would be." She nodded to him and turned to me. "I have watched you mature to this moment, great-granddaughter. You have experienced much pain, as your father did. Now you are ready, just as he was." She smoothed her robe and lowered herself onto one of the cushions. "You both are, even as you each doubt it."

Steam spiraled from the spout of the clay teapot that now appeared in her hand. I could smell the aromatic herbs and honey with which she had seasoned the brew.

"You will have tea, won't you?" she asked as she poured into the identical three bowls now clustered at the center of the table. "I have prepared it with extra honey. I know you like it that way."

"It-it's just like in The MoonQuest," Ben repeated.

"Come, children. It will get cold." She motioned to us. "This tea is so much better when it is hot."

In the next instant, Ben and I sat at the table with Eulisha in the midst of the light shaft. Or, rather, some version of us was there, because I still felt Ben's hand on my arm on the cavern floor as we gaped at the MoonQuest-like scene playing out in front of us.

"Which cup will you take?" She looked at the Ben in the vision, but seemed, at the same time, to be looking at the Ben next to me. Both Bens fidgeted uneasily. "You, Q'nta. You also have a choice to make."

If there were still two of me, I could no longer sense the Q'nta on the cavern floor. All I knew was the three-legged table, Ben perched nervously on the cushion to my left and my great-grandmother relaxed but alert on my right. Eulisha gestured at the tea bowls, which, now, were no longer identical. One was gold, one was silver and the third, green clay. Each had a black double chevron etched into one side and was blank on the other.

"You go first," Ben said to me.

Eulisha shrugged. "However," she said.

I studied each bowl, trying to remember how my father had chosen in a similar situation in The MoonQuest.

"You cannot swim the same river another has swum," Eulisha chided. "You are not the other. Nor does the river stay the same. New waters call for new ways. Each Elderbard must make her own passage through the stream." She turned to Ben. "His own passage." She touched the teapot. "Come, now, children. The tea grows cold and the hourglass is running out."

"Does it matter which?" I asked.

"Only if it does," she replied.

Without thinking, I picked up the silver tea bowl. Only it was no longer silver and no longer a bowl. Instead, I held the crystal, the Heart of the Star, in both hands. I held it but didn't, for what I really held was the light radiating from it. The crystal itself hovered weightlessly above my palms. "Astel Lev," I whispered. Eulisha nodded ever so slightly. She turned her attention to Ben.

"If you chose the silver," he said, seemingly unaware that I held anything other than a tea bowl, "I've got to choose between the gold and the green." He turned to Eulisha. "Right?"

She said nothing, her expression impassive.

Ben's eyes darted from the tea bowls to her and back again, his hand hovering over each in turn. He repeated the process five times, then five more. On the next, his hand lingered longer over each, more thoughtfully. Finally, he pulled the gold bowl to him, so forcefully that tea sloshed over the side. He lifted it to take a sip and started when instead of a tea bowl, he realized that he held the light radiating from a braided white- and yellow-gold circlet, the Ring of Unity.

"Astel Elohia," he said reverently. "Mana kae, ka'ohn."

Eulisha smiled. "Kihanna koh-hay," she replied to Ben. Astel Lev dropped into my hand; Astel Elohia, into Ben's. The teapot and green bowl vanished.

"It is time," she said. She gazed from crystal to circlet and out into the blackness beyond where we sat. "It most assuredly is." She turned to Ben. "Do you see yet what your mother holds?"

Ben stared at me, still seeing the silver bowl.

"Look through the ring."

He peered through it and his eyes opened wide with wonder. Silently, Eulisha took both the crystal from me and the circlet from Ben and placed them, an arm's length apart, over the center of the table, where they floated glowingly.

"Astel Elohia is more than the Ring of Unity," she explained. "It is also the Ring of Inner Vision. When the time of your SunQuest comes, it will reveal to you the truth of the story…and the story of the truth… if you let it. Astel Lev," she turned to me, "lies at the heart of all that is. As you listen to it, it will help you to see what needs to be seen — with your heart, not your mind. Its guidance will see you through your StarQuest…again, if you let it…if you let your heart *be* your mind."

"How?" I shook my head in frustration. "I don't know how…or what…or where. I'm not even sure I understand why."

"It is best not to know too much to soon." A voice, quavery with age and immediately familiar, wafted down toward us. I looked up. A gauzy face, bearded and wise, trembled in the light.

"F-father?"

"Your memory returns, my child. Much will return with it," Toshar said, "including the future."

"The future?"

"It is best not to know too much too soon," he repeated. "It is best to know only that the story continues and to follow where it takes you." Eulisha nodded up at him and smiled. "Do you remember those words, daughter? Grandson?"

"The MoonQuest," we replied in unison.

He laughed and that suddenly familiar sound unleashed a flood of childhood memories…and tears.

I am a small child, sitting nervously on Ryolan Ò Garan's knee. He whispers gentle prompts into my ear as I stumble through the story and song we have prepared for my mother and father. When I am done, both my parents leap to their feet and clap enthusiastically. Then Toshar sweeps me from Garan's lap and swings me through the air, laughing and singing…

I'm older now, dancing with my father at the feast celebrating a naming. Twins. Redheaded twins. Son and daughter of Uncle Yhoshi and Tante Fynda: Fidrik and Margola. I dance with many other boys and men, even with some girls. Yet only my father smiles at me as though no one else exists in the world but me, laughs with me as though nothing matters but our time together, and swings me through the air, singing…

I'm older. It's my wedding. I'm too big for my father to pick up and swing through the air. And now someone else matters to me as much as he does: Akila, whose look and smile touch me even more deeply than Toshar's. Even so, Toshar still laughs and sings as we dance, and when he places my hand in Akila's and Kyri declares us wed, tears of love mingle with his laughter as he sings his lullaby to me one last time.

Alla ka tchù, tia à

Alla ka tchù, tia à

Alla ka tchù, tia à

"The song," I whispered. "You knew."

"Alla ka tchù, tia à," he sang softly. "Yes, child. I knew."

"Why didn't you say anything?" I clenched my fists angrily.

"What could I have said? I knew. But I did not know what I knew. Just as with The MoonQuest, I know more now. That is why I am here. Eulisha too. That is why you are here. Both of you. Even now, I know only what I know. Not the whole story. Never the whole story." He smiled sadly. "Nor do I know its ending. No one knows its ending. Not even Prithi."

He laughed without mirth. "After all this time, I still want to know the ending. Can you believe that, Eulisha?"

"What we want and what is do not always match up in the moment, son of my son." Eulisha said. "They always do in the end."

Toshar grinned. "Well, Grandmother, if you set another place at that table of yours and bring back the tea and my cup, I will join you and tell my daughter and grandson what I know of what is and what is to come. I warn you, though, children, it will not be enough to satisfy you. More than likely, it will also not please you."

seventeen

My father was right. It wasn't much, and it did not please me. As he floated down on the light, his body took shape and substance, becoming solid enough that the first thing he did was enfold me in a fierce hug.

"I am *so* proud of you, Q'nta," he whispered before releasing me. "And Ben." He held Ben at arm's length before embracing him too. Ben wriggled awkwardly in Toshar's grip. "You have your father's light. Yes, definitely his light. I wonder…" He released Ben, glanced at Eulisha, shook his head. "Never mind that for now."

"Did you know my father, sir?" Ben asked.

"Sir?" Toshar laughed. "I am your grandfather, boy. No need to call me sir. Grandfather, if you are ready to do that. Toshar, otherwise. Not Ko'lar. I've had enough of that."

"Once a Ko'lar, always a Ko'lar," Eulisha chided gently.

"Oh, I know. I would not be here with you otherwise. However, three of us are Ko'lar and the fourth," he pointed to Ben, "will certainly be one one day. A little too confusing to be calling each other Ko'lar, don't you think?" He lowered himself onto a fourth cushion that took shape beneath him. "Now, Eulisha, where is that famous tea of yours?"

The story my father told us over tea was as disturbing as it was strange. Ben and I were not so much in a strange place as in a different time: a time before Toshar's time. Our disappearances, Ben and mine, had been orchestrated by Bo'Rá K'n, who had hoped to preempt The MoonQuest's success by altering its prehistory.

"His first mistake," Toshar explained, "was in underestimating a mother's love for her child."

"What do you mean?" I asked.

"Bo'Rá K'n could take away your son and your memory but, strong as he is, he does not possess the power to erase what is buried in your heart," said Eulisha, topping up my tea. "That love reunited you and Ben in the same time and place instead of keeping you separate, which was his plan."

Ben ignored his tea and drummed his fingers on the table. "So, now what? We're here. You're here. Bo'Rá K'n made a mistake. How do we get home?"

Toshar shrugged.

"You don't know?" Ben's drumming rattled teapot and cups. He stared at Toshar.

Eulisha gently covered Ben's hand with hers.

"I am sorry, Ben," Toshar said. "I told you that what I would tell you would not please you. Or satisfy you."

"There's more," I said stonily. "It's not just that we might never get home, is it?" I turned to Eulisha. "What aren't you saying?"

"Do you remember the song?" Eulisha asked.

The heart and ring

Apart must wing

I pushed Eulisha's hand off Ben's and replaced it with mine. "No."

Toshar touched my shoulder. "Q'nta, my child, you don't understand."

I shrugged him off coldly. "No, Father. *You* don't understand. You never lost a child. Ben was taken from me once. I will not let you take him away from me again."

I jumped to my feet, determined to find a way out of this nightmare tea party and away from the cavern. We might never get back to Q'ntana. That didn't mean we had to be apart.

Eulisha watched impassively as I pushed against the invisible barrier that surrounded the light shaft. Ben held his head in his hands. Toshar looked sadly from me to Eulisha, waiting for her to speak.

Exhausted, I dropped back to my cushion. "Please," I moaned. "Let us get away from here, away from quests, away from everything." I gripped Ben's arm so tightly he winced. "Just let us go."

"I understand how you feel," Eulisha said. She refilled my teacup and nudged it toward me.

I jumped up again, knocking over the table. Tea spilled everywhere. "You don't." I shouted. "You can't."

Eulisha mopped up the mess, righted the table and refilled our cups. She sipped from hers. "I also lost a child. Your grandfather. Toshar's father. He went missing when Toshar was a boy. I never saw him again. No one did."

I dropped back to my seat, ashamed. Eulisha stared into the blackness, into the past.

"I lost two children, really" she said softly. "I also lost Zakk. To Bo'Rá K'n. He did not disappear as your grandfather did. He might as well have." She turned back and forced my eyes to meet hers. "So you see, my dear. I do understand. More than you know."

"If you know, how can you ask me to do this? You can't," I cried.

Ben rose. His face was white. He shook. He stared angrily, first at Eulisha then at Toshar. "You made us choose without telling us there'd be consequences," he shouted, jabbing at the crystal and circlet, which still hovered above the table. "Was it a choice 'for all time,' like in The MoonQuest?"

"Ben…" Toshar reached for him but Ben pushed his hand away.

"You're as bad as Bo'Rá K'n," he said icily. "I don't care what you say or do, you can't make us do what you want."

Toshar sighed. "No, Ben, you're right. We cannot." He stroked his beard thoughtfully. "You both must listen to me carefully." Ben's mouth shot open. "Please. If after I have said what I must, you choose to abandon your quests, we will not stop you."

For the first time since we joined Eulisha, her face looked troubled. Toshar cut her off before she could speak. "They must choose of their own free will, Eulisha. Otherwise, none of this can have any meaning." To Ben and me he said, "You are right to be angry. For Elderbards, we have not explained ourselves very well. I will do my best to do better now."

Toshar coughed and sipped his tea. Then he stood and walked slowly around the table as he spoke.

"Bo'Rá K'n expected that his actions would overturn the prophecy of the Fayr'Owyn and the Heart of the Star. Ben would be gone for all time and Q'nta would have no memory. Instead, they played into the prophecy." Toshar quickened his pace. "Now, Bo'Rá K'n is even angrier than when I encountered him during my MoonQuest. Angrier and more determined than ever to control both Astel Lev and Astel Elohia, which would destroy their power for good forever." He stopped between us and reached for the crystal with his right hand and the circlet with his left. Holding them without speaking, he gazed from one to the other, then replaced them. "If Bo'Rá K'n succeeds," he continued, his eyes now on me, "the line of bards of which we are all part will be extinguished from history."

"It will be as though none us ever existed," Eulisha added. "Bards and stories will not perish, because bards and stories will never have been."

"I don't understand," Ben exclaimed. "We can't just vanish."

Eulisha started to respond but Toshar interrupted her. "You did once. You can again. This time not for a time. For all time. Do you understand now?"

Ben dropped to his pillow and said nothing. He reached for his tea bowl and raised it, letting the steam bathe his face before sipping. He drank slowly until it was all gone. He held his cup out for more. Eulisha poured him a second cup, then a third. On the fourth he turned to Toshar.

"Where was I after I left Q'ntana as an infant, before I turned up here?" He looked up at the opening in the cavern ceiling. "Up there."

Toshar glanced at Eulisha. She acknowledged his look with a nod then watched Ben closely as Toshar replied. "Nowhere."

"I still don't understand. How—"

"Without your mother's love, you would have ceased to exist, Ben. For all time."

Ben swallowed hard and gulped down the last of his tea. "Bo'Rá K'n can do that?"

"Not on his own," Eulisha said.

"Nor always successfully," Toshar added, "or you would not be here now."

I reached for Ben's hand.

"Bo'Rá K'n no longer knows the meaning of love," Toshar said.

Eulisha patted Toshar's hand. "And he has forgotten the meaning of courage."

Toshar continued. "The success of all his plans relies on fear and fury. Only love and courage can conquer them. Do you understand now?"

"What about Akila?" I asked quietly. "Why couldn't my love bring him back?"

"I am sorry, Q'nta," Toshar replied. "Even had Bo'Rá K'n been responsible for Akila's departure, there is nothing stronger than a mother's love for her child. Nothing."

"If we agree," I said slowly, "how will it happen? And when?" Tears streamed down my cheeks.

"Soon. The moment you make the choice to accept Astel Lev and The StarQuest, and the moment Ben chooses Astel Elohia and The SunQuest."

"Then what?" Ben asked. His voice was hoarse. "If we say yes, will we ever see each other again?"

Toshar looked down, reluctant to meet either set of eyes.

"Prithi help me," he said. "I don't know."

* * *

What choice did we truly have? I could cling to Ben until Bo'Rá K'n achieved his twisted purpose, at which point we would both disappear as though we had never been. Or we could proceed, apart, and pray that we would survive our individual quests in a way that reunited us.

Ben came to his decision quickly. Either that or he was more stoic than I could manage to be. At first, I clung to my son and wept. Then, I raged — at Toshar and Eulisha, at Bo'Rá K'n, at Prithi...at anything and anyone I could blame for my despair. In my pain, I even wished that Ben had never been born or, that if he'd had to be born and taken away, that he had never returned. Those wishes dissolved as soon as I remembered the joy of his birth and the exhilaration I experienced when he called me Mother and fell into my arms.

In the end, I did what I had known all along I would and must do.

"Yes," I said simply. "What now?"

"These are different journeys than the one I undertook, my children," Toshar said. "More difficult ones, as well. I know that, and wish it were otherwise." He touched my shoulder tenderly. "A parent wants nothing more than to protect his children from danger and harm, Q'nta. Yet I stand here, not only unable to offer you that protection but preventing you from offering it to your son." He shook his head sadly. "When The MoonQuest was done and I reluctantly accepted that Bo'Rá K'n was not, that he lived on somehow, I prayed that he would never again touch the lives of those I loved. For the rest of my life, I believed my prayers had been answered. You were born... and you were so beautiful." He stroked my hair. "We lived happily, you and me and your mother, in a kingdom that had never known such peace and prosperity, that had never been so rich with story...a

115

kingdom that I knew would embrace you when it was time for you to carry your great-grandmother's legacy forward."

"Your legacy, Toshar," Eulisha interjected.

"That too." He waved his hand dismissively. "When you met Akila, married and became with child—" He touched Ben's arm and smiled wistfully. "With *this* child. When that happened, I knew that all was well… I thought I knew that all was well, that I could die in peace and move on to other realms, set off on other journeys, and bequeath the Elderbardship to each of you in turn."

"Once you had fixed The MoonQuest on parchment, Toshar. Only then."

Toshar nodded. "True, Eulisha. True." He sighed. "I was wrong. It is so easy now to see how wrong I was. I did not see it at the time. Not until Ben vanished. By then, I was no longer alive and the story was no longer mine to write. Because of that, there was nothing I could do. Only grieve — for each of you and for Q'ntana." He placed one hand on Ben's shoulder, the other on mine. "Until now."

Holding my tears back, I saw the love in my father's eyes and recognized it as the same love I felt for Ben. "I'm sorry, Father," I whispered.

"I, as well," he replied.

Toshar pressed down more firmly on my shoulder. "Are you ready, my children?"

We nodded.

"'Heart and ring / Apart must wing," he recited. "That is why you must. The time may come when they will be reunited. That has yet to be written." He passed the Heart of the Star to me, the Ring of Unity to Ben.

"On the count of three, Q'nta, hold Astel Lev against the center of your chest. Whatever you feel, do not move it away. Ben, you will do likewise with Astel Elohia, only you will hold it against your forehead, between your eyes."

"One… Two—"

"Wait, Father."

"Yes?"

"Thank you and…I love you."

"One day we will dance again, child. I promise." Toshar smiled sadly. "Now?"

I shook my head and gazed at Ben through the tears clouding my vision. "Ben… We've never danced, you and I, but…but we will." I swallowed a sob. "I love you, Ben."

Ben stood straighter. He grinned. His eyes were bright. "We're ready, Grandfather," he said in a clear, steady voice.

"Wait," I said.

"What is it, child?" Toshar asked. "Time…"

I looked at Ben, the son I hadn't even remembered having until… No, I couldn't think that. "Remember one thing, my son. Your heart."

"What about it?"

"Whatever else is going on around you, wherever your SunQuest carries you, your heart is true…is truer…is truest."

He nodded, still smiling.

"Now, Father."

"*Three.*"

Lightning blindingly bright stabbed the ground between us with an earsplitting crash. Everything shattered: teapot and cups, table and stools, the shaft of light that had held us in place. Perhaps even the cavern itself, for I thought I heard rocks smashing. For an instant, I worried about Pri'Malaka and his Stone People. Then an excruciating blend of agony and bliss battered against my heart. Relentlessly.

I couldn't think. I couldn't breathe. I couldn't move. I was dying. I was sure of it. The light grew brighter and brighter. My breath grew shorter and shorter. Pain stabbed at me, choked me. Ecstasy enfolded me, embraced me.

Then it stopped. All of it. Everything.

Sound and light. Pain. Bliss.

I felt nothing.

I saw nothing.

I slept.

When I awoke, my chest ached and my hands were empty. I lay on the cavern floor, in the center of a pool of light.

Alone.

eighteen

"**B**en?"

I had forgotten where I was, forgotten what had happened. I knew only the Star Rock beneath me, the raised platform formerly at its center now empty. The Star Rock glowed faintly with a diffuse star-shaped blue light. Everything else was blacker than black.

"Ben?" I groped into the dark. No one was there. The only response was the distant drip-drip of trickling water.

Dribble-*drip.*

Dribble-*drip.*

Dribble-*drip.*

In a rush of anger, exhilaration and panic, I remembered. Where was the Heart of the Star? I had been holding it against my chest. Now, my hands were empty and it was nowhere to be seen. Had I lost it already? And Ben? Where was he? An aching emptiness overwhelmed me as I fretted about where his SunQuest might have taken him.

Now what? How do I get out of here? Where do I go? What do I do?

Even the crack of daylight that had pierced the cavern ceiling earlier was gone, not that I could have reached it even had the opening still been there.

I closed my eyes and waited. For something. For anything.

Dribble-*drip.*

Dribble—

It's raining. A steady drizzle that beats lightly against the stone terrace of a grim castle on a bleak starless night.

I know I have seen this castle before. Where? First one, then two, then a dozen kep'chas emerge screechingly from brooding, low-hanging clouds to circle its blackened turrets. Now I recognize it: S'kryssna S'kyaga's Castle Do'am.

The terrace is V-shaped, bound by a decaying castle wall on one side and stone balusters on the other two. Carved into each baluster is a coiled snake, its head jutting out from the column, its tongue darting out from a distended mouth.

S'kryssna S'kyaga slinks onto the terrace. She wears a black, hooded, fur-trimmed robe embellished with dulled-silver runic markings. She glances around, as though sensing an alien presence. Satisfied that she is alone, she turns slowly and raises her face to the sky. The little I can see of her creamy unblemished skin shines in the rain.

"Hoss-eeyah ka-am seeya na sempah," she chants. Again, louder: "Hoss-eeyah ka-am seeya na sempah." Then, as she walks the perimeter of the terrace, her fingers trailing on the balustrade, a third time, louder still, "Hoss-eeyah ka-am seeya na sempah."

Where the balustrade reaches its apex, she stops and hisses, "c."

As one, the baluster snakes come alive. Other than yellow mouths and red tongues, they are still the wet gray hue of the stone. They writhe hissingly toward their mistress, coiling and uncoiling around her in an ecstatic dance so sexual that I am embarrassed to watch. At the same time, I cannot turn away. This vision will not permit it.

A brilliant light explodes in the distant sky, accompanied by a faint rumble of thunder. S'kryssna S'kyaga looks up at it and frowns. The light plummets earthward, toward the terrace. As one, the snakes cease their gyrations. They surround their mistress, erect, protective and alert. In a flash brighter than any midday sun, the light falls to earth in front of S'kryssna S'kyaga. The light disperses and—

Ben!

His empty hands are pressed to his forehead.

S'kryssna S'kyaga says nothing. Her flash of stunned surprise passes almost immediately.

Ben looks around, startled. He doesn't know where he is. Then he does. Whether from my visions or his, he recognizes the sorceress and her citadel. Before he can do or say anything, the snakes close in around him. Their circle constricts, tighter and tighter, until he disappears from view.

"Ben!" I think I scream, but no sound emerges. All I hear is the low rumble of a faraway laugh and the dribble-drip of an unrelenting drizzle.

Dribble-*drip.*

Dribble-*drip.*

"Does she still sleep, I wonder?" Pri'Mala's voice returned me to the cavern. It reverberated softly in counterpoint to the dribble-drip of water somewhere deep in the darkness. "How long has it been?"

"Too long," Pri'Malaka replied, his deeper voice still booming, even as he whispered.

Dribble-drip-*drip*.

I opened my eyes, unnerved by what I had just seen and confused by the voices, which pulled me back to my first memories of the Co'an house.

Dribble-drip-drip-drip.

"Too long for what?" I called out.

The dripping drew nearer, grew more insistent.

Dribble-drip-*pshhhhh*. *Crack!* A distant chunk of rock calved from the cavern wall and smashed to the ground with an earth-shuddering crash.

Pri'Mikana giggled.

"What's going on?" I shouted.

"We are being freed, dear one," Pri'Mala replied, her voice sparkling with joy. "*You* have freed us."

Confused, I stepped off the Star Rock and out of its light.

"Stay within the light." Pri'Malaka thundered.

I leapt back.

"There is no time for this," Pri'Malaka muttered.

"There must be, husband. She must know. Before she embarks, she must know."

Pri'Malaka coughed and another far-off boulder gave way noisily.

"Time is short, Q'nta. But Pri'Mala is right. There are things you must know. The question is, which things." Rumbling, not-quite audible arguments passed between husband and wife as the dripping and rock-crashing drew nearer. "Very well," he said at last.

"Listen carefully, Fayr'Owyn, and do not interrupt with the many questions you will have. Time is now shorter than ever and you cannot stay here much longer. The Ma has found her way back into these caves. Her waters will rise, the Ko'Ba will fall and we shall be free."

"Thank Prithi," Pri'Mala sighed. "And thank *you*."

Me? What had I done? Whatever it was would surely kill me. There was no light beyond this Star Rock and I could see no way out through the impenetrable dark beyond it. Panic pushed bile up my throat. I gagged and my eyes darted in all directions.

"Oh, you need not worry, dear one," Pri'Mala said, reading my thoughts. "You will leave safely. Of course, you will. We will carry you with us. Only you must let Pri'Malaka speak his piece. Time truly is short."

Now I was certain I would die. How could a disembodied voice carry me anywhere? I sat down, hugged my legs, dropped my head to my knees and tried to ignore the sounds of destruction exploding around me.

"You have freed us and we can never fully repay you for that, Fayr'Owyn," Pri'Malaka continued hurriedly. "But your StarQuest is only now beginning and the journey ahead is long and perilous, more perilous now that you carry Astel Lev within you."

"In me?"

"No questions, Fayr'Owyn. I am sorry." To Pri'Mala and Pri'Mikana, he said, "It is nearly time. You know what to do."

Another rock crashed, so near that I flinched, releasing the water's dammed up trickle into the roaring whoosh of a flooded river. I looked up, still saw nothing and hugged my knees more tightly.

"You cannot be harmed as long as you remain within the light of the star," Pri'Mala said reassuringly. "Nothing can get through to it."

Pri'Malaka continued. "Alas, the Star Rock cannot protect you once you leave here. It has other work to do. As for you, you will be in constant peril until your StarQuest reaches Completion. From Bo'Rá K'n and from S'kryssna S'kyaga."

"Their power is great," Pri'Mala said.

"It is," Pri'Malaka added. "So is yours. Greater than you know. Greater than you believe. Do not doubt that power. Theirs or yours. Theirs to inspire hatred and fear. Yours to inspire love."

Pri'Malaka raised his voice to be heard over the cacophony. "You wonder where to go and what to do. You will find all the answers in your heart. Only in your heart. That is where Astel Lev resides for now, until you are able to return it to Reesa Kam'ana."

I tapped my chest. It felt tender where I had hugged the crystal to it.

"Remember, Fayr'Owyn," Pri'Malaka continued, "never choose with your mind. Listen with your heart. Trust with your heart. If you remember nothing else, remember that."

The need to remember anything for long seemed futile as the devastation moved nearer. I stood and watched, at once enthralled and terrified, as white-capped breakers beat relentlessly against the invisible curtain of protection that surrounded me. When the first boulder shattered against the star's perimeter and pelted noisily into the roiling water, I shut my eyes and tried to imagine myself somewhere else. Anywhere else. Yet I couldn't drown out the angry explosions… or my fears. I worried that the barrier wouldn't hold. I fretted that water and rocks would ultimately spill over the top and onto me. And my stomach bound itself in knots as my mind tried unsuccessfully to figure out ways to escape.

You will find all the answers in your heart. Only in your heart. I heard Pri'Malaka's words again through the clatter and tried to calm my ragged breathing. Pri'Mala's too: *We will carry you with us.*

The next convulsion shook the ground so violently that my eyes shot open, just in time to witness the cavern's ceiling fracture. A slice of daylight illuminated more of the hellish devastation unfolding outside my oasis. Volleys of hail-like rocks pummeled frothing, boiling waters, which, in turn, lashed up against the cavern walls. When the light overhead abruptly brightened, I started. Two ceiling slabs — one massive, one half its size — had come unmoored. I watched, horror-struck, as they plummeted toward me. Now, I would die for sure. My first instinct was to close my eyes again. Grim fascination won out. An instant later, some invisible force aborted their descent. I held my breath. Everything else stopped too. The water calmed. The rocks stilled. The cavern brightened.

"Well, then," said the largest of the slabs, "I think it is time we got you out of here." The voice was Pri'Malaka's.

"Hold on tight." The smaller slab giggled.

The slabs, I realized, were not suspended in midair. Rather, they were perched atop the star light-shaft. The rock beneath me shuddered, jiggled. A tiny crack appeared at the star's inner edge. It jiggled some more and the crack spread, following a path just inside the perimeter until it, too, formed a perfect star. Another jiggle and the Star Rock wrenched free of its surroundings.

"Now?" the rock beneath me called up. It was Pri'Mala.

"Now," Pri'Malaka replied.

Slowly, the Star Rock ascended. As it did, the protective curtain beneath us disintegrated. Water eddied in agitatedly.

"Are you able to travel a little quicker, my love?" Pri'Malaka asked. "Time."

The slab jerked up, knocking me off my feet. The water, angry again, rose nearly as quickly as we did and smacked against the sides of the cavern. Rocks broke loose and beat down around me. With a deafening roar, an entire wall collapsed into the churning water. The resulting swell slammed against the invisible barrier with a bone-jarring thud, tossing me off Pri'Mala and onto Pri'Malaka.

"We-ee-ee-ee!" Pri'Mikana squealed with delight as the waters rose and heaved us into the cloud-studded sky. As we cleared the cliffs, the Ko'Ba caved in on itself, imploding thunderously into the Ma.

A moment later, stillness reigned, all evidence of the Ko'Ba erased for all time.

THE QUEST BEGINS

I lay, damp and breathless, on a mist-shrouded plain. Gentle haze blurred everything, absorbed all color. The sky was white. The ground, snowy but not cold. In the mid-distance, a lone tree, giant and arthritic, was gray.

The stone slabs that had been Pri'Malaka, Pri'Mala and Pri'Mikana were gone. I remembered passing through a cloud just as the Ma calmed below us. Then I blinked my eyes and here I was. Alone.

With nothing to see or do, my thoughts returned to Ben and to my most recent vision. Was what I had "seen" true? Was Ben with S'kryssna S'kyaga? Did that mean his SunQuest had already failed?

It could be. The Q'ophar's voice echoed through the mist. *Or not.*

More riddles.

You know what you need to know. What you want to know is not the same thing.

"It is when it comes to my son," I countered aloud.

"Nonsense." This voice wasn't the Q'ophar's. It was a squawk, at once shrill and throaty. "Utter nonsense," it screeched again, more forcefully.

The creature that took shape out in the mist stood many times my size, his winged torso clothed in multicolored plumes. Tawny fur coated an enormous head, pillar-like legs and massive paws. A golden mane that trailed to the ground framed a face at once fierce and gentle, whose most prominent feature was a single star-shaped eye in the middle of his forehead. Black as night, the eye gazed at me with a peculiar blend of ferocity, compassion and fire.

"It's not nonsense," I retorted, too angry to be startled.

"Nonsense," he growled. "All nonsense. Failure is nonsense." He shook his head and mane in a bellowing laugh. As his mouth yawned open, teeth and tongue vanished into a black maw, and a tiny light blinked on at the back of his throat. The light brightened into an image.

The image came alive. It was a round, white-stucco house and two Co'ans. One swept the stoop while the other took a polishing cloth to the front window. It was Coanra'a and Coanri'i's house, rebuilt. My heart raced hopefully, until I realized these were other Co'ans. The creature's jaws snapped shut.

"There is no failure. There is no success. There is only what is." He nodded, as though satisfied with his point. He turned to go.

"Wait!" I rushed toward him.

He stopped when I was halfway and swiveled his head all the way around to face me. "Yes?"

"You have to tell me about Ben. Please. Is he all right? Does S'kryssna S'kyaga have him? What about his SunQuest?"

"I am tired of that question," the creature replied, licking his back feathers.

"Which one?"

"Any one."

"But—"

"Too many buts." His voice took on a shrill edge.

"But—"

"There are no buts," he thundered.

"But what—?"

He flicked his feathered tail. Puffs of down floated up into the mist and disappeared. "Enough questions. Trust the answers you have. Trust them and move on."

"But how—?"

He roared angrily, again turned to go.

"No," I cried, strangely unafraid. "You—"

"No," he snarled menacingly. "*You.*"

I wanted to scream in frustration. Instead, I unclenched my fists and took a deep breath.

"Breathe," he said. "Yes. Good."

I exhaled and what emerged was something between a sigh and stifled shriek.

"Is Ben dead?" I whispered.

"There is no death. There is only life. And the Heart of the Star."

The Heart of the Star. I had forgotten…

"You know who I am," the creature added in a softer voice.

I stopped my head in mid-shake. I *did* know. "You're Tashek. My father knew you. Wait. Weren't you—"

From the corner of my eye I saw a bird of fire, its feathers gold and crimson flutes of flame. Then I saw a mighty lion, its roar dissolving the bars that caged it.

"Many forms, many faces," Tashek replied. "Toshar saw what served him. You see what is right for you." Again, I caught a glimpse of bird and lion. "Ben will see what he sees. Or not."

"Ben. You've seen him?" I asked eagerly.

"No questions."

"But—"

"Or buts." He padded toward me. "Are you ready?"

"I—"

"Of course you are. Climb up. It is time to move on."

He lay down with his rear legs extended out behind him and his tail slapping loudly on the ground.

"Well?"

"Where are we going?"

"More questions?" he snapped.

"If you weren't Tashek," I muttered.

"If I were not Tashek," he retorted, "where would you be?"

I pulled myself up onto his back.

"Hold on tight, Q'nta Ko'lar Fayr'Owyn of Q'ntana."

I clutched his mane and braced myself.

He took off with great loping strides. The gray expanse of nothingness around me never shifted. If I hadn't seen his legs move and felt his muscles quiver, I would have doubted that we moved at all. No wind riffled my hair or Tashek's mane. His feathers lay as flat as if he were asleep.

"Perhaps *I'm* asleep," I thought as my eyelids resisted all attempts to keep them open and as my head sank into his downy neck feathers. I felt Tashek's rear legs flex as he leapt up. I was aware of a soft breeze tickling the back of my neck and of the gentle motion of his wings. But I was too tired to open my eyes. Too tired…too tired…too tired…

I am a young girl, alone in a lush, overgrown forest glen. Not entirely alone, for birds hidden deep in the foliage hoot their welcome. I come here often — always alone, though never at dusk. Not until now. M'nor will rise in her fullness tonight, though not for me. Not in this place that veils sunlight by day and moonlight by night.

The light, already weak, weakens further. Greens dull to brown and browns to gray before all melts into a velvety black that muffles all sound. If birds are still here, they wait silently, as do I. For what?

I feel for the mossy ledge that is my usual seat. Even sightless, I know every crack, bump and ridge of it. Or do I? Am I seeing in the dark what was invisible in the light? My fingers trace out an ancient rune I've never noticed before. Although I press my nose to the ledge and strain my eyes, I see nothing. I close my eyes as I continue to trace the letters. Absolute darkness feels more comfortable from behind closed lids.

Alla ka tchù, tia à

My father's lullaby. I hear it faintly as my fingers follow the rock's worn etchings. I hear it faintly on the soft breeze that emerges from nowhere. My father's lullaby...but it's more than that. What is it? A memory from the past? From the future?

I lie down and rest my head on the stone. The melody caresses my face, ruffles my hair and, feather-like, tickles my cheeks and eyelids. The words not only waft around me, they move me — backward and forward in time.

Alla ka tchù, tia à

The memories and visions are vague, too vague to grasp. After a while they scatter into the night.

Alla ka tchù, tia à

Alla ka tchù, tia à

Soon, the song fades too, and all is silent once more. My eyes open a slit. Gray light greets them, shockingly bright to eyes expecting lightlessness. I see no forest, no grove, no rock — only an infinite achromatic emptiness. The breeze, too, is gone. All that remains is my faint memory of a timeworn chant and the nose-tickling fur and feathers of a giant winged creature.

Then I remember.

twenty

"We are here," Tashek announced. "Again."

I looked around. Nothing had changed, not even our distance from the tree. We could easily have traveled nowhere at all. Tashek crouched and rolled to one side, forcing me off his back. With a startling squawk, he shook himself so violently that body, fur and feathers became a fiery blur. When his shaking stopped, he had shrunk into a brilliantly colored bird small enough to hop onto my shoulder. Toshar's bird of fire. He squawked again.

"The dream. The dream. Remember the dream!" he screamed into my ear. "Do you?"

"Not so loud." I rubbed my ear. "Sort of. The forest. The chant. Was that really me?"

"Was and is. Was and is." Tashek nodded his head vigorously. "Again."

He flew to the tree and back again, racing around my head dizzyingly. "We're here," he repeated. "Again."

I swatted at him. "You mean I've been here with you before?" He nodded again. "In the dream?"

"Dream and not dream. Real and imagined," he screeched. "All one." He flapped his wings. Fireworks sparked around him. I leapt back. "All one. All one. All one." He bobbed his head rapidly and resumed his orbit around me, flying so quickly that he blurred into a circle of cool flame. Finally, he slowed and lit atop my head. He jumped up and down, tangling his claws in my hair. I tried to shoo him away but, screeching still, he dodged my swipes.

"Come down from there. You're hurting me."

"Hurt but never harm. Hurt but never harm," he chattered, pulling and knotting my hair.

"Stop it."

"Look," he shrieked and tugged at my hair, pulling me toward the tree. He disentangled himself and pushed himself into my face. "Look!"

An ancient, worn, wood-plank door formed an arch in the tree's massive trunk. Just about my height, it had a wrought-iron ring-pull at its center.

"P'rtulle," Tashek screeched again. "Maya Ko. Now!"

"Now what, Tashek?" I swatted at him again. "Can't you just be still and talk to me?"

Tashek flew to the door. He perched precariously on the ring-pull, then buzzed back and around me again before returning to the top of my head. He yanked mercilessly at the tangle that was my hair.

"If you want me to open the door," I said wearily, "can't you just say so? Like a normal—" I shook my head. "Never mind."

Tashek dropped onto my shoulder and flapped his wings noisily. "Maya Ko. *Now!*"

I touched the ring-pull. A shiver ran through me. I looked at Tashek. He nodded vigorously. The door was damp and swollen, as though it had not been opened in a long time. I tugged at the ring as hard as I could. I couldn't budge it.

"I can't."

"Can. Can, can, can!"

"How?"

"Astel Lev. Astel Lev. Astel Lev!"

"How?"

Tashek bounced off my shoulder and whizzed around my head three times, before butting his head into the center of my chest.

"Ouch! Why did you do that?"

"Astel Lev. Astel Lev!"

"Oh." I touched my hands to my chest, closed my eyes and inhaled deeply, trying to make contact with the crystal that, somehow, was now inside me.

"Astel Lev," I whispered. "What do I do?"

Nothing.

"Astel Lev?"

"Fayr'Owyn," Tashek squawked. "Fayr'Owyn! Fayr'Owyn! *Fayr'Owyn!*"

"What? Oh." I took in another long, slow breath and spoke again — not to the Heart of the Star, but to the Mayo Ko, the door.

"I am the Fayr'Owyn. I carry the Heart of the Star back to Reesa Kam'ana. In whatever way it serves Astel Lev, my journey and The StarQuest, let me through." With my eyes still closed, I reached for the ring pull. "Please," I added.

My fingertips touched metal. The metal dissolved. I opened my eyes.

The door was gone. A giant cutout shaped like the tree opened into a rolling meadow dotted with vibrantly colored wildflowers. Tashek returned to my shoulder.

"What is this place?"

"A feather," Tashek replied, flitting in my face.

"What?"

"A feather. Pluck a feather." Tashek hovered in front of me, his wings barely moving.

"Won't it hurt?"

"Won't hurt you a bit." He sniggered.

"Which one?"

"The one that reminds you of home, of course."

I had no idea what Tashek meant. I knew even less what home meant. It would be pointless to ask.

Even though all his feathers seemed identical, each the same size and blend of rainbow colors as the next, I felt drawn to the feather at the tip of his right wing. The feather brightened and radiated heat as my finger hovered over it. The heat spread into my hand, up my arms and throughout my body. My finger grazed the feather, and it released effortlessly into my hand. As it did, Tashek vanished.

Home. I gazed through the tree-opening. *Is that where I'm going?* As if in answer to the question, sounds drifted through the opening into this place of stillness: the chirrup-chitter of singing birds...the crackling croak of river doats...the whiny yammer of angry flaigens. All strangely familiar yet oddly alien...and unnerving in ways I couldn't identify.

Why am I so scared? It makes no sense. I'm more than scared. I'm paralyzed. I can't lift my foot. I don't want to pass through the Maya Ko. I don't dare.

How can I be this frightened? I'm more frightened than when I didn't know my reflection in the Co'an's mirror...more frightened than when I first saw the Q'ophar...more frightened than when I realized I might never see Ben again.

I knew the way forward, but not what it meant. I knew the way forward, but not where it would take me. I knew I carried the Heart of the Star but not why. I knew I carried it, but not where to take it. I knew I was here to fulfill a prophecy, but I didn't know how. I knew I was Q'nta, Ko'lar and Fayr'Owyn, but not what any of that meant.

"Tashek," I moaned. "Come back. Please."

Silence.

"Ben," I whispered. "Where are you?"

No answer. Despite the animal sounds floating toward me from that other world, I felt alone. Desperately alone.

Absentmindedly, I stroked Tashek's feather. It was soft, downy as a baby's hair. A baby's hair...my baby's hair...Ben...

My mind flew back to Ben. Not to the young man I might never see again...to the gurgly infant of another time and place. I smiled at that memory and at the memory of all the smiles of those long-ago days. I remembered how Ben's birth had eased the heaviness of a father's death and a husband's disappearance. I remembered what it was like to be Elderbard, and I remembered stories I had told. I remembered my mother and Uncle Kyri. I remembered Castle Rose.

I remembered Q'nta.

I remembered everything.

The one that reminds you of home.

I stroked the feather.

"Thank you, Tashek," I whispered.

The feather fragmented into sparkles that glistered twinklingly in my hand, floated up into the mist and were gone.

twenty -one

I stepped through the Maya Ko and onto the soft, dry dirt of a shimmery red-earth ribbon of road. After the dark, damp chill of the Ko'Ba cave and the empty colorlessness on the other side of the Maya Ko, the sun-warmed air here felt good on my face and the sun-baked soil squished pleasantly into my sandals and between my toes. I looked back: The misty world I had just left, and the tree-opening back into it, fluttered into nothingness, as though they had never been.

The road, which began where I stood, looped and laced through the countryside ahead of me before it melted into the blue haze of faraway peaks. In the middle distance a river unspooled alongside the road, glinting in the early morning light. Between river and mountain, the vista darkened into dense forest.

If didn't know where this StarQuest needed me to go, I did need to go somewhere. I began to walk. I had taken only a few steps, or so it seemed, when the panorama of river, forest and mountain evaporated into an endless meadow of brilliantly colored wildflowers. Even the road had altered. It now shot straight through these wind-riffled clusters of purple, pink, yellow and fuchsia. They rippled across the plain like waves on a multicolored sea, all starkly illuminated by the unyielding light of a midday sun.

Midday? How was that possible? The sun had been hugging the horizon when I crossed into this place. Now it was directly overhead. Was I walking backward in time? Was I walking at all? My feet moved but the groupings of flora that carpeted the fields on either side of the road never changed, however I adjusted my pace or direction. Perplexed, I scored a large X in the road next to a tall, purple coneflower and continued forward. The X never left my side and the floral vista never moved. Only the sun seemed immune to the strangeness on the ground. It continued its journey, setting at last into distant flowers. As the sky blackened into night, I collapsed next to my X and wept in frustration, cursing Tashek and the Maya Ko for having delivered me to this impossible place. Soon, I was asleep.

I stand at the junction of two intersecting roads. It's dark, moonless. A jumbled scattering of stars sheds just enough light for me to discern the shadowy, pole-like trees arrayed in military formation along each road. Not a whisper of wind disturbs the silence. Even my breath feels like an intrusion. I look from left to right, front to back, but each road is identical. Each tree is identical.

The sky lightens and black fades to indigo, taking the stars with it. Rays of white, tangerine and pewter angle up from the craggy, crenelated summits of the distant peaks that mark the terminus of each arrow-straight roadway. A discordant cacophony of tweets, chirps and twitters erupts from the trees' dense foliage. In a cloud of color, the leaves burst up into the sky, circle overhead and fly off in four matching lines into the brightening dawn above each set of mountains.

Trees are bare. Roads are dusty and gray, apart from scattered clumps of pocked black rock that thrust up through the dirt. At first, the rocks seem randomly placed. As I turn, turn and turn again to face each road, I see that the rocks, too, are set identically. Even the mountain vistas on the far horizon are indistinguishable from one path to the next, with every jag and edge the twin of its neighbor. I know I must step forward, but I don't know which is the right road, can't be sure if one is more real than others, feel certain that if I step onto the wrong one I will disappear. As I turn, faster and faster, the dirt beneath my feet wears away and I find myself standing on a stone slab, black as the nearby rock clusters. Here, though, the markings are not pitted scars, they're glyphs. I trace their lines and curves with my finger and again hear the chant:

Alla ka tchù, tia à

Faint at first, the chant grows louder as I rub my finger into the grooves, which deepen the harder I press, until my hand, wrist, forearm and elbow can slide into the fissure formed by one line of a single symbol.

Alla ka tchù, tia à

Alla ka tchù, tia à

The harder I push, the deeper into the earth I burrow and the fuller the chant.

Now, the sky is but a thin, blue slit far above my head. I follow a softly glowing stone path that soon refracts into a dance of rainbow colors that swirl around me. Strangely, the path supports me, even though it lacks any discernible substance.

"Step closer, child," I hear. The words weave themselves through the music. I know it's Àna, but I cannot see her. "Closer. Just a few more steps…"

Those few steps carry me past the dancing light, which still undulates behind me. In front of me, Àna's silvery iridescence glimmers in the blackness.

"Closer still."

I edge forward, my nose a hair from hers.

"One more step."

"Into you?"

"One more step, child."

I step forward.

Alla ka tchù, tia—

A flash of light explodes around me and knocks me off my feet. I don't land on anything. I fall. Hurtle. I should be frightened. I'm not. My free fall slows, slows, slows…

I float…first through darkness then through a succession of scenes. This resembles my dream in the Co'ans' house, yet it is different because I move through people as well as through landscapes. Each time I do, I become that person, just for the moment it takes to pass through. That moment lasts a lifetime.

The first time, afraid that I will slam into a young boy and kill him with the force of my fall, I try to steer myself away. When I can't, I shout at him to move. Frail and malnourished, he huddles in his doorway, oblivious to my approach.

"Have I become a kep'cha with this boy as my target?" I worry, just for an instant. Because in the next, I know nothing of kep'chas, or of Q'nta. My name is Eyfor and, too weak from hunger to move, I wait for whatever spoiled meat scraps might be tossed into this alley for strays. I lurk in the shadows, praying I won't be seen…knowing that being seen means being beaten. It's too late. They see me. I—

A flare of excruciating pain, then an abiding joy.

Eyfor's body is a crumpled, immobile heap in the gutter, and I'm falling again. The entirety of the experience has lasted no longer than a breath. It happens another time in the next breath. And another in the one after that. Different places. Different people. Different lives. So many times that I can barely distinguish one from the next.

Still I float and fall — living in one breath as prince, in another as peasant;

husband one moment, wife the next; as slayer and slayed…as soldier, thief, bard and priest…in temple, tent, alehouse and alley. I live each experience and all of them, again and again and again. And again.

Still I float. Still I fall.

Each individual looks and sounds different. Even so, after a while, I rec-ognize them all. Not by their looks. By their hearts. Because their heart is my heart. Because my heart is their heart. The Heart of the Star.

Alla ka tchù, tia à

Another blinding flash. A painful thump in my belly.

Alla ka tchù, tia à

"Ahem," a distant voice calls…a man's voice…thin and reedy…

Alla ka tchù, tia—

"Ahem." My eyes shot open. For an instant I was confused. Where was Àna? Where was the music? Where was I?

A pebble pelted me in the stomach. It came at me from across the road.

"What—?" I sat up and swiveled around. I saw no one.

Another pebble, this time lobbed from somewhere off to the right, from among the flowers. I turned again. Still no one. But I did see my X and knew, unhappily, where I was.

"Here." The same male voice, now to my left. I turned. No one.

"Here." This time from behind me. Still no one.

"Look up. Look wa-a-a-y up." I gazed up toward the sky. Nothing. "Now, down."

I looked down, increasingly annoyed.

"No. More down. Down, down, down, down, down."

I crouched. Tiny sparkling stones mixed with the dirt winked at me like thousands of distant stars in a vermilion sky. My heart quick-ened. I remembered the star within me. What was this voice? Could it be the Heart of the Star speaking to me? Would the Heart of the Star speak like this?

"Pick a flower," the voice ordered.

"Astel Lev?"

"Pick a flower," it repeated.

No, it couldn't be the Heart of the Star. That voice would come from inside me. This one seemed to be coming from every direction but inside me.

"Where are you? Who are you?"

"First pick a flower. A purple one, I think. Yes, a purple one. It has no stink."

"No stink?"

"Yellow's good and red is nice. But purple is the one with spice."

"Why? Which one?"

"Any purple one you see, but a purple one it must be. Don't wait. Or hesitate. Pick a flower for the power."

"Do you always have to talk in rhyme?"

"Rhyme, rhyme, all in—"

I reached for the purple flower nearest to my X, jerking back in pain when I touched it. My fingers were swollen and red.

"That's the spice. That's the spice. It's much better if you taste it." He paused. "In a stew you'd want to baste it."

"I don't want to baste it," I said, sucking my fingers and trying to remain civil. "I don't want to taste it. To be honest, I'd much rather waste it." The pain had subsided and I pulled my fingers from my mouth. All redness and swelling had vanished. "Prithi save me. Now I'm talking in rhyme."

"Pick it first then take a taste. Take a taste so there is no waste. Petals first, one by one. Then leaves and stem, until it's done."

I wiped my fingers on my sleeve. I searched again for the source of the voice. "If you won't let me see you…" I stood, shrugged and strode off, taking my X and unchanging vista with me.

"Alas, alas," he moaned, his voice starting to fade, "naught comes to pass."

I stopped. "Where are you going? Why can't I see you?"

"You cannot see unless," he whispered raspily, "unless in your belly the flower be."

"And if I never see you?" I asked tartly.

"From this place you'll never flee. A purple flower is the key."

"The key to what?"

"The key to thee. The key to me. The key to free. But free you cannot be unless…unless…unless…"

"Unless I eat the flower?" I asked. "Hungrily?" I added, groaning inwardly at the rhyme.

No response.

"Unless I eat the flower?" I repeated.

Again, no response.

I knelt down and plucked a purple flower. My fingers tingled. Did I dare eat it? If I didn't and the voice was right, I might never leave this place. If I did, the "spice" might kill me. Once again, I seemed to have no choice. I stuffed the flower into my mouth.

For a moment, everything went black. Then, fingers of light poked through my awareness, in the same pastel hues as the flowers had been — purple, pink, yellow, fuchsia. The fingers slowly widened, fanned out and merged, until all was light again, but hazy, vague, unfocused.

"Hallo." The voice was no longer quite so thin.

"Where are you?" I squinted through the fuzziness and made out a wide, toothy grin. "Who are you?" My voice sounded strange to me — husky and gravely, as though I hadn't spoken in many days. My head felt as though someone had stuffed it with rocks. My vision was still cloudy, though as I stared into the haze, a figure began to take shape. And a peculiar figure it was.

Tom Dirqs, as I would soon learn him to be, stood a few heads shorter than me, his squat trunk supported by stumpy legs. His skin looked hard and woody like tree limbs, even as they were soft and yielding to the touch, like flesh. Under black coverall shorts studded with multiple, bulging, oddly shaped pockets, he wore a pink jersey and purple-spotted white bow tie. His shoes were mismatched, bright red on his right foot, forest green on his left. His eyes, too, were mismatched: one sapphire, one sunny yellow. Framing his expressive face was a mop of stringy red-brown hair.

"Hallo, hallo. You move too slow." He patted each of his pockets in turn until he found the one he was looking for. "You be needing a drink…to keep you in the pink." He pulled out a tiny red flagon and thrust it at me. "A sip is all, and you'll stand tall. Just one swallow—"

I gulped down the sweet, syrupy liquid. Whatever it was, it cleared my head and focused my vision.

"— and you'll be ready to follow." He seized my hand and, with unexpected force, jerked me forward. "Come, come. The time has come. Lift your legs and start to run."

I shook my hand free and raced after him, struggling to keep up. As quickly as we ran, we appeared to make no progress: My X never moved.

"Faster," Tom Dirqs shouted back at me. "Faster, faster…or this place will be your master."

I didn't see how I could. My chest ached. My heart thumped in my throat, parched from breathing so hard. Still, I managed to nearly catch up with Tom Dirqs.

"A few more steps and then you're done. Run. Run. Run," he exhorted.

An unexpected force sucked me forward with a booming pop. It thrust me right into Tom Dirqs and pushed both of us out onto a low, grassy bluff overlooking a broad river. Tom Dirqs continued over the edge.

twenty -two

"Do you need help?" I called down into the river. From the way Tom Dirqs thrashed in the water, I couldn't tell whether he was swimming or drowning.

"Blvadbakabug," a gurgly voice burbled up at me through the splashing. "Blvadbakabug."

I kicked off my sandals and dove in after him.

"Blvadbakabug." Tom Dirqs waved me off with one arm and paddled away with the other, making more noise than distance. When I reached him, he slapped maniacally at the water, trying to prevent me from towing him back to shore.

"Blvadbakabug," he sighed, water bubbling from his mouth, as he finally surrendered into my arms.

*   *   *

"Are you all right?" I panted as we lay drying on a more accessible stretch of shoreline. Tom Dirqs's face and clothes were caked in mud.

"Right as rain," he muttered, turning his back to me. "Don't I be looking it?"

"What just happened? Why did I have to eat that flower?"

"All in the past."

"Fine. Who are you? Where are we?"

He coughed up some water. "If you look just right, you can be seeing past the end of this world, clear through the next and well on into the one beyond that."

"What?"

"You be done with Karà Haitu," he declared.

"What?"

"I said—"

"I know what you said. I just don't unders—"

"Tom Dirqs."

"What?"

"Tom Dirqs. My name. Not that it be making no difference. Not no more. Not nohow."

"Glad to meet you, Tom. I—"

Tom Dirqs jerked up to sitting and stabbed me in the leg with a pointy finger. "My name," he said, enunciating each letter, "be Tom Dirqs. A full package. TomDirqs. TomDirqs. TomDirqs. Would you want me to be calling you Q?" He pronounced it Kuh. "Would that be satisfying you? Would you answer to that?" He harrumphed.

"I'm truly sorry, Tim Dirqs. I didn't mean to offend you. If it's Tom Dirqs you want to be—"

"It's not Tom Dirqs I *want* to be," he insisted. "It's Tom Dirqs I *be.*"

Q, as in Q'nta? "How do you know my name?"

Tom Dirqs opened his mouth then snapped it shut it. He looked away.

"Tom Dirqs?" I touched his shoulder. "How do you know my name?"

No response. He sat statue-still.

"Tom Dirqs?"

I shrugged. He would either answer me or not. It either mattered or it didn't. There was little I could do in the moment to force an explanation. I stood, brushed myself off and studied our surroundings. Two dozen paces from where we rested, a rutted path followed the stately, gently curving river in both directions. In the mid-distance a vast treeless plain narrowed into a mountain-walled canyon. In the far-off haze beyond that, I could barely make out the craggy peaks of a forbidding mountain range. It did seem as though I could see beyond this world and into others, worlds I recognized even less than this one.

"Your rhyming. What happened to it?"

"Would you rather I be poetizing?" he asked irritably. "I'd think you'd be done with it. I know I be." He lay on his back and stared inscrutably into the sky. "You shouldn't have been saving me," he mumbled at last. "You should have been leaving me to be floating away."

"Why would I do that?"

"Because I be bad. Very bad. Very, very, very bad. I do *not* deserve to be saved." He closed his eyes.

"What do you mean?"

"I tried to… I was going to… Really, I had to…," he blubbered. "I couldn't. I still could… Could I? No, I can't. Can't can't can't can't. Now, what will be happening to me? No. No. No. No. *No!*" He rolled onto his stomach and pushed his face into the grass, which muffled his words. "It don't be mattering now. I will be killed for surely. You too, probably." He sighed loudly. "I just be lying here and waiting."

I dropped down next to him. "What are you talking about? Why would anyone want to kill you? Or me?"

Tom Dirqs fumbled through all his pockets, muttering incoherently. When he reached the final one, he pulled out a small, polished glass sphere, icy blue and veined with gray. He waved it in front of my face before hastily stuffing it back, this time into a different pocket. Before he did, I caught a glimpse in it of a grim, gray castle perched atop a craggily forbidding mountain, its angular towers piercing the dark, threatening sky. Kep'chas circled its topmost turret.

"Castle Do'am," I whispered. My heart quickened.

Ben? Are you there? If not, where are you?

Tom Dirqs pushed himself up to an awkward sitting position, his eyes wide with fear. "You know?" he gasped.

"Know what?"

"Nothing."

He lay back down on his side and ignored me.

"You know something," I insisted.

He balled himself up into as much of a fetal position as his figure would allow and shook his head violently.

"What's that glass stone and why did I see Castle Do'am in it?"

"That stone be no stone," he breathed. He glanced around furtively, then patted all his pockets until he again found the one with the stone. He pressed his hand firmly against the fabric.

"Let me see it."

He clenched the sphere through his pocket. "If I take it out, she—" He clamped his hand over his mouth and looked away.

"She? S'kryssna S'kyaga?"

Tom Dirqs stiffened.

"She what?"

"This be worse than I thought," he wailed. "Worse, worse, worse, worse, worse." He sat up and twisted his fingers into knots.

"She what?"

"She will be seeing us," he whispered hoarsely.

"I see," I said icily.

"You don't. You don't be understanding."

"I think I do." I slipped my sandals back on.

"Castle Do'am," he moaned.

"What about it?"

"That's where she be prisoning the Grandmother. She will be killing her if…if…if— I…if I don't…" He looked away.

"If you don't deliver me to her?"

Tom Dirqs snuffled loudly.

"Is that how you knew my name?"

He nodded.

"Is Castle Do'am also where S'kryssna S'kyaga has Reesa Kam'ana?"

His eyes crossed and his eyebrows popped up to the top of his forehead. "Reesa Kam'ana? There be no Reesa Kam'ana. She be one of the Grandmother's sleepy-time stories. Like Kumba or Pri'Malaka. Or the Fayr'Owyn."

"She's not a story. I've seen her. In a vision."

"The Fayr'Owyn?"

"Reesa Kam'ana. She's real, and she needs my help." I paused. "Our help."

Tom Dirqs stood and walked around me. "The Grandmother's story says only the Fayr'Owyn can be seeing visions of Reesa Kama'ana." He stopped and regarded me carefully. "It be a story. All of it." He studied me again, shook his head and plopped back down. "Naw."

I said nothing.

"If you've been seeing Reesa Kam'ana and if Reesa Kam'ana be needing your help," he said quietly, as though working out a complex cipher, "then—"

I said nothing.

He looked up at me sharply. "Naw," he said again.

"What do you know about the Fayr'Owyn?" I asked.

"She be a story," he replied stubbornly.

"And in the story?"

"I don't remember. Yes, I do. She be carrying the Heart of the Star? Yes, the Heart of the Star. To Reesa Kam'ana." He touched the center of his chest. "She be carrying it here. It glows for the Fayr'Owyn," he explained.

I touched the center of my chest not knowing whether anything would happen. Something did. A faint glow radiated out and lit up my hand.

"You! You *be* the Fayr'Owyn?" He stared at me disbelievingly. "Naw." He dropped to the ground in tears. "*You* be the Fayr'Owyn. Oh my stars. You can't be. Say you're not. Please be saying you're not."

"I can't do that."

Tom Dirqs blinked hard. "Oh my. This be truly worse than I thought. Much worse. What have I done? What *have* I done?" He tried to stand, tripped over his legs and toppled over. "I be a worthless sligg," he wept into the grass. "Worse than that. Can you ever forgive me, Fayr'Owyn?"

"That depends."

"Depends?" he asked cautiously. "On what?"

"On whether you take me to Castle Do'am." Whether Ben was there or not, I felt certain that Reesa Kam'ana was. She had to be my primary concern…or there would be no Ben. Or me.

Tom Dirqs shook his head vigorously.

I nodded mine, equally vigorously. "Wasn't that what you were going to do?"

"I— No. Yes. I don't know. Maybe." He shoved his hands in his pockets, touched the sphere and yelped. He yanked his hands free and it rolled out onto the grass. I scooped it up before he could. This time, I saw nothing.

Tom Dirqs grabbed for it. "You can't be. You mustn't be. She—" He pointed a quivering finger at the stone and whispered. "She be watching us."

"Through this?"

He nodded.

"Then I'll get rid of it." I raised my arm to hurl it into the river.

"No!" Tom Dirqs shrieked. "She'll be knowing."

"Knowing what?"

"That I've told you. That I be betraying her."

I looked through it one more time before stuffing it in my pocket. Again, I saw nothing. I tugged on his arm.

"Let's go."

"Go?"

"You're taking me to Castle Do'Am. Remember?"

He pulled his hand free and sat on it.

"No. I never. I can't. I mustn't. You're the Fayr'Owyn. She be killing

you. She be killing me. I wish I had never— But the Grandmother…"
He burst into tears.

"You were lying in wait for me, weren't you," I asked, "in that Karà… Karà…"

"Karà Haitu. I hate that place. It does awful horrible things to people. Like make them be talking in silly rhymes. They call it the 'sticking place.' That's why it be so hard to leave."

"You didn't answer my question."

Tom Dirqs looked at me dolefully. "If I'd a-known who you were… really—"

"You wouldn't have believed it. S'kryssna S'kyaga didn't tell you?"

"S'kryssna S'kyaga? I'd be fainted stony dead if I ever saw her. They say she has the most beautiful face in all of M'ranna. But her eyes. They be pale blue and hard as rocks. Cold as glass too. Her eye, actually. She be missing one. It—" Tom Dirqs's eyes bulged then squinted shut.

I retrieved the glass sphere from my pocket. "Like this?" I asked.

He trembled and opened his eyes.

"That's her *eye*?"

Tom Dirqs's head jerked up and down. An icy chill shivered through me.

"Can she hear us too? Has she heard everything we've said?"

"I— No. I mean yes. I mean— Oh, Fayr'Owyn, I don't know what to do."

"I've had enough," I said. "Into the river with it."

Tom Dirqs grabbed my hand. "No, Fayr'Owyn. Don't. Let me explain."

"Tell me everything this time or I swear I'll throw you in after it."

"Oh my," he sniveled. "Oh my, oh my, oh my."

"Well?"

"A thorag," he sobbed. "The Grandmother…" He searched half a dozen pockets before he found his handkerchief, a giant square of bright yellow linen randomly spotted with orange polka dots. He pressed it against his face and trumpeted into it.

"The eye. How does it work?"

"S'kryssna S'kyaga, she can't be hearing. Only seeing, and not always. If it be in your pocket or if it be like this," he closed my fist over it, "she can't really be seeing. She be knowing where you be. Sort of. She be knowing who be with you. Sort of. But she won't be seeing. It's not even that she be knowing where *you* are. She be knowing where her eye is."

"So if I left it here…" I glared at him. "Or put it back in your pocket and threw you both into the river, she couldn't follow me?"

Tom Dirqs shook his head glumly.

"What else?"

A thorag had found him, he recounted, huddled in the ruins of the Grandmother's house after she had been taken by a kep'cha. If he didn't take the eye and if he didn't agree to lure the Q'nta woman he would find in Karà Haitu to Castle Do'am, the Grandmother would be tortured to death.

"I've got to be keeping the eye," he insisted, "or she be knowing you've kenned to her plan."

"And that you've told me everything."

"She be finding out anyhow," he whimpered. "She has spies everywhere. I be a dead Dirqs."

"If you're so sure that you're going to die for what you have done, you might as well die doing something worthwhile," I said.

Tom Dirqs dropped his eyes.

"If you're lucky, maybe you won't die at all."

"Oh, I'll die at all, for surely. Question is, will it be quick and easy or slow and horrible-ific? I be choosing quick and easy. Just pitch me back into the river. Then be going back where you came from. Please."

I examined the eye one more time. In the briefest of flashes, I caught a glimpse of S'kryssna S'kyaga, a silver patch over her empty left eye socket, standing on her turret balcony. If Tom Dirqs hadn't lied to me, S'kryssna S'kyaga couldn't hear me. Still, I had to ask. I turned away from Tom Dirqs and whispered under my breath, "My son. What have you done with my son?" Before I could complete the question, her image faded.

"Castle Do'Am *is* the way back," I announced. "The only way back." I pulled Tom Dirqs to his feet. "For both of us."

twenty-three

For three days Tom Dirqs barely spoke to me, replying in little more than monosyllables whenever I tried to engage him in conversation. Mostly, he walked with his eyes focused either on the sky or back over his shoulder, watching for kep'chas above us or ageets behind us. Ageets, he had explained in a rare spurt of loquaciousness, were M'rannans terrorized by S'kryssna S'kyaga into spying for her. In some cases, she held family members hostage in the Castle Do'am dungeon. In others, she had a parent, child or spouse killed in their presence to demonstrate her power over them.

"That be making me an ageet," he said morosely, then fell silent. He refused to speak again for the rest of the day.

The river path ultimately carried us to a road as red as the one in Karà Haitu. Here, unlike in Karà Haitu, we moved forward, if sluggishly. Any time we approached a village, for example, Tom Dirqs insisted we detour around it. "Most are filled with ageets," he muttered. As well, with his eyes focused everywhere but in front of him, he bumped into rocks and trees constantly and fell over frequently. When I dared suggest that he pay closer attention to what lay ahead of him, he glared at me, so wrinkling his brow that his eyes almost disappeared into his forehead.

As the sun traveled from east to west those first days, we passed alongside several lakes and crossed two rivers in gently rolling countryside. Every now and again, when we crested one of the knolls, the jagged spikes of the Do'am Mountains would rise into view in the far distance, poking through the sinister storm clouds that always roiled around them. No castle, though. Not yet. It was on the far side of the range and across the Great Water, Tom Dirqs explained edgily. In those moments, it was hard to see how we could ever cross those mountains and penetrate the evil that veiled them. Then our road would drop us back into the valley and the menace would recede… until the next time.

On the evening of the third day, we settled into a copse of o'aka trees — tall, dense and bearing clusters of fist-sized red fruit. A meandering rill provided us with drinking and washing-up water and fallen leaves served as both mattresses and blankets. For the first time, we risked a small fire, which cast an eerie, shadow-speckled light on the ground and tree trunks. We sat in an uneasy silence, listening to distant hoots and howls and watching the sky darken through the weave of tree limbs.

"We have a long way to travel together," I said softly. "It would be better if we could get along somehow."

Tom Dirqs stared silently into the embered remains of our fire, grinding his teeth and poking listlessly at the ashes with a stick. "I don't want to be being here," he grumbled.

"I know you don't. Me neither. Not really." A flickering coal burst into flame. "But I don't see that I have a choice."

"No choice?" he snapped. "What about me? What about my choice?"

I almost lashed out at him and reminded him that he had lost his choice when he accepted S'kryssna S'kyaga's eye. Instead, I took a deep breath, searched through the treetops for stars and, once I found them, for familiar constellations. Then I remembered what Co'anra had said: without Reesa Kam'ana, there were none.

"Do you miss the constellations?" I asked.

He looked up. "I never seen 'em," he said. "The Grandmother storied about them lots. She also never seen 'em. She heard tell about them from her Grandma, and back down the line." He dropped his head. Tears spilled through his fingers and onto the ground. "I be missing the Grandmother."

I reached for one of his hands. He started to pull away, then grabbed mine. He looked like a little boy, fearing what he most desired, desiring what he most feared.

"Getting Astel Lev back to Reesa Kam'ana will be difficult enough," I thought. "Will we even be able to find Tom Dirqs's grandmother, let alone rescue her?" Before I could come to a resolution, I heard myself say out loud, "I don't know how, but if your grandmother is in Castle Do'am, we will find her. If we find her, we'll get her out."

Tom Dirqs pulled his hand free and walked to the edge of the clearing. "Why would you be doing that for me? I have been bad and mean and—"

"Frightened." I joined him. "It's easy to do bad things when you're frightened. But you know what?"

He gazed up at me quizzically.

"It's just as easy to do good things."

"I don't know…"

"Helping Reesa Kam'ana is a good thing. Right?"

He nodded.

"So is saving your grandmother."

"But-but it not be possible. Both not be."

"The only certain thing I know, Tom Dirqs, is that we will fail if we do nothing. If we try, there's at least a chance that we will succeed."

"Teeny tiny, tiny teeny little bits of a chance."

"Still, a chance."

Tom Dirqs squeezed his right eye shut. He circled the fire three times in one direction then three times in the other, this time with his left eye shut. "That's what the Grandmother be doing when she can't decide something," he said, both eyes now closed. "She goes around one way for one choosing then around the other way for the other. She says that by the time she be stopping, she knows what to do."

"Does it work?"

He shrugged. "I never be trying before."

*　*　*

The sound of o'aka fruit pelting to the ground woke me with a start. Tom Dirqs was shaking them out of the trees with a sturdy branch. He had already heaped three small piles and was starting on a fourth. Next to him were four hollowed-out gourds and a red-stained rock.

"If you be hungry," he called out without stopping, "pound more of them o'akas into that empty gourd."

I crawled over to the gourds. Inside one was a pasty mash of fruit. Two of the others were half filled with water.

I rubbed my eyes drowsily. "What are these for?"

"Soup." He hauled the last of the o'akas to where I sat. "O'aka soup, sweet and red. Just the thing for after bed."

I looked at him crossly. "You're not starting to rhyme again, are you?"

"O'aka soup, sweet and red. Just the thing for after bed." This time he sang it, in a full, gratingly off-key voice.

"It be a song the Grandmother sang." He found another rock and pulped more fruit into the empty gourd. "You'd be rathering I say it and not sing it." He laughed. He spooned some pulp into one of the water-filled gourds and stirred vigorously. The result was a lumpy potage.

"'Drink it up, all the way. Give you strength throughout the day.' That's what she sang, she did, for me and my cousins." He prepared another bowl for himself, took a sip and added a bit more water. "Not as smooth as the Grandmother's," he pronounced. "But near as tasty. Like?"

I did. It was tasty, and filling.

"I've been thinking," I said, as I helped myself to seconds.

"Me too." Tom Dirqs wiped the red from his mouth with a large o'aka leaf.

"You go first."

Tom Dirqs shook his head. "No, you."

"I'm not going to make you come with me." I pressed on when Tom Dirqs tried to interject. "I want you to come, not just because you know how to get there from here. But the Fayr'Owyn shouldn't be forcing. It's not right."

Tom Dirqs smirked at me.

"What?"

"There be more?"

"Well, yes. Even if you don't come, I will try to help your grand-mother. Just tell me what she looks like."

"No need," he giggled.

"What do you mean?"

"I be coming. That's what I be wanting to speak." He nodded firmly. "Whether we can help the Grandmother or not, I be coming."

He shrugged me off impatiently when I tried to hug him. Instead, he gathered the gourds, rinsed them in the rill and lobbed them deep into the woods. Then he filled as many of his pockets as he could with o'aka fruit, refilled my water skin and pulled me to my feet.

"It be better if no one knows we been here," he said. We scattered the leaves we had gathered for our bed and did our best to restore our campsite to its natural state. When we were done, he scrutinized the copse meticulously, adjusting a rock here and a twig there. Satisfied, he bobbed his head and smiled. "Be ye ready?"

*   *   *

We had left the road behind and journeyed cross-country, easy on open farmland. Now, though, we were even more vulnerable. "It be not kep'chas you have to fear mostly," Tom Dirqs explained as he again scanned the sky. "It be thorags."

If on its own, a kep'cha was nearly blind, its thorag pilot had vision so acute it could see for leagues ahead. A thorag would spot us and would target us with its kep'cha long before we could see it. By the time it flew into view, it would probably be too late for us. I remembered Co'anra and Co'anri; my stomach turned. The good news, he said, was that we were safe from S'kryssna S'kyaga's thorags and kep'chas as long we carried her eye and traveled as she expected us to. Unfortunately, rogue creatures were far worse than hers. Thorags hunted living flesh for sport and to feed their kep'chas. A thorag, he continued with a shudder, preferred fresh, bloody organs. Hearts, mostly.

The sun had already dipped below the horizon when Tom Dirqs pointed to a silhouetted farmhouse to the west. Through the day he had steered us around farm buildings, just as we had avoided villages previously. Here, though, the kep'chas had already been. A clean horizontal cut had sliced away the top half of the house, which had settled in mounds of dust and debris inside the bottom half. A copper-colored barn stood two hundred paces from the ruins. Although its main door was ajar, something had punched two giant holes in the side walls.

"Kep'cha," Tom Dirqs muttered as he stepped through the opening and into the barn. Whatever animals had lived in the stalls had long since fled, except for a lone gita'a that lay recently dismembered by the door. "Thorag," he added, holding his nose while throwing hay onto the corpse. Vampire flies buzzed angrily at their disturbed dinner, but the hay cut the smell.

"Maybe we should sleep outside," I said, doubtfully watching Tom Dirqs set up hay beds in the loft, as far from the dead animal as possible.

"We be safer here. Kep'chas have been. Less likely to be coming back." He climbed down from the loft and looked around for something he clearly thought should be there. When he found it, it was a small wooden cup. "I never know a farmer who don't drink a shot of py'aka liquor to be cutting the chill at milking time." He drank half the pungent concoction and passed it to me. It was strong and bitter and burned my throat. Once in my stomach, it suffused me with calming warmth.

Back in the loft, we covered ourselves with hay, more to dull the stench than for warmth or protection and promptly fell asleep.

It's dawn. Tom Dirqs still sleeps. I open my eyes to the sound of bleating, munching and tail-slapping. I crawl to the edge of the loft. Four three-legged gita'as twitch their heads as they chew loudly on fresh hay. Three of the gita'as stand chest high, with short, brown-splotched, coarse gray hair and a single dull-orange horn atop a flat-topped head. The fourth is smaller, only waist-high. Its hair is longer, softer and cream-colored, and its horn is polished ivory. They pay no attention to me as I climb down and exit the barn.

Like with the barn, the farmhouse is undamaged: a pale-green, two-story wooden structure with a dark green gabled roof and window frames and doors the same copper hue as the barn. The window closest to me is open, and breakfast smells so tantalizing waft out toward me that my stomach grumbles dolefully. As I draw nearer, a medley of mealtime chatter and clatter competes with the morning chirps of birds arrayed along the dwelling's eaves.

"No school today, Mariah." The voice is a man's.

"Again? I miss my friends."

I approach the window and peek in, unseen. Although I have never seen any of these people before, I'm startled to realize that I recognize them all. The schoolgirl, in her mid-teens, is Mariah. Full-figured with freckles and pigtailed hair the color of the barn, she pouts at a long rough-hewn table with her uncle, Micah M'renna, and five burly farmhands. The youngest and slightest of these, just a few seasons older than Mariah, is Leq. Keeping the table supplied with platters of hot food is housekeeper Magritta, her face stern but loving, her gray-streaked hair pulled back in a severe bun.

"You do what your uncle says, Mariah," Magritta scolds.

"I can walk Ka'Ona, Uncle. Right?"

Micah M'renna shakes his head. Of stocky and muscular build, his thinning hair is a duller version of Mariah's. His right forearm bears a cir-cled-star tattoo. "Not safe. Kep'chas took out Oreeka Village yesterday."

"I have to milk her."

"One of the boys can do it."

Leq grins eagerly at Mariah. I think maybe he has a crush on her. "I will, miss."

Mariah pays no attention to Leq. "But Uncle, I'm the only one who milks Ka'Ona."

"I want you here in the house with Magritta."

"But—"

"Listen to your uncle, Mariah," Magritta says, bustling in with a steaming pitcher of ma'ika.

Mariah ignores her.

"What about you?" she asks Micah M'renna. "If it's not safe for me, it's not safe for you."

Micah M'renna pats Mariah's hand. "You can miss school and Ka'Ona can miss her walk. We cannot miss our harvest or there'll be no food for any of us...or for Ka'Ona."

Micah M'renna stands up. The farmhands stand too, even though most are still eating. They hastily wipe their mouths and follow the farmer to the door. Micah M'renna turns back. "Promise me, Mariah. You will not leave the house."

Mariah's pout turns into a reluctant half-smile directed at Leq. "Never mind, Leq. Ka'Ona will never forgive me if I let someone else milk her. She can go one day without milking." She jumps up and hugs her uncle. "I can milk her tomorrow, though, right?"

Micah M'renna hugs her tightly. "We'll see, Mariah," he sighs. The men leave through the front door and head for the barn. They don't notice me. A few moments later, they lead the three adult gita'as out of the barn toward the fields.

Mariah helps Magritta clear the dirty dishes. With washing-up sounds clinking and clanking noisily from the kitchen, Mariah returns, peers out the window to make sure no farmhands have lingered behind and clambers out. She stops, looks right at me with a confused expression then shakes her head. I open my mouth to speak but say nothing. I realize that whatever she senses, she cannot see me. Although I'm not sure why that should be, I am relieved that there is no need for me to explain my snooping — the same kind of snooping Ben that did with his Co'an neighbors and that I swore I would never do. Mariah glances around to make certain no one sees her, runs to the barn. I follow, wondering if Tom Dirqs is also invisible to her.

When I slip in after her, Mariah is sitting on a stool, milking the smallest of the gita'as and singing softly. Ka'Ona's head droops placidly. She bleats softly to Mariah's melody, her eyes half-shut.

"Ble-e-e-e-e-e...ble-e-e-e-e-e..."

Ka'Ona's head jerks up. Her eyes gape open. "Ble-e-e-e-E-E-E!"

"What is it, Ka'Ona?" Mariah puts her arm around the gita'a's head and scratches under her chin.

"Ble-e-e-E-E-E-E! "BLE-E-E-E-E-E-E!"

Ka'Ona ducks out from Mariah's embrace, kicks over the milking pail and darts to the window.

Mariah does not hear it yet. I do. Kep'chas. In an instant, seven are overhead, all piloted by thorags. An instant later, they slice through the farmhouse, shrieking euphorically. A woman screams. Magritta. Then silence. The kep'chas are gone.

Mariah sobs, her hand over her mouth to stifle the sound. She races for the door but freezes as six of the kep'chas return, flying low over the ruined house. Micah M'renna is lashed to one, Leq and his fellow farmhands to each of the others.

The seventh kep'cha is right behind them. It swerves toward the barn. Mariah drags Ka'Ona toward a large haystack by the ladder to the loft. Bleating insistently, the gita'a breaks free. She butts Mariah into a smaller haystack in the far corner under the loft.

Before I can climb back up to warn Tom Dirqs or hide myself, the kep'cha blasts through the wall. Its needle nose stabs Ka'Ona in the throat. She staggers, falls to the ground, still alive, blood spurting from her throat and mouth. A thorag leaps from the kep'cha's back, slashes the gita'a's chest with claw-like hands, rips out her heart and devours it in a single gulp.

Blood still dripping from its mouth, the thorag emits a spine-chilling howl and remounts the kep'cha, which punches a hole in another wall as it takes off in full screech.

Shaken, and knowing I can do nothing for Mariah, still hiding in the haystack, I climb the ladder to check on Tom Dirqs. Before I reach the top, I black out.

A blinding flash. Needle-like splinters poke and prick at me. A distant voice calls a name...my name. A fetid smell assaults my nostrils. I—

"Be you okay?" Tom Dirqs shook me awake. "You be tossing and turning so much I feared you were going to roll down into that." He pointed to where vampire flies still buzzed angrily around the buried gita'a.

"I had the oddest dream. I— Wait." I scrambled down the ladder to where, in my dream, Ka'Ona had pushed Mariah. Tom Dirqs followed.

"Mariah?" I poked at the haystack gently. "Are you in there?"

At first I heard nothing but the wind whistling through the holes in the barn walls and the drone of vampire flies. Then, a quiet whimper.

"Mariah?"

I clawed through the hay. At the very back, huddled into the corner, Mariah wept softly. When she saw me, she gasped.

"You! But—" She tried to back away. There was nowhere to go.

I extended my hand. "I'm a friend. We both are. I'm Q'nta and this is Tom Dirqs. We want to help you."

"I-I saw you," she stammered. "I know I did. But you weren't there."

"Who be you, girl?" Tom Dirqs asked. He turned to me. "Who is she?"

Before I could answer, Mariah crawled out of the haystack. "Who am *I*?" She tossed her head and sunlight glinted off her hair. "Who are *you*, and what are you doing here when anyone with any sense would be as far away from this place as possible?"

She stepped past us, picking straws out of her clothes and hair, and scanned the barn knowingly, seeming to scrutinize each stalk of hay to determine what was out of place. Her eyes rested on the makeshift grave and her mouth tightened when she saw the vampire flies.

"Ka'Ona?"

"I beg your pardon?" I asked.

"Ka'Ona. The gita'a. Is she…?"

I nodded.

"Did you…?"

I nodded again. The girl sniffled and wiped her eyes with the back of her hand.

"Thank you, whoever you are." She dried her hand on her coarse-weave jumper, bowed her head and sighed. She looked up sharply. "You didn't eat of Ka'Ona, did you?"

Tom Dirqs shook his head fiercely.

"Well," she said, "if you buried Ka'Ona, you can't be ageets. But you," she said to me, studying me closely," how did I see you when you weren't there?" She touched my arm lightly, still not certain I was real. "How do you know my name?"

"Be you knowing about the Fayr'Owyn?" Tom Dirqs asked back.

Mariah eyed him suspiciously. "Why?"

"Be you knowing or not?"

Mariah considered how best to answer. She glanced at the holes in the wall and down at Ka'Ona's grave. "It's a— a story," she replied slowly. "Only a story. Why does it matter?"

"It be more than a story," Tom Dirqs declared, pushing me toward her. "This be she." Mariah's eyes opened wide. She stared at Tom Dirqs then at me. She inspected me from head to toe and back, then looked back at Tom Dirqs.

"Nah," she said, shaking her head.

"Yah," Tom Dirqs countered, nodding his.

"Meet Q'nta Ko'lar Fayr'Owyn of Q'ntana." He grabbed Mariah's hand and slid her palm over mine. "Truly. That's how she be knowing things."

"I'm sorry about your uncle, Mariah. About everything."

"Uncle?" Tom Dirqs interjected. "What uncle? What everything? What other things be you knowing?"

Once outside, away from vampire flies and the stink of rotting flesh, Mariah ran to the ruins of her house and collapsed in tears. I gently pulled her to her feet and led her and Tom Dirqs to a well at the far edge of the farthest field, where I told Mariah and Tom Dirqs my dream.

"That's what happened, exactly what happened," Mariah said in amazement when I was done. "You *were* there. I saw you, just for a minim. Then you were gone. How could you be there and not be there? How could you dream it?"

"She be the Fayr'Owyn. That's how," Tom Dirqs snapped.

"I don't know myself how I see what I see and know what I know. Part of it must be about being the Fayr'Owyn and carrying the Heart of the Star. The other part..." I stopped. What had just occurred was unbelievable enough. To add that I was an Elderbard from the future... That would be too much for Mariah. Maybe even for Tom Dirqs. "What will you do now?"

"It be not smart to stay here," Tom Dirqs said. "If kep'chas and thorags be kenning that they missed someone, they be back." He looked up at the sun. "For us too, if we not be leaving here soon." Thorags don't like to fail, he added, because S'kryssna S'kyaga didn't like them to fail.

"Are you really going to Castle Do'am?" Mariah asked. "That's where kep'chas take them, isn't it?"

Tom Dirqs nodded.

Mariah stood and brushed bits of straw from her jumper. "I have to go with you. To find Uncle Micah M'renna and Leq and the others."

I didn't answer. We couldn't leave her behind. On the other hand, once S'kryssna S'kyaga discovered that Mariah was traveling with us, she would know that Tom Dirqs had betrayed her.

"What should we do?" I asked Tom Dirqs.

He refused to offer an opinion, regardless of how hard I pressed. "You be the Fayr'Owyn," he said. "This be your StarQuest."

"I be— I am the Fayr'Owyn," I agreed. "But this is our StarQuest. What I don't know is: Is Mariah part of it?"

"You be the Fayr'Owyn," he repeated stubbornly. "Wait." His face lit up. "Ask the Heart of the Star."

"Astel Lev? I—"

Tom Dirqs ran around me excitedly. "It be inside you, right?" He poked my chest.

I nodded, not understanding what he was getting at.

"Ask it. If it be inside you, you can ask it."

"Like asking my heart?"

"Like asking *the* Heart."

I closed my eyes, placed my palms, one over the other, on my chest and visualized Toshar guiding me to hold the Heart of the Star in that same way. Ben had been there. That was the last time I had seen him. My eyes watered. Where was he? How was he? How could I have let him go?

"Focus." The voice was Ben's and my eyes shot open.

"Ben?"

Tom Dirqs regarded me uneasily. Mariah stared. The sun continued its march across the sky.

"We needs have an answer," Tom Dirqs prompted gently. "The day be fleeing and we cannot be spending another night here."

"I know. It's just—" I shook my head. "Never mind." Once again, I closed my eyes and returned to that moment with Eulisha, Toshar and Ben, to that moment when my only awareness was of the crystal I had been holding against my chest. I closed my mind too, to chattering doubts that would distract me if they could.

"You quest well, Fayr'Owyn," I heard from within me, in a voice that was almost Àna's, but not quite, almost mine, but not quite, "and your travel complement is complete."

"Complete with Mariah or without her?" I asked back.

"Complete *now*," the voice replied. My chest felt hot. My head felt light. I feared I would faint. The feeling passed.

I opened my eyes. Tom Dirqs and Mariah watched me curiously.

I took Tom Dirqs's hand and held out my other hand to Mariah. She smiled shyly and took it.

"Thank you," she murmured.

"S'kryssna S'kyaga will have to be knowing sooner or later," Tom Dirqs said. "Might as well be now."

I hadn't looked at S'kryssna S'kyaga's eye since stuffing it in my pocket back at the river. I pulled it out and stared into it. Once again, I saw Castle Do'am's grim bleakness. This time, though, the scene shifted. Now I was seeing into a dark, dank, high-ceilinged dungeon cell, weakly lit by a rusty-barred opening to the sky.

Reesa Kam'ana, drenched from the relentless rain drizzling in from her cell's barred skylight, stands chained to a wooden post, her face a blend of sadness, detachment, resignation and strength. She glances toward me, nods slightly.

The cell door clangs open. S'kryssna S'kyaga strides in, her eyepatch now blood-red to match her black-cloaked gown. She is flanked by two guardsmen bearing spiked clubs and scythe-like daggers with jagged, sawtooth blades, all smeared with dried blood. Heads shaved, they wear washed-out gray chain mail emblazoned with a coiled black snake. The same sinister mark is tattooed on their right wrist. A second tattoo, a crossed club and dagger, brands their left cheek just below the eye socket. Their eyes, identical to S'kryssna S'kyaga's, are soulless and empty. Neither S'kryssna S'kyaga nor her guardsmen are aware of my half-presence.

S'kryssna S'kyaga grimaces in distaste, wrinkles her nose at the odor and curtsies mockingly. "My lady of the stars. Are you comfortable?"

"I have what I need," Reesa Kama'ana replies evenly.

"Not what you desire."

"What I desire is not in your power to grant me."

"It will be."

Reesa Kam'ana gazes up to the sky. Drizzle turns to downpour. Rain streams down her face. S'kryssna S'kyaga steps back to avoid getting wet. Reesa Kam'ana closes her eyes. A dreamy look suffuses her face.

"How the stars must miss your voice…that sweet star chant. You must teach me your song…for when I possess the Heart of the Star."

"You will find your own song, I have no doubt," Reesa Kam'ana replies, her eyes still closed.

S'kryssna S'kyaga laughs. "Of course. You have no song anymore. A Star Chantress with no Star Chant. How tragic. No Star Chantress at all would be even better."

Reesa Kam'ana opens her eyes, lets the rain fill them. "If you could find a way to kill me, I have no doubt that you would." She tilts her head to face S'kryssna S'kyaga.

"You are right, Star Chantress. I cannot kill you. Not yet. Not until the Heart of the Star is mine. That day comes. When it does, you will regret not having helped me when you could."

Reesa Kam'ana raises her face back up toward the sky. "What will be will be." She again closes her eyes.

Furious, S'kryssna S'kyaga gestures to one of the guardsmen. He leaves. When he returns, he is snapping a cat-o'-nine tails.

"Is that so? How about what is, right now?"

The guardsman whips Reesa Kam'ana without mercy. S'kryssna S'kyaga watches, smirking. Her amusement turns to rage when Reesa Kam'ana barely flinches and makes no sound.

"What will be, will be just as I command it," she shrieks and storms out.

Downpour becomes deluge, washing out the scene.

I passed the eye to Tom Dirqs. "Do it," I said.

Tom Dirqs set the eye on the lip of the well, picked up a rock and raised it over his head. He looked at me. I nodded.

The rock smashed down. The eye bounced to the ground, intact.

The rock smashed down again, harder. Again, the eye survived undamaged.

A third time, with more force. This time the eye shattered. Shards exploded skyward. A shrill scream stabbed the air. We covered our ears and fled the scene. The scream continued to echo toward us as we ran, as fast and far as we could.

Now that S'kryssna S'kyaga knew that Tom Dirqs had betrayed her, we sought a path she would not expect or anticipate.

If there was such thing.

twenty-four

If there was such a thing, we didn't find it soon enough. Kep'chas suddenly blackened the far distant sky, a blackness that spread and neared with each breath. There was no time to wonder how they had targeted us so swiftly, no time to wonder how to hide ourselves. In the midst of flat, open fields concealment wasn't an option.

"Kep'chas be hating water," Tom Dirqs offered in a tiny voice, his entire body quaking with terror.

"There isn't any anywhere near here," Mariah responded. She stared anxiously at the approaching fleet.

"Not even a pond or watering hole?" I asked.

Mariah shook her head, her eyes still fixed on the kep'chas. They were near enough now that we could hear their wings flap and whir, could see their grim-faced pilots.

Tom Dirqs blinked hard. "Run," he blurted out.

I grabbed his sleeve before he could take off. "Wait," I said.

"For what?" He tried to shake me off.

I heard something...a wordless inner voice, the same voice that had spoken to me by the barn. I pulled Tom Dirqs and Mariah to the ground and spread myself over them as best I could. Shutting eyes and ears to the danger, I focused on the voice.

"Astel Lev?" I whispered.

The answer came as a vision, as a lifetime of joys rushed into focus, blurred and receded: lessons with Garan...picnics with Uncle Yhoshi, Tante Fynda and their twins...the day I met Akila...our wedding in the garland-strewn Castle Rose courtyard and my Elderbard-naming in that same pink-stone cloister...Ben's birth and finding him again, and myself, in the strangeness that was M'ranna...

The cacophony of shrieks and yowls was now too loud for my memories to compete. I opened my eyes. Scores upon scores of kep'chas massed overhead, wailing shrilly. One pulled free from the ranks and dove screamingly toward us. An invisible force rebuffed it. The kep'cha somersaulted, righted itself and aimed for us again. Repelled again, it turned tail toward Castle Do'am. Another kep'cha tried, then another and another, until the last, its thorag keening into the wind, flew off, screeching. Through it all, Mariah wept softly and Tom Dirqs ground his teeth.

Mariah was still crying when I helped her up.

"What happened?" she asked.

"I don't know," I replied. I didn't. I had just done what I felt the Heart of the Star was telling me to do.

Tom Dirqs stared at me gape-mouthed. "It be true!"

Mariah wiped dirt-encrusted tears from her cheeks. She looked uncomprehendingly from Tom Dirqs to me. "What is?"

Tom Dirqs watched the final black specks shrink and disappear. "Maybe they not be knowing."

"Who? What?" I asked.

"The thorags. S'kryssna S'kyaga."

"What are you talking about?"

"The Grandmother," he replied in a faraway voice.

"You're not making any sense," Mariah snapped.

"It be only a story…" he replied, still staring into the sky. "I keep thinking the Grandmother's stories be only stories…"

"Like the story of the Fayr'Owyn?" I asked. "What story are you talking about now?"

Tom Dirqs shuffled his feet. "I should have been saying before. I should have been telling you what I be thinking I be knowing."

It took all my self-control not to grab Tom Dirqs by the shoulders and shake the story out of him. Mariah felt no such restraint. I pulled her off him.

"Okay," he mumbled. "But don't be going angry at me."

"Just tell us," Mariah and I shouted in unison.

"It be said that she who carries the Heart of the Star cannot be directly harmed by S'kryssna S'kyaga or by anyone or anything acting on her orders. It be said too that those in the sphere of the Fayr'Owyn also have some kind of protection." He paused. "Them's the Grandmother's words, from her stories. They not be just stories?"

"What kind of protection?" I asked.

"I don't be knowing that. The Grandmother never said." He

dropped to his knees. "Forgive me, Fayr'Owyn, for not saying nothing." Tears trickled down his cheeks. "Help me to be finding the Grandmother so I can be begging her to forgive me for not believing her stories." He pulled Mariah down next to him. "We will be serving you, Fayr'Owyn. Whatever it takes to release Reesa Kam'ana, we will be serving you on your StarQuest." He elbowed Mariah. "Right, Mariah?"

She nodded dumbly. "Will you protect us, Great Fayr'Owyn?" she asked meekly.

"Get up. Both of you." I pulled them to their feet. "Fayr'Owyn or not, my name is Q'nta. I've told you before: This is our StarQuest, not my StarQuest. So, no more kneeling or acting like I'm queen of something. I'm not."

Tom Dirqs shook his head firmly. "But Fayr'Owyn—"

"If you won't call me Q'nta for me, call me Q'nta because it's safer if all of M'ranna doesn't know about the Fayr'Owyn. At least, not yet. Tom Dirqs?"

His shaking head revolved into a reluctant nod.

"This is even more important: Can you remember any more of your grandmother's stories that you think you don't believe?"

"I don't know. I'll try to be remembering others, Fayr— Q'nta. I will now. I promise."

"Please. Our lives could depend on it."

*　*　*

It was dusk when we reached the base of a broad escarpment. Exhausted, we stumbled up to its cliff-top summit. The sun was low in the west, bathing the wasteland below us in a deceptively golden glow. But wasteland it was — a vast desert flatland that extended to the horizon, interrupted by only a handful of desiccated oases.

"This is as far as I have ever explored," Mariah said. "I've never dared go down there, into the desert."

"Do we have to go that way?" I asked Tom Dirqs.

"The Deserts of Afflayon be only way I know to the Do'am lands," he replied.

The Deserts of Afflayon? Even the name sounded like an affliction. How would we get to the other side of it? Maybe I could offer protection from kep'chas — as long as Tom Dirqs and Mariah lay underneath me. Yet even a Fayr'Owyn couldn't conjure up food, water and shelter

167

in a scorching desert. My stomach grumbled loudly, as it unhappily recalled that it had experienced no food since morning.

"I know a place, I think," Mariah said. "For shelter and water. Food, sort of, too."

"Let's do it," I said, glad for any excuse not to have to think about the next day's desert crossing.

We zigzagged down a rugged path toward the desert floor, stopping halfway, at a rocky shelf that ended abruptly at a sheer vertical cliff. A giant black boulder filled much of the ledge. It looked as though some giant had dropped it there to conceal a broad entrance into a dim, dank cave. A sloping passageway, slimy with seepage and treacherously slippery led to a luminous pool, lit from somewhere in its seemingly bottomless depths and bordered by mossy slabs and hunks of rock. From there, all we could see of the cave opening was a distant sliver of sky.

"How would you even know about this place?" I asked after we had drunk thirstily from the spring and sated our hunger on the surprisingly tasty moss that Tom Dirqs scraped away with his knife.

"I'm not sure," Mariah replied slowly. "Not from recent times. I know that. But when we were up top looking at the desert, I had a sudden memory of it. From a dream, maybe? Maybe from when I was a little girl? I don't know. I just knew it was here." She splashed water on her face. "This water too. And the moss." She shook her head. "I'm just sorry it's so wet here. It's not going to be very comfortable…"

"Wet means that no kep'chas will bother us. Right, Tom Dirqs?"

He nodded.

I stretched out on a mossy ledge. "Anyhow, it doesn't matter how wet we get tonight. The desert sun will dry us off tomorrow." However true that was, I wasn't at all looking forward to the next day's desert trek. Still, as Tom Dirqs had pointed out, we knew of no other route. "We'd best get some sleep."

I dozed, drifting between a vague awareness of whispered conversation and hazy dreams. Several times, I woke with a start, convinced I was still at the Co'ans' and wondering why I was so wet. Then I would tumble back into that shadow world between waking and sleep, a world where all I seemed to do was walk through a fog that never cleared, toward a destination that never made itself known. When dawn leached into the cave, my joints ached from the damp and my back spasmed from my restless turning on a rocky bed whose mossy surface had offered only minimal padding. I was spent, but more sleep seemed unlikely. I eased myself up from my slab and knelt by the spring, praying that enough icy water splashed on my face would revive me for the day ahead.

I was wrong.

For a while, I watched Tom Dirqs's eyelids flutter and twitch in dream as he snored gurglingly on the other side of the pool. Mariah, curled up next to him, made no sound at all. Her chest barely rose and fell, and she looked so peaceful that I wished I could let her sleep through to the end of this StarQuest. I would have to wake them soon, though. Once I did, we would have to face that endless desert and its relentless sun, on a journey that felt doomed. Even if we could elude the kep'chas and S'kryssna S'kyaga's magic to make it across that empty expanse without dying of hunger or thirst, even if we could make it all the way to the Do'am lands and through them to Castle Do'am, what then? And even if, through yet more miracles, we managed to bring The StarQuest to the Completion the Q'ophar had spoken of, then what? Now that I remembered where I had come from, would I ever see it again? Would I ever see Ben again?

I sighed wearily, threw more water at my face and stared into the pool. A distant hum insinuated itself between the water's gentle rustle and Tom Dirqs's soft snorts. I forced myself to my feet and followed the sound back up to the cavern opening, my sandals struggling to gain traction on the greasy stone. The noise grew louder. I recognized it, and my heart jammed up into my throat.

When I peeked out around the black rock, my fears were confirmed. Blocking all view of sky above and desert below was a nearly solid phalanx of kep'chas, their wings throbbing angrily, their thorag pilots waiting stonily, not yet aware of my presence.

"You be looking awful," Tom Dirqs said when I returned to the spring.

"You would too, if you had just seen what I did."

I led them back up and showed them. "We're trapped," I whispered urgently.

Mariah blanched and gasped loudly. A thorag noticed. A piercing screech sliced the still air.

Tom Dirqs thought for a moment. "No," he said. "We be trapped. They can't be hurting the Fayr'Owyn." He pushed me back toward the entrance. "It be best that you be leaving without us, that you be going on your own."

I shook my head. "We don't know if they're S'kryssna S'kyaga's kep'chas. If they're not, the Heart of the Star won't protect me. Even if they are— It doesn't matter. I can't leave you two here."

Mariah swallowed hard. "Tom Dirqs is right," she said shakily. "The StarQuest is more important than me or Tom Dirqs. You've got to go. You've got to try."

Other thorags joined the first in a chorus of bloodcurdling screams.

"I'll tell you again: This is our StarQuest. Your grandmother is counting on you, Tom Dirqs. Mariah, Micah M'renna needs you. There's got to be a way."

I peered through the dark into the tunnel that continued beyond the spring. Could that be a way out? A rhyme from my father's MoonQuest popped into my head.

The Maze of Horusha, where evil dwells

There's but one way out, where the death bell knells.

I shuddered. "This isn't Horusha," I said to myself.

Besides, they did get out. It looked hopeless. In the end, it wasn't. That's where Toshar, Uncle Yhoshi and Tante Fynda found Garan, my Garan. What did he always tell me about Horusha? He told me The MoonQuest so many times in so many ways. He always said the same thing about Horusha. What was it?

"*The darkest path is the one with the most light. And the most hopeless path is the most hopeful. Trust that when the way seems blocked.*"

"The Maze of Horusha…"

"What?" Tom Dirqs asked.

"A story," I replied. "An ancient one…that hasn't happened yet."

An explosion of smashing rock aborted our exchange, blasting deafeningly toward us. It was a kep'cha, its wings effortlessly slicing through the cavern walls, the insistent caterwauls of its thorag prodding it forward.

Mariah screamed. It was all I could do to not join her.

Think, Q'nta. We can run into the tunnel or stay and fight. If we run, the kep'cha will just cut through the rock and follow us. If we stay… No, don't think. Thinking won't save us. This is beyond figuring out. Astel Lev? What do I do, Astel Lev?

I scooped up a loose rock and hurled it at the kep'cha. Then another and another. Mariah and Tom Dirqs stared at me as though I was crazy…then lobbed their own. Either our aim was good or the kep'cha was just too big to miss. Regardless, we hit it more often than not. It yowled angrily, but its thorag forced it on and it obeyed…until Tom Dirqs's pitch slammed into its gelatinous green eye. The kep'cha bellowed in pain and flapped its wings blindly, shearing more rock from the cave walls. Thrashing in pain, it threw the thorag from its back, reeled helplessly and fled. Undeterred, the thorag scuttled toward us. We heaved more rocks. Not agile enough to dodge them, the thorag collapsed, bloodied, fewer than twenty paces from us.

Before we could think, a score of drooling, squalling thorags careered in after it…too many to be repelled by our increasingly desperate volley of rocks. It didn't matter. It wasn't us they were after.

As one, they pounced on their injured brother, ripped him open, then devoured him, alive.

Horror struck, we couldn't move.

Only when they were done, did they remember us. Blood dripping from their mouths, they snarled toward us.

"Thorags. Are they afraid of water too?" I asked through clenched teeth.

Tom Dirqs shrugged helplessly.

I splashed water at them. They bared their teeth, growled… hesitated.

Nothing to lose.

"Hold your breath!" I shoved Tom Dirqs and Mariah into the pool and dove in after them.

The water swirled around us, sucking us deeper and deeper, muting the thorags' angry wailing, until the sound melted into the whooshing rush of the eddying current.

*　　*　　*

"Oomph. Watch where you be going." Tom Dirqs sputtered as I smashed into him, Mariah collided with me and we all toppled into a sopping, confused heap.

We were soaked, yet on dry ground. We had tumbled onto the earthy, broad top step of a spiral staircase. Rather, we had tumbled onto each other. A warm, caressing breeze wafted up toward us, radiating a faint powdery glow, as though all the dust particles that hung in the stairwell were tiny, dim lights. Within a few breaths we were dry. Above us, a rippling, skylight-type opening revealed the top side of the pool and the menacing leer of a thorag. It leaned in, saw us and screeched. It leaned in farther. Too far.

The water frothed, bubbled and steamed when the thorag fell in. Moments later, bones stripped of all skin and tissue rained down around us.

Mariah screamed. Tom Dirqs screamed. I screamed.

The last to fall was a grinning skull. It shattered when it smashed into the ground.

twenty-five

The staircase spiraled down, down and deeper down, illuminated by the specks of light, which brightened and multiplied the deeper we descended. When, finally, the steps ended, we stood on the Star Rock I remembered from the Ko'Ba. It now filled a vast hall lit by eight enormous chandeliers suspended from a far-distant ceiling. No flames topped the chandeliers' gilded tapers. Instead, stars sparked brightly from wicks that never burned down. Brilliantly colored tapestries of abstract star-design screened three of the cavern's walls. The fourth was no wall at all. It was a giant opening into a velvet night.

As if blown there on a gust of wind, hundreds upon thousands of light specks converged dancingly on the raised platform at the center of the star-shaped slab. Together, in a strange but pleasing harmony, the light specks sang the Star Chant.

Alla ka tchù, tia à

Alla ka tchù, tia à

Still singing, the light specks swirled into a vortex of sparkling silver that formed Àna. Mariah gulped. Her left fist flew to her mouth. She stole a quick glance at me and when she saw me smile reassuringly, stared at Àna. Trancelike, she stepped past me, her right arm outstretched.

"Are you…are you…?" Mariah touched Àna's hand then pulled back in fright. "Are you real?" she whispered.

Àna laughed, a tinkling of glass bells so childlike that I laughed too. "You know me, Mariah M'renna. Good." She nodded, satisfied.

"But— But—"

"From your dreams, I know." She motioned for me and Tom Dirqs to join her and Mariah at the center of the Star Rock. "Dream and waking are one, child. There is no difference. They merely inhabit different forms of the same reality." She extended her hand toward

Mariah. "You may take my hand, Mariah M'renna, if it will comfort you."

Sobbing, Mariah fell into Àna's arms. "What I dreamed was true?"

Àna stroked Mariah's hair. The girl's weeping subsided into hiccups, then silence. "Know that just as all is possible in dream, so all is possible in waking. You must believe that, all of you, or your StarQuest will not achieve Completion."

With Mariah folded into one arm, she opened the other to me and Tom Dirqs, who regarded Àna curiously.

"Àna," I said.

"Fayr'Owyn."

"You knew."

"Of course. As did you."

"And about Ben?"

"That too."

I knew it wasn't the question to ask at that moment. I couldn't help myself. "Have you seen him?" I asked hopefully.

"Come," she said.

Tom Dirqs and I stepped closer.

"A mother's desires for her child must not get in the way of his life…or hers."

"What does that mean?"

"That I have seen him. That there is nothing more I can say."

I gazed into the dark night beyond the fourth wall.

"Will I see him again?"

"What will be seen will be seen. That too is all I can say."

Throughout our exchange, Tom Dirqs scrutinized Àna from every possible attitude and angle. Before I could argue with Àna, he interrupted.

"I know you too, don't I? Be it from dreams? Like Mariah?" He circled her, his head tilted so far that his ear nearly rested on his shoulder. "No. It not be dreams," he said, scratching his nose. "I've seen you, though. I have. Haven't I?"

"Once upon a time," Àna replied. "A very long time ago."

A wide grin broke out on Tom Dirqs's face and he jumped up and down excitedly. "With the Grandmother," he shouted. "Right? Right? With the Grandmother?"

"With the Grandmother." Àna smiled. "You stood no higher than my knees. Even so, you knew me by name. Just as Q'nta did when she first saw me and remembered nothing about herself." She released Mariah, who wiped the last of her tears on her sleeve. "Just as Mariah did in her dream."

"Knowing this day would come," she said, "I appeared to many people, young and old, seeking the StarQuesters of future time for some, past time for others." She winked at me. "This is that time. This is Star Time." She swiveled slowly, spinning with increasing speed. "Only you three knew me. Thus, you are the Star Ones."

"Excuse me," Tom Dirqs argued. "Q'nta be the Star One. We just be traveling with her to find our families."

"No, Tom Dirqs." She spun so quickly now that all we saw of her was a silver blur as she sang.

Star Ones' hearts can conquer time
Can love the lights back into line
Star Ones journey for the quest
Their hearts will show them all the rest
Star Ones know the pattern broke
Will only mend when words are spoke
Words of heart from one star true
Through the mouths of you and you
And you

As she sang each "you," a bolt of lightening struck the floor, creating a counterclockwise swirl of fire around Àna.

Fire lights the journey's quest
Then lights the way for all the rest
Hold it up, then pour it out
Let it burn up all your doubt
Let Kumba's flame consume the fear
Let Kumba's be the voice you hear
Guiding you on starry way
With courage bright throughout your day
Until the moment when you part
The journey's end: A brand-new start.

"Who are you?" I cried.

"I am the Star Chant," Àna replied from within the silvery blur.

Alla ka tchù, tia à
Alla ka tchù, tia à

As she repeated the Star Chant, stars danced off their tapers into the night beyond the fourth wall. Àna rose above the fiery swirl, which formed into a luminous dragon beneath her, six claws on its left feet, four on its right.

"Kumba," I whispered loudly.

The dragon ballooned rapidly in size until it seemed it would more than fill the cavern. We darted toward the open fourth wall, afraid we would be consumed by it. We were. Kumba had expanded more quickly than we could run.

Heat more scorching than anything I had ever experienced seared through me. I couldn't breathe. I couldn't see. I shrieked with pain but couldn't hear my screams. I groped for Mariah and Tom Dirqs but touched no one. Nothing.

It felt like lifetimes. Yet an instant later, it was over. The pain. The fire. The light. The tapestries, too, were gone, as were the chandeliers. All that remained was a large starlit cavern open to the night. And a single chalice, black as the sky, its base fused to the stone-slab floor.

The Nayr.

*　　*　　*

It was a long time before any of us spoke. We sat in stillness, staring at The Nayr, aware that what we had just experienced had altered us in ways we couldn't articulate. Only when stars faded into morning's light and the sun's early rays reflected back at us from the chalice did we look up at each other. Mariah's skin glowed, as though she had scrubbed and scrubbed and scrubbed it, and her eyes sparked with life and laughter. For once, her smile was sure, not shy. Tom Dirqs, too, seemed more alive, more confident. He wore clean new clothes, as did we all.

Backpacks bulging with food, knives, spare clothing, flints and other necessities, and oddities, sat next to us on the Star Rock. Among the oddities in my pack was a large spool of crystalline thread. Mariah's included a silver needle. Tom Dirqs's had a small glass hammer. Hanging from each backpack was a water skin filled with icy, lemon-scented water. Tom Dirqs took a long pull on his and sighed contentedly.

"You be different," he said to me.

Mariah nodded. "There's a light around your face like...like... Candlelight?"

"Starlight," Tom Dirqs corrected her without hesitation.

"Starlight," I repeated softly. One final star winked out as the sun's rays shot into the sky. "Maybe it's that I'm not afraid anymore," I said.

"It feels like I've been so afraid for so long…that I would never see my son again…that I would never find my way home…that we'd fail. Now… All that… It's gone."

Hold it up, then pour it out.

Let it burn up all your doubt.

"Me too," Tom Dirqs said. "I been afraid I wouldn't be seeing the Grandmother again. I been afraid S'kryssna S'kyaga would send her guarding-men to break my arms and legs and cut out my tongue, like she did…" He swallowed hard. "Like she did to the Father."

"Your father?" I asked.

Tom Dirqs nodded. "I been there. Hiding in the closet with the Grandmother. I seen it." He snuffled.

"Oh, Tom Dirqs." He waved me off. "Thank-ee. I be good now. I got you, and we're going to be saving the Grandmother." He smiled sadly. "I was afraid we'd be failing too. No more. Now, we be good. Whatever happens, we be good."

Let Kumba's flame consume the fear

Let Kumba's be the voice you hear

Mariah stared into the chalice. "This is Kumba's cup?" she asked.

"You know about Kumba?" It was said that The Nayr had been forged at the beginning of time by Prithi, who gave it to the dragon Kumba at Q'ntana's birth. The Nayr had sat in my Elderbard's study, in my father's before that. Its place was always on the black-marble Table of Prophecy that served as our writing desk. I saw The Nayr now, in my mind's eye, next to Toshar on the morning I found him dead. His face, finally at peace, rested on a cushion of ink-filled pages, his fingers and beard spotted with the remnants of his MoonQuest. Like now, The Nayr's shiny black surface reflected back the early rays of the sun. Of the suns.

The *suns*? How could I have forgotten? Two suns: Aygra, the father, and B'na, the son. *Two* suns. How was it possible that only one sun shone in M'ranna's sky when two would shine in Q'ntana's? Mariah was speaking. Something about a dream. I couldn't hear her. All I heard were the words "two suns" over and over in my head. I knew it was important. I knew there was a key within it that would unlock so much. What *was* it?

"…and that was the second dream," Mariah said, "the one with this chalice in it. Kumba too."

I refocused on Mariah. "Did the chalice have a name in your

dream?" It seemed silly, but I wanted Mariah to know The Nayr's name without me telling her, as though that tiny piece of information would somehow bond us even more deeply than, clearly, we already were.

"I think so. Only it was a long time ago." She frowned. "You know how dreams can be. Some things you remember, some you don't." She shook her head. "This is a don't. I'm sure I knew it in the dream. It's gone now."

"What about you?" I asked Tom Dirqs.

"The Grandmother told me about the Kumba, for surely." He ran his index and middle fingers absentmindedly around the rim of the chalice. "Nothing about no cup."

As his fingers pressed down more firmly, the chalice sang, a haunting melody that was at once infinitely joyous and impossibly sad. Startled, he pulled his hand away. The singing stopped. He gaped incredulously at his finger.

"Do it again," I said.

Tom Dirqs rested his finger on the cup's parchment-thin edge but refused to move it to make more music.

"It did that in the dream," Mariah said. "It sang just the same." She hummed the melody.

"What about the name," I asked. "Do you remember it now?"

Still humming, she closed her eyes.

"The Nayr," she said softly, then repeated with certainty, "The Nayr. In the dream someone was making the chalice sing. Like this." She propelled Tom Dirqs's fingers around the rim and again hummed along with the music. Her face took on an otherworldly cast as the chanting continued, her hand still guiding Tom Dirqs's.

"No!" Mariah's eyes shot open. "How?" She stared at Tom Dirqs, dumbfounded. "That someone," she gasped. "In my dream. It was you."

* * *

We took turns making the chalice sing, though none played it as expertly and sweetly as Tom Dirqs could. We sang too, learning to match our tone and cadence to The Nayr's and to each other's, feeling for the first time the same unity in our StarQuest as we were discovering in our voices. As we sang, it seemed that it was our voices that pushed the sun up into the sky, unveiling this new world through which we would journey. Farm fields and desert were gone. In their place was a thick evergreen forest: tall pinna trees with trunk-hugging, needle-like leaves that broadened into a flat canopy at their apex. A narrow, sun-dappled path wound through the trees and disappeared into dark woodland.

The more the world beyond our cave brightened, the more the cave darkened. Soon, only a flickering circle of light from the stone around The Nayr offered any illumination. It continued to burn as The Nayr jiggled free of its base and I placed it in my pack. And it continued to glimmer as we stepped onto the path and into the forest. The light winked through the weave of trees for a short while. Then the forest enveloped us, and it was gone.

*   *   *

By nightfall, we knew only that we headed vaguely west. The forest hadn't thinned, the path hadn't altered and our way forward was as uncertain as ever. However, Kumba's fire must, indeed, have consumed our doubts and fears, for not a single word of hesitation passed our lips through the day. Our only chatter was idle, focused on the unusual creatures that watched us watching them, then skittered away noisily when we approached. None of us had ever seen a seven-legged animal before, let alone one that was yellow with purple stripes and spiky fur. Nor had we come across hoppers, as we called them: tall, red-plumed, long-necked birds with no wings that bounced across our path on a single coiled leg, clucking disapprovingly. Then, there were the insects: Larger than a fist and as colorful as a rainbow, they hummed extraordinary harmonies with each other, buzzing around our heads curiously when we tried to join in. Only when the sun set and we were gathered in a rare clearing around a fire expertly built by Tom Dirqs, were we alone, the only sound the crackle of flame on wood.

"I don't care if S'kryssna S'kyaga be sending all her kep'chas after us," Tom Dirqs asserted, "I be ready for them." He bit a hunk from a cheese wheel and chewed it carelessly.

"As long as they don't cut down this lovely forest," Mariah said. She nibbled on a slice of bread. "The kep'chas, I mean. I've never seen anything as beautiful as this." The graceful pinna trees had been joined by clumps of squat shrubs with bright red limbs and multicolored leaves.

I had eaten all I'd wanted — a few slices of meat and some fruit. Now, I stared thoughtfully into the fire, pinpricks of uncertainty poking through my earlier confidence. We had no idea where we were or whether we were still even in M'ranna. Tom Dirqs could no longer guide us. How would we find Castle Do'am? Would S'kryssna S'kyaga's kep'chas find us first?

Tom Dirqs spit some rind into the fire. It sizzled. "If Àna and The Nayr be sending us this way," he declared, "it must be right."

"The Heart of the Star will show us the way," Mariah added. "It must want to go home, back to Reesa Kam'ana."

"I'm sure you're right. Both of you. Thank you. It's just that—" I shook my head. "I'm just tired. It will all be clearer in the morning. I'm sure it will." I lay down where I sat and closed my eyes. When I awoke, it was still dark. The night air was cold and I edged closer to the fire's ember-remains. Tom Dirqs and Mariah were curled together for warmth, breathing in soft unison. The forest was so still that I jumped when a lone *caw* screeched across the sky.

"Is that Bo'Rá K'n?" I wondered silently, recalling how he had appeared as a crow to my father in The MoonQuest. "Is he looking for us? Does he know we're here?" I threw some earth over the glowing coals, even as I knew that if Bo'Rá K'n sensed our presence, my fear not our fire would give us away. I swallowed hard and fixed my attention inward, on the Heart of the Star. It was hard not to let my terror of Bo'Rá K'n overtake the truth of Astel Lev. Yet I knew I couldn't. If Toshar had walked through his fear to the other side of it, somehow I had to notice my fear before Bo'Rá K'n did and get past it before he could act on it. Somehow. But how?

"The 'how' is not for you." The voice hissed and sizzled from deep within the fire ring, from the final ember, the only one that had escaped my panicked attempt to hide the fire from the crow. "Come closer," it said.

The coals were still comfortably warm as I leaned in and stared into the orange glow. It flicked, fluttered and sputtered. Was I imagining it, or did I see the flap of flaming wings and the nod of a fiery-plumed head?

"Tashek?"

The ember sparked and flared.

"You're on the right track," it crackled. Then it sputtered, fizzled and was no more. In its place was a shiny shard of crystal, cool as the night air. I held it in my fist as I lay back into dreamless asleep. When I woke, the crystal was gone.

twenty-six

"On the right track?" Tom Dirqs retorted later that morning when I shared my Tashek story. "There be no track."

He was right. Our path had long ago petered out, replaced by a forest-floor covering of ferns and ivies. A thick weave of tree limbs created a mesh-like canopy overhead.

"We be lost," Tom Dirqs moaned. "What's to be done?"

Mariah tapped on a tree trunk. "This tree looks familiar."

"They all be looking the same. A tree be a tree be a tree. Castle Do'Am could be anywhere." He stabbed his index finger in random directions, kicked at one tree then another, then dropped dejectedly to the ground.

Mariah tapped the tree again, gazed thoughtfully up into its cross-hatch of leaves and branches, then shinnied toward the top.

"What do you see?" I called up when she had disappeared from view.

"Forest. Forest. Forest. More forest. No mountains. No castle. Just trees."

She was halfway down when I heard it. Smelled it too. Felt its salt-tang on my tongue. Ocean. *Ocean*? No one else heard or tasted anything. No one else smelled anything other than decaying leaves under our feet. Was I losing my mind? Or could it be a message from Astel Lev? It had to be Astel Lev. I had to trust that it was.

"Go back up."

"Okay," Mariah said, "but there's nothing to see."

"When you get up there, look past the forest."

"Past the forest? What do you mean?"

"Don't look with your eyes. Look with your heart."

"I'll try, but I'm not sure what to do."

"Trust, and you'll know."

Mariah disappeared into the upper foliage. Tom Dirqs and I waited below in anticipatory silence. The sound, smell and taste of the sea were stronger now.

"Mariah?"

A moment later, she rejoined us. "You were right," she exclaimed. "At first I didn't know what to do. Then I closed my eyes and looked into my heart. When I opened them again, it was there."

"What was? What?" Tom Dirqs poked her arm. "The sea?"

"No, not at first. At first all I saw was a heavy mist where the trees had been. That way." She pointed south. "So I closed my eyes again. This time I touched my hand to my heart. Like you do," she said to me, "with Astel Lev. When I opened them this time, it was there."

"The sea?" Tom Dirqs. He jumped as high as he could, as though that would let him see what Mariah had.

"Yes," she said, "The sea. Past the forest to the south is a cliff. It juts out over the ocean. I heard it, like you did. I smelled it too. It's there. It's really there."

We hacked our way through increasingly dense and silent woods. The forest creatures that had reappeared at dawn had vanished, as had the twittering chatter of the morning's birds. Only the occasional distant *caw* broke through the still, a little louder each time. The others found nothing menacing about the crow's call. The others didn't know what I knew of Bo'Rà K'n, and I chose not to alarm them by sharing it.

Two days and two nights later, we stepped from forest onto a rocky promontory overlooking a mist-shrouded sea. Behind us, the trees formed a barrier so fortress-like that we wondered how we had managed to navigate our way through it. Ahead of us was nothing, only a craggy headland that ended in a sheer drop toward unseen but thundering waves.

This was the right track?

I stepped toward the cliff edge. A loose chunk broke off under my foot. Tom Dirqs grabbed onto me just in time, or I would have spilled down the escarpment after it. As I tumbled back into his arms, the spool of crystalline thread slipped from my pack. A rainbow prism of light refracted off it.

"Well?" a voice, glass-like but strong, issued from the spool. "What are you waiting for?"

After all I had experienced in M'ranna, I should not have been startled by a talking spool. I was. I stared at it openmouthed.

"I-I—"

"Do you have the needle?"

"The needle?" I repeated dumbly.

"The needle. Do you have it?"

Mariah rummaged through her pack and pulled it out.

"This?" she asked, her voice trembling.

"And the hammer?" it asked.

The hammer. I prodded Tom Dirqs. He gaped, wide-eyed, at the glittering thread and couldn't respond. Mariah retrieved it from his pack.

"Good. Just in time."

The ground quavered and another hunk of cliff crashed into the sea.

Tom Dirqs recovered from his stupor. "Let's be going back," he cried.

From deep in the forest, kep'cha screeches mixed with a faint buzzing and crashing floated toward us on wind that also squalled in from the open sea, swirling a thick fog around us.

"There is no back," the spool responded without emotion.

Another tremor, slightly more powerful than the last, shook more rock free.

"There is only hammer, needle and thread. Now."

"What do we do with them?" I shouted over wind, waves and kep'chas.

A slender arrow of sunlight pierced the mist, spotlighting a narrow fissure next to the spool.

"The Fayr'Owyn is to thread me through the needle held by the girl, as the Dirqs hammers it into the sunlight," it ordered.

Mariah and I did as we were told. Tom Dirqs raised the hammer high over his head.

"No, Dirqs-man. No force. Just a tap. If you break needle or hammer, I cannot help you. If I do not help you, no one can."

The buzzing from the forest grew louder. Trees smashed into each other and crashed thunderously to the ground.

Next, I was to secure thread to needle with a simple knot and unspool the thread. It was hard like glass but supple and pliant like twine.

"Does the Dirqs have a knife?"

Tom Dirqs nodded.

"Cut me."

"Cut you?"

"If you can."

He couldn't. When he set knife to thread, his knife blade broke.

"That is how strong I am," it said. "Now, pull on me."

I tugged with all my strength. Tom Dirqs and Mariah pulled too. We couldn't free thread from needle or needle from earth.

"That is how secure I am. Nothing in M'ranna is stronger or more certain than I. Nothing. Plus," it added, "I am always the perfect length."

"The perfect length?" I asked. "For what."

"For whatever is required of me."

"And that be…?" Tom Dirqs asked.

"Now," it continued, ignoring Tom Dirqs, "secure the spool to the stem of The Nayr and fling us over the cliff."

The Nayr? I can't just throw it off a cliff.

"You can and you must," the crystal thread insisted, reading my mind. "It will find its way into the future…as will you…if you trust. You must trust."

Reluctantly, I did as instructed.

"Why?" Tom Dirqs asked nervously. "Why be we needing to trust you, to trust your strength?"

"You know why, don't you Fayr'Owyn."

I did, and I didn't like it. How could we lower ourselves down on the crystal thread? How could we trust that not only would it not snap but that it would drop us somewhere safe and not smash us to a bone-shattering death against what was left of the cliff?

"You can't seriously want us to—"

"I want nothing. It is what *you* want."

"No," Tom Dirqs declared. Mariah went pale as the mist.

The ground rumbled again, more violently. A giant cliff slab broke free not ten paces from us. It pitched into the sea with such force that the resulting upsurge soaked us.

"Where will you take us?" I asked.

"Where you not only need to go but choose to go."

Tom Dirqs squinted over the precipice and shuddered. "I not be choosing *that*."

"What do you choose?" the Thread asked calmly.

Another slice of escarpment broke off. Then another. The kep'chas' destruction gusted dust, dirt and wood chips into our faces from the forest.

"What do you choose?" it repeated. "If you choose The StarQuest, there is only one choice and only one way. Down."

I tugged again at the thread. I couldn't budge it. Running it through my fingers, I followed its length to the very edge of our known world. Although mist veiled the ocean, the crash of thrashing waves suggested that it was a long way down…a very long way down…to a very violent meeting of rock and sea.

"Are you sure you can hold us?" I asked doubtfully.

"I have already told you: Nothing in the land is stronger or more certain than I. You either trust or you do not. There is—"

"No halfway in between. I know."

Tom Dirqs and Mariah looked at me inquiringly. "The Moon-Quest," I said. "I'll explain later…if there is a later."

"There is no comfort on the quest and no inherent right to feelings of safety," it added. "Your sole choice is quest or no quest. All else flows from that. *What do you choose?*"

"I must choose The StarQuest," I said soberly, though not happily. I turned to Mariah and Tom Dirqs. "My choice doesn't have to be your choice. Whatever you decide, I respect it. I will still do my best to rescue the Grandmother and Micah M'renna."

Kep'chas and thorags yowled in shrill cacophony. They were nearly through what remained of the forest.

"You will not be safe here for long. Your earth quakes and the kep'chas approach. You must act now or face the consequences."

As if to underscore the thread's point, the ground shook so violently that we were knocked to the ground. If I hadn't already been gripping the thread and if Mariah and Tom Dirqs hadn't grabbed onto each other and onto me, we would all have been pitched over the cliff.

"We can climb down, one at a time," I said. You—"

"No," the thread interjected. "All at once or not at all. There is no time for half-measures."

A loud *caw* slashed through the other sounds.

"The Fayr'Owyn first," the thread ordered. "After her the girl, then the Dirqs-man. All together. Now."

Clutching the thread, with Mariah behind me and Tom Dirqs behind her, I crawled to the precipice, trying to make myself as light as possible. As I peered over the edge, a breeze caught the thread and it quivered, catching a stray sunbeam. It was like holding onto a dancing rainbow. Breathtaking though it was, I still gave the thread one final wrench. The ground around me shuddered, groaned, rumbled. I tightened my hold on the thread. It was the most solid thing to cling to. I held my breath and the earthquake subsided, only to start up again a moment later.

Whatever courage I thought I had mustered evaporated as the rock beneath me heaved and rippled. I didn't dare look back to see how Mariah and Tom Dirqs were reacting. All I could do was to hold onto the thread, so tightly that my fingernails bit into my palms. I shut my eyes and held my breath, waiting for this latest tremor to pass. It did, but with such a thundering jolt that my eyes shot open.

Ahead of me, all was as it had been. Somehow, the precipice was intact. Behind Mariah and Tom Dirqs, who pressed up against me in terror, was nothing. The forest was veiled by a pall of dust. And the chunk of headland that had connected us to it had cracked and crumbled into the ocean. All that remained was just enough rock to hold the three of us, the needle and the crystal thread.

"Now," the thread urged. "It must be now, or it will be too late."

Still gripping the thread, we stood. Our sunbeam had disappeared behind the dirt-streaked mist. Tom Dirqs and Mariah huddled behind me. A sudden gust of wind and salt spray whipped my face with a cawing sound. The thread lashed wildly in my hands. An icy chill seized me. I began to tremble.

"It is *mine*," the wind howled, trying to free the cord from my hands. "It is mine and I will have it."

It was more than wind. It was breath. It blew at me from a mouth so dark and cavernous I could lose myself in it…if I let that happen.

"It is *mine*," it roared again. "It is mine and I will have it. All of it is mine. The land. The people. You. You, especially, are mine. I will have it all, and you will not stop me. You cannot stop me."

The wind stopped as unexpectedly as it had begun. There was no sound — not ocean, not kep'chas…only a silence so complete that I couldn't ignore the chill whisper that shivered through me.

"You cannot escape me." Bo'Rá K'n's voice was hushed, but contemptuous, angry and cold. "Your StarQuest is doomed."

The wind rose again, slapping and jostling, doing its best to rip the cord from my hands.

"I will prevail."

"No!" I shrieked with all my force, yet still barely able to hear myself.

I tugged gently to alert Mariah and Tom Dirqs and, holding fast to the thread, I let the wind push me off the cliff. The storm ceased. All was silence. Again. I hung — we hung — suspended over a clear, calm sea whose breakers had stilled, whose mists had cleared.

Once again, the sun shone. The thread responded, flashing brilliant sparks of color into the motionless air around us. If Bo'Rá K'n still railed and threatened, his fury could not touch me here. All I knew was this crystal thread, its multihued refractions and Mariah and Tom Dirqs swaying gently above me.

Any other thread would have cut our fingers. Any other cord would have burned them. This thread was different. It held us. It *was* us. My palms tingled as the cord entered my body, separating to run up each of my arms to my shoulders, curve up through my neck into my head, then cascade into my torso, where the two branches twined, twirled and swirled in the center of my chest before dropping down each leg and out the bottom of my feet. I was serene and unafraid and, as I glanced up, saw that Mariah and Tom Dirqs were similarly at peace.

Our peace was short-lived. A razor-sharp whine severed the stillness. It was a kep'cha, gnawing at the cord. I screamed. Not from terror but from a fierce pain that confirmed that thread and I were one.

"Astel Lev!" I cried out, focusing all my intention, attention and awareness on the Heart of the Star within me. "Let it go. Let the crystal thread go home."

Nothing happened. The kep'cha still whined and chewed somewhere above me. Pain still shot through me. Then, with a loud crack, thread and needle released from their anchoring point in the rock. The kep'cha flipped and smashed into the cliff face. Its thorag hurtled into the ocean, which consumed it with a sickening hiss and fizz. At the same time, the thread reeled out through Tom Dirqs and Mariah then through me as, unsupported, we plummeted seaward after The Nayr to the sound of mocking laughter.

twenty-seven

Water spumed toward me in a froth of rage. Someone was screaming. Me? Mariah? Tom Dirqs? Faces flashed before me: Ben… Akila… Garan… Eulisha… My parents… Ben again, first as an infant, then as I had seen him last. Where was he? Would I die before seeing him again? Would I die before I knew how old he was?

I don't even know my son's age…or mine…

How much more twisted could time get? I started to laugh, not because it was funny. It wasn't. It was tragically absurd. *I* was tragically absurd. Laughter turned to panic…panic to tears.

I slammed into the water.

My next awareness was of flailing arms and choking brine. Somehow, my head pushed out of the water, just for an instant. I coughed up seawater and foundered again. I forced my eyes open into the ocean, despite the stinging. I saw no sign of Mariah, Tom Dirqs or The Nayr, only blue-green swirls of foam-flecked water.

I tried to swim back up to the surface but an unassailable force dragged me down. Deeper…deeper…deeper. I struggled. I kicked. I punched. The force was too strong. Certain I would die, I wept, my saltwater merging with the ocean's. Finally, I had no choice. I had to let go, to let the sea carry me where it would. That letting go moved me to a place of inner calm. I now saw myself as seaweed, floating on the current…unconcerned with outcomes…certain that one day I would wash up on a beach…knowing that, until then, there was nothing to do but glide and sail. If only I could breathe, I would be fine. If only I could open my mouth and breathe…

Wait. I *was* breathing. I was underwater. My lungs no longer ached. My cheeks were no longer puffed. My mouth…it was *open*.

Prithi save me, my mouth is open!

Water flooded my mouth and lungs. Coughing and flailing, I

propelled myself back toward the surface. *It's too far. I'm not going to make it. I'm going to die.*

"You can breathe. You *can* breathe." It was as though the water spoke to me. "Forget that you can't. *Forget that you can't.*"

My chest was ready to explode.

"How can I breathe?" I shouted silently. "How can I forget?" My lungs shrieked with pain.

The water spoke again, in a barely comprehensible gurgle. It spoke of the moons Ben had spent floating in my belly. Ben did not know he couldn't breathe, it said. He did not know how to breathe or how not to breathe. He just floated and swam in his salty ocean, and was.

My mind and lungs argued. My heart spoke louder. It made no sense, yet made all the sense in the world. Somehow, I relaxed. The more I relaxed, the more I forgot that I needed to breathe. The more I forgot, the less I did need to breathe. Without understanding how, my body was getting what it required. If I thought about it, I would realize it was impossible and I would drown. So I stopped thinking. Instead, I swam. I swam as though I had swum this sea all my life. I swam past rich corals, lush, leafy fronds, puffy sponges — all swaying and pulsing with a vitality that invigorated me and made me want to go farther, deeper. I swam past a colorful array of peculiar creatures — fish in all shapes and sizes, some with only a single eye, others with as many as twelve; multicolored seahorses with four legs, a tail and fins; pointy-nosed, feather-clad delfians; and all manner of sea-floor crawlers, scuttlers and scramblers.

They were peculiar, but also strangely familiar, as was this coral outcropping…and now this one. If my early explorations had been aimless, now I seemed to know where I was going…and what I would see when I got there. For example, I knew that beyond that next ferny forest lay a castle-like complex of caves and openings hollowed out of a massive, rough-hewn boulder. I was right. As I swam past the ferns and an imposing stand of coral, there it was: Castle Fynn.

*   *   *

"Welcome. Welcome, Q'nta Ko'lar of Q'ntana. Q'nta of the Astel Lev. Q'nta of The StarQuest. Welcome Fayr'Owyn." Fynn'Qya rose from his ornate throne and spread his fins, pausing for dramatic effect. "Welcome *back.*"

Fynn'Qya was a thor'qya. More to the point he was The Thor'Qya.

In fact, as far as he was concerned, he was THE THOR'QYA: a massive, fishlike creature that stood upright on his rear fins, his puffed-up belly of gold and silver scales shimmering blue and crimson whenever he moved. In addition to the two gold-flecked blue eyes on either side of his bloated face, he had a third, just above the slope of his snout-like nose. Each eye operated independently, which made watching him an unsettling, almost dizzying experience. The blue eyes ignored me. Instead, they darted all over his subsea chamber, determined to miss nothing. The eye in the center of his forehead, larger and more piercing than the others, stared unblinkingly at me, shifting colors as he spoke. Dull gray at first, it brightened to a sparkly silver as he grew more animated. Flitting about him were mini-pyramid pods of rainbow oval fish that stilled their movement each time he spoke, only to resume their water ballet once he was done.

"Do you remember me?" he asked, all three eyes focusing on me so intensely I blushed.

"I-I—"

Fynn'Qya interrupted my stammering with a single *HA* so exuberant I thought the scales would shake loose from his body, like the Q'ophar's had.

"You will remember these," he said and flicked his fin at one of the fish pods. It tore away, as if on a vital mission, returning immediately with Mariah and Tom Dirqs, who breathed here as naturally as I did.

"We be breathing," Tom Dirqs exclaimed. "How be we breathing?" He paused and alarm filled his face. "Be we drown-dead? We be drown-dead!"

Fynn'Qya gaped at Tom Dirqs and chortled. "You can't. Not in my kingdom. It's illegal."

"Drowning is illegal?" I asked

"It's the law. I should know. I made it."

"But how?" I asked stubbornly.

"They told me you were as much Questioner as Quester."

"Who? Who told you?"

Fynn'Qya pressed his lips together. An instant later he exploded into loud guffaws. "Another question! Don't you know you already have all the answers you need?" He poked a fin into my chest. "In there. The Heart of the Star. It's all there. Didn't they tell you?"

"Who?" Tom Dirqs demanded. "Didn't who be telling us what?"

Fynn'Qya shook his head. "More questions. You've got the answers,

I tell you. All of you. I told you that a long time ago."

"No," Mariah insisted. "You're wrong. We only just got here. Don't you remember?"

"Don't *you* remember?"

We looked back at him blankly.

"Questioners, all of you. Who, I wonder, is the Star Questioner?" Fynn'Qya roared with laughter and orange tears bubbled down from each eye. "Forgive me," he heaved, short of breath. "I should not play with you like that. I just can't help it." A low rumble bubbled up from his belly. We jumped back, expecting another eruption. "No," he said, and forced himself to swallow the laugh. "Enough of that. It's just so…so…"

The explosion pushed through despite his best efforts. Once again the waters around him seethed into an eddy of orange.

"Do you know what's going on?" I mouthed impatiently to Tom Dirqs.

He shrugged. Mariah covered her mouth. She didn't want me to see that she was laughing too.

I stepped up to Fynn'Qya and glared into his central eye. "Whatever the joke," I snapped, "I think…I think…I think…"

I couldn't help it. Fynn'Qya's laughter was so infectious that I started to giggle. Before I knew it, I was laughing uncontrollably and crying those same orange tears. My feet lifted off the ground and launched me into a back flip. I didn't land, I floated, bounced and somersaulted some more — backward, forward and sideways — bumping into Mariah and Tom Dirqs, who laughed even harder than I did, our tears clouding the water until we could see nothing at all. I don't know how we managed to avoid crashing into Fynn'Qya or the rocks. We jounced, each in our own orange cocoon, growing lighter and feeling freer as all tension and anxiety washed away. I wondered briefly, as Tom Dirqs had done, whether we were "drown-dead" and in some watery afterlife. I let the thought go. It didn't matter. It didn't matter whether we were alive or dead, whether this was real or a dream. Whatever it was, it was magical.

When had I ever felt this free before? I asked myself floatingly.

Ben.

Heavy as stone, I dropped to the ocean floor. Water filled my lungs. I coughed and tried to hold my breath at the same time, but found I could do neither.

Ben!

Everything went black.

*   *   *

"You dreamed me," Fynn'Qya said, with a twinkle in his center eye. The other eyes, satisfied that I wasn't hurt, darted off on their own, tracking the busyness that swarmed around us in this makeshift infirmary. Tom Dirqs and Mariah smiled with relief and squeezed my hands. We each wore a star-shaped shell pendant strung on crystal cord. My shell was pink and silver. Mariah's was pale violet. Tom Dirqs's was white and gold.

"When you were a child," Fynn'Qya began.

I jerked up. "I remember now. When I was a child, you came to me in the night."

"No, child that you still are, you came to *me*." The twinkle brightened as he reminisced about the frolicsome swims we had shared.

"It was just a dream, though. Wasn't it?"

The twinkle dimmed and his face darkened. "Did you learn nothing from that fool, Garan?"

"I loved him. Please don't call him a fool."

Fynn'Qya smiled sheepishly. "Forgive me. I am too quick to judge. I remember Garan dismissing those dreams we shared. Did he even believe in dream-reality?"

"Oh, Fynn. Of course, he did. He was just jealous of you. He wanted all my learning to come through him."

"So you know there is no such thing as 'just a dream,' do you not?"

"I did once. Then I didn't…until Àna reminded me. Reminded us."

"What changed?"

"Akila…then Ben. Then Ben again."

Tears welled in my eyes. Not orange tears of joy. Clear tears of pain.

"Is this a dream? Is there even a M'ranna? Is there even a Q'nta? Were Akila and Ben ever real? Are you?"

"Does it matter?"

"It has to."

"Dream and not dream. Real and imagined. All one." The words issued from Fynn's mouth, but in a squawk. Tashek's.

The water around Fynn'Qya wavered, blurring his face and body and obscuring Castle Fynn. For a moment, his scales merged with Tashek's feathers. Then they both vanished, taking Castle Fynn and the ocean with them. Only Tom Dirqs and Mariah remained, holding my hands and smiling encouragingly.

INTO THE COIL

The sun hung low on the horizon, casting ripples of fading golden light over the countryside. Cotton clouds edged in a pinkish-gray glow hovered motionless overhead. A few birds, black against the sky's final flush, offered the only movement in this day's dying hour. The only sound too: a mournful wailing that heightened our anxiety. Even our driftwood fire burned with an eerie stillness. No pops. No crackles. No sputters. No spits. Nothing to suggest that it was real. Or that we were.

We sat on a fine-sand beach that stretched changelessly into the infinite distance. In front of us, a barely breathing ocean slipped noiselessly forward then back, offering no hint whether its tide was arriving or departing. Behind us, pale cliffs thrust craggily into a darkening sky. Too sheer to climb, with no ground-level fissures for shelter, their aspect was more hostile than protective. Anyone could spot us from above and, sandwiched between rock and sea, we were vulnerable from all sides.

We hadn't built the fire to dry our ocean-soaked clothes. There had been no need. Our clothes were dry and salt-free when we opened our eyes from what could only have been a dream but wasn't. How could it have been when we each had identical memories of our undersea experience and each wore Fynn'Qya's shell pendants? In fact, we hadn't built the fire at all. It was already burning noiselessly when we opened our eyes.

I fingered my pendant distractedly and tried to make sense of what had happened. We had given up talking about it — or anything — when our conversations kept swimming in circles with no resolution. Instead, we watched the sun set, ate silently from the same backpacks we had left behind when we dropped down the crystal thread, and brooded.

When darkness fell, we tried to sleep. None of us could. So when M'nor rose full and bright over the cliffs, we smothered our fire with sand and set off along the beach. We walked through the night, saying little, until the moon set into the ocean. We wanted to keep walking, but the stars weren't bright enough to light our way. So we curled up against the cliff and, finally, slept.

The sky was barely light when merciless sheets of rain lashed us awake. Our clothes and packs were already sopping and we could barely see each other, let alone the beach, through curtains of water that cascaded down from the heavens. Brooding, low-hanging clouds filtered the morning's already meager ration of daylight. The ocean, so benign the previous evening, advanced toward us menacingly, spewing salt spray in all directions.

At first, we huddled together, hoping to wait out the storm. That strategy was short-lived. When the first furious swell hurled itself onto the beach only paces away from us then only barely receded, we ran. There was nowhere to run to, except along the narrowing strand between sea and cliff. Still, we ran.

Thunder crashed explosively and bolts of lightning speared the ocean, filling the air with a slightly burnt odor. Still, we ran, trying to outrace the ocean and outpace the lightning.

If thunderbolts could aim with malicious intent, these did. Clumps of sand erupted into the falling rain as lighting struck the beach at our heels. Volleys of rock crashed into our path as lightning struck the cliff walls to our side. Still, we ran.

Wet sand scraped our skin. Wind ranted in our ears. Insatiable waves lashed their frothy tongues at us. Unstable in the deluge, the cliff crumbled into chunky mud at our feet. Still, we ran.

"I can't," Tom Dirqs panted after what seemed an endless, pointless race. Sopping sludge eddied at his feet. "You. Go. On."

"Not without you," I shrieked into the storm.

A breaker slammed into us, thrusting us toward the collapsing cliff. When it retreated, it dragged a flailing Tom Dirqs back with it. "Don't. Come. After. Me!" he shouted. "No reason...all of us...die..." A titanic swell engulfed him and he vanished.

I dove after him. Mariah dove in after me. All we could see of Tom Dirqs through the murky muck was his red shoe. I struggled toward it against rough and dirty water that pulled it away from me more quickly than I could swim. Mariah and I took turns shooting up to the surface for air, one of us always watching for that shoe. Was Tom Dirqs still attached to it? If he was, was he already dead? Regardless, would we swim so far out to sea that we wouldn't be able to make it back — with or without Tom Dirqs?

My arms ached. My eyes stung. Mariah, too, strained.

Something pulled at my hair. The shell necklace. I twisted my head to untangle it. Fynn'Qya. If he had been more than a shared dream, could he help us now? Could he bring back the Q'nta who knew how to breath under water? This Q'nta didn't. I tapped Mariah's shoulder and swam up for air. I was so stunned by what I saw in the near distance that I swallowed a mouthful of water. Gagging and coughing, I kicked my legs hard to get Mariah's attention. A moment later, she was treading water next to me, pounding my back, as startled as I was.

twenty-nine

Tom Dirqs reclined on the back of a yellow-green baleya. "What ho," he shouted when he noticed us. "Look at me."

A school of rainbow ovals leapt up and over him, landing with splash on the other side of his baleya. Before I could reply, a second baleya pushed itself up from under me. A third surfaced under Mariah. I barely had time to grab on to its loose, blotched skin before it thrust itself above the water's surface and pitched toward Tom Dirqs's baleya.

Apart from a few scattered scales on its large winglike side fins, each baleya was mostly smooth and just large enough to hold one of us comfortably. Its rear tail fin rotated slowly, more quickly for speed.

"What ho," Tom Dirqs exclaimed again as our baleyas glided up next to his. The ocean stilled and the water became so clear that I could see leagues below, where the oval fish now swam sinuous ballet-like patterns. Of storm, shore, murk and muck there was no sign. Only sun and sea, baleyas and us.

"What— How—?" I sputtered, still too stunned to say much else.

As if in answer, the water around the baleyas bubbled and boiled — orange.

"Then he be real?" Tom Dirqs asked.

"Then he be real," I replied.

In the next breath, the baleyas sped off in rotating V-formation, each taking a turn at the front and singing so loudly that we couldn't hear each other to speak. It was a whining, whistling, squeaking sort of song that, though not at all melodious, was strangely comforting. Every now and again, the ovals would resurface, squeak softly in tune with the baleyas, then disappear back into the sea. They always disappeared when flocks of white-chested gandas crossed the sky, especially when they circled low over the water, hunting for food. When one bird spotted something appealing, the whole flock cannoned into the water en masse, only to emerge moments later in full screech, their wings flapping water into the air.

It was all refreshingly monotonous and relaxing, lulling us into a dopey doze, until a lurching stop woke me to an unwelcome sight: If kep'chas preferred to avoid the ocean, they felt no such reluctance on land. The beach ahead was black and buzzing with kep'chas and thorags, their angry impatience all too evident. In the middle distance behind them loomed the Do'am Mountains, a cloud-shrouded Castle Do'am perched bleakly atop the tallest of the peaks. Somehow, we had come around the back side of the mountain range, bypassing the Do'am Lands altogether.

"We knew this to be a possibility," my baleya said to the others. They had moved out of formation and touched nose-to-nose-to-nose instead. Kep'chas whined and screeched loudly from the shore.

Baleyas could talk? Had I known that, there were so many questions I would have asked.

"I say we do what we were asked to do and no more, Freya," Tom Dirqs's baleya replied. "Drop them on the shore. Period. What say you, Treya?"

Mariah's baleya snorted. "Letter of the word or spirit of the word? I know which I would prefer, but..."

"But what, Treya?" Freya, my baleya, asked.

"You are in charge, Meya," Treya said.

"Only nominally," Freya countered.

"Nominally or not," Meya said, "do we obey the letter of our word or its spirit?"

"Can I say something?" I asked.

"No," all three baleyas shouted in unison.

"Why not?" I asked. "It's us you're talking about."

"Contrariwise," Freya snarled. "It is us we are talking about. Letter of the word, I say."

"Spirit of the word," Meya said softly. "Fynn'Qya meant for us to deliver them to the shores of Do'am *safely*."

"Good point," Treya said thoughtfully. "If that is the case, why did he not say so?"

Freya hooted and flapped her fins. "My point precisely."

Mariah stroked Treya's head.

"What is it, girl?" he snapped. "This is none of your affair."

Mariah smiled. "You're right, Treya. This is *your* affair. What I want to say is about you, not us."

I watched Mariah curiously. She continued stroking Treya's head.

"More to the left, girl. Yes, that's right." Treya sighed contentedly. "All right, fine, then. What is it you have to say? Be quick."

"If you leave us on the shore, will you be able to get away quickly enough so the kep'chas don't get you too?"

"Why would the kep'chas go after us?" Freya asked grumpily.

I stroked her head just as Mariah was doing with Treya. Freya moaned with pleasure.

"Because you've kept us safe all this time," I replied. "They wouldn't appreciate that, would they?"

Freya said nothing. Instead, she turned her head so I could stroke her in a better place.

"Let's just drop them here," she said to the others. To me, she asked, "Can you reach under my neck?"

Tom Dirqs had followed our lead and was stroking Meya. "Then you won't even be following the spirit of your word, will you? Not if you be dropping us in the middle of the sea."

"It is not the middle," Freya retorted, with little conviction.

"What is it to be?" Meya asked. "Spirit or letter?"

Freya twisted her head so I could reach her chin. "I do not like to say it," she said. "Truly, I do not. But the girl speaks sense. They all do. What do you say, Meya?"

"Treya?" Meya asked.

"I agree with Freya," he said. "Spirit."

Meya shook her head free of Tom Dirqs's scratchings and let out a bone-chilling wail. Freya and Treya joined in. The kep'chas, in constant motion since we had first sighted them, stilled. Their thorags gaped at us.

"Lie flat on your stomachs, dears," Meya said.

"Lay your face against our neck skin and keep your mouth pressed open against it," Treya added.

"Hold on," Freya shouted.

Their tail fins ejected, gyrated up and over our heads, aimed for the beach and pierced three kep'chas. They and their thorags tumbled screechingly to the ground as Meya, Treya and Freya plunged head-first into the water.

It was hard to keep my mouth open. But Treya was right: By

breathing into the baleya's skin, I could stay underwater indefinitely. The trick was in keeping a tight seal around my mouth, so that no water could seep in.

There was no V-formation here. The baleyas barreled straight down, side-by-side-by-side, sending water bubbles streaming up after them. Only when we were in sight of the ocean floor did they rearrange themselves into a single line with Meya at the head.

The sea bottom raced up at us. Tom Dirqs stiffened as Meya careened toward it. They would slam into the rocks and we would be next. Was Mariah still behind us? Had Treya been smart enough to veer away? Would she be able to complete The StarQuest on her own? The only mercy for me and Tom Dirqs was that it would be a quick death. But why?

Unable to scream, I kicked at Freya. She ignored me. If I rolled off my baleya, I would still smash into the rocks. Eyes wide with terror I watched Meya and clung so tightly to Freya that she squirmed with pain. Too bad, I thought. There will soon be pain enough for us both. I shut my eyes. I wouldn't watch Tom Dirqs shatter against the rocks. I wouldn't watch my death either.

Nothing happened.

No impact.

No bone-shattering pain.

Nothing.

And I felt no water rushing by me, only air.

Gingerly, I opened my eyes a slit. What I saw defied reality. Just to be certain, I closed and opened them again. Wider. Tom Dirqs, still on Meya, now sat up. That's because instead of diving through water, we dove through rock as though it was water. As though it was air.

I sat up too. I could breathe. I looked back. Mariah was still behind us, looking as mystified as I felt. I waved at her.

"What's going on?" she shouted, though I could barely hear her through the wind whistling past my ears.

I shrugged. I stroked Freya gratefully. "I'm sorry I didn't trust you," I murmured into her skin.

She jiggled in reply, though I couldn't be certain whether she was annoyed or was accepting my apology.

Tom Dirqs turned around and shouted something. All I could make out was the word "Do'am."

"You're not turning us in to S'kryssna S'kyaga, are you, Freya?"

No reply.

After a time, we slowed down and leveled off. Soon after that, the baleyas again "swam" next to each other, Meya in the middle. Freya still wouldn't respond to my questions, but now Mariah, Tom Dirqs and I could hear each other.

"Has Meya told you anything?" I asked.

Tom Dirqs nodded.

"Well, what?" Mariah demanded.

He leaned into Meya, whispered something into her skin, then listened.

"Okay, hmmm," he said.

"Tom Dirqs?" I asked.

"Meya asked me to be waiting," he replied. "I don't know all the story and she says it be better if she be telling it." He listened again to Meya. "She says Freya and Treya aren't being mean. They know it's Meya's tale to be telling." Once more he put his ear close to Meya. "It won't be long, she be saying. Not long at all."

It wasn't. When we stopped, the rock and earth that had been so permeable previously solidified around us. There seemed no way out.

"There is, dear ones," Meya cooed reassuringly once we had dismounted and stretched. "This is our last safe place to talk before..." She looked at Freya and Treya. "Will you complete the journey with me? You do not have to. I can continue alone if I must."

"Before what?" I asked. "The rest of the way to what?"

"You know I did not want to come, Meya," Freya said. "Nor do I particularly want to continue." She looked at me with a strange combination of affection and disdain. "Regardless, I have grown to, well, not exactly like this human, but to find her bearable. If she really is the Fayr'Owyn (and it is hard for me to believe that anyone as weedy as she is could be the Fayr'Owyn), I am for it. Treya?"

The other baleya nodded.

"Fine, then," Meya said. "We know what must be done. Regardless of consequence?"

"Regardless of consequence," Freya and Treya replied.

"I don't mean to be rude—"

"Then do not be, Fayr'Owyn," Freya snapped. "If that is who you are. Let Meya speak. She speaks for us all."

"I'm sorry," I said. "It's just that we don't know where we are or where you're taking us. How do we know we can even trust you?"

Meya sidled up to me. "Fair and true. Fair and true. Freya?"

"Very well, Fayr'Owyn. I am sorry. We are all on edge."

"These are on-edge times, they are," Treya added.

"Let's stir up some food for you first," Meya said. "Treya, can you take care of that? Food first. Afterward, we can get you geared up for…for what is next."

Treya repositioned himself at the center of the enclosure. His body pulsed as he hummed, a low gargly thrum that deepened first into a growl then into a booming rumble that reverberated in my stomach. The rumble turned into a guttural grunt, the grunt into a high-pitched squeak that ignited a light so blinding that it forced our eyes shut. When we reopened them, a mouthwatering array of fruit, nuts, fish and sweetmeats was spread on a bright-colored cloth before a grinning Treya.

"How did you do that?" Mariah asked.

Treya winked.

Until we saw the food, none of us had realized how hungry we were, and we attacked the spread with such vigor that it didn't seem there would be anything left. When we were nearly done and the food almost gone, I realized that the baleyas had eaten none of it. I stopped, put one hand on Tom Dirqs's arm and the other on Mariah's, and said, with no little embarrassment, "I'm so sorry. We've been horribly thoughtless. We've eaten all the food."

Meya laughed. "No, no. This was all for you. We do not eat this food. Air and seawater is all we need. We have been eating. Finish it, if you are still hungry. Do."

We did. Every last morsel. To my amazement, we felt neither sleepy nor bloated. Rather, we felt surprisingly energized and ready, or so we thought, for whatever it was that was to be next.

"Castle Do'am," Meya said. "We have passed beneath the Do'am shores and are now under the very mountain that supports the castle."

"We be *under* Castle Do'am?" Tom Dirqs blanched.

Mariah squirmed.

"Very far under," Meya replied.

"Still too close," Freya grumbled.

Meya slapped Freya with one of her fins.

"Fine," Freya barked. "But you are not going to convince me that this is a good place to be."

"No one said that it was," Treya pointed out. "Now that we have arrived, let us do what we must and get gone. This is not a good place. Even as far down as we are."

It didn't feel at all good. Or maybe it was just knowing that Castle Do'am sat on top of us that made it feel so menacing.

"What is next?" I asked warily.

"What is next is for us to be gone from here before S'kryssna S'kyaga realizes that we are here," Freya said. "She will, you know. She always does."

A chill shuddered through me.

Meya turned to Treya and nodded. Treya positioned himself at the center of the enclosure and began to spin, rising up silently through the rocks until he was just over our heads. A dazzling swirl of multi-colored light spiraled down from him to where we stood and another eddied up into the rocks above him. There was no flash this time when Treya was done. Instead, the light continued to spiral after he slowed and stopped. He hovered overhead, flapping his fins as though conducting some silent, invisible orchestra.

When his fins stilled and the light faded, we were each wearing slacks, a tunic and light boots.

Above him, an opening had been punched through the rock.

"No weapons?" Tom Dirqs asked nervously.

"Are they all this stupid?" Freya snapped. "Did we come all this way and risk our lives for halfwits?"

"Tom Dirqs is right," Mariah said. "How can we take on S'kryssna S'kyaga without weapons?"

Freya groaned. "How can you be so foolish, girl?"

Meya slapped her. "That is enough, Freya."

"Whatever," Freya grumbled. "Can we get on with this?" She turned her back on us.

"That's correct," Meya said. "No weapons. You carry whatever weaponry you need in here," he said, touching our hearts with the tip of his fin.

"Blah, blah, blah," Freya muttered. "Can we go now?"

"I still don't see—" Tom Dirqs started.

"Your job is not to see," Freya snapped.

"Freya is right," Meya said, "though her manner is unforgivable."

"Do not apologize for me. Just get on with it."

Treya glanced up through the rock opening. "Freya is right again. I cannot hold this portal open for too much longer."

Meya nodded. "You know about the Heart of the Star?"

"Somehow, I have to get it back to Reesa Kam'ana?"

Freya rose up on her tail and glared down at me. "Are you sure you're the Fayr'Owyn? Because the real Fayr'Owyn would know—"

"What the real Fayr'Owyn does know," I retorted. "When you carry the Heart of the Star inside you, you can tell me what the real Fayr'Owyn would know. Until then, what I do know is that you're the one who's holding us back with all your grumbling."

Tom Dirqs slapped me on the back approvingly. "You be telling her, Q'nta."

"You're just a mean old grump," Mariah added, emboldened by my outburst.

Freya clapped her fins together and laughed. Meya joined in.

"Now that is the power of the Fayr'Owyn," Freya replied approvingly. "That is the force that will get you through the Coil and that is the mettle that you will need to take on S'kryssna S'kyaga."

"Th-the Coil?" Tom Dirqs stammered, wringing his hands. "It be r-real?"

"Oh, yes," Freya said matter-of-factly.

"What's the Coil?" I asked.

"Nothing much," Freya replied.

"Nothing much?" Tom Dirqs screeched. "Nothing much? How can you say it be 'nothing much?' It be only the worst place in all of M'ranna."

"Tush," said Freya.

"Tush? *Tush*? You be sending us through the Coil? No one has ever made it through the Coil without going mad." Tom Dirqs dropped to the ground, crossed his arms over his chest and pressed his lips together. "There's got to be another way. You can be swimming through rock. Take us a different way."

I looked from the baleyas to Tom Dirqs. Mariah was close to tears. "Will someone tell me what this Coil is and why we need to pass through it?"

"Ask *her*," Tom Dirqs spit, pointing a trembling finger at Freya.

Treya flicked his tail and cleared his throat. "This," he said, indicating the portal opening with his fin, "is the way into the Coil. It is a spiral passageway that is the only way up to Castle Do'am."

"The Coil is your only chance," Meya said. "Kep'chas guard all other routes. You will never make it alive any other way."

Tom Dirqs harrumphed. "If we be making it alive with no minds, what use will we be being to anyone?" He paused. "What use will we be to the Grandmother?"

"If you make it alive with your hearts intact, you will be of great use to all M'ranna, including to the Grandmother," Meya replied softly.

"What *is* this Coil?" I asked again, impatiently.

"It be filled with all the horrors you can imagine…then more on top of them," Tom Dirqs said. "It be your worst nightmares, all in one place. That's what the Grandmother be telling me, in her stories."

"Your companion is correct," Meya said. "In part." Fluttering her fins, she gestured for us to draw nearer. "In order for your hearts to triumph, in order for the Heart of the Star to triumph, you must walk through your deepest fears. The Coil will help you do that. Tom Dirqs is correct," she added. "No one else has survived the Coil."

I looked at her with alarm.

"At the same time, no one before has been the Fayr'Owyn or has traveled with the protection of Astel Lev. I will be frank with you: It is the most dangerous part of your StarQuest. Once you have passed through it, though, you will be uniquely equipped to deal with S'kryssna S'kyaga and bring your StarQuest to Completion. That is your goal, is it not?"

I nodded. The others did too. Their heads barely moved.

"Then, truly, you have no choice."

Freya ferried us up, one by one, to Treya, who, with uncharacteristic gentleness, conveyed us to the stone ledge outside the portal entrance to the Coil. On his final run, Treya deposited a coil of rope, a single unlit torch and three small packs of food at our feet.

"Link yourselves together with the rope and do not untie it until you pass beyond the Coil's magic," Treya instructed. "The rope will absorb some of your fears and counteract some of the effects of this place."

"Your fears may make you distrust the others," Meya added. "The rope will hold you together in love when fear threatens your connection."

"The torch will light itself when you need it most," Freya said. "There is no point in trying to light it otherwise. Conventional firelight cannot survive the Coil's magic."

"As Fayr'Owyn, you must go first, always bearing the torch in front of you," said Meya. "Even though it will not cast any light, it *will* light your way."

"Do not put it down," Treya added. "Never put it down."

"Never?" I asked, dubiously.

"Never," Freya declared.

"One more thing. About the torch," Meya continued. "You must hold it in your right hand. Always in your right hand."

"Right hand." I nodded. "What about food? You haven't given us very much. Does that mean it won't be a long journey?"

"It will seem long," Freya replied. "Lifetimes long."

I shivered.

"It is best if you eat as little as possible through your time in the Coil," Meya explained. "Food will slow you down and feed your fears. Eat sparingly and for energy only. Eat before you pass through the portal and then only when you must."

"Not for comfort," Treya added. "Never for comfort."

Tom Dirqs was uncharacteristically silent. Mariah wept softly. For my part, I wondered what I could possibly fear so much that facing it might cause me to lose my mind…or to give up on life. What could be worse than, as a mother, losing your son not once but twice? I hugged myself as I tried to conjure up fears more terrible than never seeing Ben again.

"There is nothing you can do to prepare for the Coil," Meya said, reading my thoughts. "All you can do is remember." The three baleyas had descended again to the floor of our rocky refuge. They looked like tiny toys from our aerie and had to bellow to be heard.

"The fears?" Mariah asked. From her pale, tight face, it was clear that hers had already begun playing out in her mind.

"You do not have to try to remember the fears," Freya replied. "They will find you without any prompting."

"The love," Meya added. "All you can do is remember the love."

thirty

The portal rock was muddy yellow, with sharp, jagged shards jutting out from it at odd angles. Through it we could see nothing. Only blackness. Before they left, the baleyas had offered us only a single comfort: S'kryssna S'kyaga would be powerless to harm us from the moment we stepped into the Coil until we emerged at the other end, not far from Castle Do'am's dungeons.

"Small comfort," Tom Dirqs groaned. "Why should she be caring when the Coil be far more evil than she is?"

"The Coil is not malevolent, Tom Dirqs," Meya pointed out. "Nor are your fears, unless you give them that power over you."

Tom Dirqs looked unconvinced. He pushed his hands deep into his pockets and hunched his shoulders. He squinted into the blackness. "What if I already have?"

Freya flapped her fins impatiently. "Then you are doomed."

"Prithi be saving us," Tom Dirqs muttered.

As if it were water, the air around the three baleyas rippled and wavered. Before we could say goodbye, they were gone, leaving us squashed together on the narrow ledge. The darkness beyond the portal was like a fourth presence, dominating our thoughts with its sinister silence. As Treya had instructed, we linked up with the rope, waist-to-waist-to-waist, and I held the torch up with my right hand as though it were lit. I forced my mind to focus on my heart and, trying to ignore my fear of the fears ahead, I stepped through the portal. Once we were all through, the cavernous space behind us filled in with rock. There was only one way: forward through the Coil.

*   *   *

"This isn't so bad," Tom Dirqs said. "I'm not being afraid of a single one thing yet."

"There's been nothing frightening yet, has there?" Mariah snapped. I couldn't see her, but her tension was palpable.

We had been trekking up the Coil for what seemed forever, encountering nothing but stillness. At first, we had been edgy. Would we face demonic monsters? Would the rock path give way and plunge us into a chasmic abyss? Would S'kryssna S'kyaga get to us here, despite what the baleyas had said? Could my deepest fears drive me mad? Could they kill me? What about Mariah's and Tom Dirqs's? Could one person's nightmare harm the others? When talking it through repeatedly brought us no answers, we climbed in silence.

The Coil's unrelenting darkness, initially worrisome, was proving to be no problem. Its dirt floor was even and free of obstacles. Its walls were smooth and an arm's length apart — near enough for us to feel guided and safely enclosed; not so near as to feel suffocating. Slowly, my anxieties eased. Could the Coil's malign reputation be something S'kryssna S'kyaga had manufactured to discourage this access to Castle Do'am? It didn't make any sense…nor did much else. Tom Dirqs, too, had relaxed. He had stopped grinding his teeth — a grating habit that always broadcast his agitation. Now, he whistled through his teeth. Although equally annoying, I took it to mean that he was relaxed and untroubled. Only Mariah remained tense. She spoke in monosyllables and gripped so tightly on the rope that I could feel it tugging at me.

Her anxiety tugged at mine. Where was Ben? Was he up ahead, in Castle Do'am? In S'kryssna S'kyaga's dungeons? I shuddered. I hoped not. I hoped the vision I had seen of him on the castle terrace hadn't been real. Had it been? Mariah continued to tug and Tom Dirqs to whistle, but I was barely aware of them. Instead, I focused on the vision of a shadowy dungeon cell that floated in front me as I walked.

A single ray of light beams in from a barred opening in the ceiling, far out of reach. Stone walls are stained with long-ago-dried blood. Ben tosses and turns on a thin, filthy bedroll. He jolts awake, drenched in sweat. His clothes are ragged, his face is smeared with dirt. He trembles, feverish. He pulls himself up, painfully, and looks up. Sunlight fills his face. It seems to revive him, give him strength.

"Ben," I cry softly.

He jerks around, as though he has heard my voice. But he sees nothing. He returns his gaze to the sunlight.

"I am Ben Ko'leya, son of Q'nta Ko'lar Fayr'Owyn, grandson of Toshar

Ko'lar, great-grandson of Eulisha Ko'lar." His chant is rote, as though he has repeated it so many times that he can speak it without thinking. "I am Ben Ko'leya, son of Q'nta Ko'lar—"

The cell door clangs open. S'kryssna S'kyaga strides in, flanked by the same two guardsmen who had accompanied her to Reesa Kama'ana's cell in my vision through her eye. Her patch is gone, her eye restored. Ben ignores them.

"…son of Q'nta Ko'lar Fayr'Owyn, grandson of Toshar—"

"Is that lineage supposed to impress me?" S'kryssna S'kyaga sneers.

"…Ko'lar, great-grandson of Eulisha Ko'lar." Ben turns to face S'kryssna S'kyaga. "It should," he says.

S'kryssna S'kyaga laughs. "It will take more than a doomed line of bards to impress me." Contempt drips from her voice.

"I still have nothing to say to you. Why are you here?"

"To remind myself why I despise you and your mother. I will get my hands on her too. Don't you doubt it. When I do, the Heart of the Star will be mine. This land too. All of it. Forever. Then, I will find a more permanent way to deal with you. For right now, I have a friend who so wants to keep you company."

She pulls her sleeve back to reveal a tattoo on her right wrist: a coiled black snake. She strokes the tattoo, hisses a few lines of sibilance. The tattoo comes alive on her arm. It uncoils, hisses and snaps at Ben. He backs away.

"The Ring of Unity," she snarls. "What is it? What does it do?"

"I told you. I don't know."

She shakes the snake from her wrist. It slithers toward Ben, hissing.

"Give it to me. I want it. I will have it."

The snake slides up the wall next to him, darts its tongue at him. Ben's face is pale, sweating. He cringes.

"I don't know how."

The snake's tale coils around Ben's leg. He tries to shake it off.

"I-I am Ben Ko'leya, son of Q'nta Ko'lar—"

The snake's tongue scrapes his cheek.

"…Fayr'Owyn, grandson of—"

"No," she says with icy calm, "perhaps you do not." She watches the snake tease at Ben for a few moments longer, smirking at his discomfort. The guardsmen stand motionless on either side of her. "Not that you would help me if you could. Would you, bard?"

Finally, bored, she extends her arm. The snake coils onto her wrist and shrinks back into the tattoo. "I shall return. Count on it." She spins around

and leaves, followed by her guardsmen. The cell door clangs shut behind them.
"…Toshar Ko'lar, great-grandson of Eulisha Ko'lar."
The light fades. Ben's voice fades. The dungeon fades.
He's gone.
Ben!

thirty-one

Mariah jerked on the rope. I winced. I was back in the Coil, once again not certain whether what I had seen of my son was real or an expression of my fear.

"What is it, Mariah?"

No answer.

"Tell me what's wrong."

No answer.

I didn't know what else to say to either calm her or get her to reveal why she was so upset. While I hoped that whatever she was feeling wouldn't manifest as one of the Coil's nightmares, I was reluctant to risk my own tenuous equilibrium by pushing too hard. So we continued to walk, Tom Dirqs's increasingly shrill and off-key whistling our only accompaniment.

* * *

Mariah tripped, lost her balance and fell. The rope wrenched me backward. I fell into Mariah from the front just as Tom Dirqs crashed into her from the back. We all tumbled into a heap on the dirt path. My torch rolled away into the darkness.

"Now see what you've done," Tom Dirqs groused.

"See?" Mariah shrilled. "*See*? I don't see anything. That's the point, isn't it. I don't *see* anything. But I'm hearing too much." She poked Tom Dirqs in the chest. "That whistling." She struggled with the rope, now tangled in our arms and legs. "Over and over and over and over. The same tune. Loud. Off-key. In my ear. Over and over and over."

"You could have asked him to stop," I offered gently.

Mariah ignored me. "It's bad enough to be stuck in this place. To be stuck here and tied to him—" She tugged again on the rope, trying to unsnarl herself.

"Yow," Tom Dirqs squealed. "Stop pulling. You be hurting me."

Mariah yanked harder. "It's less than you deserve for hurting my ears so bad with all that screeching you call music." She fumbled with rope. "I can't be next to him. He's...he's— What comes out his mouth is even worse. It hurts my ears and it hurts my head. I need to get away from him." She attacked the knots. "I'm untying myself."

"*No*," Tom Dirqs and I shouted in unison. We groped for Mariah's hands and held them in place as she wrestled against us.

"You're hurting me," she whimpered when she stopped struggling.

"I be showing you what hurt is." Tom Dirqs pinched her wrists as tightly as he could. Mariah screamed and pulled herself free. She pressed herself against me.

"That's enough, Tom Dirqs," I said.

"She be crazed," he muttered. He untangled himself and crawled off to retrieve the torch, which, fortunately, hadn't rolled very far.

I put my arm around Mariah and held her close. Her face was feverish. She trembled. "What are you afraid of?" I asked.

"The dark," she breathed. "Why can't we light the torch? Just for a little while? Just until—"

Tom Dirqs thrust the torch into my hand and his face into Mariah's. "With what? Be you hiding a flint somewhere? Be you?"

"If I was, I'd— I'd—" She burst into tears.

I pushed Tom Dirqs away.

"She be starting it," he muttered.

"Which dark are you afraid of, Mariah?" I asked, ignoring Tom Dirqs. "All dark? Or just this dark?"

"All dark," she managed through her weeping. "They came in the dark."

"Who?" I asked.

"They came in the dark, and when they left it was more dark." She shuddered. "Now they're going to come again." She squeezed into me as though if only she could disappear inside of me, then all would be well. "They always come again."

Tom Dirqs's face softened. "Who?"

Mariah gulped out a final sob. "I didn't always live with my uncle. I had parents once...once upon a time. And a brother..."

"Once upon a time?" Tom Dirqs asked.

"It was so long ago that it seems like a story now...or a dream." Her jaw tightened. "No. More like a nightmare." She started to cry again in soft, smothered moans.

"What happened?" Tom Dirqs's voice cracked.

"It wasn't guardsmen, like…like…" Mariah touched his arm. "I'm sorry."

"Me too," he sighed. "Truly."

"It was the middle of the night. But it wasn't dark. Not yet. The moon was bright. You could see for leagues across the fields, all the way to the lake. The gandas were dancing on the water. They always do when M'nor is full." She paused, a half-smile playing on her lips as she remembered watching the night panorama unfold from her window. Her smile froze. "Then the sky went black. No moon, no stars. And the sound. It was like nothing I had ever heard before. Screeching, howling, yelping, yowling. Loud. So loud that covering my ears barely muted it. I didn't know what it was. Not then. You see, I'd never seen kep'chas or thorags before, or heard them. But I knew that whatever it was couldn't be good." She began to shake again. "If only I had…" She pressed her face into my tunic.

I stroked her hair. "If only you had what?"

She swallowed hard and continued, her voice deadened by the fabric. "My room was next to the kitchen. That's where the trapdoor to the cellar is. Was. I was so scared. I didn't know what else to do."

"What did you do?" I tilted her head so that her voice wouldn't be so muffled.

"It was dark in the cellar. Like this. No, worse. It was even darker after…after…" She buried her face in her hands and sobbed loudly. "After the house fell onto the cellar door," she whispered through her hands.

"Kep'chas?" Tom Dirqs asked.

Mariah nodded. "The house was dust and dirt and debris. Everything in it was rubble." She paused. "Everyone in it. Just like Uncle's house." Her voice rose to a keening wail. "Twice," she shrieked. "Twice I could have saved my family. But I was a coward. I only saved myself. I couldn't even save Ka'Ona. Now they're all dead. Or worse."

She pushed herself away from me and again clawed at the rope. "I have to die. It's my turn now. It's only fair. I have to die before you die and it's my fault. Again."

Tom Dirqs laid his hands gently but firmly over hers. "We be needing you."

She shook her head stubbornly. "I'll only let you down, like I've done everyone else. It's better this way."

I added my free hand to Tom Dirqs's. "You had to live."

"No!" she exclaimed and pulled her hands free. She started to worry again at the rope then dropped them impotently into her lap. "Why?" she murmured.

"Remember what Àna told us? Told you? You're a StarQuester. You had to live. For this."

"For us," Tom Dirqs added.

She stood and turned away, staring into the Coil's empty blackness.

I rose next to her. "Remember what Treya and Meya said? We mustn't untie the rope. We have to stay together and work things out. If we don't, we will never make it out of here. If we doubt each other or ourselves, S'kryssna S'kyaga wins. Bo'Rá K'n wins. If they win, we're all doomed, including Micah M'renna." I pulled Tom Dirqs to his feet. "Tom Dirqs is right. It is about us. But it's about more than the three of us. It's about Reesa Kam'ana and the stars."

"And the Heart of the Star." Mariah exhaled deeply.

Tom Dirqs handed me the torch and touched my arm gently. "It's about Ben too, isn't it?"

"It's about everything. Nothing will survive if we fail. There will be no Ben. No Q'nta. No MoonQuest or StarQuest."

Mariah looked at me quizzically. "How can that be?"

"The Fayr'Owyn be a bard, from the future," Tom Dirqs explained. "That's what the Grandmother always said." He turned to me. "Right?"

"The future? That doesn't make any sense. The future hasn't happened yet." She stood in thoughtful silence for a few breaths. "Has it?"

"It has for me," I replied.

"I don't understand. What's 'bard?'"

"You don't know bards?"

"They be storytellers, yes?" Tom Dirqs asked.

"That's part of it," I replied. "Everyone in my family is a bard. As far back as anyone knows." I paused. "Not as far back as M'ranna, I guess."

Mariah shook her head. "What do you mean? How can you be here when you haven't been born yet?"

I shrugged. "All I know is that Garan — my tutor — he always said that time was not a straight line. More of a spiral, like this Coil. I knew he was right even if I didn't really understand it. Not with my mind. I'm not sure I do now. All I know is that my past is M'ranna's future. Its distant future."

"Is it scary to know the future?" Mariah asked.

I flashed back over all that I had experienced since landing on the Ko'Ba and on my life in Q'ntana before that. Then I thought about the Coil, about the baleyas' warnings and about S'kryssna S'kyaga, who could be waiting for us right now at the other end.

"The future I know *is* scary. Was scary…for me. But it's too far off to make any real difference to us here," I said. "Whatever is going to happen now, here in the Coil, is the only thing that matters, right now."

"More nightmares?" Mariah asked.

"Maybe not for you," I replied, "unless Tom Dirqs starts whistling again."

"No more," Tom Dirqs said gravely. "I'm sorry if my whistling be making you scared or mad. I be done with it."

"No, I'm the one who's sorry," Mariah said. "I don't know what got into me. I know the whistling helps you not be scared. Maybe I should try it?"

"Maybe if you whistle loud enough you won't be hearing mine."

Mariah laughed.

Tom whistled nervously, then stopped.

"It's okay, Tom Dirqs. See?" Mariah whistled with him, in dissonant counterpoint.

I clapped my hands to my ears. "Nothing," I shouted over the din, "could be scarier than this."

We laughed, hugged, untangled ourselves and set off again, up the Coil.

thirty -two

"**Y**ou're a storyteller, right?" Mariah asked.

"A bard. Yes."

"Can you tell us a story while we walk?"

Tom Dirqs stopped whistling. "Yes, Q'nta Bard Fayr'Owyn. A story. That's what we be needing to be less fearing."

A story… How long had it been since I had allowed one to flow through me? How long since I had let those magical words *once upon a time* launch me on a journey with unknown friends to unknown lands? Losing Ben when he was an infant hadn't stopped my story-telling. It made me tell them differently, though. I told stories because I was a bard, because it was expected of me. I hadn't let them unravel from my heart on their own power. That's what my father had learned on his MoonQuest. That's what Garan had taught me. That's what I had expected to teach Ben so that, in the right time, he could take my place as Elderbard, according to the Law of Balance.

From father to daughter, mother son
The mantle passes, the balance is done

But Ben had vanished long before the teaching years could begin only to reappear once most of them had passed. Now he was gone again. On a journey of his own? Or suspended in time yet again?

"Once upon a time—" I coughed hard, experiencing such a binding tightness around my chest that I felt certain I would die. Tom Dirqs and Mariah pounded me on my back. I shook them off. I wasn't choking, nor were my lungs congested. It was my heart, itself both choked and congested.

"Mending to be done," Co'anri had pronounced. Mending *had* been done: to my memory and to my courage. I could not have remembered what an Elderbard was without the former, and I could not have embarked on this StarQuest as the Fayr'Owyn without the latter.

Truly, I had traveled a great distance within myself since waking up in M'ranna. Even my heart had mended some when Ben and I reunited as mother and son. But the mending had been too tentative to survive another forced separation.

Now with increasing despair, I realized that stories had lost their place in my heart a long time ago, when I first lost Ben. Perhaps they might have returned once he did. But he was gone again before I could find out. The void I felt in the center of my chest, I was unnerved to discover, was from much more than Ben's absence. It was from Story's absence, an absence I had barely noticed and now grieved far more than I could bear.

"I can't," I croaked. "They're gone. My stories..." Great coughing, heaving sobs wracked out of me. Mariah and Tom Dirqs murmured soothing words of comfort, but I was inconsolable. Toshar had grown into his stories. I had grown up with mine then abandoned them. Now I was a bard with no stories. How could I even call myself a bard?

"It's over," I moaned.

"No, Fayr'Owyn," Mariah crooned. "It's never over. You taught me that."

"I was wrong. If I have no stories, I'm nothing."

"You be having us," Tom Dirqs said. "You always be having us. As long as there be a StarQuest and we be part of it, you be having us."

"The Fayr'Owyn is a bard. Without stories, I'm no bard. If I'm not a bard, I'm no Fayr'Owyn. If I'm not the Fayr'Owyn, there's no StarQuest. There can be no StarQuest."

"You be having at least one story," Tom Dirqs said. "I know you do."

"What story? You heard me. I could barely get out 'once upon a—'" I burst into tears again.

Tom Dirqs gazed thoughtfully into the darkness. "Once upon a time," he began, in a voice not fully his, "there was a bard who arrived in M'ranna from a far-distant place and time with a mission more important than the stars."

"Her mission *was* the stars," Mariah added.

"*Your* story, Q'nta Fayr'Owyn, Elderbard of Q'ntana. That be the one story you do know, and it be the story we most need to hear."

"Why?" I breathed.

"It's the story of the StarQuest," Mariah said. "That's why."

"This be *your* nightmare, Q'nta," Tom Dirqs said. "Losing your stories."

All the horrors you can imagine…then more on top of them. Wasn't that what Tom Dirqs had said about this place? How could losing my stories be my nightmare? How could I put my stories before my son? Before The StarQuest? What kind of mother was I? What kind of Fayr'Owyn was I?

Remember The MoonQuest.

The voice was Kumba's. I knew it, even though I had never heard it.

Remember a moon that went dark for want of stories.

Remember a land that lost its soul for want of stories.

Remember a heart that lost its light for want of stories.

"What about Ben?" I shouted silently at the dragon. "That's what destroyed the light in my heart."

Had you let them, your stories could have rekindled the same light in you that they did in M'nor.

"Stories restored the moon. They won't bring back Ben," I argued stubbornly.

Are you so sure?

I said nothing.

Your stories are your legacy…to your son, to your companions…to your people…to your land. Your stories are your hands and feet…your bones and skin…your heart and lungs. Your stories are the blood and air that course through you, giving you life. Your stories are life. Without them you are barely alive. Without them you have barely been alive. You were alive, once upon a time, Q'nta. You can be once more…if that is your choice. Is that your choice?

"I don't know."

It was, once upon a time…

"Once upon a time," Tom Dirqs began again, in concert with Kumba, "there was a bard who arrived in M'ranna from a far-distant place…"

Could I not even tell my own story? How could I be so much like my father after so many seasons? Had I not learned the lessons of his MoonQuest?

"It's what you said to me," Mariah offered. "Whatever's scaring you now, you have to push through it, so we can face whatever's next. You can't let it destroy you. If it destroys you, it will destroy us too."

I sighed, then inhaled deeply. It felt as though I was breathing in all of the Coil, all of what had brought me here and all of whatever would be next. With a noisy wheeze, I let it all go and focused on those four words that underlay so much of my life and so much of who and what I was.

"Once upon a time," I began haltingly. My throat closed. My chest tightened. I shut my eyes and continued. "Once upon a time, there was a bard named Q'nta who arrived in M'ranna from a far-distant place. Once upon a time there was an Elderbard named Q'nta. This is her story."

I recounted the story as it had unfolded for me, starting when my eyes opened in the Co'ans' house and continuing, for many turns of the Coil, until it merged with the present moment. As I spoke it, I relaxed and fell into the old, long-forgotten rhythm of storytelling. Even though I knew this story before I started it, I still allowed it to have its way with me, to be told as it would be told, not as I would choose for it to be told. Through it, I remembered my life in Q'ntana more clearly and sensed my StarQuest more completely. I also felt Ben in my heart more fully, despite his absence. When I was done, I felt the return of an old inner peace that had begun to crack when Akila disappeared and that had vanished completely when Ben followed. I knew that my stories had come back and would never leave me again. I knew I would see Ben again. I knew, too that whatever lay ahead, our StarQuest would succeed to Completion.

I opened my eyes and hugged Mariah and Tom Dirqs. This time, my tears were joyful. "In the end, with the Heart of the Star restored, the stars once more found their mooring…and so did Q'nta."

Time passed. How much, none of us could guess. We didn't stop to eat. We weren't hungry. As for a rest break, it was out of the question. I was reluctant to do anything that would keep us in this place a breath longer than necessary. Instead, we continued nonstop up the relentless spiral, grateful that we hadn't lost the torch, relieved that Mariah and I had survived what the Coil had thrown at us…yet still on edge. Would it be Tom Dirqs's turn next? Would Mariah and I be spared additional nightmares? However long we walked must have been long. My arm throbbed from carrying the torch.

"Just one more step," I repeated silently, hoping that my mantra would soon prove true. Very soon. Meantime, I worried about Tom Dirqs. He had stopped whistling a while back, nor was he grinding his teeth.

"Tom Dirqs?"

No reply.

"Tom Dirqs?"

Again, nothing.

"Mariah?"

"Uh-huh?"

"Is Tom Dirqs all right?"

"I— Eeeeyaaah!" Something pulled her back into Tom Dirqs, then me toward her.

Instead of dropping the torch to brace myself, I clutched it more tightly, with both hands. I slammed into Mariah. She yelped in pain.

An ear-piercing yowl cut her off. Then another. It was Tom Dirqs. "He be coming after me," he shrieked. "I know he is. You've got to be helping me. We've got to get out of here." He squinted into the blackness, pointing a shaky finger at the void. "No," he shouted. "Not you." He staggered back the way we had come, dragging me and Mariah behind him with a strength he had never before demonstrated. We pulled back. He collapsed at our feet.

"What do you see?" I asked. "Who's there? I don't see anything. Do you, Mariah?"

She shook her head fearfully.

"How can you not be seeing anything?" he whimpered. "How can you not be seeing anyone? How can you not be seeing *him*?" Tom Dirqs stood and fumbled with the rope. Fortunately, we had tightened all knots during Mariah's panic, and his fingers shook too much to loosen them. He keened, so loudly that the sound echoed eerily all around us, one howl overlapping the last and then the one after until the Coil reverberated with fear.

His eyes bulging with terror, he lunged at me, grabbing my leg. "Oh no," he shouted. "Oh no. Oh no. *Oh no!* I won't be going. You can't be making me."

"What is it, Tom Dirqs? What's going on? What's happening?"

Tom Dirqs clasped my leg in a viselike grip. "The Fayr'Owyn will be protecting me," he sobbed into the darkness. "You can't be taking me. Protect me, Fayr'Owyn. Please. You must be protecting me. Mariah too. She's being next. I know she is." He released my leg and dove at Mariah. She gasped in surprise and pushed him off. Whimpering and muttering incoherently, he crouched behind me, folding himself into a fetal ball.

A loud whoosh blew through the tunnel. It sounded like a tornado, yet Mariah and I felt no movement. The wind seemed only to affect Tom Dirqs, who clung to me from behind as some powerful force visible only to him tried to pull him free.

"You've got to be saving me, Fayr'Owyn. It's going to get me. Once it gets me it will be getting her. Maybe you too. Prithi, let it not be taking the Fayr'Owyn." He gulped loudly. "Or me. Especially not me."

I turned to face him.

"No, no. Don't be moving. Please don't be moving. You mustn't be moving."

"Tell me what you see, then. Tell me what you want me to do."

"If you can't be seeing it, I be dead. *Dead.* We all be. It be over." With one hand still clutching at me, he used his other to burrow into the ground and throw dirt on himself. "It be over," he murmured. "Over and done. Done and over."

The wind-sound whooshed again. Again it tugged at Tom Dirqs. Mariah crouched next to him, humming a soothing, lullaby-like melody. He trembled violently but he stopped digging.

"The Dirqs is right," a voice boomed through the tunnel, loosening rock from the walls and stirring up the dirt on the path. "It *is* over. If not in this moment, then in the next. If not in that moment, in the one following. Your ending is coiled in the twists and turns of this very place, ready to spring up and devour you. Ready. Always ready."

Tom Dirqs howled again. Mariah wept.

Dust swirled around my feet and up into my face and hair, choking me. My eyes stung. My scalp itched. Whatever its purpose, the wind seemed to have no interest in moving me. The same wasn't true for Tom Dirqs and now for Mariah, who had attached themselves to me, trying to avoid being swept away by a force I still didn't fully feel.

"It is *not* over," I shouted back at it. "You can blow and blow and blow, but all you blow is filthy, dusty air. You could not defeat my father and you cannot defeat me." I raised the torch higher. With a flash, it lit itself — a flame that was all colors all at once. The tunnel that had been masked in shadow exploded into light. Ahead, a sickly green, trunkless face with black, blank eye sockets and an empty gaping mouth stared back at me, breathing out the fetid gusts that tried to pry loose a cowering Tom Dirqs and Mariah.

Torch in hand, trailing Tom Dirqs and Mariah behind me, I strode toward the face. "You know you cannot destroy Tom Dirqs or Mariah as long as they stand with me, Bo'Rá K'n," I shouted into the wind. "And you know you cannot destroy me as long as I carry Astel Lev within me." I didn't know it. All I knew was that I was safe from S'kryssna S'kyaga. But I prayed it was true.

A flaming tongue shot out of Bo'Rá K'n's mouth. It whipped toward me, stopping before it could touch me.

"I could destroy you with this torch," I said, more calmly than I felt, wondering how I knew it and whether that too was true.

Bo'Rá K'n roared. Fiery snake tendrils flicked out at us.

"Do it," Tom Dirqs shouted.

"Do it," Bo'Rá K'n goaded.

"You would risk your power to destroy me?" I asked.

Bo'Rá K'n's mouth snapped shut.

"I didn't think so." I stared deeply into his eye sockets, willing myself not to be drawn in. At the same time, I turned my attention from my mind and all its fears and let my awareness drop into the Heart of the Star.

The dust stilled. The wind stilled. Everything stilled. All I knew was the Heart of the Star. All I knew was my heart.

"I love you, Bo'Rá K'n," I whispered, surprising myself with those unlikely words.

The green face wavered. Its fiery tongues extinguished. Its mouth snapped shut.

"I don't like you." The fading stopped. "But I love you."

With a barely audible sigh, Bo'Rá K'n's face disintegrated. I burst into tears.

* * *

"You be *loving* him?" Tom Dirqs asked incredulously. "That-that *thing*? How could you?"

"He would have killed us," Mariah said, still shaking. "Why didn't you kill him?"

We sat side by side, our backs against the rock wall, our fingers playing in the loose dirt of the path, still linked by the baleyas' rope. The torch, still brightly lit, hovered of its own accord in front of us.

Why hadn't I killed Bo'Rá K'n? Was it possible to kill a Tikkan dreamwalker, even one who now chose to traffic only in nightmares? Plunge the torch into his face and he would have been harmed in some way. Of that I was certain. I would have been harmed even more. I knew that too. Wouldn't it have been worth the risk to find out? Without Bo'Rá K'n, there would have been no call for a Fayr'Owyn or a StarQuest. Without Bo'Rá K'n, King Fvorag could never have silenced Q'ntana and there would have been no need for Toshar's MoonQuest. Without The MoonQuest, there might have been no Eulisha, no Toshar...no Q'nta, no Ben. The same consequence as a failed StarQuest. The implications and potential outcomes tied my mind in knots. I shook my head to try to clear them.

"I don't know," I said. "The words came out of my mouth, only it wasn't me saying them. It was Astel Lev that spoke and Astel Lev that lit the torch."

Tom Dirqs shook his head. "Astel Lev be knowing what Astel Lev be about. If it had been me..."

"That's why it's not, Tom Dirqs," Mariah said thoughtfully. "That's why it's not me either," she added before he could argue. She turned to me. "That's why it's you. That's why you are the Fayr'Owyn. That's why Astel Lev was entrusted to you."

I laughed. "I don't know about that. If it *had* been me, I might have taken that torch and burned him right up. It wasn't me, though. It was the Heart of the Star."

"It *was* you," Mariah insisted. "You let Astel Lev take charge. That's why you were able to do the right thing. If it had been me… Well, I just don't know." Her voice trailed off.

"Was it the right thing?" I asked, still not certain. Would it have been worth erasing from history my family and all bards to prevent generations of tyranny and abuse?

"Mariah be right," Tom Dirqs said grudgingly. "It had to be the right thing. Or Astel Lev wouldn't have been putting those words into your mouth. It's just that—"

"It's just that you will never know, will you?" Mariah interrupted. "It doesn't matter now." She stood up and dusted herself off. "What matters now is that we keep moving or we will never be free of this horrible place."

"Mariah's right again," I said. I stood and reached for the torch, but it moved forward on its own, illuminating the path before us.

Tom Dirqs inspected the rope and double-checked all its knots, chuckling to himself. "We don't be wanting any escapes, now, do we?"

"Are you ready, Tom Dirqs?" Mariah asked impatiently. "I want to get out of here."

He examined the rope one last time. "Aye."

Following the torch, we resumed our journey up the Coil, grateful now for its light.

"You *sure* you be loving him?" Tom Dirqs asked after a while. "Do we be having to too?"

The torch stopped. I stopped.

"Yes, Tom Dirqs. I think so."

He shuffled his feet in the dirt. "I'm sorry, Fayr'Owyn. I don't think I can be doing that."

"You don't have to like him. You don't have to like anything about him. You don't have to like what he does, what he says or how he acts. But if we don't love him, if we don't love the dreamwalker he still is, deep inside—"

"Very, very, very deep," Tom Dirqs muttered. "Very."

"If our hearts can't somehow touch his heart, we're no better than he is." I thought back to all I had felt when I watched kep'chas destroy the Co'ans' house — that unsettling mix of horror and pleasure. "I wonder," I added softly, "if we *are* any better than he is."

thirty-four

With the torch lighting our way, our progress accelerated noticeably. We would soon find ourselves in the deepest reaches of Castle Do'am and face-to-face with its mistress and a new set of dangers.

"We're almost there, you know," I said.

Mariah and Tom Dirqs nodded. The Coil now tightened so rapidly, that we seemed constantly to be turning.

"You know that I have no idea what we're to do when we get there, don't you?"

They nodded again.

"You will," Mariah said.

"If you don't, the Astel Lev be telling you," Tom Dirqs insisted.

This time I nodded. "I'll be listening," I said, "as best I can." I strained to hear something, anything. "I'm listening now. I don't hear anything."

"Not time, is it?"

"What?" I stopped, stunned. The voice was neither Mariah's nor Tom Dirqs's. It had a raspy, guttural quality to it, but no body attached to it.

"Who are you? Where are you?"

"Here." The torch stopped and tilted in a semi-bow. "Me."

"Y-you can talk?" I stammered. Would I ever get used to the strangeness of this place? First a talking spool of crystal thread, now this.

"Far better than you, it would seem."

"But-but—"

"As I was saying." The torch straightened up and continued ahead of me, bouncing jauntily. "Not time yet, is it?" it repeated.

"For what?"

"Why, to know what is next!"

A fireball leapt toward me out of the flame. I jumped back, knocking Mariah and Tom Dirqs down. I fell on top of them. The fireball swished around us, ultimately landing on the ground in front of me. It shook itself, hopped a few times, did a backward somersault and squawked loudly.

"Tashek!"

The fireball re-formed itself into the diminutive bird and bowed.

"Ever at your service, Fayr'Owyn."

"But-but—"

"You must work on those conversation skills of yours, Fayr'Owyn, if you plan to continue calling yourself a bard."

"Was that you all along? Have you been with us the whole time?"

Tashek squawked again and did a little dance. "What is 'all along?'" he asked. "What, for that matter, is 'time'? I am here now and that is all that should matter. Now," he said, preening his feathers, "will you present me to your friends or are you losing your manners as well as your speech?"

Still startled, I introduced Mariah and Tom Dirqs. He hopped onto each of their heads then perched atop the torch flame and bobbed at them. "You have heard of me, I presume?"

"I-we—" Mariah stuttered.

"You are as eloquent as the bard, I see," he interrupted. "Never mind. There is work to be done. Talk-work. That's why I am here. That's why you are here. That's why *it* is here." He pecked at the center of my chest with his orange beak.

"You have nearly made it through the Coil — with hearts strengthened and minds intact. One more trial—"

"Another one?" groaned Tom Dirqs. "Haven't we been trialled enough? Isn't there enough that be waiting for us on the other side, inside Castle Do'am? Why more trials?" He stamped his foot. "No more trials."

Tashek hopped onto Tom Dirqs head and pecked at his scalp. Tom Dirqs tried to smack the bird away, but Tashek was too quick for him, dodging and ducking Tom Dirqs's clumsy swats.

"Some minds," Tashek said, "may be *too* intact." He pecked three more times, then burst into flame just as Tom Dirqs finally made contact.

"Yow," Tom Dirqs screeched. He stuffed his singed hand into his mouth.

"You do not *have* to lose your minds to the Coil," Tashek said when he dropped back to the ground, "though it is not necessarily a bad thing." He poked under his wing with his beak and stamped his claw twice. "Where was I? Oh, yes. The Coil." He stared frowningly at Tom Dirqs. "I am not the architect of the Coil, Tom Dirqs. I did not design it. I do not own it. I did not even send you to it. But in it you are. In it I am too — come all the way through this wretched place to help you. Here I am, and what do you do? Complain. Complain, complain, complain." He flapped his wings and hovered above the torch. "Why, I have a good mind to go back the way I came and leave you to, to…to whatever it is I leave you to." Tashek dropped into the flame and merged with it.

"That wasn't helpful, Tom Dirqs," I said.

"That's for sure," Mariah added.

Tom Dirqs pulled his fingers from his mouth and clenched them in his other fist. "I said one thing. Only one. How was I to know he would be taking it such a bad way? I just be tired of so much trialling. Was it wrong to be speaking that?"

"Me too," I said. "But he came here to help us, Tom Dirqs. You know we can use whatever help we can get. Maybe if you apologized?"

"Is he still in there?" Mariah pointed to the flame. It spurted and guttered.

"Are you being in there, Mr. Tashek?" Tom Dirqs asked into the fire. It didn't respond. He turned to me questioningly.

I shrugged. "Try."

Tom Dirqs edged as close to the flame as he dared. "If you be in there Mr. Tashek… Even if you're not, wherever you are, I be sorry. I be sorry I spoke from my head and not my heart. I be sorry I tried to hit you. I forgive you for hurting me."

Mariah glared at him.

"No, no," he corrected himself. "You're not needing me to forgive you. I deserved it, and I be sorry." He held both his hands over his heart. "From my heart."

The flame held still for an instant, then spiraled up from the torch head, its uppermost tip re-forming itself as a Tashek. He squawked once, nodded at Tom Dirqs, then resumed as though the incident had never occurred.

"You have nearly made it through the Coil — with hearts strengthened and minds intact. One more trial: the most important trial." He squawked again, so shrilly it hurt my ears, as he flew back into the flame, which flickered, wavered and dimmed. In the resulting half-light, the torch broadened and grew arms and legs that covered themselves in a coal-colored robe. Its flame re-formed itself into a head, with a mane of long red hair framing a pale face that radiated even more light than the torch fire had.

"One more trial," she said, her voice sultry and sizzling. Her eyes, black as her robe, sat on high cheekbones that cast her hollowed cheeks into shadow. A string of diamond-like stones glittered around her neck.

Tom Dirqs edged as far back as the rope would allow, tugging at it so we would move back with him.

"B-be you the trial?" he asked shakily.

She stared silently at Tom Dirqs then burst into gales of laughter that echoed through the Coil's passages. The more she laughed, the more her necklace brightened until before long it was all that was visible of her. As brusquely as she had started, she stopped.

"If I were the trial, little man" she snapped, "you would not want to survive it."

"Who are you, then?" I asked. "What happened to Tashek?"

"I am No'An'O," she replied. "I am mistress of the Coil and keeper of the Do'am p'rtulle."

"Are you here to help us?" Mariah asked.

"My job is to protect the p'rtulle." She dropped down into the ornate, overstuffed armchair that appeared behind her, tented her long, scarlet-nailed fingers and spoke. "In the times before this one, there was no castle above us. In its place was a vast, peaceful paradise, filled with all manner of flora and fauna. It was known as the Pergosà."

No'An'O looked around as though expecting to see something that wasn't there, frowned. A delicate, gold filigreed table appeared to her right. On it steamed a glass of tea. Next to the glass, four star-shaped, sugar-dusted biscuits stacked themselves on a silver plate. With glass in one hand, she dunked a biscuit into the amber liquid and nibbled at the moist bits. She then sipped at her tea, frowned and returned glass and unfinished biscuit to the table.

"Do you know Kumba?" This question she directed to me.

"We all do, ma'am," I replied.

She stared at each of us in turn, studied her long, pointed fingernails, then continued. "You stand in the birthplace of Kumba. Did you know *that*?"

I said nothing.

"I thought not." She smiled smugly. "This Coil you travel through was Kumba's body before — well, before there was anything else. When Prithi freed Kumba into Creation, Kumba's first stop was the summit of what you know now as Do'am Mountain. It was Kumba who planted the trees that first bore the stars, and it was Kumba who tossed those stars into the heavens, in the patterns you now know as constellations.

"When Prithi had need of Kumba for other tasks, he sent for my sister to tend the gardens and mind the stars. She then called on me to guard the p'rtulle entrance into that sacred place, into the Pergosà."

"Your sister?" I asked.

"Reesa Kam'ana," she replied disdainfully, as though to a halfwit.

"If you are Reesa Kam'ana's sister, you must help us. We're here to save her." Mariah rushed toward No'An'O but stopped cold when No'An'O fixed her with an icy glare.

"Reesa Kam'ana cannot be my concern. Not anymore. My job is to ensure that only the pure of heart step onto the Pergosà's sacred ground."

Tom Dirqs draped his arm around Mariah. "You aren't a-doing much of a good job," he snapped and pointed up. "That be no paradise up there. That be a prison. And your sister be its chief prisoner."

No'An'O stood and shook her head angrily. Sparks flew from her hair, briefly illuminating the tunnel ahead, then extinguishing. She pointed a finger at Tom Dirqs. He shrank back in fear. She glared at him as she sank back into her chair. "My job is not to help or hinder. That was the Agreement. I will tell you what I know. I will do what I can. Do not ask for more or I will not even do as much as that."

I pulled Mariah and Tom Dirqs back next to me. "I'm sorry, No'An'O. We all are. We don't know about any Agreement. We don't know much of anything. All we know is that we're grateful for any hel— For anything you can tell us."

No'An'O harrumphed loudly. Table and contents vanished. A curled-up k'nrah appeared on her lap. It purred as she scratched it absentmindedly.

"I, too, did not invent the Coil, Tom Dirqs, nor my place in it. Nor did I invent the trial. My task is to administer it. Nothing less, nothing more." The k'nrah awoke, stretched, purred and licked No'An'O's face. She pushed it away. It disappeared.

"In early days, the trial was put in place, as I said, to ensure that only the pure of heart could enter the Pergosà. That no one before now has ever journeyed far enough to experience it is of no matter. Today, although that is still partly its function, for Do'am Mountain is still sacred ground, it will serve a different purpose: to strengthen you to meet S'kryssna S'kyaga and survive your time in Castle Do'am."

I swallowed hard.

"I cannot spare you from what lies ahead. That is not my job, not according to the Agreement. All I can do is warn you to be on your guard."

"Can you tell us what to expect?" I asked.

"Or how to prepare?" Mariah added.

"Is there anything special I can be doing, ma'am?" Tom Dirqs asked.

"The one thing I can tell you," No'An'O replied, "is to trust the magic. Unconditionally. Forget this at your peril. But remember this: The magic that presents itself may not be the magic you seek, or even the magic you desire. Magic knows none of that. Magic simply is."

"I'm sorry, ma'am. I don't understand."

"You will." Her eyes drilled into each of us in turn. "Another thing: One of you might not survive this trial. Another of you might not survive Castle Do'am. It has not yet been written that this is so. But it is possible. It is always possible."

Mariah and Tom Dirqs paled, stared at each other then at me, and then back at No'An'O.

"Which? Who?" I asked. "How?"

"I have already said too much. It is not my story to tell." She looked around, scowling. The tea glass reappeared in her right hand. She sipped it slowly, focusing all her attention on the steaming liquid. When the glass was empty, she tossed it into the air, where it burst into light fragments. "One more thing and one more only: Whoever survives — be it the trial or Castle Do'am, be it one of you, two of you or all of you — who ever survives *must* continue. Once the loss of one is clearly imminent, the survivors must not hesitate. Hesitation will spell certain death for you all and certain doom for your StarQuest." She stared again at each of us. "You may feel heartless in your actions. Know that you are not being callous. You are being true — to each other and to your StarQuest. There is no other heartful truth that matters."

She rose and her armchair collapsed into the earth. She stepped toward us.

"Do you understand, Mariah?"

Mariah nodded.

"Do you understand, Tom Dirqs?"

He wrung his hands. "Yes, ma'am."

"And you, Fayr'Owyn. Do you understand?"

I thought of all that had already been lost and all that would be lost if we failed.

"I do."

"Then do as I say. Untie the rope."

I didn't know what to say, given how firmly Treya had insisted that we stay bound together. "That's the one thing we cannot do, ma'am, not until we have left the Coil's magic behind."

No'An'O pursed her lips and squinted at me. "This is my magic, not the Coil's. Do what you want. The choice is yours, Fayr'Owyn." She began to dissolve from the feet up. "The choice is yours, too, to die, which, undoubtedly you all will if you attempt the trial tied together like that."

"Wait, please," I said.

No'An'O's dissolution halted mid-chest. She glowered at me.

"Are you sure this is the only way for us to get into Castle Do'Am?" I asked.

"You try my patience, Fayr'Owyn."

I sighed. Once again, I seemed to have little choice. While we struggled with knots we had deliberately tightened to prevent one of us from separating from the others, No'An'O's body re-formed itself and she drummed her fingers impatiently on a legless tabletop she flicked into existence for that purpose.

"This is not a game," she said, watching with displeasure from the armchair that rose up to meet her. "You are wasting my time…and your own."

I ignored her and pulled out my knife.

"No!" She leapt up and snatched the knife from my hand. "The rope cannot be cut. It must be untied." She tossed the knife into the tunnel, sank back into her chair and waved her arm at me. "Get on with it," she said. "But be quick."

Tom Dirqs cursed softly. Na'An'O raised one eyebrow at him. We all held our breath. Would she glare Tom Dirqs into oblivion? Instead, she picked a piece of lint from her cloak and ignored us.

Our fingers scraped and bleeding, we presented the rope to Na'An'O. "Why would I want your filthy rope?" She wrinkled her nose. "No. You must burn it, and your clothes and everything you have come with."

We backed away uncertainly.

"This is no time for modesty. If you are to survive the trial and step into the Pergosà, you must be purified."

Tom Dirqs crossed his arms defiantly. "Was S'kryssna S'kyaga purified? Did she have to burn her clothes and go through some trial?"

No'An'O flew to her feet. Fire flashed in her hair and burnt in her eyes. Her voice was icy calm. "*If* you survive the trial, foolish man, Prithi can decide if you merit sparing. If it were up to me—" With one step she was at his side, her hands clapped tightly to either side of his head. Tom Dirqs didn't vanish. Instead, his clothes appeared in a heap next to the rope. Embarrassed, he dropped his hands to cover his genitals and backed into the shadows.

"Who is next?" Na'An'O barked. She looked from Mariah to me. "If I have to undress you, I cannot promise that it will be as painless as it was for the Dirqs."

Shakily, Mariah and I shed our clothes and laid them, with our packs, atop Tom Dirqs's.

"The rope," No'An'O ordered Mariah. "On top." Trying to cover herself with one hand, Mariah placed the rope on the heap of clothes. "Truly, there is no point covering yourselves. You have nothing I have not seen before and, frankly, nothing I much care to see again. As for each other, you will need your hands free if you are to make it through the trial alive." She shrugged. "Your choice."

Next, she had us each pluck a lock of hair from her head. Once freed, the strands burst into flame. We dropped them on the pile of clothing and formed a circle around it as, smokelessly, it burned down to ash that was instantly cold. We rubbed the ash all over our faces and bodies and joined hands again. No'An'O nodded and popped into the center of the circle.

"Ko-hay ah. Amma-ken. Toh-hee annah-hoh," she intoned three times, once in front of each of us. On the final syllable she vanished.

"Now, what?" Tom Dirqs asked miserably. With No'An'O went our light. Our eyes, accustomed first to the lit torch then to the illumination from No'An'O's face, struggled to adjust to the absolute blackness she had left in her wake.

"Don't unlink hands," I said. "We have to stay in physical contact or we might lose each other."

As our eyes adapted to the darkness, black lightened to deep gray. We couldn't see other clearly, but we could make out shapes and shadows.

"I suppose," I said, "the only way is ahead." Holding hands, we edged forward. The ground was soft and sandy, making walking without shoes less treacherous than it might otherwise have been. It was still slow in the dark. As the Coil continued to tighten, the passage narrowed and narrowed yet more, until we could only sidle forward with our backs to the rock...until there was nothing on any side of us but solid rock.

There was no way forward. Or back.

We were trapped.

thirty-five

Tom Dirqs and I released Mariah's hands. There was no danger of losing anyone in a space that barely allowed us to breathe. As one, we attacked the wall, groping blindly for even the tiniest opening. But three pairs of hands could find nothing that two single hands hadn't.

No one spoke. Mariah whimpered softly. I could feel Tom Dirqs's anger rising but didn't know what to say to preempt it. He would blame No'An'O. He would blame the baleyas. He would blame me. Maybe he was right. Maybe the baleyas and No'An'O had been sent by S'kryssna S'kyaga. Maybe the betrayal had preceded the Coil. Had I been too trusting? Had I misread the Heart of the Star?

When the tension finally exploded, it wasn't Tom Dirqs who sparked it. It was Mariah. I had been so immersed in my own thoughts and self-blame that I hadn't noticed that she had stopped crying, hadn't noticed the silence.

She thrust her face in Tom Dirqs's. "Don't you dare say one word against the Fayr'Owyn," she spat. "Not one word. I know what you're thinking, Tom Dirqs. I can hear all the blaming going on your head. Just stop it. Stop it right now." She poked him in the chest with each word. "All your blaming won't get us out of here."

Tom Dirqs inhaled deeply and held his breath. He released it noisily then looked away.

"What if No'An'O be tricking us?" he asked quietly. "What if we've done this all wrong?" He gulped and sniffled. "We're going to be dying in here, ain't we?"

"No." The word escaped from my mouth before I could stop it. I didn't know how we would make it through this trial. Somehow, we would. "No one is going to die here," I insisted.

"But No'An'O—"

"No'An'O said a lot of things. There's only thing one we need to focus on, and that's how we get out of here and complete the trial. Successfully. All of us. Alive." I closed my eyes and tried to connect with Astel Lev, the one thing the fire could not take from me. "The only way that's going to happen is if we stop bickering and start loving."

Mariah kissed Tom Dirqs on the top of the head. "The Fayr'Owyn is right. I'm sorry, Tom Dirqs."

Tom Dirqs squeezed my hand and Mariah's. "Me too."

I squeezed back. "This is not about trying to figure anything out. This is about thinking with our hearts, not our heads. Still…" I looked up, trying to pierce the darkness overhead, than looked back down at Tom Dirqs. "Do you think you could—?"

"Be climbing up top your shoulders to see if anything is up there?"

I nodded and knelt down. A moment later I was bracing myself against the stone wall and Tom Dirqs was poking into the inky void over my head. A moment after that, I no longer felt his weight on my shoulders.

"Tom Dirqs?" I felt for his feet. They weren't there. *"Tom Dirqs!"* I shouted his name again and again, until I was hoarse. Mariah too. When we could shout no more, we collapsed into each other's arms, sobbing.

*　*　*

Tom Dirqs was gone. No'An'O had been right. I had been wrong. I knew it wasn't my fault. I still blamed myself.

"Maybe he found a way out and is looking for help?" Mariah asked, more to cheer me up than because she believed it.

"Maybe," I replied, maintaining the pretense.

Now what? Mariah wanted climb on my shoulders, too, to see where Tom Dirqs had gone. I wouldn't let her. We had already lost one. I wouldn't lose another.

"No'An'O didn't say one of us would die," Mariah said slowly, "only that one of us wouldn't survive the trial. Couldn't she have meant something else?"

I shrugged. The only positive aspect of Tom Dirqs's absence was that it left enough room for us to sit, which we did, if almost in each other's laps.

"You said we had to think with our hearts, to not try to figure things out. What does Astel Lev say?"

I did my best to go to that deep inner place that had served me in the past. Or had it? Maybe Astel Lev was an illusion and No'An'O had tricked us. Maybe the baleyas had betrayed us and we would die here. Just as Tom Dirqs probably had. Hopelessness enveloped me in a darkness even blacker than that which surrounded us.

I don't know how long we sat, crushed into each other. I know Mariah said things. I could hear the soft, singsong hum of her voice somewhere in my awareness. From the rise in the hum, I imagined she was asking questions. From the pressure of her hand on mine, I know she was trying to reassure me. Yet I could make out none of her words. My mind was elsewhere. And my heart... Well, my heart had clamped shut. I blamed myself for what had happened to Tom Dirqs. I felt responsible for Mariah and blamed myself for getting her into what was now, clearly, a hopeless situation. I blamed myself for every choice and decision I had made that had brought us to this place. I blamed myself for letting Ben be taken from me a second time.

Ben.

It had all begun with Ben. Ben's disappearance and reappearance. Remembering Ben. Remembering him as my son. Remembering myself as his mother. Could I have prevented that second disappearance? If I had done something different, would we still be together? Maybe I no longer trusted No'An'O and the baleyas. Could I stop trusting my father and grandmother?

"They weren't real," a voice in my head whined. "Why trust them?"

"Did they *feel* real?" another, fainter voice asked.

I thought back to those moments under the Ko'Ba. To Ben. To the moment I first sensed Eulisha's presence, and Toshar's. Ben didn't doubt that they were real. I didn't either. Then.

Voices battled within me. In my head. In my heart. My voice. Others' voices. Which did I trust? Which could I trust? Ben. I could trust Ben. If I could trust no one else, I could trust Ben. Had that truly been Ben? The last time I could have been certain, he was an infant. Could this nearly adult Ben have been an impostor sent by Bo'Rà K'n? What was true? Was anything true?

Your heart. Your heart is true. Is truer. Is truest.

A new voice. What was it?

Your heart. Your heart is true. Is truer. Is truest.

It was *my* voice. My words to Ben, just before he...just before we... Just before I let him go. Then, more voices...familiar voices from recent days...from past days.

In order for your hearts to triumph, you must walk through your deepest fears. The Coil will help you do that.

Let your heart be your mind.

Astel Lev lies at the heart of all that is. If you turn to it, it will help you to see what needs to be seen — with your heart, not your mind. Its guidance will see you through your StarQuest…if you let it.

Turn to Astel Lev, Eulisha had said. Could I still do that?

"Astel Lev."

"What?" Mariah asked.

I shook my head and closed my eyes. Closing my ears to the cacophony of voices was more difficult. Somehow, I managed to drop my awareness to a place where they took on the same unintelligible hum as Mariah's had.

Astel Lev.

Astel L— I remembered what I had forgotten: that unless I completed The StarQuest, not only would I never see Ben again, there might never be a Ben…or a Q'nta. Whatever else mattered, that had to matter most. I had to succeed or I would deny my son his life.

I had to succeed or I would deny story its life. Once again, I knew that without heart there was no story and without story, no life would be worth living. Not even Ben's. I sighed and opened my eyes. Darkness and walls were gone. So was Mariah.

Mariah!

CASTLE DO'AM

thirty-six

I sat, still naked, on a golden cushion in a mist-shrouded chamber, squinting to adjust to this sudden return to light. Next to me, a fountain of rainbow water burbled musically. A lythe strummed softly somewhere out of view. Although I saw no one else, I sensed that I wasn't alone.

"Mariah? Tom Dirqs?"

No reply.

"Who's here? Where am I?"

Again, no reply.

I tried to stand but something weighted me down. I couldn't move. The music swelled as more lythes joined the first. As it did, some of the mist cleared, revealing scores of identical fountains, stretching as far as I could see. The chamber was still empty, yet I felt someone close by.

"Tom Dirqs? Mariah?"

"You are here to complete your trial." No'An'O faded in and out of view, an ethereal presence hovering mistily in the fountain spray. "They must complete theirs as well." She paused. "Or not." She had nearly washed away when only her mouth reappeared. "One thing: Do not move from where you are." Then she was gone.

Don't move? I couldn't even cross my legs, let alone get up. I sighed and closed my eyes. The blend of lythe and gushing water made me drowsy. My head dropped onto my chest.

I stand at the underground entrance to Castle Do'am. Are Mariah and Tom Dirqs with me? I feel their presence but cannot be certain as I don't see them. All I see is a heavy wooden door braced with strips of iron. Carved into its dark, aged planks is a single star flanked by a pair of roses and crowned by a coronet. More stars, clustered in unfamiliar constellations, circle this central motif. Scrolling up out of the coronet is a roll of parchment. Whatever letters were etched into the parchment have largely worn away.

I try to decipher the words, but they are too faint. Instead, I touch my fingers to what remains of the letters. The washed out phrase lights up, in a language I don't understand. Before I can pull my hand away, its light shoots into my finger, along my arms, into my shoulders and down into my heart, where it swirls in a spiraling eddy of warmth before flashing simultaneously up and down — out the top of my head and down into the earth beneath my feet. As it leaves my body, the door itself softens into light. Hundreds of faces flicker in the light. My face is among them, as are many I recognize and most I do not. The light flares brighter and brighter until I have to shield my eyes.

When I look again, door and light are gone. In their place grim-faced guardsmen stare back at me with empty, soulless eyes of washed-out blue…the same armored, snake-tattooed men I saw in Ben's cell and in Reesa Kam'ana's before that. There are more of them now. Many, many more. So many that their number seems to stretch endlessly into the infinite distance.

Behind me, the Coil folds in on itself and vanishes into nothingness. All that is left is the square of dirt under my feet and the wall of evil in front of me.

A scream births deep in my belly. I catch myself and stop before it erupts into sound. I will not give in to my fear. Instead, I call on the Heart of the Star to act as my eyes. I gaze deeply into the blankness of those dulled-blue eyes and into the blackness of those bleak guardsmen-hearts. From one guardsman to the next I stare, taking in each in turn with a determined intensity I never knew I possessed. At first, the guardsmen meet my stare, glaring back at me with an eerie blend of vacuousness and venom.

"Astel Lev," I murmur softly. "Help me. I need more."

The same warmth I felt in my heart moments earlier rushes into my eyes. Now I see past the blankness and blackness. Now chain mail falls away… tattoos dissolve…weapons clatter to the ground.

The guardsmen's flat, uniform eye color gives way to the full spectrum of depth, shade and hue. I know that were I to look with my eyes, not with the vision of my heart, nothing would have changed. The guardsmen would be as they had been. I know, too, that I dare not let my awareness rest there, even for a breath. My vision focuses instead on heart truth.

I step forward. I'm no longer deep underneath Castle Do'am. I am on the stone-paved road that winds up Do'am Mountain, through a phalanx of guardsmen, to the forbidding gate of S'kryssna S'kyaga's citadel. The men, now no longer guardsmen, part to let me pass. When I reach the summit, I touch one hand to my heart, the other to the gate. The gate swings open.

"Q'nta? Wake up." Mariah shook my shoulders gently. "Where are we? Is Tom Dirqs here too?"

I opened my eyes. Mariah stood in front of me, no longer naked. Nor was I. We both wore tunics, leggings and sandals in the same gold hue as the banquette cushions. I stood — I could now — and embraced her. As I did, images flashed through my mind, of Mariah naked and on horseback. Of Mariah's trial…

One hand clasps the reins of a silver stallion, the other grips a wind-rippled standard: a midnight field upon which sits the constellation of a woman, with its brightest star as her heart. Mariah's horse rears before an army of guardsmen so vast it extends beyond the horizon. Clad, armed and tattooed identically to the guardsmen in my vision, the men stare impassively at her.

"Make way," she cries. "Make way for the standard bearer."

Her horse brays loudly, snorts, bares his teeth. The guardsmen hold their ground. Mariah whispers something into the horse's ear. He tosses his head and stamps his front right hoof three times.

Still, the guardsmen are as stone.

"Oman ki-hanna oma-ay," she whispers then sings the song of The Nayr. Her voice is sweet and bell-like at first, like the tinkling of a gentle brook. The brook becomes a river and the river an ocean as her voice heightens, strengthens. The ocean is now a tempest, thundering from her in peals of song.

A giant thunderbolt drops from the heavens and impales the ground between her and the army. Day is now night.

Still singing, Mariah rides up the thunderbolt then beyond it. Now suspended in midair, she hurls the thunderbolt back into the sky and leaps back to earth.

The guardsmen grow restive. Mariah shakes the rein. Her silver horse tosses its head once more and presses forward. For a moment, it's not clear whether the guardsmen will relent. They do, parting to let her through. Heads bowed, some crying, they drop their weapons.

She gallops past them into the night as the stars in her standard fling themselves up into the velvet sky.

Mariah pulled back from the embrace, awestruck. "That's it. That's what happened. I thought I was dreaming it. But it happened. I know it did. How did you know? How did you see it?"

"I don't know. When we hugged just now, when our hearts touched, it was as though I could see into your heart with mine. That's the only way I can explain it."

We hugged again, just to see what would happen. Nothing did. Instead, I told her my dream.

"It wasn't a dream, any more than mine was," Mariah insisted. "It must have happened. It must have really happened." She laughed and squeezed my hand.

All around us, fountains plashed pleasingly, merging with Mariah's laughter and with the strumming of the still-unseen lythes. The mist had completely dissipated and everything in the chamber seemed brighter, more vibrant. The water's colors were more luminous, the gold fabric more glittery. Overhead, silver vondas cooed from branches unattached to any trees. None of it seemed real. At the same time, it all felt more real than anything else I had experienced on this journey.

"Tom Dirqs. Where is he?" I asked.

"He isn't here with you?"

Relief at our reunion turned to alarm.

Had Tom Dirqs failed his trial? No'An'O had warned us that this might happen. Or was he still in the midst of it? Were we to wait or go…where? It wasn't as though we saw a clear exit from this endless-seeming chamber, with its cookie-cutter clusters of fountains edged with gold cushions. The music, too, continued at the same volume and from the same unseen lythe players. We set out to search the chamber, determined not to lose sight of where we had begun, in case Tom Dirqs turned up there. But with every fountain and its surroundings indistinguishable from the last, we quickly lost all sense of place and direction. Frustrated, I collapsed on the nearest banquette, only to see Tom Dirqs's reflection staring back at me from the water instead of my own.

"It be about time," he said irritably.

Startled, Mariah peered into the water.

"Where are you?" I asked

"Where be I? Where be you?"

Mariah stick her finger into the fountain.

"Stop that," Tom Dirqs shouted. "You poked my eye. Maybe you'd like me to poke your eye." A twiggy finger stabbed out of the water. Mariah dodged it before it could jab her.

I swatted at Tom Dirqs's finger. It felt watery, insubstantial. "How do you see us?"

"In this awful fountain. The water be looking like swamp sludge. It be tasting awful too, and I be so thirsty."

When I described where we were, Tom Dirqs confirmed that he was in gritty, gray version of it. Plus, he was still naked.

"I be on your shoulders," he said, "and before I be knowing it, I be in this room. It be all gold when I got here." He gazed glumly around. "It not be gold no more."

As he explained it, he'd had the same experience with No'An'O as we had. His dream, though, had quickly turned into a nightmare when he had seen the guardsmen and tried to flee.

"I couldn't even be doing that part right," he groaned. "I tripped. On a tree root. I fell flat into a mud puddle. A guarding-man be scooping me up and hauling me to Castle Do'am. When I woked up, all gold here be gone."

He wiped his eyes, smearing more mud on his cheeks. "I be the one," he cried. "I failed my trial. I didn't trust the magic. Now I'm the one you must be leaving behind." Large tears streaked down his face and plopped into the fountain, rippling and distorting his reflection. He rummaged for a handkerchief before realizing he had none, then cried some more.

"There was more, wasn't there?" I asked. I knew what he would say before he said it. I also knew that he had to be the one to tell it.

"What is it?" Mariah asked gently.

"I—" he bawled, so hard he couldn't speak. Finally, he stopped crying, hiccuped twice and washed his hands and face in the dirty fountain. When the water settled and we could again see him, his face was streaked with slime. He tried to smile, but his fear and grief seeped through.

"They dropped me in Castle Do'am, in front of a dungeon cell," he whispered hoarsely. "It be horrible, worse than any nightmare." He turned away and continued with his back to us. "It be S'kryssna S'kyaga. She be laughing. Loudly. Hideously. At me. Because I wouldn't... Because I couldn't..." He looked back through the fountain at us. "She'd been torturing the Grandmother. The Grandmother didn't scream when S'kryssna S'kyaga be breaking her arms. She just be staring back with a dreamy look and a bit of a smile. As if it didn't matter none."

He smashed his fist into the water. His face shattered into a thousand pieces. "It be mattering to me. More than anything else, it be mattering to me. So I screamed. I screamed because she didn't. The Grandmother didn't. Then S'kryssna S'kyaga took a knife and held it to the Grandmother's tongue. Then, I be seeing the Grandmother's fearing. S'kryssna S'kyaga be seeing it too. That's when she be laughing, S'kryssna S'kyaga. She looked at me, S'kryssna S'kyaga. 'You know how to stop me, Tom Dirqs,' she said. 'But you will not, will you?' She be cackling horribly, like the witch she is. 'You cannot, can you?'"

The fountain water had settled and Tom Dirqs was sobbing again. "She be right," he bawled. "I couldn't. I couldn't be saving my own grandmother." He wiped his eyes with the back of his hand.

"The words would not have been enough," I said. "You would have had to mean them. It's not your fault."

He glared at me. "Whose fault be it, then?" His eyes softened and he looked sadder than I had ever seen anyone before. "I be failing the Grandmother and I be failing you," he moaned. "I don't deserve to be being part of your StarQuest. You be better off without me." He stood and walked away from the fountain.

"Wait!"

"What for?" he called back to me without turning around. "No'An'O be warning us about waiting. I not be coming, so I'd better be moving on. You too."

"I don't understand," Mariah said. "What couldn't you say?"

"I love you."

"To your grandmother?"

"No," he replied. "To S'kryssna S'kyaga." He kept walking and, in a moment, was gone.

<h1 style="text-align:center">thirty-seven</h1>

Mariah was ready to dive in after him. I held her back. Tom Dirqs was gone. No'An'O had been right. Would she be right about one of us not surviving Castle Do'am too? I looked at Mariah and knew that she wondered the same thing. Neither of us said anything. No'An'O had also said not to hesitate. Had we waited too long? Were we as trapped in our space as Tom Dirqs was, perhaps, in his?

"I said so many horrible things to him and now he's gone," Mariah said. She gazed into the water, now a still whorl of color. "I'm sorry, Tom Dirqs," she whispered. A single tear formed in the corner of her eye and spread to her lashes. She blinked once and the tear fell free. It didn't drop, it floated feather-like toward the fountain. When it landed, the water swirled, spiraling slowly at first, then more and more quickly until a silver opening formed in the center of the eddy.

The walls of the whirlpool rose. Its eye beckoned…gleamingly… hypnotically. Before I could stop her, Mariah dove in. Before I could think, I dove in after her.

The water roared around us as we tumbled headfirst into its dry center point. Silver deadened to gray then black. The water twisted around me, thundering so loudly that it hurt my ears.

All of a sudden, the noise stopped, the water disappeared and I landed — on my feet, next to Mariah. Although back in The Coil, its rock walls and earthen floor were behind us. We found ourselves on interlocking green-marble tiles surrounded by a delicate stonework tracery etched with luminous gold and silver markings that suffused the space in a delicate glow. In the center stood an empty circle bounded by identical points of clear crystal, all pointing inward. Beyond the crystal circle was the ancient, wood-plank door of my vision, unguarded.

A gong pealed three times. Its baritone boom echoed against the stonework for many moments as white smoke curled up and into the circle from the tips of the crystal points. When the reverberation had faded to silence and the smoke cleared, a woman stood before us. She was tall and shapely, with flaxen hair that rippled down her back. Her blue eyes sparkled between a smooth brow and high cheekbones. Her nose was straight without being harsh, and her lips, full and red, curved into a gracious smile. She wore a simple, long-sleeved white robe scooped at the neck and tapered at the waist. A single pearl, large and opalescent, hung from a silver chain just above her breasts.

She was startlingly beautiful, the most beautiful woman I had ever seen.

"Welcome," she trilled. "Welcome to my home." She smiled warmly and opened her arms to us.

This is S'kryssna S'kyaga? The most wicked and feared woman in all M'ranna? How can it be? She isn't the serpentine sorceress of my visions, nor anyone else I have ever encountered. If she's not S'kryssna S'kyaga, who is she? And why does she welcome us so cordially to Castle Do'am? Maybe this isn't Castle Do'am at all. Where are we? What's going on?

"Come," she said in a voice delicate as a butterfly. "Come into the circle. You will be my most honored guests, dear ones. For as long as you choose. Come." She gestured for us to join her.

Captivated by the woman's elegance and allure, Mariah stepped toward the crystal circle. The woman raised an arm to help her. As she did, her sleeve hitched up to reveal a small tattoo: a coiled black snake.

S'kryssna S'kyaga. The guardsmen. My visions.

I wrenched Mariah back and we fell to the floor, watching in horror as S'kryssna S'kyaga's tattoo expanded and came to life, just as it had done in my vision of Ben. As it uncoiled and stood, hissing, on its tail, its red tongue flicking angrily, everything about S'kryssna S'kyaga turned ugly. All color leached from her clothes. Her hair turned black and stringy, the strings writhing into a mass of slimy snakes. Her features hardened. Only the pearl pendant continued to glister. Crabbed fingers clutched it angrily.

"If you will not be my guests," she screeched, "you can be my prisoners."

Acrid smoke streamed from the crystal tips, thickening until all we could see of S'kryssna S'kyaga was her face.

"You will be my prisoners." She smiled cruelly through the smoke that now obscured most of her face. "You are my prisoners."

When the smoke cleared, the floor had lost its luminosity, the crystals were dulled, the stonework was scorched and S'kryssna S'kyaga was gone. Only the harsh smell remained.

Mariah and I clung to each other, trembling.

"I miss Tom Dirqs," she whispered.

I missed him too. He was stubborn, moody and unpredictable. But he made me laugh when things seemed most hopeless. I could stand to laugh now. I could stand to feel fearless, as fearless as the woman in my vision who had stared down all those guardsmen. I didn't feel fearless. S'kryssna S'kyaga had left me with a glacial chill in the center of my chest. There was no way back. We couldn't return through the Coil. The only way forward that I could see was the door, and it was locked. Even if I could find our way through, how would we find Reesa Kam'ana? And if we did, how could we defeat S'kryssna S'kyaga?

"Tom Dirqs would have told us a bad joke," I said.

"Or make me so mad I'd want to strangle him."

"In the end, he would have made you laugh."

"Do you think we'll see him again?"

"I don't know, Mariah. I don't know much of anything, it seems."

"What about Astel Lev? Can you ask it?"

I tried. I closed my eyes against the fearsome darkness and searched inside for the Heart of the Star. I couldn't find it. It was as though S'kryssna S'kyaga's presence had encased it in an impenetrable block of ice.

"You have to find a way to Astel Lev," Mariah said.

I slumped down next to the door. Mariah was right. Astel Lev knew the way. It would guide me, if I could only reach it.

A story. Tom Dirqs's voice. *That's what we be needing.*

"Tom Dirqs?" I called out hesitantly.

"He's here?" Mariah asked hopefully.

I shook my head. "Do you think a story will help?"

"I don't know. Stories always helped your father."

They had, over and over again, through his MoonQuest… throughout his life. Whenever I'd had a problem, he would tell me a story. If it was a big problem, he would encourage me to tell one of my own and find the answer within it.

"Well, Father," I murmured, "this is one of the biggest problems yet."

Then tell me a story, daughter. Now that you have found your stories again, that is where you will find your answers. Not in my stories. In yours.

Yes, I had found my stories again. Could they do for my StarQuest what they had done for Toshar's MoonQuest? I sighed. It was worth a try.

"Once upon a time," I paused. I wasn't sure I could do it. I started again. "Once upon a time..."

Mariah smiled encouragingly.

"Once upon a time," I started a third time, "there was a star. High up in the heavens this star shone, twinkling smilingly at anyone who noticed her. So eager was she to twinkle that she was always the first visible each dusk and the last to wink out each dawn.

"The star called herself Àna. She had chosen her own name, as all stars do. But she had not known that in the ancient, long-forgotten stellar language, *ana* meant songstress. Ironically, if there was one thing Àna loved more than anything else — more, even, than twinkling — it was singing.

"The problem she faced was that stars did not sing. It wasn't that they could not. It was that they did not. Singing was considered vulgar and brazen, something to be discouraged at the earliest age.

"At first, as a child, Àna would not be discouraged. She could not understand why such beautiful sounds were not allowed. She could not understand why it was forbidden to make such sounds when it felt so good to do so.

"'It is not about feeling good,' Àna's father scolded. 'It is about doing what is right.' He scowled, but only for a moment as scowls dull a star's twinkle. 'Singing is not right. So you will not do it.'

"Àna argued. She even argued in song. To no avail. Her father was adamant and so, eventually, like all child-stars before her, Àna was silenced. Unlike all child-stars before her, though, Àna could not smile if she was silent. If she could not smile, she could not twinkle. Unfortunately for her, if singing was banned, twinkling was required.

"'You must twinkle,' her father chided. 'All stars twinkle and so you must. All stars twinkle,' he added before Àna could reply, 'and no stars sing. You must do one, never the other. Singing,' he added disapprovingly, 'is all right for the moon, that M'nor. Not for a star. Never for a star.'

"Àna's mother said nothing. She knew her husband was right. She knew, too, that her daughter was right. Unable to reconcile these thoughts, she watched Àna lose more of her luster each day.

"One day, some seasons later, when Àna was barely visible in the sky, alone because no star would partner with such as her, she found herself drifting toward the moon. M'nor was full that night — full in light and full in song.

"'Mir M'nor m'ranna,' the moon sang. 'M'ranna ma Mir.' Her voice was as clear and full as her light, and Àna found herself transfixed by M'nor's words and melody. She drifted closer and closer. As she did, she grew sadder and sadder. For M'nor's voice reminded her of her own voice and reminded her, too, of all the joy that song had once brought her. It reminded her, as well, of all the sorrow brought on by her silence.

"'Will you not sing with me, young Àna?' M'nor asked.

"Àna looked around fearfully. Her father did not approve of the moon. 'Steals all our light,' he muttered whenever it was full. If he saw her talking to M'nor, he would be furious. If he heard her singing with M'nor… She couldn't imagine what he would do.

"'Please?' M'nor begged. 'It gets so lonely singing alone. I could teach you my song…'

"Àna thought she might like that, even as she knew shouldn't.

"'Mir M'nor m'ranna,' the moon sang. 'M'ranna ma Mir.'

"'No,' Àna whispered. She looked away. 'I can't.'

"M'nor laughed. 'Of course not. How silly of me. You must teach me yours.'

"'Mine? I have no song.'

"'Of course you do. Are you not Àna?'

"'Y-yes.'

"'Then you must know what Àna means, little one.'

"'Means? It's a name. It means nothing.'

"'Is that what that ridiculous star told you?'

"Àna glared at M'nor. 'He is my father. It's not right that you speak of him that way.'

"'Is it right that he stop the Star Chantress from living her destiny? From singing her destiny?'

"Àna was confused. Chantress? Destiny? 'What do you mean? What has my father to do with any of this?'

"'Your father has stopped you from singing the song that will arrange all the stars in patterns and help bring Elohia to the land.'

"Àna was torn. In some deep place in her star heart, she knew M'nor to be right. She knew, too, that she had always known it. Yet her father…her mother…

"'It is simple, Star Chantress: Your light is nearly gone. Only song can bring it back. Your song. If you do not sing it, you will die. Perhaps you believe that the death of a single star does not matter. You will tell me that stars die every day, just as new ones are born every day. You will tell me that stars roam the heavens freely and will ask me why clustering together into patterns should matter. You will ask and tell me these things and I will tell you that you must know the answer for yourself and that you can only know that answer once you allow the Star Chantress you are to live through you, once you allow the Star Chant you already are to sing through you…once you surrender to your destiny.'

"Alarmed by all M'nor had said, Àna fled. Yet each night she returned, drawn by M'nor's haunting song. Each night, she expected M'nor to repeat her appeal. But M'nor never spoke of it until one night many moons later when, softly and hesitantly, Àna joined in M'nor's song.

"'Mir M'nor m'ranna. M'ranna ma Mir.'

"Àna's voice stunned even M'nor with its incandescence.

"'Mir M'nor m'ranna. M'ranna ma Mir.'

"The more she sang, the more confidence Àna gained. The more confidence she gained, the louder she sang. The louder she sang, the more luminous she grew. When Àna had regained her childlike glow, M'nor stopped singing.

"Barely aware of M'nor's silence, Àna continued.

"'Mir M'nor m'ranna. M'ranna ma Mir.'

"'Mir M'nor M'ranna. M'ranna ma Mir.'

"'Well done, Àna,' M'nor interrupted. 'You have learned my song, and you have learned it well. Now you must teach me yours. You will tell me you do not know it. You do. It lies in your star-heart. In the Heart of the Star.'

"'You are wrong,' Àna countered, even though she knew the moon was right. 'I have no song of my own,' she added, even though she knew she was wrong. With those words, her glow paled and her joy with it. 'My father…' She could not continue.

"'Your father will come to accept the new way,' M'nor said.

"'He will not,' Àna said sadly.

"'Then he will die,' M'nor said simply.

"'Then he will die.' Àna recalled all the joys she had experienced while singing and all the pain brought on by the silence her father had imposed. 'Then he will die,' she repeated aloud, 'if he must. If that is his choice.' She closed her eyes to the skies — to her star friends and family and to her moon friend. She closed her eyes to the skies and opened them to her heart.

"'Yes,' she heard M'nor say, but it was faint, overpowered as it was by the song that rose within her.

"She sang, softly at first.

"*Alla ka tchù, tia à.*

"She sang again, more surely.

"*Alla ka tchù, tia à.*

"This time, her voice spanned the heavens.

"*Alla ka tchù, tia à.*

"When she opened her eyes, M'nor was shedding tears of joy and all the stars had begun clustering themselves into patterns that Àna knew in her heart, even though she had never seen them. All stars but one. For even as Àna sang, no stars joined her. Instead, points of light formed from within her, creating the constellation of a radiant woman, with the original Àna as her heart.

"As Àna continued to sing, now accompanied by M'nor and all the stars, this new constellation drifted earthward, until it landed in the garden paradise that Kumba had prepared for her, into the Pergosà. From that moment forth, she held the constellations in place with her Star Chant as Reesa Kam'ana, the Star Chantress.

"*Alla ka tchù, tia à.*

"*Alla ka tchù, tia à.*

"*Alla ka tchù, tia à.*"

I opened my eyes, still singing the Star Chant. Mariah joined in. The silver and gold inlay on the marble floor glowed, more brightly the louder and fuller we sang. Then, in the center of the crystal circle, a single, dazzling eight-pointed star carved itself into the green marble. We stepped onto it, still singing.

Alla ka tchù, tia à

Alla ka tchù, tia à

Alla ka tchù, tia à

The star sang with us, glowing brighter and brighter, until we could see nothing but it and each other...until, in a blazing flash, its light shattered into millions of mini-stars that arced colorfully around us then extinguished. When the fireworks were done, the castle doorway was open. No guards blocked our way.

<h1 style="text-align:center">thirty-eight</h1>

Absolute stillness. Our heels on the stone-slab steps registered no sound. No noise of any sort reached us from elsewhere in the castle. Even our breath and heartbeats seemed muted as we climbed. So when the door we had passed through swung shut with a subtle click, it was as though a clap of thunder had exploded. We jumped, grabbed on to each other and then laughed nervously when we realized what had happened.

The broad, curving staircase rose up a windowless tower through many turns of the spiral until it reached an intricate wrought-iron gate decorated with two star-bearing trees. Its dragon latch yielded easily and we stepped through into a long, broad gallery rich with color and luxe. Massive candlelit chandeliers of glittering crystal hung from a heavily gilded ceiling. A thick carpet, meadow-green and bordered with realistic berry bushes, ran the length of the passage. Bright, ornately framed oil paintings depicting lush orchard and garden scenes covered its gold-inlaid ebony walls, separated at regular intervals by fussily carved tables of white kama wood inlaid with elaborate patterns, also of ebony. Translucent stone bowls overflowing with ripe, aromatic fruits sat invitingly atop the tables.

"We mustn't," I said as Mariah reached for a cluster of thomé.

"I'm hungry."

"I know. Me too. But we can't."

Mariah sighed. "I know."

When had we eaten last? Days ago, it seemed. The farther we walked, the harder it became to tear my eyes from the fruit bowls and to ignore their enticing perfume. When, with hands in pockets and eyes focused on the floor in front of us, I thought we had conquered temptation, the paintings shimmered to life. Condensation beaded on colorful fruits that hung plumply from swaying tree limbs. Birds hopped from branch to branch. The paintings' sun-warmed air felt so moist and languid that light perspiration beaded on the back of my neck. Each scene looked authentic enough that I was certain that we could have stepped into it had we tried. What helped hold us back was the silence. Despite the movement, not a sound emerged from those picture-lands. No birds sang. No leaves rustled. It was real yet not. Enticing yet eerie. It was S'kryssna S'kyaga's lifeless imitation of the Pergosà.

As we continued forward, doors replaced tables between the paintings. Tall as the artwork, each was a single plank of heavy, dark wood punched through near the top with a thin strip of iron bars. All were locked.

Before long, a low, moaning sound leached into the silence from behind the doors. Another. Then another. Words too…

"Help me…"

"Save me…"

"Free me…"

As the cries intensified, filthy arms, cut and bruised, some missing fingers, strained toward us through the doors' barred openings. Tried to touch us. To stop us.

"Help me…"

"Save me…"

"Free me…"

"Fayr'Owyn…"

I stopped, trying to see who knew me by that name. But I could see no faces through the shadowy grates. Only arms, hands, fingers.

Mariah gasped. "Uncle?"

"Mariah. You've come. Thank Prithi."

She shook free of my hand and ran toward an arm that bore a circled-star tattoo.

"Is that really you, Uncle?"

"Help me…"

Was this S'kryssna S'kyaga's dungeon?

We have to free these prisoners. All of them. The Grandmother too. She must be here. Will I know her without Tom Dirqs?

"How do we release you, Micah M'renna?" I asked.

"Fayr'Owyn?" Two eyes peered longingly down at me.

"Fayr'Owyn," the other prisoners echoed loudly, all competing for my attention. Arms waved more desperately. Voices echoed against the walls. My head throbbed.

"Get one of the tables," Micah M'renna shouted above the clamor. "Have Mariah climb up. As soon as she touches my hand, I'll be free. Thank Prithi, I'll be free."

The tumult was unbearable. Men bellowing. Micah M'renna hollering to be heard. Mariah calling to her uncle as she dragged a table across the carpet toward him.

"*Stop*," I hollered. No one heard me. The commotion only grew louder, more distressed.

"Help me…"

"Save me…"

"Free me…"

"Fayr'Owyn…"

I clapped my hands to my ears. The din barely dulled. I had to think. Something was not right. Not about Micah M'renna, not about any of this.

"…the dungeons," Mariah shouted.

The baleyas had said we would end up not far from the Castle Do'am dungeon. Was this it? Could our next step to success be as simple as touching Micah M'renna's hand? *Was* it Micah M'renna's hand. Mariah seemed so certain. Could she be wrong?

Alla ka tchù, tia à

The Star Chant sang softly inside me.

Alla ka tchù, tia à

I repeated it aloud once, then twice more, louder each time, with my palm against the center of my chest. What I saw next was difficult for my mind to accept. The scene didn't change, but it was as though someone had dropped a gauze curtain between it and me. The sound, too, remained — muffled. Mariah was half behind the gauze and half with me, pushing the table into place in front of Micah M'renna's door.

Alla ka tchù, tia—

It wasn't real. Like the paintings, it was an illusion. However, also like the paintings, it felt absolutely real. I tugged on Mariah's arm, trying to pull her back to my side of the curtain. Then my eye caught another hand gesturing from the next door. A young hand. Ben's.

"Ben," I sobbed and lurched toward him.

Alla ka tchù, tia à

He is not real. None of this is real.

"It's so real" I cried in silent reply.

My heart was torn — half pulling me toward Ben, the other half knowing that nothing I was seeing was real and that the only safety lay in grabbing on to Mariah and racing as fast and far from this scene as I could.

But Ben…

"I love you, Ben," I whispered. I swallowed hard, seized Mariah's hand and pulled her behind me. "It's not real," I shouted as she struggled against me.

She broke free and started back. I caught on to her tunic and wrenched her toward me with all my strength. The gauzy effect thickened. The gallery scene behind it stilled to silence and dimmed, nearly disappearing into the shadows. Only Mariah and I remained, in a grotto-like space barely lit by a single wall-mounted torch that flickered, guttered and smoked.

Sobbing, Mariah kicked and scratched me.

"How could you?" she wailed. "How could you leave him there?"

"Alla ka tchù, tia à. Say it with me, Mariah."

She shook her head stubbornly.

"He wasn't real. None of it was. Like the pictures. Alla ka tchù, tia à. Say it and you will see what's real."

"I don't want to say it. I don't want to see what's real. I want my uncle. I want Micah M'renna." She collapsed in a teary heap. "I want to go home."

I crouched next to her. "This is the way home. The only way. Alla ka tchù, tia à."

She hiccuped and nodded. "I know. I knew it back there. But I wanted to believe. So badly I wanted to believe."

Rest, I thought. We need to rest. I doubted that this was a safe place. Still, it had to be safer than where we had just been. Besides, I could see no immediate way out.

"Try to sleep," I said. "I'll keep watch."

Mariah slept long and deeply, and the time passed slowly. As much as I wanted to sleep too, I knew it wouldn't be wise. I needed time to think. We had made it through the Coil, which was good. We had lost Tom Dirqs, which was not. More of S'kryssna S'kyaga's cunning and Castle Do'am's cruelties loomed ahead. Ahead, too, were Reesa Kam'ana and the end of our StarQuest. It would end, one way or the other. Success seemed so unlikely, yet I didn't dare view it as impossible. Too much depended on it. My future depended on it, including those parts of my future that, in a bizarre twist of time, I had already lived. Ben's future too. His very existence. Bards, storytelling, Castle Rose — their fate all lay in my hands, hands that did not feel capable enough to hold it.

"It is not your hands that must hold it, my dear. Not your thoughts either." Àna glittered twinklingly into view. Had I fallen asleep? Was I dreaming her? I looked around. Àna's presence was the only thing around me that had changed. The torch flame still guttered. S'kryssna S'kyaga's Pergosà gallery was still etched into the deep shadows beyond the grotto. Mariah still slept, her even breath calming me.

Àna floated toward me, her luminescence draining away some of the castle's menace. She touched one hand to my forehead, the other to my heart. My mind stilled and my heart opened. "Yes," she said. "Your heart."

She sat next to me and passed her hand over the damp stone floor. Pale yellow thread unreeled from her palm and wove itself into a simple cloth that fluttered to the ground. She passed her hand over the cloth and a strand of silver formed into a star that wove itself into the cloth. From the star emerged two bowls of steaming broth, a large heel of bread and chunks of assorted cheeses. I tore into the food, saving half for Mariah.

"You cannot win with your mind," Àna said as I ate. "S'kryssna S'kyaga's is not only sharper than yours, but more guileful. If you rely on what you think will ensure your success, your StarQuest will be over in a trice. S'kryssna S'kyaga knows this and will do all she can to cast your heart in the same stony mold as hers. Listen to your heart, Fayr'Owyn. Listen to yours, and to Mariah's as well. Listen, too, to S'kryssna S'kyaga's. She can no longer hear it but, with Astel Lev's help, you can. Once you do, all you need to know shall be known."

She began to fade. "I cannot stay much longer here, or I shall die. Castle Do'am weighs too heavily on me. Not its past as the Pergosà. Not its future as…" She shook her head, smoothed her robe and stood. "You have one question. Ask it. Then leave you I must. The weight is more than I can bear."

I had so many questions. Questions about Tom Dirqs. Questions about how to get into the castle, about how to find the dungeons and release the prisoners, about how to defeat S'kryssna S'kyaga and restore Reesa Kam'ana. Too many questions, as I had been often told. Yet one haunted me more deeply than any of the others.

"Will I see Ben again?"

"What does your heart tell you?"

I closed my eyes and let my awareness drop to that place where the Heart of the Star and mine were one.

Ben's infant eyes stare at me with an intensity that is hard to meet. I cannot avert my eyes, for this is the first time I see him, as the midwife holds him up then hands him to me.

I'm spent. I have been screaming and pushing, it seems, all my life. Screaming against a pain far deeper than any I have known. Pushing harder than any other labor I have known.

I cradle the child that named himself Ben even before he was born. His stare pierces through all I have ever thought I knew to the place of all I truly know. To my heart. He blinks once, then his eyelids flitter shut. He, too, has worked hard. My eyes close as well.

Together, we sleep. Together, we dream. Of a time when he is gone and a time when he returns. Of a time when I am gone and a time when I return. Times of heartbreaking sorrow. Times of profound joy. And, always, times of love.

My eyelids quiver open. My arms are empty. Àna is gone.

thirty-nine

Although I could see a faint, sketchy outline of S'kryssna S'kyaga's gallery, I couldn't pierce the grotto's shadows to return to it. The grotto's walls didn't look solid, but they were. It wasn't that I desired to return to the gallery, but I saw no other way to reach the real Micah M'renna, the real Ben and Reesa Kam'ana. As Mariah ate, I circled the grotto again and again, trailing my hand along its greasy walls, searching for any kind of clue — an odd marking, an unusual dry spot, a peculiar chink. Nothing. When I was done, I dropped to my knees and did a similar survey of the floor. Again, nothing. I looked up. The torch cast too dim a light to see the ceiling, if there even was one.

The torch? I loosed it from its bracket and examined it. No Tashek. No No'An'O. Nothing unusual. Discouraged, I replaced it, sank to the ground next to Mariah and ripped a hunk of bread from the loaf.

Àna's cloth. There was something about the cloth. About the star she had woven into it. I pushed the remaining food onto floor and scrutinized both the star and its weave. Again, nothing unusual.

"Wait," Mariah said. She pulled me onto the cloth, onto the silver star. "Say it," she said.

"What?"

"You know what." She touched the center of my chest.

I took Mariah's hand and held my other hand to my heart. "Say it with me. Sing it with me."

Alla ka tchù, tia à

The star expanded underneath us, filling the grotto space.

Alla ka tchù, tia à

Slowly, the star began to rotate.

Alla ka tchù, tia à

Gaining speed, the star spun up and through us, taking the grotto's walls with it.

Alla ka tchù, tia à

We stood once more in S'kryssna's S'kyaga's gallery.

The prisoners were gone. The doors were still locked. The paintings were just as they had been: motionless-once-again views of a hyperreal but illusory Pergosà. Or were they? As we walked past one after the next after the next, the pastoral scenes jumbled, kaleidoscope-like. When they settled, the pretend-Pergosàs were gone. In their place hung torture scenes so grisly, so eerily real, that we could almost smell the blood, sweat and terror depicted in them, could almost hear the wrenching screams as limbs stretched and bones snapped.

My stomach heaved. Yet grimly fascinated, I could not look away. Instead, I gaped at one painting then the next, sickening at the sadistic imagination S'kryssna S'kyaga must possess to have commissioned these grotesque scenes. In one, a young woman hung from a stone wall from her heels, her intestines trailing out of a slashed belly. A guardsman stood next to her with a bloody scimitar. She was still alive. In another, a guardsman beat an elderly man with a mace. In a third, a boy and girl lashed together to an iron post writhed as a guardsman poked at them with flaming torches. In a fourth, a guardsman amputated a young man's hands; his face was barely recognizable pulp. Mariah dropped to her knees and vomited. Holding her, bile rising to my throat, I was sure I would be next.

A pair of sparkling silver slippers appeared next to Mariah's vomit. A fitted sequined gown rose up from the slippers. S'kryssna S'kyaga, once again arrestingly beautiful, towered over us. I started to pull Mariah to her feet. S'kryssna S'kyaga kicked us back down.

"You have made a mess in my playroom," she purred. "Hadn't you better clean it up? Yes, I think you must. Absolutely." She pointed a slender, manicured finger at the floor. "Ka-hass," she hissed. The puddle of vomit rose and poured itself into Mariah's mouth. Choking, she tried to spit it back out. "Ka-hass," S'kryssna S'kyaga repeated. The vomit forced its way down Mariah's throat.

"You will not mess up my playroom." She wiped her hands distastefully on a cloth that materialized for that purpose then dissolved. S'kryssna S'kyaga still loomed above us. "You will not upset my plans." She gestured to four of the nearest paintings. Its guardsmen came to life, stepped out of their still inert images and pressed toward us.

I rose and pulled Mariah close. "You cannot harm either of us as long as I carry the Heart of the Star," I announced, with more courage than I felt.

"Harm you?" S'kryssna S'kyaga smiled sweetly. "Why would I want to harm you?" She glared at a guardsman. "Take them," she barked.

"You can't," I said. I closed my eyes and connected with the Heart of the Star. Warmth rose up and filled me. I squeezed my eyes tighter. The warmth turned to light that expanded beyond my body to enclose Mariah's. When I opened my eyes, Mariah was clinging to me and weeping, two guardsmen stared at us impotently. Their colleagues lay unconscious on the floor. S'kryssna S'kyaga's eyes flamed.

"She can't hurt us," I whispered to Mariah.

"No?" S'kryssna S'kyaga shrieked. As we watched in horror, her head sunk into her shoulders and each of the loose silver threads of her robe lengthened and thickened into silver-scaled snakes with trident tongues that snapped angrily at us.

Mariah screamed.

All that remained of S'kryssna S'kyaga was a knot of snaky tendrils. They circled writhingly around us, enclosing us in a slimy, sibilating mass. But they could not touch us, which angered them even more. Their bloodshot eyes flared furiously. Their black tongues darted venomously. Mariah clung to me. We trembled, making ourselves as tiny as we could.

"Push back," a voice from within me whispered. "You are the Fayr'Owyn. Push back."

Tentatively, I raised my free hand and pushed it out toward the snakes. They hesitated, then backed away, hissing with rage. They pressed so close together that nearly all light from the gallery was gone. Only the light from the Heart of the Star remained, as unyielding as if it were solid.

I extended my arm fully, palm outward. "Astel Lev," I said. The light brightened around us, gaining a pinkish hue that caused the snakes to recoil in confusion. "Astel Lev," I repeated. The snakes shriveled and receded back into S'kryssna S'kyaga's robe. A moment later, her head reappeared.

"Very well," she said icily. "I concede your power. If you are wise you will also concede mine." She nodded at each of the four guardsmen. As one, they melted back into their paintings. Then she assessed me thoughtfully. "Perhaps I cannot detain you. Not yet. But nor can you stop me." She stepped as near to us as Astel Lev's light would allow. "I *will* have the Heart of the Star. Count on it."

That last word carried the force of a whip-crack. With it, the candles guttered and flared and one of the doors between the paintings flung open. She swept through it and was gone.

*   *   *

The gallery seemed never to end. Neither did its horrors. Still shaking, we couldn't help but stare at painting after painting after painting, each more grotesque than the last. The farther we walked, the longer the corridor seemed to extend and the newer the paintings seemed to be, some still carrying the scent of fresh oils that mingled sickeningly with the smell of blood.

"What did she mean by 'playroom?'" Mariah asked.

I shook my head. I did not want to know.

Mariah gasped loudly and clutched my arm. She pointed to two adjacent paintings and vomited again. Tom Dirqs was in one, Micah M'renna in the next. Stripped naked, their bodies covered with lacerations and pus-oozing welts, they were upside-down, lashed to spiked wooden wheels. Tom Dirqs's face was distorted, his eyes screwed shut and his mouth distended into a silent shriek. Micah M'renna was missing a thumb and part of an ear. Dried blood matted his hair and chest. The longer I stared at the Tom Dirqs painting, the more it came to life. The wheel turned. Tom Dirqs screamed. Guardsmen laughed. S'kryssna S'kyaga appeared, touched the wet blood on Tom Dirqs's battered face then sucked her finger and smiled. She giggled. Her giggles became cackles. The cackles screeched louder and louder. Like a mask, her beauty fractured and fell away, shattering on the stone floor. What was left was too horrible to describe. What was left was me, staring out from the picture at the Q'nta in the corridor.

This time, I vomited too and collapsed to the ground next to Mariah.

The Heart of the Star

forty

We staggered to the end of the gallery and out onto a V-shaped terrace, the bottommost of a series of triangular terraces that stepped up the jagged mountainside toward the looming bulk of Castle Do'am. I recognized it as the snake-balustraded terrace of my vision, and it chilled me to realize that if the terrace was real, so must my vision have been. If my vision was real, then Ben had to be here in the castle. Somewhere. Alive or dead.

I would find him. Somehow.

As though carved from the mountain itself, the castle's grimy gray stone merged into the perpetual gloom of a threatening sky. In those distant heights, kep'chas circled the castle's stiletto turrets, occasionally diving down toward the upper terraces before swooping back up again. There was no visible way off this terrace, save scaling the sheer rock face…or returning to the picture gallery. An icy wind whipped at us, whining angrily. We shivered, unable to move forward, reluctant to go back.

I started toward the far edge of the terrace, as far from the gallery door as possible, but stopped twenty paces away. The snakes that coiled around the balustrade were harmless stone ornaments without S'kryssna S'kyaga's sorcery. Yet I couldn't shake the image of them having come to life to threaten my son. I kept my distance.

A thorag spotted us and aimed its kep'cha downward. I pulled Mariah to the pavement with me. The stone was cold and damp against my face. I closed my eyes and tried to see the Heart of the Star. All I could see was Tom Dirqs's pulpy face. Seconds before crashing into us, the kep'cha's steely-eyed thorag steered it back up and into the clouds.

"Back there in the gallery," I shouted over the wind, "that was the real dungeon."

"What do you mean?"

"The paintings. They aren't paintings at all. What's in the pictures…
It's real."

Mariah turned white.

"Then…"

I nodded.

From some hidden depth of strength, her face set in determination,
she turned back toward the door.

"I know," I said. "But how? How do we unlock the enchantment?"
Despair washed over me. Perhaps S'kryssna S'kyaga could not harm
us directly. All that spelled was stalemate. That would not free any
prisoners or save Reesa Kam'ana or get me home. Or help me find
Ben.

Mariah touched the center of my chest. "It's all there. How we free
Micah M'renna, Tom Dirqs and the others. How we get up into the
castle. How we do it all." She put her arm around me. "How you find
Ben." She marched me back toward the gallery door. The dungeon
door. Once there, she forced me to look into her eyes. "I don't care
what you saw in that painting. You're not S'kryssna S'kyaga. You're
not the thorag that killed your friends. You are Q'nta Fayr'Owyn,
Elderbard of Q'ntana, keeper of Astel Lev. Whatever it is, you can do
it. Not by yourself. Not even with my help. But because you hold the
Heart of the Star. Because it's part of *your* heart now."

I knew she was right. Yet I felt none of those things. I felt only
impotence…and shame for that impotence.

"Do it for Ben," she whispered.

"That's not fair."

"If this was about fair, we wouldn't be here. You wouldn't have lost
Ben and Akila. There would be no S'kryssna S'kyaga and no Bo'Rá K'n.
I would still be living with Micah M'renna. No," she added softly. "I
would still be living with my brother and my parents."

I looked up. A formation of kep'chas hovered menacingly overhead
then dropped toward us in deliberate descent.

"That's what happens when you lose heart," Mariah said. She
dragged me inside — away from squalling winds and screeching
kep'chas, back into the hall of horrors.

How could I not feel powerless next to this? Still, I knew Mariah
was right. Somehow, I had to get past that. Somehow, I had to find my
heart again.

I walked up to the Tom Dirqs picture. The scene had grown more horrific, something I hadn't believed possible. Tom Dirqs had been removed from the wheel. Now, he hung upside-down as S'kryssna S'kyaga herself turned the crank that slowly lowered him toward a vat of bubbling viscosity. Tom Dirqs screamed in terror. I covered my ears and closed my eyes.

Mariah pried my hands free and touched my eyelids. "You have to look. We both do. If we don't, we *will* become S'kryssna S'kyaga."

I opened my eyes. S'kryssna S'kyaga was now the torture master in all the paintings. From each one, she grinned malevolently at me.

"The Heart of the Star," I heard, whether from Mariah or somewhere else. "Listen to the Heart of the Star." My gaze softened.

I am S'kryssna S'kyaga. Some part of me must be…just as some part of me must be the thorag.

I was horror-struck, then sickened — with myself. I wanted to flee. I knew I couldn't. S'kryssna S'kyaga cackled.

Louder. Louder. Louder.

All the S'kryssna S'kyagas from all the paintings hooted and sniggered in a cacophony of derision.

"The Heart of the Star," I heard again. Somehow, I pushed the laughter aside and listened. Somehow, I pushed the laughter aside and loved.

My heart opened. It was as though a giant drawbridge had dropped and a heavy portcullis had been raised. Emotion flooded through me. Tears streamed down my face. Even though I knew Mariah was there, I was barely aware of her presence. My only awareness was of all the S'kryssna S'kyagas as, once again, their facades cracked.

"I love you," I whispered to the scores of Q'ntas that emerged. "I love you," I repeated, louder, more certain. "I love you," I said once more.

"Say it with me," I urged Mariah, suddenly aware of the look of revulsion on her face — directed not toward the paintings but toward me.

"How can you?" she cried, her earlier resolve gone. "What are you saying?"

"You have to."

This time it was Mariah who tried to shut out what she saw and I who forced her to look.

"I can't," she sobbed. "It's not me up there."

"It is," I countered. "You must."

She pointed at the painting next to Tom Dirqs's. "Micah M'renna," she whispered hoarsely. "Me."

I put my arm around her. "I know. That's why you have to do it. Can you?"

Mariah shook then nodded her head numbly.

I looked back up at the paintings with a mix of disgust and defiance.

"I love you," I called out. This time I was aware of Mariah saying it with me.

Colors swirled around me: the pinks of earlier, now streaked with green, blue and ivory. The colors brightened, grew more vibrant. The floor shook. A gust of wind blew the gallery door open and extinguished the chandelier candles.

The walls shuddered. Another gust of wind. One painting tumbled from the wall and smashed to the floor. A second. Two more. Four more. Six more.

The wind eddied the swirling colors into a kaleidoscope of shapes and shards that knifed through the gallery, shredding everything they touched. More paintings fell as the walls supporting them collapsed into clouds of debris.

One final gust swept everything through the gallery…until there was no gallery. Until there was only me, Mariah and an astonished Tom Dirqs and Micah M'renna, standing on an empty terrace.

Micah M'renna dropped to his knees and bowed his head. "I knew you would come, Fayr'Owyn. That's all that kept me alive…knowing you would come." He looked up at me, his body broken and brittle, his eyes wet and bright. "I'm ready to serve you. Tell me how."

My heart broke. This once-solid man could barely keep his balance. He swayed as the wind thrust itself angrily at him, swallowing his words. His eyes were hollow. His face was drawn. He trembled with palsy.

"I wish we could have gotten here sooner," I said. "I wish—"

"I'm alive, Fayr'Owyn. Mariah is alive. That's enough. More than enough."

Mariah helped him to his feet and threw her arms around him.

Tom Dirqs had stood shyly to the side. Now he limped toward me. "I let you down, Q'nta. Fayr'Owyn. I let myself be frightened and now we be trapped. Again. Only now you be stuck with two useless burdens instead of two men who could be a-helping you with your StarQuest."

Even as I opened my arms to him, I worried that he was right. I was grateful he and Micah M'renna had been spared. Still, I wondered why they had not gone where the other prisoners had — wherever that was. For Mariah's sake, it was good her uncle was here. Yet he and Tom Dirqs were so crippled they could barely move, let alone keep up with whatever next awaited us. I shrugged. It wasn't up to me. None of it was. It was up to Astel Lev, the Heart of the Star. I was merely a vessel, a vehicle.

Not true. You are the Fayr'Owyn. I can be nothing without you. And you cannot awaken to your destiny without me. Now is the time.

The voice came from deep within my chest and echoed loudly throughout my body, so loudly I was sure everyone else had heard it. If they had, it paled in immediacy next to the four bellowing kep'chas that hovered directly overhead. Balanced precariously on each was the corner post of a large iron cage the size and shape of the terrace. On the next gust, the kep'chas pulled away. The cage plummeted toward us.

Once it landed, there would be no escape. With sheer cliff walls above and below the terrace, there was no way to avoid being caged.

Astel Lev spoke again: *You are the Fayr'Owyn. You cannot awaken to your destiny without me. Now is the time.*

Now.

Could I stop the cage? Did I truly possess that kind of power? Was that part of my destiny as the Fayr'Owyn?

An open heart knows no limits.

An open heart knows no limits. Carrying Astel Lev next to mine couldn't hurt either. With one on hand on my heart and the other palm facing up toward falling the cage, I repeated the Star Chant.

Alla ka tchù, tia à

Nothing happened.

Alla ka tchù, tia à

Still nothing. The grate was nearly on top of us.

Micah M'renna rose painfully, placed both his hands on my heart and sang out with me.

Alla ka tchù, tia à

The grate's fall slowed, faltered.

Mariah and Tom Dirqs placed their hands on top of Micah M'renna's. We chanted together.

Alla ka tchù, tia à

Alla ka tchù, tia à
Alla ka tchù, tia à

The wind stopped. Sunlight thrust through the clouds. A single ray hit the cage. It shattered. The ray pushed earthward and enfolded all of us. In one instant, Micah M'renna and Tom Dirqs were healed of their wounds. In the next, a crystalline staircase formed in the center of the beam. Castle Do'am and the Do'am Mountains faded behind its brightness. All we saw were glittering steps leading so far up into the sky that they disappeared in the sun's glare. Tom Dirqs and Micah M'renna raced up the staircase, amazed at the restoration of their physical prowess. Mariah and I followed, too stunned by the turn of events to speak.

"Oh, my stars." Micah M'renna stopped partway and pointed to the heavens.

Tom Dirqs jumped up and down excitedly. "The stars," he shouted. "The stars!"

When we caught up with them, we gasped with wonder. The staircase ended at the Star Rock, only now it was studded with pale starlike lights. At four of its eight points stood Toshar, Eulisha, Àna and Ben. The Grandmother stood on the raised platform at its center. Above them, the sky was night-black.

Ben! He saw me and beamed a smile brighter than that of any single sun. In a flash, I saw a vision of him being pulled from his cell and up to the Star Rock on the same ray of light that had created our crystal stairway. My heart broke as I knew for certain that all I had seen of him on the Castle Do'am terrace and in its dungeon must have been true. At the same time, I reveled in his release. Whatever had happened to him at S'kryssna S'kyaga's hands, he now looked whole, fit and happy. I longed to shout his name, to run to him.

It wasn't time.

As though pulled by some invisible force, Mariah and her uncle moved to fill two of the empty points, on either side of Toshar. Tom Dirqs, his eyes focused longingly on the Grandmother, drifted to another of the points, next to Àna. There was one point left, between Eulisha and Ben. If I could have run to it, I would have. I knew it wasn't mine. The center point was, where the Grandmother stood. I didn't know what to do. I didn't see how I could take her place. It didn't feel right.

No one spoke. They all watched me, except for the Grandmother, whose gaze was fixed on the empty sky. She nodded at something unseen by the rest of us, turned slowly to me and smiled warmly. I took a step toward her and her smile broadened. When I reached her, she took my hand in hers, as twig-like as Tom Dirqs's

The Grandmother was short, shorter than her grandson with a face so ghostly white she barely looked alive. Yet her dark eyes twinkled vibrantly. She wore a robe as white as her skin, embroidered with gold and silver stars and a shiny black pendant with a silver star embedded in its center.

"Welcome, Fayr'Owyn. We have storied long years for this moment."

She stepped away to the final empty star point. As I took her place, the Star Rock began to rotate around me. As it spun more quickly, it threw the star-lights on its surface up into the sky, where they twinkled uncertainly in patternless clumps.

"You are the Fayr'Owyn," they sang. "Now is the time."

The time for what? I had yet to defeat S'kryssna S'kyaga or rescue Reesa Kam'ana. I didn't even know where they were — or where Castle Do'am was — in relation to this place. Then, all at once, I did know.

I raised my arms to the stars and sang

Alla ka tchù, tia à

The Star Rock stilled.

Alla ka tchù, tia à

Now, I spun. Faster and faster. Then faster still, until everything around me blurred then vanished. My dizziness was short-lived. As I spun I felt more sure of myself, my power and my destiny than at any time since waking up in the Co'an house all those lifetimes ago.

Alla ka tchù, tia à

The spinning slowed then stopped. The Star Rock was gone, along with everyone on it. Instead, I stood behind S'kryssna S'kyaga in Reesa Kam'ana's still-intact cell. S'kryssna S'kyaga turned sharply when she sensed my presence. Her face clouded. Her eyes blazed with hatred and, in a brief flash, fear. Reesa Kam'ana blinked twice and jerked her head to the side. Her wrists were chained to a wooden post set into the mold-streaked floor.

"It's time, S'kryssna S'kyaga," I said, not sure where my words came from.

She glared at me. "It's time to destroy you. Guards!"

The door to the cell clanged open and a dozen guardsmen rushed in. They stopped when they saw me.

"You cannot kill me. You know that." I turned to the guardsman. "Leave us."

"Stay," S'kryssna S'kyaga commanded. "Seize her!"

The guardsmen looked from one to the other uncertainly then pushed one of their number at me. With one hand pressed against the center of my chest, I held my other palm up. The guardsman stopped. I took his hand and touched it to my heart. He dropped to his knees.

"My lady Fayr'Owyn." He bowed his head. "How can I serve you?"

"What is your name, guardsman?"

S'kryssna S'kyaga backed away, pushing one guardsman after another toward us. They rushed at us, only to be blocked by an invisible barrier.

"Cormel, my lady."

I looked into his eyes, which darkened from their bland gray-blue to a deep green.

"Your truth name is Ka-Rey. Rise, Knight Ka-Rey of Astel Lev."

Cormel's eyes watered. He kissed my hand and stood.

"How do I serve you, my lady Fayr'Owyn?"

"By serving not me but the Heart of the Star, which is your heart, Knight Ka-Rey. By opening your heart and doing what needs to be done."

He nodded and moved to block S'kryssna S'kyaga, who had nearly reached the cell door.

"Stand aside," she snarled.

Ka-Rey spread his arms and legs to bar her passage.

"Ka-hass," S'kryssna S'kyaga screeched. Black smoke filled the doorway. When it cleared, Ka-Rey was still there. She waved her arms angrily. The door rattled but held. Ka-Rey still blocked it

"Take him," she ordered those guardsmen still loyal to her.

"No," I said softly.

The guardsmen halted.

"*No?*"

I shook my head and walked toward her. The guardsmen, too stunned to stop me, broke ranks to let me through. "No," I repeated.

"Take her," she shouted. "Or I will turn you all into slime ants and let you feed on each other." She stamped her foot so forcefully that the room quaked. Then she churned her heel into the stone. "That is what I'll do to the last of you."

The guardsmen hesitated. Then the burliest shoved the youngest and slightest at me. I smiled and opened my arms to him. Sobbing, he fell at me.

"I-I'm Gorkat," he whispered. "Please don't hurt me."

"You were Gorkat." I touched his heart. "From this moment forward, you are Ka-Tika, Knight of Astel Lev."

He nodded.

The remaining guards backed away.

"Free Reesa Kam'ana, Knight Ka-Tika."

Ka-Tika looked questioningly at Reesa Kam'ana's shackles.

"Touch each manacle to your heart, Knight. If your heart is pure, the cuffs will dissolve."

"Ka-hass!" S'kryssna S'kyaga roared. But her roar choked off into a cough. She waved her arms again, then again. Each time, her magic weakened yet more. Finally, the cell door ceased its rattling and the only smoke spewed from her mouth, along with a phlegmy, throat-clearing hack. The guardsmen watched their mistress's weakening in wide-eyed confusion. A few came to me to be knighted. The rest pressed their backs tensely against the wall farthest from both S'kryssna S'kyaga and me.

As Ka-Tika freed Reesa Ka'mana, I moved toward S'kryssna S'kyaga.

"It's not over," she hissed.

"I think it is." I opened my arms to her.

"Bo'Rá K'n," she screamed.

"He cannot help you now."

"Bo'Rá K'n," she screamed again.

"He can only destroy you."

I moved toward her, my arms still open.

S'kryssna S'kyaga edged back.

"The Heart of the Star. I'm ready to give it to you. Isn't that what you want?"

"Q'nta! No!" An echo of disembodied voices — Mariah's, Tom Dirqs's and Micah M'renna's — bounced against the stone from the Star Rock, wherever it was.

S'kryssna S'kyaga looked at me strangely. A half-smile played on her lips. "After all this, you're ready to just give it to me." She stepped toward me.

I raised my hand to stop her. "There's one condition."

"Oh? You are in a position to set conditions?"

"I believe so. I'm certain it's a condition you will agree to."

"To possess the Heart of the Star? Why not?"

"Q'nta! No!" My friends were frantic.

"Can't you be stopping her?" Tom Dirqs wailed.

I looked S'kryssna S'kyaga in the eye. "You think I'm naive. You think I don't know you will agree to anything."

"So?"

S'kryssna S'kyaga's voice was stronger, more confident. Her guardsmen crept back toward her.

"You think I don't know that you plan to break whatever promise you make?"

S'kryssna S'kyaga smirked. The cell shook. Her grin widened. "If you know all this, you are naive."

"No. You're the one who is naive."

"Ha! State your condition. Whatever it is, I agree. And once I possess the Heart of the Star, you are dead."

"If you say so."

"I do."

She turned to the guardsmen I had knighted. "You too. Slowly. Horribly. Painfully."

"I die willingly for my lady," Ka-Rey stated.

"I, as well," Ka-Tika added.

The others nodded solemnly.

"Fools," she muttered. "Everyone is happy to die and the Fayr'Owyn too? What could be better. Out with it, Fayr'Owyn. My patience wears thin."

"Here is my condition, which you must agree to when you are in my embrace and Astel Lev is moving from my heart to yours."

"Get on with it."

I gestured for Reesa Kam'ana to join us. "Once the Heart of the Star is in your possession, you must immediately pass it back to Reesa Kam'ana."

S'kryssna S'kyaga gawked at me then burst into gales of laughter and dropped into a mock curtsy. "Yes, my lady. Of course, my lady. Whatever you say, my lady." Her voice hardened. "Get ready," she snapped at the guardsmen. "As soon as the fool embraces me, she will lose her power. Do not wait for my order. Just kill her. Kill everyone except Reesa Kam'ana. Her, I still need." She indicated Ka-Tika and Ka-Rey. "Make theirs painful." The men sneered and laughed cruelly.

Knives unsheathed, guardsmen surrounded me and S'kryssna S'kyaga, and Reesa Kam'ana and Ka-Tika. A third group faced off against Ka-Rey and the other knights.

"Are you ready?" I asked.

"Are you?" S'kryssna S'kyaga retorted.

I opened my arms. "Repeat after me: I, S'kryssna S'kyaga…"

"I, S'kryssna S'kyaga…"

We took one step closer together.

"…do swear in all solemnity that, in the moment our bodies separate, I will return the Heart of the Star…"

Beads of sweat formed on S'kryssna S'kyaga's forehead. Her heart thumped loudly.

"…do swear in all solemnity that, in the moment our bodies separate, I will return the Heart of the Star…"

She stepped into my arms. No one breathed. The guardsmen watched curiously. The knights, soberly. Reesa Kam'ana nodded slightly.

"…to Reesa Kam'ana, its rightful guardian…"

A flash of light exploded from the center of our chests where they touched.

"…to Reesa Kam'ana, its rightful guardian…"

The light swirled around us in a blinding eddy, dissolving the cell's ceiling and walls and letting in the night air.

"…and that I will no longer seek her or it out and will free her to live, in peace, wherever she chooses."

The light fragmented into an infinite array of mini-stars that hovered around and above us.

"…and that I will no longer seek her or it out and will free her to live, in peace, wherever she chooses."

The stars danced and twinkled. I withdrew my arms and stepped back.

S'kryssna S'kyaga dropped her arms and grinned malevolently. In less than a breath, her grin turned to grimace. She clutched at her chest, as though overcome by a terrible pain.

"Seize them," she managed to croak. She pitched forward, grabbing onto a guardsman for support.

Hypnotized by the stars, the guardsmen — including the one whose shoulder she clung to — ignored her.

"I-I," she stammered, trying to get their attention.

S'kryssna S'kyaga's eyes hardened. She staggered toward me. *"You—"*

Her fists clenched and pressed to her chest, she let out a shriek so piercing that the whole castle, what remained of it, shook.

"What. Do. I. Do?" S'kryssna S'kyaga managed to gasp.

"Open your heart," I replied.

"How?" she croaked. Tears streamed down her face.

The Star Rock swooped down from the darkness, an empty space at its center. It hovered overhead, positioned itself, then landed so that Reesa Kam'ana, S'kryssna S'kyaga and I stood at the center opening. Toshar, Mariah, Micah M'renna, Ben, the Grandmother, Eulisha, Àna and Tom Dirqs still stood at the star's eight points. Guardsmen and knights scattered to its outer perimeter to avoid being crushed.

I smiled at Tom Dirqs. He smiled back with the biggest grin I had ever seen. "Tom Dirqs," I asked, "can you open your heart to S'kryssna S'kyaga in spite of what she has done to you and to those you love?"

His smiled dissolved. He struggled for an answer. I knew that he longed to be able to say "yes" and that he also desperately wanted to say "no." He started to speak several times then clamped his mouth shut and looked me pleadingly.

"Mariah?" Her eyes filled with pain. She said nothing.

"Micah M'renna?"

"I want to, Fayr'Owyn, but—"

S'kryssna S'kyaga gasped in pain.

"Grandmother?"

"Where I am, where Toshar and Eulisha are, there is only love. Nothing else."

Tom Dirqs gasped. "You be— You mean you—?"

"Yes, child. I died in a cell much like this one was. I did not die at S'kryssna S'kyaga's hand. Nor was she present. But her hand directed the hand that ended my body's life." She nodded at Ka-Rey. His shoulders drooped. He looked away in shame.

Tom Dirqs wailed mournfully. "No, no and no! I cannot be loving that—that—monster." He struggled to leave his star point. An invisible force held him in place.

"I be killing him," he shouted impotently. "Let me free so I can be avenging the Grandmother. Her too." He pointed a trembling finger at S'kryssna S'kyaga. "Let me at her, Q'nta. Please. Let me at her." He covered his face and sobbed.

"Look at me, Tom Dirqs," I said gently.

He looked up hesitantly.

"All of you."

S'kryssna S'kyaga moaned with pain. It took every ounce of her strength to remain standing.

"You cannot forget what this woman has done. You must not forget it."

S'kryssna S'kyaga tried to look fierce but only whimpered.

"You must see beyond the body that did what it did. You must see past the mind that did what it did. You must see the heart that even now struggles to open." I touched S'kryssna S'kyaga's chest. She winced.

"Only love can restore the Heart of the Star to Reesa Kam'ana. Only love can restore the celestial pattern. Only love can restore the timeline that will free you and M'ranna. Only love can send me and Ben—" I swallowed hard, for I suddenly realized that Ben would not be coming home with me. With great effort, I regained my composure. "Only love can send me back to Q'ntana, which waits for its Elderbard. Only love can birth the Elderbardship that must begin in this time, if there is to be a Q'ntana for me to return to."

I stopped, stunned. Ben, the first Elderbard? My mind tried and failed to grasp how he could be both my son and my ancestor. I could see him struggling with the same incongruity. It was futile to try to extract sense from it. I continued.

"Ben, my son, can you love S'kryssna S'kyaga in spite of what she has done?" I spoke with the strength of an Elderbard even as I listened with the uncertain heart of a mother.

Ben, whose voice I had not heard in so long, smiled. My heart melted. "There is so much I do not understand, will perhaps never understand. I do not understand how I can come from a long line of eloquent, heartful elderbards and, at the same time, be its founder. Still, if I have learned anything from all of you — and from you, too, S'kryssna S'kyaga — it is that I can live with what I don't understand." He paused. "I can love it too." He looked directly at S'kryssna S'kyaga. "And I can love you."

He turned to Tom Dirqs, Mariah and Micah M'renna. "If I am to be your Elderbard, I ask for your love."

They smiled and nodded eagerly.

"That our new partnership be founded in love, I ask that you open your hearts to the one who has hurt you the most. Can you, Tom Dirqs?"

Tom Dirqs looked from Ben to me to S'kryssna S'kyaga.

"I-I—" He fidgeted, chewed his thumb and sighed. "Yes," he said at last. "I can."

S'kryssna S'kyaga clenched her teeth. As pale as she was, she grew paler still.

"Mariah?" Ben asked.

"I promise to try," she whispered.

"It cannot be about trying, Mariah," Ben pressed gently. "Can you do it? Can you do it now?"

Mariah looked from Tom Dirqs to her uncle. "Can you?" she asked.

"I can, child," Micah M'renna replied. "I must. If I can't, if I don't, there is no future. Not for any of us. Can you? Will you?"

Mariah hesitated, then nodded and half-smiled. "Yes."

"Mother?"

I nodded.

"Can you, S'kryssna S'kyaga?" Ben asked. "Can you open your heart to yourself?"

S'kryssna S'kyaga's face contorted. Her eyes narrowed then widened. She looked as though she would faint then righted herself, still clutching at her chest. Her mouth yawned open and a scream even more piercing than the one that had shook her castle erupted into the sky. Her mouth was still wide open when the sound stopped. Finally, she crumpled into Reesa Kam'ana's arms.

No one spoke. No one breathed. Though lit, the stars ceased their twinkling dance. For a moment, it seemed as though nothing was happening. S'kryssna S'kyaga's face was still contorted with pain. Reesa Kam'ana's was still impassive. Then, first one star then another and another spiraled through the two women and across the Star Rock into Àna, who was absorbed into the star stream. The river of stars then swirled back to and through Reesa Kam'ana before exploding out of her in all directions. Twinkling once again, they clustered far above the Star Chantress's head.

When the two women separated, they were both different. S'kryssna S'kyaga's face and eyes had softened, stripped of their cruelty, menace and pain. She stood straight, but humble. A soft halo glowed just above her head. A radiant Reesa Kam'ana smiled broadly and snapped her fingers. The halo sparked into a crown of stars that lowered itself gently onto S'kryssna S'kyaga's head. S'kryssna S'kyaga touched it disbelievingly.

Reesa Kam'ana turned to me. "Fayr'Owyn?"

"Long live, Karenna Kihanna," I shouted. "First queen of Q'ntana!"

"Long live, Karenna Kihanna," Eulisha, Toshar, Ben and the Grandmother shouted back. Tom Dirqs, Mariah and Micah M'renna gaped at me in stunned silence.

"Queen?" S'kryssna S'kyaga stammered. "I cannot. I must not. It's not right. I don't deserve—"

"As crowned by the stars," Reesa Kam'ana replied. "It is they who have chosen their queen. I may be their guardian, but I am also their servant. As are you. We both are, now."

"Karenna Kihanna?"

"Your truth name, Your Majesty," I replied, "as Q'ntana is this land's."

"Named," Toshar interjected with pride, "for Q'nta, the Fayr'Owyn whose StarQuest has now achieved Completion."

It happened in an instant, an instant that seemed to last forever. The stars that had clustered over Reesa Kam'ana's head zoomed dizzyingly in all directions. When the final star stopped, the constellations were once more in place in the sky.

"But they're different!" Micah M'renna exclaimed.

"As they should be," said Reesa Kam'ana. "For so is everything else." She snapped her fingers three more times. On the first snap, the bald, craggy peaks of Castle Do'am softened into the rounded hills of my Q'ntana home and kep'chas were no more. On the second, what remained of Castle Do'am transformed itself into a pristine, pink-stoned castle. On the third, we found ourselves inside the castle, in an Elderbard's turret study: Ben, hunched over his writing table, Queen Karenna Kihanna at his shoulder.

Micah M'renna, Mariah and Tom Dirqs burst into the room. Ben leapt up and embraced them. Karenna Kihanna smiled and withdrew. A moment later, Ben and the others chased laughingly after her.

I say "we," but Toshar, Eulisha, the Grandmother and I weren't really there. Or maybe Ben, Mariah, Micah M'renna and Karenna Kihanna weren't really there. Or maybe I was the only one who was there. For in the next moment, I gazed up from my pages of parchment to realize that my candle had nearly burnt out, my fingers were black with ink and my only company at this late hour were the twinkling stars of a Q'ntana night, grouped in the familiar constellations of my childhood.

The Worlds of The StarQuest

Afflayon (ah-*FLAY*-on) — Desert region of M'ranna

Ageets (ah-*JEETS*) — S'kryssna S'kyaga's reluctant spies

Akila (ah-*KEE*-lah) — Ben's father

Alla ka tchù, tia à (alla ka-*CHEW*, tee-ah *AH*) — Ancient Star Chant

An Kora Mount (ann *KOH*-rah) — Hill outside the Co'an village where the Kora Kì grows

Àna (*AW*-nah) — Embodiment of the Star Chant; a star in one of Q'nta's stories

Astel Elohia (*AA*-stel ell-oh-*HEE*-yah) — The Ring of Unity

Astel Lev (*AA*-stel lev) — The Heart of the Star

Aygra (*AY*-grah) — M'ranna's sun

Baleya (bah-*LEY*-ah) — A type of sea mammal

Bela (*BAY*-lah) — A type of red-fleshed nut

Ben (*BEN*) — Q'nta's son and protagonist of *The SunQuest*

Bili'i (bih-*LEE*-ee) — A type of berry

B'na (bih-*NAH*) — The smaller of Q'ntana's two suns

Bo'Rà K'n (bo-*RAH*-kin) — The dark force at work in M'ranna

Brimiya (*BRIM*-ee-yah) — A stew popular with the Co'ans

Bylta'a (bill-*TAH*) — A tiny furry mammal

Castle Do'am (*DOH*-um) — S'kryssna S'kyaga's home. See also "Do'am"

Co'an (*COE*-ahn) — Village in M'ranna and the people who inhabit it

Co'anra (co-*AWN*-rah) — A Co'an and twin brother to Co'anri

Co'anri (co-*AWN*-ree) — A Co'an and twin sister to Co'anra

Cormal (*COR*-mawl) — One of S'kryssna S'kyaga's guardsmen; see also "Ka-Ray"

Dafna (*DAF*-nah) — Q'nta's mother

Delfian (*DELL*-fee-yun) — Sea creature that lives in the Great Water

Do'am, Do'am Mountains (*DOE*-am) — Region of M'ranna, mountain range in that part of M'ranna

Doat (*DOE*-ut) — Freshwater mammal

Ee'jin (ee-*GIN*) — Regeneration activity practiced by the Co'an people

Elohia (ell-oh-*HEE*-yah) — The unity of all things

Eulisha (you-*LEE*-sha) — Elderbard and Q'nta's great-grandmother

Eyfor (*AYE*-fore) — A young boy in one of Q'nta's visions

Fayr'Owyn (fair-*OH*-winn) — M'ranna's storied savior

Fidrik (*FEE*-drick) — Fynda and Yhoshi's son; Margola's twin brother

Filiamo (feel-ee-*AH*-moh) — A type of sweet food

Flaigen (*FLAY*-ghin) — A type of bird

Fli'aq (*FLEE*-yack) — A Co'an term that encompasses both the physical body and what we might call the aura or energy field; see also "s'ken"

Foraa'a (for-*AH*) — A Co'an broth, generally served after a s'ken

Freya (*FRAY*-ah) — A baleya

Fynda (*FIN*-dah) — One of the four journeyers on The MoonQuest

Fynn'Qya (fin-*KEE*-yah) — A thor'qya and master of Fynn Castle

Gabaya (ga-*BAH*-yah) — Co'an kitchen

Ganda (*GAN*-duh) — Seabird indigenous to M'ranna

Garan (*GA*-ren) — Q'nta's childhood tutor; one of the four journeyers on The MoonQuest

Gita'a (jee-*TAH*) — A three-legged, single-horned mammal

Gorkat (*GOR*-cut) — One of S'kryssna S'kyaga's guardsmen; see also Ka-Tika

Grandmother Dirqs (*DERKS*) — Tom Dirqs's grandmother

Horusha (ho-*ROO*-shah) — Mountain range and maze of tunnels in Q'ntana

Hoss eeyah ka-am seeya na sempah (*HOHSS EE*-yah kah-*AHM SEE*-yah *NAH* sem-*PAH*) — Invocation S'kryssna S'kyaga uses to summon her snakes. See also "ka-hass"

Jyp (*JIP*) — Shrub-like tree

Ka-hass (kah-*HAHSS*) — The word S'kryssna S'kyaga uses to invoke her magic.

Kama (*KAHM*-ah) — A white wood indigenous to the Do'am region of M'ranna

Ka'Ona (kah-*OH*-nah) — Mariah's pet gita'a

Karà Haitu (*KAH*-rah hay-*TOO*) — A enchanted place in M'ranna

Ka-Ray (ka-*RAY*) — Cormal's truth name

Karenna Kihanna (ka-*REN*-nah kee-*HAW*-nah) — Q'ntana's first queen

Ka-Tika (ka-*TEE*-kah) — Gorkat's truth name

Ken, Kenning (*KEN*-ning) — A form of intuitive knowingness

Kep'cha (*KEP*-chah) — Birdlike creature controlled by S'kryssna S'kyaga; see also "thorag"

Kihanna koh-hay (kee-*HA*-nah koh-*HAY*) — Invocation related to the Ring of Unity. See "Astel Elohia" and "Mana kae, ka'ohn"

Kiribà (kee-ree-*BAH*) — Type of fruit with red skin and flesh

Kitikà (kih-tee-*KAH*) — Twelve-legged bug indigenous to M'ranna

K'nrah (kin-*RAH*) — Small animal indigenous to M'ranna and Q'ntana

Ko-hay ah. Amma-ken. Toh-hee annah-hoh (koh-hay *AH*. ahm-mah-*KEN*. *TOH*-hee annah-*HOH*) — Invocation at the Do'am p'rtulle. See also "No'An'O"

Ko'Ba (*KOH*-bah) — Towering rock formation overlooking the Ma

Koka'i (koh-*KYE*-ee) — A type of nut

Ko'lar (*KOH*-lar) — Ancient word for "Elderbard"

Ko'leya (koh-*LAY*-ah) — Ancient word meaning "son of the sun"

Kora Kì (ko-rah *KEE*) — A magical tree that grows down from the sky

Kora-Stone (*KO*-ra) — Power source for a transco'an

Kumba (*KOOM*-bah) — The Great Dragon of Creation

Kyri (*KEE*-ree) — A king of Q'ntana

Leq (*LEK*) — A hired hand on Micah M'renna's farm

Lythe (rhymes with "writhe") — Stringed musical instrument

Ma (*MAW*) — Ocean-like body of water near the Co'an village

Magritta (ma-*GREET*-ah) — Micah M'renna's housekeeper

Ma'ika (ma-*EE*-kah) — Hot drink, often served at breakfast in M'ranna

Mana kae, ka'ohn (*MAH*-na kay, ka-*OWN*) — Invocation related to the Ring of Unity. See "Astel Elohia"

Margola (*MAR*-go-lah) — Fynda and Yhoshi's daughter. Fidrik's twin sister

Mariah (ma-*RYE*-ah) — One of the journeyers on The StarQuest

Maya Ko (maya *KOH*) — A p'rtulle on The StarQuest and The SunQuest

Meya (*MEY*-ah) — A baleya

Micah M'renna (*MIKE*-ah mih-*RENN*-ah) — Mariah's uncle

Mir (*MEER*) — The sea

M'nor (mih-*NOR*) — The moon

M'ranna (mih-*RAH*-nah) — The land where *The StarQuest* takes place

Nayr (*NAIR*) — Ancient, legendary chalice

No'An'O (no-*AWN*-no) — Mistress of the Coil, keeper of the Do'am p'rtulle

O'aka (oh-*AH*-kah) — Fruit-bearing tree indigenous to M'ranna; the fruit of the tree

Oman ki-hanna oma-ay (*OH*-man ki-*HAH*-nah oma-*AY*) — Mariah's invocation

Oreeka (oh-*REE*-kah) — Village near Micah M'renna's farm

Pergosà (pear-go-*SAH*) — Eden-like paradise

Pinna (*PIN*-nah) — Tall tree indigenous to M'ranna

Pohrià (poe-*REE*-yah) — A dim-witted animal

Prakk estafi (*PRAHK* es-*TAH*-fee) — Curse

Pri'Mala (pree-*MAW*-lah) — One of the Stone People, Pri'Malaka's mate

Pri'Malaka (pree-*MAW*-lah-kah) — Chief of the Stone People

Pri'Mikana (pree-mih-*KAW*-nah) — One of the Stone People, daughter of Pri'Mala and Pri'Malaka

Prithi (*PRIH*-thee) — M'ranna's deity

P'rtulle (purr-*TULL*-ah) — A portal

Py'aka (pee-*YA*-ka) — Alcoholic beverage popular in rural M'ranna

Py'kraal (peek-*RAWL*) — Type of fish found in the Ma

Q'nta (kin-*TAH*) — Protagonist of *The StarQuest*

Q'ntana (kin-*TAH*-nah) — The land where *The MoonQuest* and *The SunQuest* take place

Q'ophar (*KOH*-far) — A creature that's half dragon, half human

Reesa Kam'ana (*REE*-sah ka-*MAW*-nah) — The Star Chantress

Ryolan Ò Garan (*RYE*-o-lun oh *GAR*-en) — See "Garan"

S'ken (sih-*KEN*) — Diagnostic technique employed by the Co'an people

S'kryssna S'kyaga (*SKRISS*-nah skee-*YAW*-gah) — An evil sorceress

Sligg (*SLIGG*) — Worm-like creature indigenous to M'ranna

Tante Fynda (*TAWN*-teh *FIN*-da) — Aunt Fynda. See "Fynda"

Tashek (*TAW*-shek) — Shapeshifter that appears as various creatures

The Nayr — See "Nayr"

Thomé (toh-*MAY*) — Type of nut that grows in clusters

Thorag (*THO*-rag) — Flesh-eating drone-pilot of a kep'cha

Thor'qya (thor-*KEE*-yah) — Massive fish-like creature that lives on the sea floor of M'nanna's Great Water

Tikinà (tee-kee-*NAH*) — A type of fruit that resembles a brittle stick, with yellow flesh and crimson seeds

Tikkan (tee-*KAWN*) — Ancient race of "dream-weavers"

Tom Dirqs (tom *DERKS*) — One of the journeyers on The StarQuest

Toshar (*TOW*-shar) — Q'nta's father and protagonist of *The MoonQuest*

Transco'an (trans-*COH*-un) — A device that reproduces something of the power and energy of the Heart of the Star. See also "kora stone" and "Astel Lev"

Treya (*TRAY*-ah) — A baleya

Vonda (*VAWN*-dah) — Type of bird

Yàmana (*YAH*-mah-nah) — A type of fruit

Yhoshi (*YOE*-shee) — One of the four journeyers on The MoonQuest

Zakk (*ZACK*) — Toshar's uncle and Eulisha's son

Zzyzzyby (*ZIH*-zih-bee) — A type of pink cheese

Appreciation

When I began writing *The StarQuest* in 1998, mistakenly believing that *The MoonQuest*, its predecessor, was ready to be published (it would take several more drafts over nine more years for that to happen), I was single, I had barely been seven months in the United States and I was using a different name, one of the stories I tell in my *Acts of Surrender* memoir. Now, more than two decades and countless lifetimes and transformations later, I have surely forgotten many of the people who deserve my thanks at this time. To those worthy omissions, I apologize. My conscious mind may have lost track of your contributions but my heart has not, nor has the spirit of this story.

As for today, my profound gratitude goes out to all my friends, online and off, whose belief in me and *The Legend of Q'ntana* has never wavered, even when mine has. Most specifically, I am indebted to Sander Dov Freedman, Karen Weaver, Joan Cerio, Adam Bereki and Francene Shoop, as well as to Aalia Kazan, whose unique relationship with the Q'nta of this and other *Q'ntana* stories is also chronicled in *Acts of Surrender*, and Guinevere Yoseyva, who has her own singular relationship with a *StarQuest* character: Ben.

Special thanks go to Kathleen Messmer, who has shared my vision for *Q'ntana* since the moment we met at one of my earliest book signings for *The MoonQuest*'s first edition and who has expressed her enthusiasm and support for these stories in more ways than I can ever hope to enumerate or repay. Kathleen is also responsible for this edition's evocative cover image. Thanks as well to Denéa West, whose generous spirit helped make this new edition possible.

Large chunks of *The StarQuest* were either written or revised over a steaming Americano, and I am grateful to many baristas in multiple parts of the U.S. — most specifically across Southern California and in Albuquerque, New Mexico — for helping to nurture an atmosphere in their cafes that supports creativity.

Anyone familiar with me and my writing knows how important the energy of place is in my life and in my work. With *The StarQuest*, I must acknowledge the initiatory presence of Sedona, Arizona, where this book (and so much else in my life) was born; the mana of Maui (not to mention the driver's seat of Kihei Taxi's *puka* 6), where bits of the first draft found their way onto the page; Los Angeles, often a fount of creative inspiration for me and also birthplace of certain *StarQuest* scenes; Canyon de Chelly in Northeastern Arizona, where several key revelations about Ben and Q'nta bubbled up into my conscious awareness over an autumn campfire; Albuquerque, whose Sandia Mountains so often inspired me as I brought this story to completion; and Portland, Oregon, where a previous edition of *The StarQuest* was conceived and with it, an expanded vision for these *Q'ntana* stories .

Finally, to the many fans of the original edition of *The MoonQuest*: Thank you for exerting relentless if always supportive pressure on me to get *The StarQuest* finished and into your hands. I hope you found the result to have been worth the wait.

About the Author

Mark David Gerson is the bestselling author of more than twenty books. His nonfiction includes popular titles for writers, inspiring personal growth books and compelling memoirs. As a novelist and screenwriter, he is best known for *The Legend of Q'ntana* fantasy series. His other fiction includes the novels of *The Sara Stories*, set largely in Montreal, his hometown. When not writing, Mark David coaches an international roster of writers and non-writers to help them get their stories onto the page and out into the world with ease.

For more about Mark David Gerson,
and to sign up for his newsletter to learn about
upcoming *Q'ntana* books and other releases,
visit www.markdavidgerson.com

The Legend Continues...

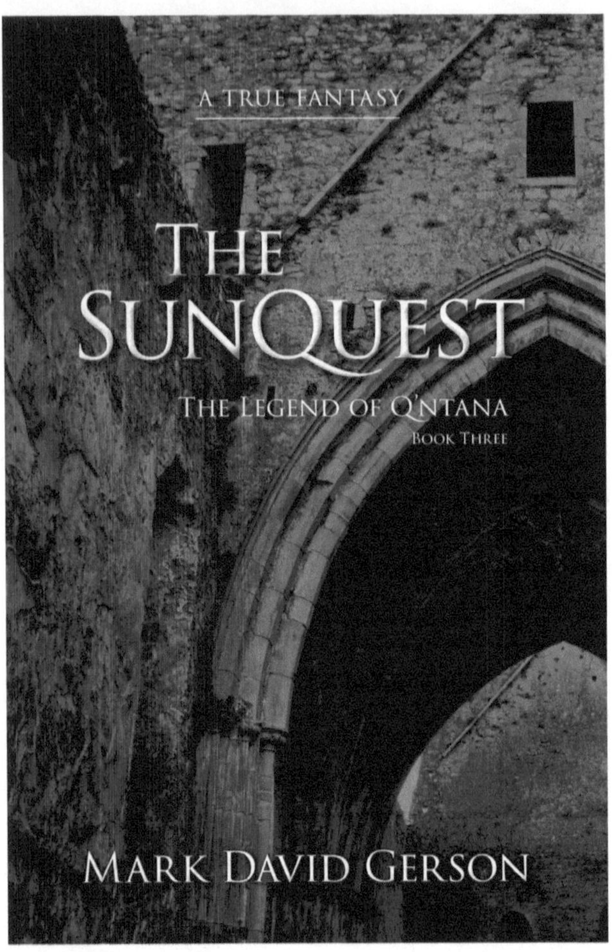

Coming Summer 2024!

WWW.QNTANABOOKS.COM

www.ingramcontent.com/pod-product-compliance
Lightning Source LLC
Chambersburg PA
CBHW060800190726
48285CB00002B/497